Other Titles by Crystal-Rain Love from ImaJinn books

Blood Revelation Series

Blood Curse
Book One

Slayer's Prey
Book Two

Slayer's Prey

The *Blood Revelation* Series
Book Two

by

Crystal-Rain Love

IMAJINN

ImaJinn Books

This is a work of fiction. Names, characters, places and incidents are either the products of the author's imagination or are used fictitiously. Any resemblance to actual persons (living or dead), events or locations is entirely coincidental.

IMAJINN

ImaJinn Books
PO BOX 300921
Memphis, TN 38130
Print ISBN: 978-1-61026-090-9

ImaJinn Books is an Imprint of BelleBooks, Inc.

ImaJinn Books was founded by Linda Kichline.

We at ImaJinn Books enjoy hearing from readers. Visit our websites
ImaJinnBooks.com
BelleBooks.com
BellBridgeBooks.com

10 9 8 7 6 5 4 3 2 1

Cover design: Deborah Smith
Interior design: Hank Smith
Photo/Art credits:
Man © Helder Almeida | Dreamstime.com
Background © Subbotina | Dreamstime.com

:Lpsx:01:

Dedication

To Von Ashby Lewis, a good friend and "fan" who demanded I keep cranking out chapters on this one. Writer's block never stood a chance.

Prologue

SOMETHING WAITED out there. Jacob Porter felt the lurking danger in every part of his twelve-year-old body. The fear twisted his gut, prickled his skin and caused the short hairs at the nape of his neck to stand on end as he eased down the alley alongside his best friend, Bobby Romano.

"Hey, Bobby, this isn't right. Let's stay on the street." The shadows seemed to dance along the brick walls lining the alley, beckoning them closer. They never should have snuck out, he decided.

"Don't be a baby, Jackie. The shortcut will get us back home quicker, before my mom notices we're gone. Do you want to get a beating?"

"No."

"Neither do I. Come on!" Bobby walked ahead, leading the way down the dark alley. Broken bottles and rotting food lined the pathway. The only light came from moonbeams which spilled over the walls, casting a dull blue glow in the narrow passage. Bobby walked ahead fearlessly, his short black hair glistening in the blue light. He'd had enough sense to pull on a blue jean jacket before climbing out his bedroom window. Jacob shivered as he walked behind, wearing only a thin white T-shirt with his jeans and sneakers. He wasn't so sure the cold was the only reason for his shiver.

They should have stayed at Bobby's house, but Bobby had wanted to see Nina. Nina worked at Foxy Lady, the strip club on Fourth Street. Bobby knew a way to sneak in after the show began, had learned it from tailing after his older brother one evening.

"Come on, Jackie, don't cha wanna see some real titties?" Bobby had asked.

Jacob had thought about it, thought about how bad Mrs. Romano would beat them both if she found out, but in the end the prospect of seeing a real naked woman had won out. Now, he wished he'd talked Bobby out of it.

The alley led to an opening between four buildings, a small clearing that provided space for the local businesses' Dumpsters. The moonlight didn't spill into that space. That was odd considering it was more open than the narrow alley. Jacob stopped in his tracks, his feet suddenly frozen. "Stop, Bobby," he ordered before his friend entered the clearing.

"What's the matter with you?" Bobby asked, turning so his dark eyes looked back at Jacob. "We have to go past the clearing and down through the other side of the alley over there. If you'd hurry up we can make it back home in ten minutes!"

Jacob shook his head. "No, Bobby. We have to go back."

"What are you talking about? Quit being a baby. Nothing's going to get us. We're just ten minutes from home. Come on!"

"No!" He felt himself wanting to cry and struggled to hold back the tears. Something was out there, waiting for them, waiting to eat them. "Something's out there, and it's going to kill us!"

Bobby rolled his eyes. "What a crybaby. We don't have time for this! My mom will be coming home from her job in twenty minutes, and the first thing she's going to do is check on us. We can't go the long way home, Jackie."

Jacob wanted to turn and leave. If he and Bobby weren't so close he would have done just that, but Bobby was his best friend. If he didn't make it to the house before Mrs. Romano came home from her job, she would give them both a good whipping. A good friend didn't cause their friend to get a beating. They also didn't let them walk alone through dangerous places.

"Bobby, there's no light there. Don't you think that's weird?"

Bobby looked over his shoulder at the opening and shrugged. "It's not even five in the morning, dude. What do you expect?"

"But, the moon . . ."

"Jackie, we can talk science at school. We gotta go. Now."

Jacob let out the breath he'd been holding, knowing Bobby was not going to change his mind. He had always been stubborn, more so than Jacob which was no easy feat. "All right, but we're running all the way home, and don't look back. Just run like your life depends on it."

Bobby grinned. "Okay, whiney-girl. Now, let's go."

Against his better judgment, Jacob ran along with Bobby, sprinting through the clearing as though the hounds of hell were on his heels, but just as they reached the other side and were about to enter the alleyway that would take them to the safety of Bobby's house, a shadow moved from the wall and blocked their exit.

Jacob and Bobby skidded to a stop; their mouths dropped open as they looked at each other.

"Jackie?" Bobby's voice trembled, his eyes wide and glossy. Jacob was no longer the only crybaby.

The shadow stepped forward and Jacob could see black eyes staring out from pale skin, pink lips pulled back over white teeth and two long fangs. Jacob blinked. He'd seen men like this before, with long dark hair and black clothes, long fingernails like a woman. He had seen men like this in really bad movies. Vampires.

Run, Jacob! Run! a woman's voice screamed inside his head, and he didn't waste time trying to figure out who was speaking to him. He did what he was told, grabbing Bobby's arm and turning away. They started to run, heading back to the alley they had just left, but Bobby screamed before they made it, and as Jacob turned toward him he froze in fear.

There were more of them, and they were feasting on Bobby. Three men and a woman plunged their teeth into Bobby's small body and drank his blood as he screamed. Jacob tried to scream too, but no sound came out. This wasn't real. It couldn't be. He was having a nightmare.

Run, Jacob! Run!

Jacob looked around for the woman he heard in his head, but no one was there, no one but the vampires, and a black cat perched on top of a Dumpster. He couldn't obey the woman, whoever she was. He had to help Bobby.

"Leave him alone!" He cried out in vain, catching the attention of the first vampire. The beast backed away from Bobby's limp body and stared at Jacob, blood covering the lower half of his face. His slow, wicked smile promised death. It was in that instant that Jacob knew Bobby was dead and soon he would be too.

Jacob slowly backed away as the vampire approached, too scared to run, too scared to move much at all. His mind was screaming that he needed to get away, but his heart was beating too fast, his legs shaking too hard. He felt a warm gush of liquid down his pant leg as the vampire reached for him.

The cat sprang from the Dumpster and, with a hiss, scratched the vampire's face before landing on all fours on the ground.

Run, Jacob, run! Do it now! The woman's words sounded like an angry roar, pushing Jacob into motion. As the cat leaped at the vampire again, Jacob turned and ran.

As he sprinted the length of the alley, he heard the other vampires screaming, but he didn't dare turn to see what was happening. Fearing they would come after him, he pushed his leg muscles as hard as he could, beating the pavement with his feet as he made it to the street. Even then he didn't stop running. Bobby was dead. He had to tell Bobby's parents. Jacob started to cry as he thought about what he would have to say when he reached their house.

For a moment, he wished the vampires had gotten him too.

Chapter One

Sixteen years later.

JAKE PORTER PARKED his black 1976 Chevy Malibu in the small church's parking lot and stepped out of the vehicle. The twilight air was cool and refreshing, reviving his tired senses. He hadn't slept well in days, lingering by his older brother's bedside, waiting to make sure Jonah would be all right before he left town on the trail of a possible killer.

He had no idea what he was up against or where to begin the search, but he knew Curtis Dunn had to be found. The psycho's evil twin, for lack of a better title, had shackled Jonah to a wall and killed several innocent women. That was enough to make him an enemy in Jake's vengeful mind.

He walked into the church, not the least bit surprised to find the doors unlocked during the late hour, despite the fact that the church was centered in Baltimore's most dangerous neighborhood. The pastor had no reason to fear the scum who walked the streets at night. He was far more powerful, having lived hundreds of years longer than the mortals who hung out on the darkened street corners. Jake knew this because he had hunted him, as he did all vampires. The only reason why this particular vamp was still breathing was because he'd helped Jake save his brother.

"Christian!" Jake called for the vampire by name, a war raging inside his body. Part of him, the part that had watched in horror as vampires drained his best friend of blood, wanted to kill Christian. He'd hunted the vampire down in an effort to do just that, nearly succeeding once before. But the part of him that had witnessed Christian destroy a demon with prayer alone held a strange sort of respect for the man, and he knew it would be wrong to kill him in cold blood.

Christian emerged from a doorway near the back of the church, his boyishly handsome face drawn into a mask of protective awareness. Jake didn't blame him for being on guard. He couldn't guarantee he wasn't a danger to the vampire. Every time he came close to a vamp he felt adrenaline surge in his veins, felt the urge to take them out like deer in hunting season.

The vampire stared at him, his dark blue eyes roaming over his body, studying him. His dark hair was short and neat, cut close to his head. He wore a nice, but inexpensive, suit, and to all who were ignorant of his true nature, he looked like a normal, completely harmless pastor. But Jake knew better. He knew just how lethal Christian could be.

"Jacob Porter, have you come to attempt to take my life once again?"

"My name's Jake, and no, I didn't come to kill you today."

"Ah, another day then." The vampire smiled coolly as he took a few steps closer, stopping at the beginning of the row of pews filling the space between them. "What is it you want of me on this evening?"

"For one thing, I'd like my gun back." Jake referred to the specially made gun with custom-crafted UV bullets Christian had taken from him after drinking his blood. His neck still throbbed at the memory of Christian digging his fangs into his skin, the fear he'd felt when he'd thought his end had come.

Christian shook his head, his eyes lit with amusement. "Now, Jake, do you really think I would keep such a weapon? It was destroyed."

Jake had figured as much, but it didn't hurt to try. "I'm not happy to hear that, Fang-Boy. I guess I'll have to figure out another way to kill this demon slash vampire thing I'm after."

"You're referring to Curtis Dunn?"

"Alfred, Curtis, whatever name you'd like to call him."

Alfred Dunn, going by the name of Curtis, and his brother, Carter, had left a pile of bodies in Baltimore parks before they came across Jonah. Jake's brother, a detective with Baltimore Homicide, had been tailing Aria Michaels when he'd been snatched out of his car and locked in the Dunn twins' basement. Jonah had been beaten to a pulp by the time Jake and Christian's vampire friends found the place. Carter Dunn didn't make it out of the building alive, but Curtis escaped while Jake tended to his brother, and the vampires saved two of their own. Now it was Jake's job to find him.

"Curtis Dunn is not a vampire. He is essentially a mortal man fighting against a demon that has possessed him and is battling for dominance."

"Oh, well, thanks for clearing that up," Jake said sarcastically. "Now give me some info I can use. Is he dangerous or not?"

"What did your brother say?"

Jake sat in one of the pews, feeling no imminent danger from the vampire, and sighed in frustration. "He said he was a real wacko, whining about being two souls in one body. Sounded like a pathetic little bitch if you ask me."

Christian grinned as he sat on the back of a pew, still several feet away from Jake. "He befriended Aria, and for a long time she hadn't a clue of his true identity. He even tried to help her once, although his attempt was utterly pathetic. If he can control the demon inside him that's struggling to take over, he will probably remain harmless. But from the way Aria described him, he seemed to be losing the battle. You must never forget that although Carter was the more evil of the two, they were still related, and it was Alfred Dunn who made the initial pact with the devil to reincarnate them through their bloodline. Without that pact, Alfred and Patrick Dunn would have remained dead rather than returning to the world as Curtis and Carter Dunn."

Jake rose from the hard pew. "Something only a coward would do, going to Lucifer for help because you're too weak to fight your own battle alone. He should be easy enough to snuff out." He turned his back to the vampire and started to leave.

"Why did you come here, Jake?"

He stopped just before he reached the door, turned around, and shrugged. "To get my gun back."

"You knew I wouldn't keep such a thing in my possession. Why did you really come?" The vampire looked at him knowingly, patiently. He had a way of relaxing Jake, making him feel like confessing his heavily guarded secrets. Jake didn't like it. Before he could decide how to respond, Christian added, "You can ask me, Jake. I hold no opinions or judgments."

Jake squared his shoulders, tried to fight off the hold Christian seemed to have over him. Then, before he could stop it, the question haunting him since the day they saved Jonah slipped through his lips. "Why was your prayer so powerful?"

Christian's eyes sparkled, and his mouth tugged up at the corners in satisfaction. "Because God listens."

"That's it? God listens?"

Christian nodded. "He listens to you too, Jake."

Jake felt anger boiling inside him. "Oh really?" Images of blood and the sound of screaming flooded his mind in a red haze as he recalled the night his best friend was savagely taken from him. "Then why do so many people die screaming? Why doesn't he hear the screams?"

"He does." Christian's eyes softened, and his voice took on a soothing tone. "But some darkness is so evil we can't possibly understand it. We aren't supposed to. We merely believe, keep our hearts true, and know deep within our soul that everything is for a reason and, if we only ask, He will not give us more than we can handle. We simply follow where He leads, and when it is our time to meet with Him all will be revealed."

Jake shook his head; the irony of receiving a sermon from a freaking vampire was too much to handle. "Whatever, Suck-Face. I'm outta here." He turned toward the exit and headed for the door.

"Wait."

Jake stilled and looked over his shoulder. "What?"

"You said it would be easy to snuff out Curtis Dunn. I can understand why you want to question him, but why kill him? His twin, Carter, was the demon who drained those women and hurt your brother."

"There was an out-of-state murder. The body was completely drained of blood. Guess what else."

"Fang marks on the neck." Christian's face lost what little color it had.

"The same way Carter left his victims." Jake headed for the door again, tossing over his shoulder, "Pray for me." He couldn't stop the sarcasm from coating his words.

Touched by the cool night air, his skin tingled as he walked toward his car, wondering what had possessed him to visit the vampire. Christian was right. He knew the vamp wouldn't leave a weapon so deadly intact. And the vampire didn't know any more about Curtis Dunn than he did.

Jake settled into the car, jerking when a soft mew came from behind him. Laughing at his scare, he turned to see his stray cat licking her paws in the back seat. The black cat had seemed to follow him since his childhood, disappearing and returning whenever it suited her, sneaking along with him from city to city.

"How'd you get in here, Alley?" Jake asked, reaching back to pick her up. He'd named her Alley after the alley where he'd first seen her, or some other cat that looked like her, the cat that had attacked the vampires and saved his life. Of course, if he'd listened to the doctors his parents had sent him to, he'd believe the cat and the vampires were all a figment of his imagination. According to them, his friend had been killed in front of him, but he'd died from a severe beating which ended in cardiac arrest, not from a vampire attack. His parents never believed him, and even Jonah thought he was insane until he ran across Christian and his vampire friends and finally had to admit paranormal beings really did exist.

Alley mewed softly and rubbed against his chest as if she could hear his thoughts, comforting him as she always did. "I'm all right, Alley. Confused as hell, but all right. We got a wacko to find. Are you coming with me?"

Alley stepped off his lap and gracefully sauntered over to the passenger seat, tugging a map open with her teeth. Jake laughed to himself. "Girl, sometimes I swear you know what I'm saying to you."

NYLA STRETCHED AND yawned at the foot of the bed after she watched Jake's eyes finally close. He had beautiful eyes, a thin band of warm caramel brown encircling a soft green. They sparkled when he laughed, but unfortunately he didn't laugh often enough. The weight of his guilt was bearing down on him.

She had followed Jake since the night the vampires attacked his friend. He'd made a vow all those years ago to track down the vampires who'd killed Bobby and avenge his friend's death. He'd researched and hunted until he found the names of three of them—Lionel, Niles, and Detra. Lionel had been his first kill. Detra was the first kill he cried over, despising himself for killing a woman but knowing inside it needed to be done. He hadn't yet discovered the name of the fourth vampire, the one who'd attempted to take him that night. Nyla prayed he never did. Demarcus was pure evil, rotten to his soulless core.

She'd attacked him that night, saving Jake but losing part of herself in the process. She had always been different, a pantherian from infancy when her mother sacrificed her to the pantherian queen, Priscilla. She had undergone a deadly ritual few survived. She was strong. She had survived and hated herself for it, more so since her encounter with Demarcus. The deadly vampire was strong and swift, and he'd managed to bite her and infect her with his curse. Now, not only was she a shape-shifter but a vampire as well. The very thing Jake hated. And an eternal link to the beast he wanted to destroy.

Nyla jumped from the bed and pattered toward the small table sitting against the wall of the motel room. Jake had tossed his maps and papers on top of it. He was going after Curtis Dunn, a man who could quite possibly have knowledge of scientific experiments that could prove gravely dangerous to mankind. Jake's laptop sat atop the desk, the light from the monitor spilling into the dark room. He'd searched the Internet for leads and pored over count-less documents taken from the Dunn twins' home. The newest victim's body was found in Louisville, Kentucky. Jake had driven here nonstop, but he'd had no idea where to go once he entered the city.

Nyla closed her eyes and focused. Her body turned into mist and within seconds she stood in the room in her human form. Shifting used to hurt. It had felt like swallowing a lightning bolt. Since Demarcus had bitten her she shifted effortlessly, quickly, without any pain at all. Unfortunately, she craved blood in human form, a characteristic she despised in herself and avoided for as long as possible, not just because she didn't like the idea of feeding off humans, but because she could feel Demarcus inside her head when she did.

Demarcus. Her sire, and the creature Jake Porter couldn't wait to kill.

She glanced over at the bed where Jake slept peacefully and forced herself to shut down all thought of Demarcus and to rein in her growing hunger for fresh blood. If she wasn't careful, the mental blocks she'd set up around her thoughts could fall, and Demarcus would creep inside her head. He'd not only know where she was but who she was with. She would never forgive herself if she led Demarcus to Jake. Jake had destroyed demons, evil spirits, and vam-pires, but she'd seen the inside of Demarcus's head and knew he was far more dangerous than anything Jake had gone up against.

Nyla sat at the desk and quietly went through the papers. Even in human form, she maintained a catlike stealth, and with her sensitive hearing, she was able to listen to Jake's breathing and would know the second he woke. She'd be in cat form before he could lift an eyelid, so the thought of getting caught in his room rifling through his things didn't scare her. Being a half-shifter, half-vampire had its perks, but she'd gladly take mortality if given the choice.

After reading through the stack of papers, she could understand why Jake had been so frustrated before finally falling asleep. There was nothing linking the Dunns to Louisville. Why had Curtis come here?

And why did she have a nagging feeling that things were going to go horribly wrong here?

Nyla shivered, trying to shake off the cold chill creeping along her spine. The feeling had started when Jake got the call from his brother, when the original murders first started. It had steadily grown stronger as the days rolled past and had intensified once they entered Kentucky. The feeling wasn't like any other sense of danger she'd experienced in the past. It was much stronger than a sense of impending doom. It was a sense of . . . impending death.

Nyla rose from the chair and stood at the side of the bed, gazing down at Jake Porter's sleeping form. She'd watched over him for years, observed him as he grew from a boy to a man. Her feelings for him had grown over time as well. As a child, she'd wanted to protect him from the dark creatures that haunted his tormented mind, doing the job his parents had failed to do. As a man, he called out to her heart, and she wanted to touch him, hold him . . . love him.

She had fallen for him. She couldn't pinpoint the how or the when, but at some point she had quit seeing the boy and only saw the strong, sexy man with the unquenchable desire for justice, and she'd fallen head over heels, or paws in her case. And he would never feel the same way about her. Hell, if he knew his pet alley cat was a shifter, he'd kill her.

Even with that knowledge, she couldn't let anything happen to him if she could prevent it. Jake couldn't walk into this looming danger by himself, and there was only so much she could do in cat form. If she changed into a panther in front of him, her cover would be blown. He'd probably put a bullet through her before she could open her mouth to explain.

There were a few hours left before dawn. She had just enough time to sneak out into the night and make arrangements. And tomorrow, Jake Porter would meet Nyla, the woman.

Chapter Two

NYLA CREPT DOWN the darkened street, staying alert for danger. She knew nothing about Louisville, had no idea how strong its shifter or vampire population was. But she knew if Curtis Dunn was here killing women to further his experimentation, there had to be a decent number of vamps and who knew what else lurking in the shadows.

She had her gun, and her knives rested in the sheaths adorning her arms beneath the long sleeves of her T-shirt, but they could only protect her if she was a better fighter than her opponent. She touched the gun where it lay in the shoulder holster beneath her leather jacket, needing the boost of courage it offered. She was thankful she was a therian and not a lycanthrope. When therians shifted, anything on them made of fabric, flesh or metal changed with them. She never had to worry about popping up naked in the wrong place or leaving her weapons behind. Two things that came in handy while traveling with Jake.

She was going to "meet" Jake tomorrow night, posing as a bounty hunter. She'd never appeared to him in human form before, afraid he would see through her, recognize her as the creature she was. But something in her gut told her she had to do this. Jake could not battle the danger waiting for him alone. His brother, Detective Jonah Porter, was in Baltimore. Jake needed an ally with him here in Louisville. The problem was that he never partnered with anyone, so she knew better than to offer her services to him in the form of a partnership. She'd have to use reverse psychology and present herself as his rival—and hope he didn't try to take her out. She'd hate to have to hurt him.

But she was pretty sure it wouldn't come down to that. And if it did . . . well, she wouldn't hurt him too much.

She reached a small motel sitting on the corner of two west end streets. She didn't need to live in Louisville to know the west end was the bad area of the city. The neighborhood was obviously home to low income residents, judging by the state of the buildings, and the fact that she'd seen several police cars patrolling the streets indicated the crime level was high. She hadn't seen nearly as many police cars near the Dixie Highway motel where Jake was staying.

She could have stayed at the same motel he'd chosen, but that would have been too coincidental. Jake wasn't an idiot. He'd know she was deliberately following him. Besides, a tough-as-nails bounty hunter would have no qualms about staying in the city's roughest neighborhood, mingling with the other badasses.

She entered the motel, walking up to the young African-American man behind the check-in counter. He had a medium complexion, with rich chocolate-brown eyes and dark brown hair divided into long cornrows. His gaze slid appreciatively over her body as she approached.

"I'd like a room for two nights, please," she said, shifting the plastic shopping bag she carried in her right hand. She'd know tomorrow whether or not she needed the room longer. It was only for cover anyway.

"Just you?"

"Yes."

The man grinned. The name tag on his shirt read Andre. He punched in something on the keyboard before him and held out his hand, stating the amount due.

Nyla reached into her pocket and extracted a small wad of bills, thankful again that she was a therian and cash stayed with her throughout her transformations. She was more thankful she did so well in poker games. Following your dream man in cat form didn't exactly pay. She counted out the right amount and gave it to Andre.

"You really shouldn't pull out your money like that," he warned her as he put the bills in the cash register and counted out her change. "Nice-looking white girl like you all alone in the hood, you're a walking target for these fools around here." He handed her the change. "Be a shame if something happened to such a pretty face."

"Thanks for the compliment and the warning, but I can handle myself," she said with a smile as she took her change.

Andre simply raised his eyebrows, as though he didn't believe her, before handing her a key card. "I can show you to your room."

"That's all right. I'm sure I can find it," Nyla said, turning to go. She could feel his eyes exploring her backside as she walked away.

The room was small and musty-smelling, the only furnishings a bed, small table, and a TV sitting on a small dresser. She'd done some light shopping at a 24-hour Walmart before looking for a motel and had purchased a week's worth of clothing and toiletries.

She dumped the contents of the large shopping bag on the bed and set to work removing the tags from the clothing. She worked fast, feeling the hunger for blood growing inside her. She hadn't fed in weeks, and she didn't know how much longer she could resist. The craving would leave her the moment she shifted, but she had to prepare her room for the off-chance that Jake would see it.

She collected the discarded tags and tossed them into the small garbage can next to the dresser, then proceeded to shake and bunch up her clothing, trying to work out the brand-spanking-new appearance.

She placed the clothes in the dresser and put away her toiletries before falling back on the bed. There wasn't any interesting art on the walls, no arresting color schemes on the curtains or the bedspread . . . nothing to take her mind away from the growing hunger inside her body.

She could just shift, change into an alley cat and run back to Jake's motel. Shifting wouldn't help her make it through the next night, though. She needed to feed, and it was best she did before meeting up with Jake. One good feeding would hold her for a week, maybe two.

She recalled Andre with his chocolate-brown eyes, all alone behind the check-in counter. She wondered if his blood was as sweet as chocolate . . .

"DAMMIT TO HELL!" Jake continued to curse violently, gripping the phone in his hand while he absorbed the information his brother had just relayed to him.

"Jake?" Jonah's voice echoed from the phone.

"Yeah?"

"Why are you so bothered by this? I mean, obviously you'd be bothered that people have been killed, but this seems like it's personal."

"I came here to stop the crazy bastard, not to watch while bodies pile up." Jake bit the words out. Another body had been found just outside Louisville. The body was drained of blood and sported two fang-sized holes in the neck. That damned possessed Dunn had struck again.

Alley mewed, rising from where she lay in a patch of morning sunlight spilling through the window onto a small square-shaped section of carpet, looking completely full and content. She must have found herself something to feast on while she went out prowling the night before. Jake still didn't recall leaving the window open. He'd have to be more careful.

"Jake? You all right, bro?"

"Yeah," Jake answered, gliding a hand down Alley's back as she jumped up on the bed, nuzzling against him. She always seemed to know when he needed comforting. "I'm just pissed."

"So I gathered. I got some good news, though. I found out the first victim's name. Janie Paxton. She worked at The Crimson Rose."

"Where's that?"

"Bardstown Road."

Jake scooted Alley off his boxers-clad lap and rose from the bed, crossing the room to the table. He took out the Louisville street map and looked up Bardstown Road. "You know anything about the area?"

"Not a thing. That's all the info I could get, and the only reason the LMPD shared it with me is because I gave them everything I knew about the suspected killer."

"Everything?" Jake raised an eyebrow, even though he knew his brother couldn't see it.

"Well, not everything. I couldn't tell them the original killer disintegrated because of a prayer recited by a vampire and that this new killer is his demon-possessed twin brother, who just happened to be his father in his previous life."

"Why not? Sounds like typical daytime talk show stuff to me." Jake sat at the table and woke his laptop from sleep mode, preparing to look up information about the club Janie Paxton had worked at. "What exactly did you tell the locals?"

"I told them what I told my guys. An anonymous tip led me to the Dunn residence, where I was attacked by Curtis Dunn. The body—what was left of it—of Carter Dunn was already there when I arrived. Curtis fled the scene after getting the jump on me, and the fact that his lab refrigerators were filled with jugs of blood was enough evidence to show that he, Carter, or both of them had killed those women."

"The blood matched the victims' DNA."

"Right."

"I'm sorry we had to leave you there." Jake recalled the night he and the vamps rescued the Dunn brothers' prisoners. He'd found his own brother chained to a wall in their basement laboratory. The woman Jonah had been trying to protect was bound to a metal table, her blood dripping into a bucket beneath it with the aid of tubes in her neck that were designed to leave what looked like fang marks. A vampire was clamped to another wall, nearly dead.

They'd rescued Eron and Aria from that basement, but unlike the vampires, Jonah needed human medical attention. There was no way Jake could have taken Jonah to the hospital as injured as he was without the cops being called and questions asked that they couldn't possibly answer. In the end, Jonah persuaded him that leaving him there to call in the "attack" was the best option.

"You had to. How else was I going to explain what happened that night without all of us winding up in the nut house?" Jonah let out a small laugh, devoid of humor. "And to think that all these years I thought you'd imagined these creatures. Demons and vampires. Shit."

"Yeah, sometimes I don't even believe the things I'm up against until I'm actually up against them."

"You be careful, Jake. This stuff you're dipping into is nuts, man. Don't get yourself dead."

"Or undead."

"Jake!" Jonah's voice clearly displayed his lack of amusement. "I'm serious. You go too far with things, always trying to prove something."

"We have the same job, Joe. My bad guys are just scarier than yours."

"Why do they have to be *your* bad guys? You don't even get paid for some of the things you do."

"I get paid for enough, and it's not about money. Why'd you become a cop?"

"To protect those who couldn't protect themselves."

"Exactly."

"No, not exactly. You're like this because of Bobby. It's not your fault they took him that night."

"That doesn't mean I can't kill the bastards." Jake's voice came out as a growl.

"Don't lose your own life trying to avenge his. You're the only brother I have."

"You be careful too. Don't get strung up on any more walls."

"I'll do my best."

"And I'll be there if your best backfires, sissy-boy."

"Back at cha, ass-wipe."

"Bitch."

"Pussy."

Jake grinned as he hit the end button on his cell phone. The Porter brothers never actually said the words "I love you." They didn't need to.

CURTIS DUNN HUDDLED in the corner of the dark room, fighting against the tremors wracking his body. The scent of fresh blood filled the air in the small room, suffocating him slowly. The vampire hanging on the north wall was so young, so . . . innocent looking. How could he do this? How could he be forced to do something so horrendous?

"Alfred, come here!"

Curtis cringed at the sound of the other vampire's voice. It was cold and harsh like its master's. He thought he'd met the purest form of evil when he'd made a pact with the devil decades before, but Demarcus wasn't far behind on the meter.

"Please call me Curtis," he said weakly, afraid he might upset the vampire more. Curtis was the good part of him, the new soul which had been given a chance when he'd reincarnated, but Alfred was embedded in some deep, dark place inside him. Demarcus was determined to bring him out.

"I don't wish to speak with Curtis. I wish to speak with Alfred. Now!"

Curtis closed his eyes as the menacing creature stood over him. He waited, fearing the backhanded slap which would send him careening across the small room, but it didn't come. Instead, Demarcus grabbed him by the skin at the nape of his neck and forced his head back.

"Look at me, you sniveling little coward," he growled, his rank, blood-fragrant breath blowing hot on Curtis's face.

Curtis opened his eyes, staring into the face of his tormentor. If he called on Lucifer, Demarcus couldn't hurt him, but he'd run from his dark master, and this was his punishment. He was being dominated by a brutal beast of a vampire who hadn't a trace of goodness left in his dark soul. If he even had a soul.

"You will do as I say," Demarcus demanded.

"I can find a cure for you without hurting anyone else," Curtis pleaded with a quiver in his voice.

"No, you can't. I am a vampire, and you must dissect a vampire to understand how our bodies differ from yours."

"Please, Demarcus. I've already drained two women for you." Curtis shuddered. "Why must I do this? Why must so many lives be taken?"

"The women are bait, and we needed the DNA sample from the first one."

The shifter. Curtis shuddered again, remembering how the young woman had writhed in wolf form as he cut into her. He'd killed her in order to save his own life, even though it wasn't worth anything. He should allow Demarcus to kill him, defy the vampire and end his miserable existence . . . but he couldn't. No matter what torture Demarcus promised him on Earth, he had turned his back on Lucifer. He was terrified of what would happen in the afterlife. He'd sold his soul to the devil. Eternal damnation couldn't be much better than what he was going through in the realm of the living, especially if he wasn't under Lucifer's protection anymore.

"What are you baiting, Demarcus?" If he was going to do most of the dirty work, he felt he ought to at least know why.

"The bitch who did this to me." He stood before Curtis, his pale skin covered in a thin film of dark fur, patches of the skin beneath peeling away in clumps. His eyes were glazed over, his lips dry and withered. The claw marks inflicted on him nearly two decades ago were still embedded in his skin. They should have healed the day after the attack, while he went through the mending stage of sleep, but they hadn't.

"How do you know she will come?"

"I see inside her when she feeds. I infected her, just as she infected me, except she infected me with a virus. I gave her power. She fights against the hunger, throws up shields to keep me from tracking her down, but she'll misstep eventually, and I'll be there."

"But how do you know the bodies will lead her to you?"

"I've caught glimpses of her these last few years. She's been following a man. Wherever he goes, she goes, if the danger level is high enough. I can't tell who he is, but I know he's a hunter."

"A vampire hunter?"

"Yes. There is always death in her mind when I see her. Death and love. I can't see the man, but I sense his presence with her. He was there in Baltimore when your twin was killed." The vampire narrowed his eyes at Curtis "And you swear you never saw this man?"

Curtis willed his heart not to beat frantically, knowing the vampire would hear it and know he was lying. It would be too easy for the monster to kill him, which was the only reason why Demarcus shared so much with him. The arrogant bastard knew he was no threat. "I only saw the vampires who rescued their friends. There were no mortals except the ones we captured."

"He was there. I felt her love for him, her fear for his life. If he was there because of the bodies found, he'll follow the bodies we leave behind here as well."

"How long must we do this? She has evaded you for sixteen years."

"You just focus on finding a cure for me. She'll slip up. She's already revealed her location in Baltimore to me. She'll reveal her location here while I'm close enough to grab her, or better yet, she'll show me the man. If I capture him she'll do anything to get him back, even let me kill her."

Chapter Three

JAKE SHOOK HIS head as he pulled into the small parking lot outside The Crimson Rose. The Bardstown Road area was overflowing with young Goths with multicolored hair and piercings in places no sane person would want to stick a sharp instrument into.

Stepping out of the car in his usual attire of black T-shirt and blue jeans, he knew he stuck out like a second thumb. At least his shirt read VAMPIRES SUCK, a little helpful with keeping in the spirit but not much. There wasn't a chance in hell he was putting on makeup or puncturing his face with metal.

The sun had set hours ago, and from the looks of it, the freaks came out at night. No matter which direction he turned his head, he saw young, pale-skinned, black or multi-color-haired twenty-somethings and teens in dark clothes. Some appeared to have more tattoos than skin; some of the females had more skin than clothing.

Admiring the view of scantily-clad women as he made his way to the club's entrance, he reminded himself that as soon as the opportunity presented itself he needed to get laid. It had been too long.

The bouncer barely checked IDs as the people filed into the dark interior of the club, so the line wasn't long. It was more like a steady rushing stream than a line.

Jake found himself inside the club in a matter of minutes. It took a second for his eyes to adjust to the red-hued light caused by strobe lights which hung overhead, sending rays of dancing crimson beams around the large room.

A mass of people were doing something resembling dancing on the dance floor, moving their bodies to the alternative music which blared from the wall speakers. Not much of a dancer himself, Jake moved over to the bar.

Janie Paxton, the victim his brother had told him about, had been a waitress at the club. She'd been abducted after leaving work in the early morning hours and found dead five days later. Jake needed to know who she had contact with during her final night of work. Dunn may have been a customer, and someone might know something about him.

Jake ordered a bottle of Budweiser, checking out the bartender while he waited for the drink. The man, thick with muscles, appeared a little taller than his own height of six-foot-one. His dark brown hair was pulled back into a low ponytail, showing off the dragon tattoo encircling his neck. Five gold hoops adorning his ears were the only jewelry complementing his simple outfit of a black muscle shirt and black jeans. He looked like the type of man you didn't want to piss off, and Jake figured coming straight out and asking about the recently deceased waitress would probably do just that.

"Here ya go," the bartender said gruffly, putting the chilled bottle on the bar before Jake.

"Thanks. Say, is Janie Baxter still working here?" Jake asked, his tone giving away nothing.

"You mean Janie Paxton?" The bartender's eyes narrowed, his hands twisted around the white towel he held.

"Yeah, that's her, I think. About five-five. Red hair, at least when I last saw her."

"You didn't hear?"

"Hear what?"

"Where you from, man?" The bartender leaned forward on the bar, resting on his fists. The expression on his face clearly indicated he was tired of people discussing the deceased girl.

"Baltimore," Jake answered, and he had a driver's license to prove it if it came down to that. "I come through here every once in a while, visited the club on my last trip. What's going on, dude? Oh hell, she's not your girl is she? I'm not trying to move in on anybody's territory."

"She was murdered," the man said bitterly, his hands relaxing. "Her body was found a few days ago."

Jake assumed his best shocked expression. "Shit, man, I'm sorry. Damn. What happened? Did they get the killer?"

The bartender shrugged his tense shoulders. "I don't know, man. She was a nice girl. I don't like gossiping about people after they've passed, so that's all I can tell ya. Enjoy the beer."

Jake held back a frustrated growl as the bartender walked away, and he pivoted on his barstool to scope out the rest of the club. He couldn't blame the guy. He remembered what it was like after Bobby died. All the kids in his neighborhood wanted to know what had happened that night, in full gory detail. It was like a damn horror story to them. He could imagine how many people had come around the club trying to get information, people who didn't even know the girl but were just fascinated by her death. Yes, he had just done the same thing, but he had a good excuse. He was going to capture the girl's murderer.

He sipped on his beer, checking out the handful of waitresses who bustled from table to table with trays of drinks and pretzels. It had been his experience that women talked more than men. It was just in their nature to be more open.

He zeroed in on a blond twenty-something with a rose tattoo on her arm and a small hoop through one of her nostrils. Her frown was too heartfelt to merely suggest she was unhappy about working. Maybe she was friend of Janie Paxton, one who might talk if she thought it would help put Janie's murderer away.

"Come here, often?"

The corner of Jake's mouth turned upward as the low, sultry voice of a woman beside him breezed into his ear. Yes, he was on the trail of a killer, but his body needed some attention too. The woman's voice was full of promises, and if she was half as sexy as her voice implied . . .

Jake's hopes for a quickie in the bathroom vanished as he turned his head and took in his new acquaintance. She was easy on the eyes, all right. Long hair so blond it shimmered, full pouting lips and glacier-blue eyes that met his. Her small breasts seemed pushed up in what was probably one of those underwire contraptions under her two-sizes-too-small, low-cut crop top, and the edge of her red thong underwear peeked out over the top of her low-rise denim mini-skirt. Long, shapely legs led down to a pair of three-inch hooker heels.

And if she were a day over sixteen Jake would eat his shirt.

"How old are you, little girl?" He didn't try to keep the disgust and anger out of his tone. The girl had more makeup on her face than could be found on a drugstore counter, and her eyes had that "I know the score, big boy, come and get it" look that no girl her age should be giving to a twenty-eight-year-old man.

"Eighteen," she answered with a giggle and had the audacity to look surprised.

"In two more years, maybe."

"Oh, really, you flatter me." She batted her eyelashes, sliding in closer to rest her hand on his thigh. "Let's go somewhere."

"I have a better idea. You go home and wait until you're a woman before you come on to a grown man." Jake extracted her hand from his leg none too gently, wondering how the club stayed open letting underage girls inside.

"I'm all woman, honey. I can show you just how much woman I am."

"Go home," Jake ordered, pushing the girl away when she moved in to cuddle up to him. He desperately needed some action, but even during his worst dry spell he'd never sink to bedding a child.

"Fine," the girl snapped, anger flushing her cheeks a brilliant shade of red, managing to catch herself before she stumbled. He hadn't pushed her hard, but he hadn't been gentle either. "My fault for assuming you were heterosexual."

"I'm hetero, sweetheart. I'm just not a child molester."

"I already told you—"

"You don't fool me, little girl. What are you looking for anyway? Money?

Are you hungry?" he asked, wondering if she'd just snuck out for the night, or was a runaway.

"I don't need your charity, jerk. I'm just looking for a good time. I thought you'd be fun, but apparently I was wrong."

Jake shook his head as she stomped away in a huff. If she was looking for someone to buy her dinner, he could have seen to it that she was fed, but if she truly was out searching for some bastard to use her . . . hell, what could he do?

Jake watched her while she scoped out the club, zeroing in on a guy with a green Mohawk and two arms full of tattoos. It wasn't the hair or tattoos that bothered Jake, but the "I just got out of prison and am looking to do anything with or without a pulse" look about the guy which put Jake into protective mode. He muttered a curse as the foolish girl started to approach the man.

He scoped the club's interior quickly, spotting a side exit. The waitress he wanted to question would most likely be working until much later. He'd have to put off the hunt for Curtis Dunn for a little while, long enough to save the underage girl from herself.

With a crazy plan forming in his mind, Jake left his unfinished beer on the bar and hurried to intersect the girl. He caught her by the wrist before she reached Mr. Mohawk and pulled her toward the exit.

"Hey!" she gasped, but kept up with his quick stride. "What's the matter? Remember how to work your equipment?"

"Yeah, something like that," he muttered, heading for the side exit, promising himself if he ever had a daughter he'd put bars on her window and a monitor around her ankle, maybe slap on a chastity belt for good measure.

"Don't worry, baby, I'll be gentle," she said mockingly, and Jake squeezed his hand tighter around her wrist until he realized he was hurting her. The last thing he wanted to do was harm the girl. It was her parents who deserved a good beating. Where were they while she was out trolling?

He pulled her through the exit and tugged her down the length of the building, rounding the edge of it so they ended up in a narrow alley behind the club. He didn't let go of her wrist until he made sure they were alone.

"I'm glad you changed your mind," she said huskily, laying her hands on his chest.

Jake forced her against the brick wall of the club, his hand tightly cupped over her mouth while he used the other hand to retrieve his Smith & Wesson M&P .40

from the back of his waistband. Her eyes widened as he pointed the gun in her face, small sounds of terror coming from behind his hand.

"Scream, and I'll blow your brains all over this wall. Understand? Blink twice for yes."

She blinked twice in rapid succession, tears streaming from her eyes. Jake removed his hand from her mouth, using it to keep her pinned against the wall.

"Please don't kill me," she whimpered. "I'm too young to die. I'll let you do whatever you want to me, just please don't kill me."

"What's your name?" Jake asked. He felt like a monster for terrorizing the girl, but if he didn't scare the hell out of her she'd run off and try to find a guy to spend the night with, a guy who wouldn't give a damn how young she was.

"Chr-Chrissy."

"How old are you?"

"Fourteen."

Sweet Jesus. "What the hell are you doing at a nightclub trying to pick up grown men, Chrissy?"

"I got nowhere to go."

Jake looked her over again. She was clean, sweet-smelling and groomed. "You don't look like you've been living on the streets."

"I just ran away a couple nights back. I was staying with friends, but that fell through and . . ."

Jake's mouth twisted into something resembling an evil smile. "So you walked into the club tonight and saw me, no tattoos and no piercings, pretty normal looking. You thought I'd be an easy target. Flirt me up and get my wallet, huh?"

She nodded, her lips trembling, snot starting to run out her nose.

"Well, congratulations. You picked up a psychopath with a gun. Kind of makes you homesick, doesn't it?"

"Oh, God." Chrissy convulsed into deep sobs, covering her eyes with her hands as though she didn't want to see what was coming next. "What are you going to do to me?"

"He's going to drop the gun and back away," a female voice said from behind him. "Slowly."

Jake's body tensed at the same moment Chrissy's eyes snapped open, hope shining bright within the icy blue orbs. Shit. He'd never even heard the woman sneak up on him. He would have whirled around, but the press of what could only be the barrel of a gun against the back of his head told him not to move a muscle.

"I can explain."

"Save it. Drop the piece."

Dammit! If the woman was a cop, he was screwed, but if she was a cop wouldn't she have said so already? Jake lowered his gun, slowly in case the woman at his back was trigger-happy, but he held it tight. No damn way was he letting go of it until he knew just what he was dealing with.

"I'm not going to hurt the girl. I'm just teaching her a lesson."

"What lesson is that?"

"Never talk to strangers."

"I think she's got it. Now drop the gun and step away from her."

Jake thought about it, actually considered dropping the gun, but it just wasn't in his nature to give up so easily. He didn't sense anyone else behind him. If the woman was a cop, he was headed for jail. If she wasn't a cop . . .

Jake backed up fast and hard, hard enough to ram the woman's hands upward, and spun around before she had a chance to recover. He aimed his gun at her and all he could think was *damn*.

Eyes the color of lilacs stared him down from within a tanned face complete with dark, arched eyebrows, a pert little nose and lush, juicy pink lips. Long, black hair flowed around her face, framing the exquisite masterpiece. It was hard to tell where her hair ended and her clothes began. Everything she wore was black. Black leather jacket, black top, black jeans and boots.

And she was pointing her black gun directly at him.

Jake saw a blur of motion to his right and knew Chrissy was trying to flee the scene. He snagged her wrist without looking and tried to pull her behind his body, but was met with resistance. The gun-toting woman had a grip on her too.

"Let her go," Jake said, low and threatening, trying to tamp down the urge to reach out and grab his opponent. The woman had threatened him, was still pointing a gun at him, and all he could think about was how well her body filled those tight black clothes—and how badly he wanted to run his hands over those curves.

"You let her go."

"I saw her first," he countered.

They stood there in the alley behind the club, pointing their guns at each other with a scared fourteen-year-old child between them, each tugging at a wrist as though they were playing tug-of-war with her body.

"Don't make me have to hurt you, Porter."

Alarm bells rang out. "How the hell do you know my name?"

The mystery woman smiled, no teeth showing. The smile did things to his lower body that made no sense given the current situation he was in. He generally didn't find himself so horny when looking down the barrel of a gun.

"I make it a habit to know those in my field," the raven-haired beauty said, never letting the Browning 9mm in her hand waver.

"You're a hunter?"

"Yes."

"What's your specialty?"

"Demons and psychotic humans." She let go of Chrissy's hand. "Let the girl go, Porter. I sought you out for a reason, and she doesn't need to be involved."

"Put the gun away."

"I asked you to do the same thing, and look how obedient you were."

"I don't take orders."

"Neither do I."

They stared each other down until Chrissy broke the silence, her voice quivering. "Look, dude, I've learned my lesson. Just let me go. I'd rather not be a witness when you two decide to blow each other away."

Jake realized how stupid they looked, like a scene out of a bad gangster movie, and took a chance. He lowered his gun, hoping the hot hunter-chick would do the same. He waited until she did before he took his eyes off her to look at Chrissy.

"What are you going to do if I let you go, Chrissy?"

"I'm going home. My psycho-parents are far better than this. I mean, they're nuts, but you're a total lunatic . . . No offense," she added, apparently realizing she'd just insulted the "total lunatic" in question.

"Remember this night, Chrissy. This could have been real, and you could have been splattered against a wall in a dirty alley. Nobody would have seen anything. Nobody would have saved you if I had truly wanted to hurt you. Do you understand that?"

"Yes," she said, and the tears started again. He wiped them away.

"And don't try to grow up so fast, kid. You're a beautiful girl. Don't turn yourself into something ugly. No man who's going to treat you good would want what you were advertising in that club."

"Okay."

"Go straight home." He let go of her wrist, and she ran like hell.

NYLA WATCHED JAKE while he watched the girl run away. He didn't take his eyes off her until she disappeared around the side of the building. Knowing him the way she did, she knew part of him wanted to personally deliver the girl to her parents.

"So demons got so boring you decided to move on to teenagers?"

"She came on to me in the club," he said, returning his gaze to her. "I snatched her up before she moved on to another guy, a guy who didn't look as if he'd give a damn that she's just a child. Now, who are you?"

"Nyla."

"That's it? Just Nyla?"

"That's all you need to know."

"I don't think so." He raised his gun again, pointing it directly between her eyes. "Try again. Who are you, and what do you want from me?"

"You know, you're really starting to get on my nerves," Nyla said before spinning into action.

She swept his legs out from under him in one smooth, fluid motion, then followed him to the ground. She saddled his waist and grabbed his wrists, holding them over his head, wrestling with him as he strained to aim his gun on her.

"You bitch."

"Manners, Jakie, manners."

"I'm gonna show you manners," he growled, straining harder to free his hands.

Nyla couldn't hold him down for long or she risked him figuring out she was not a mere human. Hating the fact she had to play the part of the weaker sex, but knowing it was necessary for both of them to survive the night, she tried to hold both his wrists with her left hand, aiming her gun at him with the right.

She'd barely made the switch when Jake shoved her off of him sideways, using her own arm for leverage. She fell back on the ground but quickly jumped up before he could train his gun on her. They circled each other, guns pointed and ready, in the dark alley.

"You know, Jakie, I think you have some major trust issues."

"Quit calling me Jakie."

"But it's so cute."

"I'm not cute."

No, he wasn't. He was a display of raw masculinity, sexy and rough around the edges. Nyla strained to control her raging hormones while she and

Jake continued to circle each other. She could still remember the feel of him beneath her body from a moment ago. She longed to have him in that position again. Preferably without the guns involved. Or the clothes.

"I'm not here to hurt you, Jake, but I will if you force me to," she cautioned him, dropping the nickname. It was too close to Jackie, the nickname his best friend had given him. She'd known that, and her ploy had worked. He was on edge. Crappy as it made her feel to hurt him, even the slightest bit, she had to do it. She had to mess with his head a little. If she let him think while he was calm and rational she might give something away, and she'd be dead before dawn. Not the best way to start a relationship with the man she loved.

"I'll ask again what it is you want. If I don't get a good answer I'm going to shoot your pretty little head off."

Pretty? Nyla practically swooned inside and silently chastised herself for it. Now was not the time to go all girlie.

"I'm hunting the bastard who killed the women in Baltimore. I know you have information about him."

"And you know this, how?"

"I was there, and I saw you. I saw you with the vampires."

His eyes widened, but if she'd blinked she would have missed it. He was starting to get suspicious. Not good.

"Yet none of the vampires sensed you."

"Neither did you, oh great vampire hunter. I followed you all the way from Baltimore. You're growing careless."

"If you truly want my help finding the guy, why did you draw down on me?"

"After the stories I've heard about you I wanted to be armed and in control when we first met."

"I've never killed a human."

"You were holding a young girl at gunpoint in an alley," she reminded him. "How was I to know you hadn't gone off the deep end?"

"You thought I was going to hurt the girl?"

"You had a gun on her. You're lucky I wasn't a cop."

He seemed to think about that. Then, with a sigh, he clicked on the gun's safety and shoved the weapon into the back of his waistband. "If you were going to shoot me, you'd have done it already."

"You think?" Nyla put her gun away, letting out a breath of relief. So far so good. "Let's make a deal. Don't shoot me, and I won't shoot you."

"Sure."

"What's with the club? Dunn a regular patron, or you just looking to get laid?"

"You know his name?"

"I told you I was after him too. The Dunns are some jacked-up demons."

He narrowed his eyes at her, just enough to make her nervous, and then cleared his throat. "Why do you need my help?"

Nyla managed to look shamed. She was a good actress. Hell, she'd pretended to be Jake's pet cat for years. "Because I haven't managed to get him yet. You got close, took one of them out, I believe. And you have more vampire kills than anyone I've heard of. That counts for something."

He nodded. "I don't work with a partner, Nyla, and even if I did, I'm not sure I trust you."

"You don't have to trust me, Jake. Just help me catch and kill this bastard."

He nodded again, then motioned for her to lead the way back to the club. Never let the other guy walk in back of you. It was the golden rule for hunters and hit-men.

"Oh, and, Nyla," he said softly from behind her as they walked toward the club, "if you give me even the slightest reason to, I *will* put a bullet through you."

Chapter Four

"I DON'T HAVE ID."

"What?"

"I don't have ID," Nyla repeated, stopping a few feet from the club's entrance. IDs were plastic. Plastic was the one material that didn't stay with her when she shifted.

"What do you mean you don't have ID?"

She turned to find Jake frowning at her, his eyes incredulous. She was on edge enough as it was. She really didn't need the attitude, and she wasn't about to explain to him all the reasons why she generally didn't need ID so he could put a hole in her body. "I said I don't have ID. I think the statement is simple enough, Sherlock."

"That's just great. They don't look hard at the IDs, but they do at least look at them. What kind of hunter doesn't carry at least one fake ID?"

"This kind. You just go back in the front way and I'll see you inside."

"And how are you getting in? The front and back exits are covered, and the side door doesn't open from the outside."

"A lady has her secrets, Jakie. Now be a good little boy, and do as I say."

Something hot and angry flared in his eyes, and she knew it was because of the nickname more than the fact she'd just given him an order. If she were in cat form she'd rub her body along his to comfort him. She wanted to rub her body against his now, but not just for his comfort.

"My name is Jake. Not Jakie, not Jacob, not anything but Jake."

"Whatever. Time's a wastin'. Let's just get in the club . . . unless you're only here to pick up a woman." Nyla tried to fight off the little flare of jealousy the thought evoked.

"One of the victims worked here," he snapped. "I need to question the employees, not to mention look out for Dunn in case he's a customer."

"All right, I'll see you inside."

Nyla turned and headed back around the club, entering the same alley they'd just left. She didn't need an ID to get inside a building, she'd merely shift and enter through a vent, window or under a door crack while still in mist form. It was another skill she'd acquired since Demarcus bit her. Before then, she'd never been able to move while in the mist state or hold it for longer than it normally took to shift into another form.

She glanced over her shoulder to make sure Jake wasn't following. So far he seemed to be buying her story. If she didn't know him well, she'd say she was in the clear. But she did know him, and she knew she'd better watch her back or risk getting shot in it. Jake no longer had any qualms about killing a female; he had no qualms about killing anyone if he thought they needed to be killed.

Nyla checked out the back of the club and found her way inside. A small rectangular set of windows high up on the wall indicated where the club's bathrooms were. She glanced around again, making sure there were no witnesses, and dissolved into mist.

JAKE MADE HIS way through the club, elbowing through the growing crush of people. His gaze fell on the back of a woman, noting the purple thong sticking out of the back of her pants, and the woman's underwear made him wonder what Nyla was wearing beneath her tight jeans. He shook his head in frustration. What he should be worrying about was how many weapons she had beneath her leather jacket, not what type of underwear she was or was not wearing.

He didn't trust her, found it odd that a hunter would just pop up out of the blue claiming to need his help, but it didn't stop his mind from wondering what she'd be like in bed . . . or on the floor, or up against a wall . . . the possibilities were endless. Damn, he needed to get laid before his mental faculties shut down altogether.

He scanned the club, searching for the object of his lewd fantasies, but didn't see her anywhere. Great. Who didn't carry ID? Something was definitely off about her. No matter how hot she was, his instincts said she was trouble.

Jake took a seat at one of the small neon green tables sitting outside the dance floor. Pushing the job back to the forefront of his mind, he waited for the waitress he intended to question.

He saw Nyla exit the ladies room and scan the club. Their eyes locked, and a sense of familiarity washed over him, but she glanced away and headed for the bar before he could figure out why he felt as if he knew her.

The sound of a feminine throat being cleared brought his attention back to the matter at hand. The waitress he'd picked out earlier stood at his side, her expression clearly indicating she'd been waiting for his order long enough. It irritated him because he didn't recall staring at Nyla that long.

"I'm sorry," he apologized, smiling to set off the dimples the ladies seemed to love. "How are you tonight . . ." Jake glanced at her name tag. "Selene?"

"Dandy. What'll you have?"

Oh-kaaay. She wasn't in a good mood. Well, he'd worked with pissed-off spirits, so he could handle a grumpy waitress. "Just a beer."

"Bottle or mug?" Selene's tone didn't change. Bags under her eyes indicated she wasn't getting much sleep.

"Bottle."

"What kind?"

"You pick, and get one for yourself. You look like you could use it."

Selene glanced up from her little notepad, weariness drawn on her face like a mask. "I've got two kids, honey. I don't have time for one-night stands."

"I'm just offering a beer to cheer you up, and maybe keep you from falling over. You got a break coming?"

"Maybe."

Jake flashed his lady-killer smile again. "Grab yourself a beer and sit down. You look like you need a breather, and some company couldn't hurt."

Selene looked at him long and hard, then walked away without a word. Jake watched her as she approached the bar, noticing that Nyla was deep in conversation with the same bartender he'd tried chatting up earlier.

Their faces were close together, her upper body stretched across the bar as though she couldn't get close enough to the tattooed hunk of muscle. Jake's fist tightened, and his jaw clenched. He recognized the reaction as jealousy, but didn't know where it came from. He'd just met the chick, and if he was going to get jealous over a woman, it would be a normal woman, not one who could easily sweep his legs out from under him and pin him to the ground.

He tried to tell himself she'd just taken him by surprise, but inside he knew that wasn't entirely true. She was a tough chick, but there was something different about her. With her speed and strength, he'd say she was a shifter, but she didn't put out that faint buzzing of preternatural power which seemed to emanate from the nasty creatures. She didn't put out anything indicating she wasn't human.

So *what* was she, and how was she making it so hard for him to pull his gaze away from her?

NYLA GLANCED AT the neon clock on the far wall, took note of how many hours had passed, and groaned. This was taking too long. She'd cozied up to the bartender, welcoming his flirting in order to get information, scoped out the club in search of Dunn, and watched in dismay as Jake chatted up the waitress, flashing his killer dimples. There was a moment when he'd covered the waitress's hand with his own, and Nyla had nearly marched over to his table and scalped the woman.

He was hers, dammit! He'd held her for years, telling her his deepest secrets, going to her for comfort when he needed it. Just because he didn't know it didn't make him any less hers.

Nyla stalked out of the club, hoping he'd notice she'd left and come looking. Hell, at this point, she just hoped he'd notice her. He'd already shared the waitress's break hours ago. For some reason he'd stayed at the same table, chatting with the blond whenever she had a lull between ordering customers.

The thought that he was interested in sleeping with the waitress flitted through her mind, and she clenched her teeth, fighting the urge to change into panther form and rip the woman to shreds.

She held on to her anger as she walked to an empty section of curb a block away from the club. For the next step in her plan to work, she needed to look furious when Jake found her, which, thankfully, turned out to be only a matter of minutes.

"Is there a reason why you're standing on the curb looking at a vacant parking spot with murder in your eyes?" he asked after he reached her side and studied her face.

"My car used to be in that empty parking space," she answered, her words clipped.

"Are you saying what I think you're saying?"

"Yep."

"You're joking."

"Nope."

"Your car was stolen?"

"Yep."

"Damn." He glanced around as though he thought her car was just misplaced, not stolen.

Nyla resisted the urge to laugh at his puzzled expression. If she actually owned a car and it really was stolen, she would be seriously pissed. She had to maintain her angry countenance in order to pull off this charade.

"I can drive you back to wherever you're staying," he said, sounding as though he really didn't like the idea. "I assume that would be my motel."

"Why would you assume that?"

"You're stalking me, remember?"

"Trailing and stalking aren't the same," Nyla responded. "And I don't need to stay at your motel to know your whereabouts." Actually, it made sense, and Nyla could kick herself for not thinking of it before.

"How could you follow me and stay at another motel?"

"I'm exceptionally talented," she answered before turning away and walking toward the parking lot and his car.

"You put a tracker on my car."

Now there was a good idea, but knowing he wouldn't find a tracking device, she said, "Maybe."

"Are you always this evasive?"

She stopped and turned to face him. "Are you always this annoying?"

"You came to me for my help, sweetheart. I don't need you, and I don't have to help you."

"You need my help too, Jakie. Do you really think you're going to get this guy all by yourself?"

"*Dammit!* My name is Jake, and I always work alone."

"You didn't kill the other twin by yourself. You had help from the vamps, or maybe you just watched while they offed him."

His eyes glittered with anger. "You weren't in that house. You don't know what happened."

"I know three vamps walked in with you, and four vamps came back out with you. I also know that one of the vamps brought you there all tied up. They were in control, not you. Maybe you're losing your touch."

His nostrils flared, and his tone was hard and ruthless as he said, "I've lost nothing."

"Then why didn't you kill the vamps? Isn't that your job?"

"At that moment, they weren't the bad guys."

"So you could accept a vampire as a friend?"

"I wouldn't say that." His face darkened, his eyes growing distant. "Come on. Accept my offer before I decide to withdraw it."

Nyla banked down her disappointment at his response to her question and followed him to where his Malibu was parked. When she'd seen how Jake left Baltimore without killing Christian, or even causing him trouble, she'd thought that maybe he was beginning to accept that not all vampires were evil. With four simple words he'd dashed her hopes. He'd never befriend a vampire, and that made it hard for her to become his lover.

"Wait a sec," he said, peering into the back of the car. He muttered something and opened the door, looking around the car's interior.

"Did you lose something?" Nyla asked, fighting back a grin when she realized he was looking for her.

"My cat. She's a little feisty."

"Feisty?"

"Feisty, as in she likes to scratch the hell out of women."

Nyla cleared her throat to keep from laughing while Jake stopped looking in the car and started scanning the parking lot. True, she had scratched up some of his female acquaintances, stopping their booty calls before they could happen. Jealous? Sure. Petty? Probably, but what was a girl to do?

"I didn't take you for a kitty-cat person."

He shrugged, continuing his perusal of the parking lot.

"Is she lost?"

"She's never lost," he answered quickly. "I've had her for years, but she's an alley cat. She likes to wander off and do her own thing from time to time. Probably has found a boyfriend around here."

"Well, if she scratches up all your female friends, maybe she thinks you're her boyfriend."

"Cats and people don't mix, sweetheart," he said, giving her a look that said he couldn't believe she'd really said something that weird. Then he shook his head. "Let's wait awhile. I know she'll probably find her way back to my motel all right, but I'd rather take her with me. Just steer clear of her as much as possible. She's small but vicious."

"I'm sure she is," Nyla murmured, struggling to keep the growl out of her voice. Well, what had she expected him to say? She was a vampire, and she was a cat. She could give up on the hope of him realizing she was his dream woman. His dream woman wasn't the furry, bloodsucking, nocturnal type. Speaking of which . . .

"The sun will be up soon, Porter, which means I've officially gone twenty-four hours without sleep. How much longer do we have to wait on this fur ball?"

The narrow-eyed look he gave her wasn't friendly. "A while longer."

Yeah, sure. Wait so she could bake like a couple of eggs in a hot skillet when the sun came up and fried her ass. She didn't do the day-walking thing unless she was in cat form. Maybe it was the fur, or just the fact that when she was a cat she was, well, a cat. When she was in human form she thirsted for blood like a vampire. The way she figured, if it walks like a vampire, talks like a vampire, well then, it probably gets extra freaking crispy when dawn breaks, so she'd rather not be standing outside when the sun decided to show its face.

"So, when you say cat you mean something exotic like a panther or tiger cub, right?"

"No, I mean cat. C-A-T."

"That's funny." Nyla angled her head to the side, running her eyes down the length of Jake's tall frame. "I never took you for a homosexual."

"What?" She didn't need to hear the outrage in his tone to know it was there. His eyes relayed the emotion loud and clear. "What is it with you chicks tonight?"

"For one, I don't like being called a small yellow bird and for two, what are you talking about?"

"Nothing."

"Someone else found out your secret too, huh?"

"What sec—" His eyes narrowed but the half-mast lids couldn't hide his frustration. "I am not gay."

"My bad," Nyla said, putting her hands up in mock surrender. "I thought only gay guys got so attached to kitty cats. My mistake."

"Haven't you ever had a pet?"

"No." When you grow up with feline DNA it's hard enough taking care of yourself, she added silently.

Daybreak was getting closer, and Jake still hadn't made a move toward the driver's seat. Pissing him off hadn't prodded him in that direction, as she'd hoped. That left Plan B.

"Jake, I seriously am worn out," she said, swaying a little for effect.

"Twenty-four hours isn't that long for someone in our field to go without sleep." Judging by the way he said it, Nyla knew he had his doubts if she truly was what she claimed to be. "Haven't you eaten?"

She did a cross between a mumble and a groan, leaning back against the side of the car, her hands cradling her head as if she were afraid it would simply detach and roll off her body.

"Are you all right?"

She mumbled some more unintelligible words, trying to sound pathetic.

"Lay down in the car and nap. I'm sure Alley will be back soon."

Dammit. The man was determined to see her fry. If they left now they'd have just enough time to reach the motel before sunrise. Nyla did the best thing she could think of.

She fell to the ground as ungracefully as a sack of potatoes.

Chapter Five

JAKE'S SCENT LINGERED in the air, but the room was empty, Nyla deduced upon first waking. She didn't remember falling asleep.

She remembered that Jake barely caught her in his strong arms in time to keep her head from cracking against the pavement. She remembered the feel of those arms holding her against the solid wall of his chest as he struggled to open the car door without dropping her, finally getting her into the backseat where he laid her down gently.

She kept her eyes closed the whole time, letting him think she'd passed out from exhaustion. Fortunately, he immediately got into the driver's seat and sped off, forgetting about Alley, er . . . her. Oh, what a twisted mess she was in.

She must have fallen asleep right after they left the club, which didn't surprise her. She'd spent last night securing a motel room and finding a human to feed from. She'd been tempted to drink from Andre, the motel clerk, to save time, but that would have been a mistake. She couldn't do the whole brainwash thing some vampires were able to do.

Instead, she'd wandered the streets and fought back her hunger until she found a bum. She hadn't hurt him, and if he told anyone about the mystery woman who bit into his neck and drank his blood nobody would believe him. It's kind of hard to believe the word of a man who talks to a Frisbee, which was what he was doing when she'd found him.

After that, she'd shifted back to cat form and ran back to Jake's motel room, eavesdropping for any information she could get her paws on.

No wonder she'd fallen asleep so easily once she was in the back of his car, the motion of the ride lulling her as gently as a mother's lullaby.

But what had she missed?

Nyla started to stretch, but her left arm wouldn't move as it should. She sat up, twisting around awkwardly to see her wrist was handcuffed to a rail of the headboard of Jake's bed.

Dammit. She quickly looked around the room. Her jacket and boots were beside the nightstand, but her clothes were still completely on. That was a plus. If she were going to get naked with Jake, she'd prefer to be conscious. How had he carried her all the way into his room and removed those items without waking her? More importantly, how had he managed to cuff her? Man, she had to be more careful . . . much more careful, she realized as she spotted her empty holster on the desk. Her sheaths, knives included, were missing as well.

She bit out a vile curse and dissolved into mist, changing back to human form once she was free of the handcuff and able to stand. Where the hell was Jake? Even as she asked herself the question, she knew the answer. She reached into her back pocket, ready to rip off Jake's head when she withdrew her empty hand. He had the receipt with her motel room number on it and was, without a doubt, at her motel rifling through her belongings.

Thank goodness she hadn't fed from Andre, whom she was sure Jake would question about her. But what would Andre say? She'd paid in cash, suspicious but not for a hunter, and she hadn't completely lied to Jake about that. She hadn't spent every minute of the past sixteen years of her life with him. She'd taken a few weeks off here and there to hunt for Demarcus and had slain some nasty vampires along the way. She might not have as many kills under her belt as Jake, but she'd definitely earned the title of hunter.

Reassuring herself that Andre couldn't tell Jake anything she wouldn't want him to know, she took a moment to review what she'd left in her room in the rundown motel. There were no personal items for Jake to find at the motel, with the exception of her underwear, so she would be all right. Unfortunately, that conclusion didn't stop negative thoughts from crowding her mind as she paced the room.

Jake didn't trust her. She hadn't expected him to, which is why she'd planned to play the role of an adversary and then somehow work her way into his heart. But she'd made mistakes. She'd planned on acting as though she hadn't followed him, but then she'd blurted out that she had. So what excuse did she have to stay at another motel? And how would she explain not having ID? She knew that Jake, and probably all the hunters, traveled with several different IDs.

Damn! How had she forgotten a detail like ID? Because she'd never needed ID to slay vampires or do anything else in her life. She just had to stay cool and not make any more mistakes, and everything would work out fine.

She hoped.

WHO WAS NYLA KATT? Jake wondered while he shoved his hands under the mattress of her bed. He frowned when he didn't find anything there—or anything useful in the entire motel room.

He sat on the bed, heaving a sigh of frustration. He'd found out her last name by bribing the front desk clerk, but who knew if that was real? A complete and thorough search of her room hadn't told him anything—except her bra size and that she had a thing for tiny, lacy black underwear, which was exactly what he didn't need to know. It was hard seeing a woman as a possible threat when all you wanted to do was bang her.

He didn't need this crap. Two women were dead, and instead of following leads on their killer, he was searching a woman's motel room. But there was something about Nyla Katt that unnerved him. There was also something oddly familiar about her, something in the way she looked at him, but he couldn't pinpoint exactly what it was. And he didn't care what story she gave him. He'd been in this business a long time, and he knew another hunter wouldn't just pop up, asking for his help the way she had.

His cell phone rang, and the sudden sharp chirping sound in the silent room caused him to jump, a clear sign he was on edge.

"Porter," he announced, placing the phone to his ear.

"It's me." Jonah's voice spilled from the receiver. "How's it going down there? Any progress?"

"Not too much. Have you got anything for me?"

"The name of the town where the second woman's body was dumped. Hicksville."

"Got anything on the vic?"

"Brunette. Early twenties. Body drained, two supposed fang holes in the neck. No identification has been made. The boys are all over my ass about this, seeing as how I supposedly had him in my grasp and let him get away."

"After the condition you were in when they found you, they can shut the hell up. It's not like they'll ever be able to catch him." Jake didn't bother hiding his anger.

"Yeah, but everyone likes to point the finger."

Jake snorted. "Yeah, I got a finger for them. You all right? Nobody's looking at you funny?"

"Everything's fine, bro. They totally bought the story I spun for them. You just handle yourself and quit worrying about me."

"I always handle myself."

"I'm not even touching that one," Jonah managed through a chuckle.

"Shut up, ass-wipe." Jake had to laugh himself. "Do me a favor, though."

"Yeah?"

"See what you can find out on a Nyla Katt." He spelled out the name.

"Do I get to know why I'm running a check on her?" Joe asked.

"Let's just say I don't know if she's more my thing or yours."

"I'm assuming that means you don't know whether she's human or . . . something else."

"Exactly." Jake let out a sigh. "She seems human, but more than human. You know?"

"Uh, no. I'm not the expert in that area. Is she dangerous?" Jonah's tone took on a hint of worry.

Jake scoffed. "More like she's in danger. It's all I can do to keep from strangling her. She's just . . . I don't know. She's not like anyone I've ever come across."

"Do you have the hots for this girl?"

"I don't get the hots," Jake bit out, irritated that he could actually *hear* the grin in Jonah's voice. "She's just a woman who popped up out of the blue, claiming to be hunting Dunn, and get this—she saw what happened the night Carter was taken out."

"What?" All trace of amusement fled. "How the hell could she do that?"

"I don't know. She said she was following me while I followed them. Yet, none of us picked up on her. She doesn't actually know what happened inside the house, but she knows Carter was taken out that night, and she knows vampires helped make that happen."

Jonah was silent for a moment before asking, "You're sure she's not a vampire?"

"She doesn't put out the vibe. I can sense vampires before I see them."

"I didn't know that."

Jake frowned, sure Jonah would have known that much. "Yes, you did."

"No, I didn't. You've never told me that."

"Whatever, dude, just find me something on this woman." Jake shrugged it off, his frustration growing. It would be dark soon, and he had a woman handcuffed to his bed that he had to get back to. Under other circumstances, that might have put a smile on his face, but he didn't think Nyla Katt was going to wake up happy, warm and willing. He was definitely in for a confrontation.

"All right, man, I'll check the woman out. Just watch your back. If she is a normal chick and she followed you all the way from here to Kentucky, you're slipping."

"Gee, you always know the right thing to say. You should have been a life coach."

"Yeah, and you should have noticed you were being followed."

Jake didn't deny the fact he'd made a potentially fatal mistake. When you screwed up that big, you didn't make excuses. You made damn sure it never happened again.

"I know, Joe. That's why I want to know who I'm dealing with."

"I'm on it," Jonah said after a long pause. "I'll get back to ya as soon as I get something. Be extra careful in the meantime, jerk."

"Back at you, cake boy."

With the conversation over, Jake rose from the bed and took a deep breath. He didn't know who Nyla Katt was or how dangerous she might prove to be, but until he did, he wasn't letting her out of his sight, he decided as he left her room with visions of lacy black panties dancing through his head.

Thirty minutes later, he found himself back at his motel standing outside the door of his room, listening for sounds. There weren't any, although he was sure Nyla was still inside. He'd left her handcuffed to his bed and put the Do Not Disturb sign on the knob so the maid wouldn't find her and call the police. Nyla probably woke shortly after he left and had tired herself out trying to get free. He'd been sure she wouldn't scream for help, knowing any chance of civility between them would be shot to hell if she did. She was probably just lying there, a seething ball of fury, waiting to unleash that anger on him the moment he walked through the door.

Jake slid in his key card and unlocked the door. He stepped inside and knew he was in trouble the second his gaze fell on the empty bed, the handcuffs dangling from the headboard. Before he could prepare for the attack, he felt an arm snake around his neck and something sharp and pointy jutted into the middle of his back.

"Don't move."

He searched the room with his eyes as he heard Nyla close the door behind him. He didn't see any evidence that she'd gone shopping for weapons, but she did have something pressed against his spine. He focused on the feel of the weapon, determining it was too small to be the barrel of a gun. He felt a tiny prick that felt like a knife tip, but judging by the amount of pressure against his back, he could turn and wouldn't suffer anything more than a nick.

"Don't try anything stupid, Porter," Nyla warned, increasing the pressure, as if she'd read his mind. "Make no illusions as to who is in control now."

"Whatever you want to believe, lady," Jake growled, starting to get really pissed. He'd battled spirits and vamps, yet he was being held at knife point in his own motel room by a woman he outweighed by at least seventy pounds. That more than chafed his ego.

"I thought we talked about those manners, Jakie. It's kind of rude referring to someone as just 'lady' when you know their name, don't you think?"

"I'm sorry," Jake managed to get out, despite Nyla's forearm continuing to apply pressure against his windpipe. Damn, the woman was stronger than she looked. "What I meant to say was, whatever you want to believe, *bitch*."

"Ouch, Jakie, that hurts . . . almost as bad as this." She accentuated her statement by tightening her hold.

Jake struggled to breathe, to fight off the dizziness, but her hold was too tight, despite the fact she had to be standing on her toes to get him in that hold. If he had any hope of getting the upper hand, he had to break away now. She was tough, but she was smaller, and he was sure he could outmaneuver her.

He quickly jammed his elbows back into her sides. She let out a gasp, loosening her hold on him while she tried to regain her breath, which was all he needed.

He whirled around, hitting her in the side with the full length of his arm. Nyla skidded across the floor, a pen falling out of her hand as she came to a stop against the wall. Jake stared at the floor, frowning as his mind grappled with what he saw. A pen?

"You held me at *pen-point?*" Jake bellowed, anger now mingling with indignity, as his gaze shot to her face.

"Yeah, and don't you feel like an ass," Nyla said, her voice low and deep as she picked herself up off the floor. There was something dangerous glittering in her eyes, something warning him not to underestimate her. "I don't appreciate being handcuffed."

"Speaking of which, how'd you get out of them?" he asked, eying her closely. He knew she was going to do something. He wasn't sure what that something was, but he did know he wouldn't like it.

"It's one of my skills," she growled as she launched herself at him, succeeding in head-butting him in the stomach.

Jake doubled over in pain, then snapped back up when Nyla belted his chin with an uppercut.

"What the—" His words were cut off as he found himself belly down on the floor. Nyla was on his back trying to pin him. He tried to roll but the feel of his own gun, taken from his waistband and then pressed against the back of his head, stopped him cold. "If that's another pen, I'm going to really be pissed."

NYLA CLICKED THE safety off Jake's gun. "Does a pen make that sound?" She laced her tone with menace, trying to cover up the fact she was still reeling from the adrenaline surging through her due to their little tussle. She'd never thought she'd get him down so easily. There was a lot to be said for the element of surprise.

"No, ma'am."

"Funny how we remember our manners when we have guns pressed against our head, isn't it?"

He let out a pretty good snarl, almost as good as an angry cat's. "Say what you have to say, Nyla."

"Why'd you handcuff me to your bed?"

"I don't know who you are. Why would I leave you alone in my room with weapons?"

"You could have just taken the weapons, which, by the way, I want back immediately, and I already told you who I am. I came to you for help, not a showdown."

"Oh, I can see that." Jake didn't bother hiding the sarcasm. She could feel tension radiating off him, knew he was struggling to keep his temper in check. She felt the strength of that tension wash over her, and something about it made her warm and hungry inside. Absentmindedly, she ran her fingers down his back, wanting to feel the skin beneath his shirt.

Jake must have noticed her loss of focus because he used that moment to roll over. She was still straddling him, and she still had the gun, but he didn't look that scared of her.

"We've been in two fights within twenty-four hours, Nyla. Why do you suppose that is?"

"Maybe you just can't keep your hands off of me," Nyla whispered, her voice low and husky, even a bit wistful. Small beads of sweat dotted Jake's brow, and she had the strongest urge to taste them. The desire to run her tongue along his skin welled inside her, heating her from the inside. She bunched his T-shirt in her hand, ready to rip it off his body, planning to free herself of her own clothing afterward.

Suddenly Jake was on top of her, and he had the gun. She was pinned and hadn't done a thing to stop it from happening, hadn't even seen it coming.

"You're not exactly an Amazon. A normal woman of your size could never have gotten me in that hold. Who are you, Nyla Katt, and *what* are you?"

Nyla knew she should have been scared because he'd reversed positions, worried because he'd asked *what* she was, like he knew she wasn't just a mere woman. She should be scared as hell because he was pointing a gun directly at her chest.

But as her eyes roamed over his arms, delighting in the way the corded muscles bulged under his skin, she realized something much worse was happening to her.

She was going—hell, had already gone—into heat.

Chapter Six

"GET OFF ME," Nyla growled from behind clenched teeth.

"How do I know you're not going to try to off me with a pen or something?" Sarcasm dripped from his words.

"Get. Off. Me." Nyla closed her eyes, trying to block out the image of him on top of her, but in her mind's eye she saw them both in several more interesting positions, none of which were incentive to stop the sudden heat pooling between her thighs. "Please, let me up," she said, opening her eyes to risk a glance at the man above her.

Maybe it was her pleading tone or the fear she was sure shone in her eyes, but with a frown, Jake slid backward, setting her free. For a second, she thought she saw guilt in his eyes, but she didn't have time to decipher what he was feeling. She had to get away from him.

She scrambled to her feet, abandoning her usual catlike grace, and ran to the bathroom, slamming the door closed behind her. She twisted the lock and turned to the sink, twisting the knob until water gushed full blast.

"Nyla?"

She ignored Jake's call and the jiggling of the doorknob as she splashed the cool water on her face. It felt as if her skin was aflame and crawling with energy.

"Nyla, are you all right?"

"I'm fine!" She winced at the harshness in her voice and gripped the edge of the sink, fighting the tremors. They weren't bad yet, but they would be unless she did something to stop them. She usually didn't get them so quickly. Her nearness to Jake while in human form must have revved up her hormones. It made sense. The Heat was usually a purely physical desire, but her feelings for Jake intensified it. Fan-freaking-tastic.

"Do you need anything?" Jake asked from just beyond the bathroom door, his tone indicating genuine concern.

Yeah, the use of your penis, she wanted to say, but instead opted for, "You could get my weapons like I asked."

"I think we should discuss that."

"I think you should do as I say before we have another altercation."

"Nyla—"

"I am in here with your razor, Jake. You can get me my damn gun like a good boy or I can come out there and go Lorena Bobbitt on your ass! Which scenario do you prefer?"

She heard his footsteps and then the door closing as he left the room. Men. Threaten them with a little penis amputation, and they'd do anything.

With Jake out of the motel room, some of the tension fueling her desire seeped away, allowing her to breathe a little easier. "Damn feline DNA," she grumbled, splashing more water on her face.

There were ways, she had come to learn, that she could hold off the Heat. Blood was one of them. Thanks to her vampire side, she enjoyed the taste of warm, flowing blood. The feel of it rolling over her tongue could be a nearly orgasmic experience, but when she fed she let Demarcus in. She couldn't feed without the monster creeping inside her head. She could feel him in there, looking through her eyes, trying to sense where she was. Why? There were only two reasons she could think of.

Revenge or domination.

Neither were appealing so taking blood was out. She'd already fed recently, and she had a firm rule about taking blood. Never twice in the same city. Thank goodness she could go weeks between feedings.

The cold water helped a little bit, soothed her heated flesh, but her insides were still a raging inferno. Sooner or later she would have to give in.

So why not just jump Jake the moment he walked through the door? He was a man. He lived for sex. Hell, thanks to her and her jealousy, he hadn't gotten any for a while. He probably wouldn't mind at all.

She stared at her wet face in the mirror and shook her head. She would not attack him like Slut-zilla, queen of the hoochie tribe. If there came a time when she could be with him in the way she'd dreamed of for years she wanted it to be his call. She wanted him to come to her, to know that he wanted her, Nyla, not the sex-starved animal she became when the Heat had her in its grip.

She'd have to wait it out. Supposedly, that could be done. It took about two weeks. Two weeks of agonizing, burning, itching, skin-crawling, tremor-inducing desire. She usually made it about four days and grabbed the closest thing with testicles.

Making it past four days in human form with Jake was impossible, how could she make it two weeks? *Dammit!*

She heard the room's door shut, then, "Nyla?"

Double-dammit! The sound of Jake's deep voice caressed her skin like silk, making the desire churn more fiercely inside her.

"Nyla?" He was by the bathroom door now, his scent wafting underneath it to reach out to her. She started to choke on desire. "I have your weapons, but I'm not going to just give them to you."

Damn him. A wave of anger crashed through her, and she could feel the Heat draw back a bit. Not much, but enough that she could breathe evenly, and that gave her an idea. If she could stay mad, use the anger to dissipate her sexual needs . . .

"Nyla?" Worry came through in his voice.

"I heard you, *dammit!*" She turned off the tap and swung around to jerk open the door, meeting Jake's steely gaze. She closed her eyes against the too-hot-to-handle sight of him standing before her and carefully dodged past him, making sure no part of their bodies touched. Skin to skin contact was so not what she needed at the moment. She needed anger.

"Are you all right?" he asked cautiously.

"What the hell do you care?" she asked, spinning around to face him, using her anger as a shield against his attractiveness. "You chained me to a frigging bed and then knocked me across the room!"

"You had a knife, or what I thought was a knife, against my back!" he shouted back, his expression incredulous.

"I did that because you chained me to a bed!"

"I handcuffed you. I did not chain you!"

"I'm sorry," she drawled scornfully. "Is there a difference?"

Jake opened his mouth as if to speak, but then must have thought better of it. Or maybe he just didn't know what to say. Nyla couldn't read him as well when she was in human form. In cat form, he was an open book.

"In answer to your earlier question of *what* I am, I am *not* a monster, Jake." It was easy letting anger roil along with those words. "I can kick your ass because it's what I've practiced for years. It's what I've trained for. I'm a hunter. I catch dangerous men and sometimes demons. You know as well as I do that I can't just slap them around. I have to hurt them. If you can't take a beating like a man, deal with it, but don't you dare start questioning what I am as if I'm something you hunt just because I bested you."

"Wait a damn second!" Jake bellowed. "You didn't kick my ass. You snuck up on me with what appeared to be a knife. We tussled, maybe, but there was no ass-kicking. You're good, but you're not *that* good."

"Oh, I'm sorry," Nyla snapped, placing her fists on her hips. "Did I hurt your sensitive male pride?"

He started to respond, and she could tell that whatever he said would be loud and smart-mouthed, but then he paused, and she watched some of the spark burn out of his eyes before he lowered his gaze to the floor. "The only thing hurting my pride is knowing I knocked you across a room, which I only did because I thought you had a knife to my back. I don't get off on smacking women around, Nyla."

Damn. So much for directing her anger towards him, Nyla thought, realizing it *had* been guilt she'd seen in his eyes when he backed away from her earlier. It was hard to be pissed at a guy who already felt like crap, particularly when he'd just been defending himself.

"You didn't hit me, Porter. It was more of a shove, and like you said, you thought I had a knife. Chivalry is nice, but when it gets you killed, it's just plain stupidity." As she spoke, she felt the desire starting to rise again. Desperately, she searched for words which would bring back some of her anger. "Besides, I'm some sort of a monster, remember?"

"I don't know what you are." Jake raked a hand through his hair and shook his head. "You're the toughest chick I've ever met, but still, you're a chick. Maybe I just don't expect a lot of fire out of you, so I'm surprised when I get it."

Nyla unfisted her hands and folded her arms. "Except for the chick reference, which is annoying since I don't recall hatching from an egg, that almost sounded like a compliment."

"Lap it up then. I don't hand out compliments often, and I still don't trust you."

"Shocker there," she commented, laying on the sarcasm, and realized she'd spent enough time with Jake that she'd adopted his smart aleck attitude.

The thought almost made her smile, which consequently made her desire ratchet up another notch. She quickly tore her gaze away from Jake's chest, fighting the urge to rip away his dark T-shirt and explore the hard planes beneath, but she found that staring up into his eyes wasn't much improvement.

Their green depths seemed brighter, the honey-brown edge surrounding his irises darker. Together, mixed with the intensity of his gaze, they stole her breath away.

"Nyla?"

The deep timbre of his voice reached out to her like a phantom hand, stroking her intimately. She tried to breathe, but the desire filled her from the inside, pushing all the air out of her lungs. She was drowning, and she wouldn't survive unless she released the pressure building inside her body.

"Nyla?" Jake reached out to her, and she felt her walls of protection start to crumble, blasted apart by the hormonal furor raging inside her.

His hand touched her arm and her insides turned liquid, causing her body to sway toward his. There was a second where, as she gazed into his eyes, she saw a matching hunger reflected in his gaze. It could have been her imagination, or maybe she was drunk on lust and everyone looked as hot and bothered as she felt, but she couldn't be sure because she only had that one second before she knew she wasn't alone in her own mind.

She snapped her eyes shut before Demarcus's power could reach them and backed away from Jake. "Don't touch me," she said, and tasted her own fear on her tongue.

She started rebuilding the metaphysical walls in her mind, struggling to push Demarcus's dark presence out and force down the Heat at the same time. It wasn't easy. Demarcus fought against her, pressing his power against hers, straining to burst through the new wall she was putting up in haste. She could feel him searching the wall, trying to find one loose brick so he could force himself in, but metaphysical walls, built with strength, power and determination, didn't give way so easily.

"Nyla."

"Shut up, J—"

The moment she started to say his name, some other voice, which didn't belong to Demarcus said, *Hide him. Don't say his name. Don't reveal him.*

She didn't question the voice. It was the same one that had sent her to that dark alley sixteen years earlier, the same voice which sent her to protect Jake. She felt Demarcus's power battering against her walls and knew he'd heard the voice too.

He tried to force her to open her eyes, but she kept them sealed shut, running blindly for the bathroom. She waited until she knew she'd passed Jake to open them and find the door, slamming it closed behind her before Jake could do something stupid like step in front of her.

Jake called out to her as she fumbled with the lock. "Are you all right? What's wrong with you?"

"Shut up!" she snapped, quickly turning on the faucet and letting the gushing water drown him out.

Satisfied that Jake was as safe as she could make him for the moment, Nyla stood before the bathroom mirror, her hands gripping the edge of the sink, and lowered her shield just enough to allow Demarcus enough access to see through her eyes.

She didn't have to feel his presence to know when he accomplished this. She looked at her reflection in the mirror and saw him the moment he was there. Her eyes were the same shape, the same shade of purple, but Demarcus had turned them bitter and cold, full of his evil.

"Stay away," she ordered him, her voice low enough that Jake couldn't hear from the other side of the bathroom door, but it was still filled with the ferocity of a mighty roar. "You can't have him, and you can't have me."

As she glared into her own eyes, she could feel his anger, his determination to destroy her, and she used it against him.

She borrowed his darkness, his deep hatred, and combined it with her fear, her anger, and her determination to protect the man she loved. She rolled those emotions into a ball and laced them with her own power, both vampiric and therian. She used the produced energy from those emotions to cast Demarcus out of her mind with one last, parting remark delivered through clenched teeth, "Go. Back. To. Hell."

Nyla opened her eyes, and the first thing she realized was she was on the bathroom floor. The second thing she realized, as she looked up into Jake's concerned gaze, was that Demarcus was truly gone from her mind.

Jake was speaking to her, asking her what happened, but she couldn't think straight enough to formulate an answer.

He scooped her into his arms, and that's when she noticed he'd kicked in the door to get to her. Then she became aware of the fact she was in his arms, and she immediately began to struggle for release.

"Stop it, crazy woman," Jake commanded, fighting against her while she kicked and squirmed, trying to get out of his hold. He managed to hold on to her until he reached the bed and dropped her none-too-gently on top of it. "There. Now, what the hell is wrong with you?"

That was a good question. She'd just been squirming in Jake's arms, and now she was on his bed, in his motel room. If the Heat had still been raging inside her, he wouldn't have stood a chance. The fact that she wasn't ripping off his clothes told her the Heat was gone. No, not gone. It was never truly gone. It was inside her somewhere, waiting, but, thankfully, for the moment she wasn't under its control.

She felt Jake's hand on her forehead and quickly jerked away, afraid his touch might reignite the flame. The moment she looked back into his eyes, she regretted the reflexive action. He almost looked hurt.

"I'm not going to do anything to you, Nyla. I was just checking your temperature. You're running a fever."

"How can you tell that by touching my forehead?"

"It's either that or you're The Human Torch." He must have recognized the confusion on her face. "One of the characters from *The Fantastic Four*. His whole body can turn to flame."

Nyla blinked and nodded slowly, realizing her eyes were burning. She *was* running a temperature. She was used to running a fever while in Heat, but the Heat wasn't burning through her now. It had to be an aftereffect of forcing Demarcus out of her mind.

"I'm fine, Porter. I must have a little bug or something."

"I'll call room service for some aspirin. You should eat something too. You're not going to be much help to me if I have to keep scooping you up off the floor."

The statement brought her head up, and her gaze locked with his. "You mean that? We hunt together. No more fighting?"

"I can't guarantee the part about no fighting. I hear I'm a real pain in the ass." He grabbed the room service menu off the nightstand and sat next to her. "What do you want to eat?"

"Steak." She didn't need to think about it. Apparently the power she'd used to cast out Demarcus had pushed down the Heat, but the power and strength she'd used up in doing so had awakened another hunger. It was just starting to make its presence known.

Jake picked up the phone to call room service after setting the menu aside, apparently having decided what he wanted. "Well-done?" he asked.

"Bloody."

He wrinkled his nose. "That's gross."

"Then don't watch me eat it."

The look of disgust on his face indicated he wouldn't. He placed their orders, including aspirin with the food, and placed the receiver back in its cradle.

"What's in the box?" Nyla saw her gun and knives, still in the sheaths, sitting on the table across the room. In front of them lay a medium-sized box.

"I know a guy who makes some pretty high-tech gear. I lost my last vamp gun, so he rushed an order to make me a new one." Jake rose from the bed and strolled across the room to the table.

"A vamp gun?"

"It uses special UV bullets," he explained, sitting down to log on to his laptop. "My brother is supposed to send me pictures of the first victim, assuming he can weasel them out of someone in Louisville's homicide department. Ah, whaddaya know. He did it."

Jake picked up the laptop and brought it with him to the bed. "Are you sure you're up for this?" he asked, seeming to study her a little too intently for comfort. "You were out cold for a moment in the bathroom. If you do that on a hunt you could put us both in jeopardy."

"I'll be fine, Porter. I have to help you catch this guy and end this thing. It's important to me."

"I know," he said, his frustrated expression stating that he recognized her determination. "But why is finding the other Dunn twin so important to you?"

Nyla held his gaze for a long minute, as she searched for an answer. Finally, she realized that the best lie would be the truth. "They nearly killed someone close to me." She wasn't lying. She was referring to his brother, Jonah. In the sixteen years she'd been with Jake, she'd gotten to know and care for Jonah too. Besides, she wasn't about to tell Jake that a little voice in her head was telling her he was in danger. He'd decide for sure she was nuts.

Jake nodded, seeming to understand her reasoning, which came as no surprise. After all, it was his revenge for his friend Bobby that had set him on this monster hunting path. "Why do you need my help?"

"You found them before I did. You had at least some part in taking out one of them. I'd be an idiot for not joining forces with you."

He leaned back against the headboard and seemed to think about that. "The vampires killed Carter Dunn. Actually, they didn't kill him. They destroyed him."

"Is there a difference?" Nyla didn't have to fake her curiosity. She hadn't actually entered the Dunn residence with Jake and the vampires, so she had no idea what had gone down that night.

"Apparently so. Seta, the female vamp you saw with me that night, fought against him with magic, and I believe she would have just killed him if she could. It was Christian, the pastor, who took care of him in the end."

"He's the pastor who brought you there?"

"Yeah," he said, and something akin to fear, but not quite as strong, washed over his face for a second. "He just prayed. Nothing special, no holy water flinging or spiritual seizures. He just prayed and poof—Carter Dunn was destroyed."

"What do you mean by destroyed?"

"It was like he blew up, not just his body, but what was in it. His charred body was left behind. Whatever was in it completely disintegrated in this blinding light."

"You're talking about the demon that possessed him?"

"Yeah . . . or his soul or something. Everything just exploded in the light." The deep frown on his face suggested he was reliving that night in his mind, but before she could comment, he gave a sharp shake of his head and returned his attention to her. "Anyway, my brother, who's a detective by the way, sent me all the intel he could gather."

Jake clicked on the email waiting to be read, but before he could read it, there was a knock on the door followed by an announcement that room service had arrived. "I'll grab that."

Nyla admired his backside as he rose from the bed, heading for the door, but remembering that the Heat could rise again at any time, she quickly looked away. She decided to focus on business, and she started to review the e-mail Jonah had sent, downloading the attached files, which contained pictures of the first victim.

Sure, she was about to eat, and bloody meat at that, but she had panther in her blood. She could stomach the sight of blood and rigor mortis and still manage to hold down her dinner.

She viewed the pictures while Jake took care of the food. "Come on and eat, Nyla, before you pass out again."

"Uh, Jake, you need to see this picture."

"You're looking at those *now*? Before you eat a bloody slab of meat? Damn, woman, you're cold."

She let the comment go as she stared into the victim's eyes, eyes a shade of amber no normal human would ever achieve. She swallowed hard when she saw the claw-like nails still protruding from the young waitress's fingers.

"Jake, forget the food for a second. I think the first victim was a shifter."

Chapter Seven

"THAT SADISTIC BASTARD," Jake bit out while pacing the floor.

"Maybe the nails are fake," Nyla offered. "The eye color could be the result of special contacts."

"Does it look fake to you?"

"No," Nyla conceded, moving from the bed to the table. They were still discussing the girl, but the smell of bloody bovine was calling to her. "However, a true shifter looks human in death. The claws should have drawn back in once she died."

Jake turned toward her the exact moment she plunged a red-tinged chunk of meat into her mouth. She watched him visibly fight the urge to gag while she savored the bloody juices sliding over her tongue.

"Damn, Nyla. You could have warned me you were going to do that."

"It's my dinner, Jake. What did you think I was going to do with it, play a couple rounds of canasta?"

He shook his head before taking a seat across from her, carefully avoiding looking at her plate. It made Nyla grin. He picked up his chicken breast, looked it over for a moment, then set it back down, opting for a French fry instead.

"You slice up and behead vampires on a regular basis, but you can't look at pictures of dead people before you eat meat or watch someone else eat rare steak. It's almost cute."

"Shut up," he said irritably. "Let's stay on the subject."

"Fine. If the victim was a were-something, why didn't her claws retract upon death?"

"Maybe they couldn't."

"Explain that."

"What do you know about Carter Dunn's laboratory?" Jake asked, daring a glance at her.

"Unfortunately, not much," she answered, which was true. She'd traveled with Jake to Baltimore, but she'd been hit with the bloodlust once they arrived, a case so bad it was unbearable, even in cat form. She'd thought Jake was just going to meet up with Jonah to discuss some possible vampires in town, so she'd headed out to find a donor. By the time she found Jake later that night, he was hog-tied over Christian's shoulders. The windows and doors to the house had been sealed up so tight with spells after they'd gone inside that she hadn't been able to find a crack to mist through, so she'd had to wait outside, praying he made it back out alive. "I know that Carter Dunn was behind the murders in Baltimore and somehow managed to completely drain his victims of blood."

"He had a lab in his basement," Jake said as he continued to eat his food, "and he liked to perform experiments. There was a vampire chained to the wall of that lab. He'd been there for months. Alfred Dunn had a personal vendetta against him."

"Alfred Dunn was Curtis and Carter's great-grandfather, correct?"

"So you've researched the family?"

"Of course." Nyla finished off her last bit of steak, letting the bloody juices sit on her tongue a moment before swallowing. "I know the twins' grandfather was murdered, and they were fathered by the man who raped their mother."

"Their grandfather, Patrick, was killed by a vampire named Eron, the same vamp they had pinned to a wall. Alfred Dunn knew Eron had killed his son, so he spent most of his life searching for him in hopes of killing him. He eventually made a pact with the devil, and because of that pact, his own grand-daughter was raped by a demon, and he and his son were reincarnated as Curtis and Carter Dunn."

Nyla leaned back in her chair, resisting the urge to lick the pinkish juice from her plate, and pretended to mull over the information she'd just been given. She already knew the reincarnation part, thanks to her superior eavesdropping skills—and the fact that people talked so openly around cats.

"This confirms my theory that the twins are demons."

"Carter, definitely. Curtis seemed to be struggling."

"Struggling how?"

"When Aria Michaels, whom Carter had kidnapped as his next victim, was chained up in his lab, his brother Curtis said something about being two souls fighting."

"So he has a good side and an evil side battling inside him?"

"Something like that." Finished with his meal, he pushed his plate away and handed Nyla the packet of aspirin she'd overlooked. "Don't forget to take these. That fever needs to come down."

"Thanks." She opened the packet and downed two pills with the help of the bottled water Jake had ordered for her. Being a shifter, they wouldn't help, but they wouldn't hurt her either. "It seems as though the evil side of Curtis is winning since these murders have started back up."

"It would appear that way."

"Something in your tone says you aren't convinced that's what's happening."

Jake shrugged as if to say what he believed wasn't important.

"Tell me what you think."

Jake seemed to ponder the question for a moment, then nodded, dedicating himself to the task. "I don't think these were normal demon posses-sions, as in cases where demons temporarily control a person. I think Carter Dunn had no soul, but was instead a real live demon encased in a human shell."

Nyla sat back, considering. "And Curtis?"

"From what he told Aria while she was captured, it seems that something happened when he was reincarnated. The demon Alfred Dunn became in Hell was reborn into a human body . . . but a new soul somehow made its way into that body, too."

"Two beings in one body? Alfred, the demon, and Curtis . . . the newborn soul."

"Yes." Jake flexed his fist. "But I'll show no mercy to Curtis Dunn. He was in that body, and he did nothing while women were murdered, and while my brother was beaten nearly to death."

"So that's why this is personal for you."

"Yes, and it's why Curtis got away. My brother had been beaten badly and was hanging on a wall when I got there. I was too focused on rescuing him and the woman bleeding to death on a lab table, as well as the fight between Carter and the vamps, to pay attention to Curtis. While all of the good guys were preoccupied, he got away."

"I see, but what has this got to do with the shifter murdered here in Louisville? You said maybe her claws couldn't change back to normal."

"Right, because of the experiments Carter performed on the vampire."

"Carter is dead. We're after Curtis."

"They're identical twins, so Carter probably wasn't the only one handy with a chemistry set. They kept Eron alive because they were working on a serum to give them immortality without having to become vampires."

Nyla sat back in her chair and folded her arms. "I get it. You think Curtis is experimenting on shifters now."

"Yes. Maybe he did something to her system before killing her, something which would prevent her claws from retracting, hoping to attract the attention of shifter hunters."

"He left fang holes again, too."

"Dunn would love nothing more than to see the vampire race wiped out. Any time he can expose them he will take that opportunity. He's trying to kill two monsters with one stone now."

Nyla let the remark go, although it cut her deeply. It emphasized that no matter what she did, she'd always be a monster to Jake, could never belong to him in the way she wanted. She needed to accept it, secure his safety, and move on. The question was, could she move on without him? Or would she be condemned to follow him around until the day he died?

She ignored the questions, knowing that only time would tell, and asked, "So, did you find out anything useful about the victim while you were schmoozing the waitress at The Crimson Rose?"

"Did you find out anything while you were cuddling up to the bartender?" he shot back.

Nyla was taken back by the sharpness of his tone, but even more so by the glint of anger she saw in his eyes.

"I had to do something while you were picking up a hottie. One of us had to get information."

"Did you?"

She started to tell him that she'd asked him first, but decided it wasn't worth the game of one-upmanship. Besides, she might get an answer she didn't want to hear. "According to the bartender, Janie Paxton was a nice girl who kept to herself. There were a few occasions when male customers got out of hand with her and she'd 'beat the crap out of them.' After seeing her claws, I'd say she was definitely shifter-strong. The bartender didn't notice any stalkers or weird guys lurking around, and he didn't see anyone fitting Dunn's description."

Jake nodded, seeming to analyze the new information, then startled her by saying, "The bartender wouldn't talk to me at all. What did you have to offer him to loosen his tongue?"

"What? You didn't see me crawl behind the bar and unzip him?" Nyla asked smartly, tired of his attitude. "What's your problem, anyway? You almost sound like a jealous boyfriend."

She saw incredulity spark in his eyes and tensed, ready for another fight, but after a moment she watched his anger dim.

"Fine." He stood from the table and began to clear it off.

"No, not fine. Did you find out anything useful from the waitress? After chatting her up the entire night you must have found out *something*."

"Who sounds jealous now?" he taunted, eyes glittering with irritation.

"Don't flatter yourself, Porter. I just want to catch this nut case and move on, so I hope all that time you spent with the waitress was more than just flirting. I don't like my time wasted, especially when lives are at stake."

"I was questioning a witness, not trying to pick her up." He closed his eyes and inhaled deeply, slowly, before reopening them, his temper barely contained. "Newsflash; not every guy you know is controlled by his libido."

"And not every woman you know has to promise sexual favors to get information."

"Fair enough."

While they'd squabbled, he'd cleared the table, and with nothing left to do, Jake fisted his hands at his sides and seared her with a look that was anything but happy.

Nyla rose from her seat. "Just tell me what you found out from the waitress so we can get on with this."

Jake looked as if he was about to make another smart remark, but apparently the cold glare she gave him made him think better of it, because he said, "I didn't find out anything helpful." He hooked his thumbs into his front pockets. "Janie was a young, single girl who liked to flirt a lot. Selene was concerned she might have been too promiscuous. According to her, there were several guys who could've followed Janie home one night and killed her. Too many for her to narrow down the selection."

"Let me guess. None of them stuck out when you gave her Dunn's description."

"Of course not. That would have made my job easier."

"Our job," Nyla corrected while she stood by the bed, looking over the pictures of the victim again.

"How can you look at those after eating bloody meat?" Jake asked in disgust.

"Some of us aren't so pussified, Jake."

"Hey—"

"Oh, don't go getting your little lacies in a twist," she interrupted. "You need to learn how to take a joke."

She heard him huffing out a breath, imagined him counting to ten, and grinned.

"What are you looking for?" he asked as he walked over to stand beside her and looked down at the bed.

"Clues, Sherlock." She looked up from the pictures to catch him glaring at her. "Do you have a plan yet?"

"I thought you were the professional demon hunter."

"As are you, and I've already conceded you are better at this than me."

Jake's eyebrows shot up before he could control his reaction. He obviously hadn't expected such honesty.

"Unlike some, I can admit when someone else is better at something, Jake."

"What's that supposed to mean?" he shot back.

Nyla let out a breath, growing more irritated by the minute. It seemed as if all he wanted to do was fight. Of course, she had been provoking him, she admitted with an inward sigh, and decided to call a truce. "It doesn't mean anything. Do you have a plan or what?"

"We need to find out Dunn's motive."

"Wouldn't it be the same as Carter's? To develop a serum for immortality?"

"I don't think so," Jake said, shaking his head. "Shifters aren't immortal."

"No, but they're strong."

"So are vampires."

"Maybe Curtis couldn't get strength from vampires, so he decided to throw a little shifter into the cocktail."

Jake shook his head again. "Think about it, Nyla. A vampire could be caught as long as he was taken during the mending stage of day-sleep. A shifter is strong whether in human or animal form."

"So?"

"So I've seen Curtis Dunn. He couldn't nab one."

"Demons are strong," she pointed out.

"Not all are physically strong, and he's not a demon . . . well, not fully."

Nyla nodded her understanding, recalling what he'd said about Dunn being a demon and a separate soul inside one human shell.

"Are you sure he's not strong?"

"I'm positive he couldn't take on a shifter, especially not a werewolf, which Janie was, judging by the color of her eyes."

"If the waitress was right and Janie was a party girl he could have slipped something in her drink."

Jake just gave her the kind of look people give you when they're too polite to call you stupid to your face.

"Yeah, yeah, I know. A shifter isn't affected by drugs because their bodies burn too much energy," she told him, "but who's to say Dunn hasn't invented something that would stay in her system? You've already suggested he shot her up with something that kept her from reverting back to full human when she died."

"It's possible," Jake conceded, seeming to mull the idea over, "but it doesn't feel right."

Which meant Jake's gut was telling him something else, and if she knew anything, it was that Jake's gut never steered him wrong. She was always amazed by how dead on his instincts were.

"What are you thinking?" She moved the pictures aside and sat on the edge of the bed, watching him.

"He had help."

"Another demon?"

"Maybe, but it doesn't feel right," he said, sitting on the opposite end of the bed. "Nothing feels right. In his own pathetic way, Curtis tried to warn Aria before his brother kidnapped her. I don't think he wanted the immortality serum, and I don't think he wanted to expose the vampires to the world."

"But Alfred did," she reminded, "and the part of him living through Curtis probably still does. Maybe Alfred has gained control."

"Or maybe someone is pulling Alfred to the forefront, letting him be in control." Jake ran his hand through his short brown hair, leaving it in a sexy mess. "I just feel in my gut there's someone else involved, but I can't figure out who it could be. As far as I can tell from my research, the Dunns were not connected to anyone in this area—no friends or family or even business contacts."

For some inexplicable reason, an image of Demarcus flashed through Nyla's mind at his words, but she quickly banished it. Demarcus had entered her head when she'd fed, and even though he had seemed stronger, closer in some way, he couldn't be involved. Demarcus loved himself too much to help someone bring attention to vampires' existence, and Curtis Dunn—or the evil spirit of his great-grandfather possessing him—was leaving behind bodies with fang marks.

"Regardless of who is helping him, there's probably a missing vampire," Jake said, jerking her away from thoughts of Demarcus.

"You really think so?"

Jake nodded. "Definitely. And you're right about Alfred Dunn. The bastard is vengeful. If he's gained control over Curtis, he could be forcing Curtis to continue the experiments with the serum. If so, he'd follow the same initial steps."

"What are you saying? That somewhere in Louisville a vampire is pinned to a wall?"

"I'm afraid so."

Nyla's heart leapt at the remorse she thought she heard in Jake's tone. "You sound as if you feel sorry for the vamp in question."

"Nobody deserves to be pinned to a wall, Nyla. Even I don't torture vamps; I kill them quick and neat."

"How decent of you." She couldn't keep the bitterness from spilling from her mouth.

"What's with the attitude? You have a problem with me killing vamps?"

"No, I've come across some pure evil ones, but do you ever wonder if maybe some of the ones you've killed just because they were vamps weren't really evil?"

Jake didn't have to answer. She saw the guilt in his eyes, before he channeled it into a cold glare.

"They're bloodsucking monsters, Nyla. They feed off people."

Nyla shrugged, focusing her gaze back on the picture of Janie Paxton's deceased body. She didn't need to see him to know Jake was shaking his head.

"Anyway," Jake said, rising from the bed. "We're going to need to find which vampire is missing. Obviously, the local vamps aren't going to talk to me."

"Obviously."

"We're going to need help."

"You know someone who has a good relationship with the vampires?"

"I know a vampire."

Nyla arched an eyebrow. "You know several vampires, Jake. The problem is you tend to kill them before they can be of much help."

Jake didn't respond to her comment, but pulled out his cell phone and punched in a number. Nyla watched in amusement as he struggled to maintain a friendly tone while speaking with Christian, the vampire from Baltimore who'd managed to hog-tie him.

"That was Christian," Jake stated, as if she hadn't already figured that part out, after disconnecting the call. "He said help will arrive soon."

Nyla just grinned.

"What's so damn funny?" he asked, scowling.

"Nothing. I think it's cute you know his number by heart."

Jake took a step forward, but Nyla held one of Janie Paxton's pictures in front of him. "Before you attempt to throttle me, take a look at this."

"What?" he bit out, snatching the picture from her hand.

"Inside the fold of her arm."

Jake peered at the picture closely, and she could see by the widening of his eyes the moment he found the scratches she'd focused on for the last several minutes.

"Those could just be simple scratches."

"Do you think some simple scratches would look like that?"

"No." Jake shook his head. "We need to know what those markings are, and they weren't mentioned in the police or coroner's report. Jonah would've told me if they were."

"So what are we going to do?"

"We're going to inspect her body ourselves."

"She's already been buried," Nyla reminded him.

"Good thing I have shovels in my trunk."

Chapter Eight

NYLA SLID HER knives into the sheaths strapped to her forearms and lifted her gun from the table.

"Are you sure—" Jake began.

"Jake, if you ask about my health one more time I swear I'm going to break your legs!" Nyla interrupted, irritated. She'd passed out once—all right, twice, if she counted the fake passing out by his car the previous night—and the man was acting like it was something that happened every twenty minutes.

Nyla slid her Browning 9mm into its holster, adjusting the straps so the holster fit tight, but not tight enough to chafe. Sure, all that was on the night's agenda was digging up some poor girl's body, but you never knew when some *thing* was going to jump out of the dark and try to take a bite out of you—literally.

"Look, you're the one who passed out twice. How do I know you're not going to get down in that hole with me and do it again?"

"You're the one who has a problem with dead bodies. How do I know you're not going to scream like a girl and pass out at my feet?"

"I don't do anything like a girl," he said defensively, leaning back against the door with his arms crossed, an action which caused his bicep muscles to bulge.

Nyla drew in a breath and let it out slowly while she willed her heart to quit skipping beats. She didn't know if the Heat was coming back or she was just suffering through the natural effect of being in her true human form in close range with the man of her naughtiest dreams. Jake simply sent her hormones into a tailspin whether she suffered from the Heat or not, which was what made it all the more dangerous. All she knew for sure was that she was suddenly very warm inside.

"Okay, you don't do anything girlish. Then let's do this," she managed to say, hoping he didn't pick up on the breathy tone in her voice.

"You look a little flushed."

"I'm fine!"

He flinched at the harsh sound of her voice which seemed to bounce off the motel room walls, and she couldn't stop herself from doing so as well. If they didn't get out of that room and get to business, they were going to come to blows again. There was just too much tension filling the air between them.

"Fine, but if you pass out again I'm leaving you behind."

Jake opened the door, angrily muttering something under his breath. Nyla followed him out, sliding her leather jacket on to cover her weapons. She'd feel better if she could have showered and changed into fresh clothes, but she didn't have anything with her.

"Do you think we can swing by my motel and get my stuff?" she asked as they walked toward his car.

"I packed up your clothes. They're in the trunk."

"You're not even going to pretend you didn't snoop through my room, are you?"

"Would you prefer I insult your intelligence by doing so?"

"I'd prefer you trust me."

Jake turned to face her, a cocky grin twitching the corners of his bow-shaped mouth. "If our relationship was about trust, you wouldn't have introduced yourself while holding a gun on me."

"That's different. Your reputation precedes you."

"And yours doesn't, which makes you all the more dangerous. It's rule *numero uno*, Nyla. Never trust the unfamiliar."

He turned away, leading her as they covered the distance to his car. Once there, he stood beside it, scanning the parking area, a look in his eye that said he was searching for someone.

Certain she knew who he was looking for, she said, "Still pining over your lost cat?"

He directed his gaze to her, narrowing his eyes into slits. "You have a thing against cats or something?"

"No, on the contrary, I think they're beautiful creatures. I've even been compared to them," she added, struggling not to chuckle.

"Whatever."

"You know, I'm not buying this unfamiliarity thing between us. I know all about your pet cat, we've tussled a time or two, and we're both hunters."

"So you say."

"What's that supposed to mean?"

"It means all I found in your motel room were clothes. Besides the weapons you currently have on, and your fighting skills, there's nothing about you that says 'hunter.' You have no identification, no credit cards, no cell phone, just a small wad of cash in your pocket and an attitude. Unless, of course, everything else was in your car, which was conveniently stolen. Funny how you didn't report it stolen."

"Would you report yours if it was stolen?"

Jake didn't say anything, but she saw his jaw clench and knew that he knew she had him.

"I can report it if you want. I can have the cops here in minutes. Let's see, Jakie. How many warrants do you have out on you? How many illegal weapons are you carrying? Shall we compare? And what do you think they'd find if they did recover my car?"

He swallowed hard and yanked open his door. "Get in the car, and let's go."

It was going to be a long ride.

Twenty minutes dragged by, feeling more like twenty hours, as Jake steered the Malibu down east end Louisville roads, traveling toward Cave Hill Cemetery. The radio was on, but the music didn't seem to reach him.

Nyla stole glances at him from the corner of her eye, started to speak a few times, but lost her nerve. She wasn't afraid of him, but she was afraid of losing him. If he got too annoyed with her and refused her help, she didn't know how she'd stay with him without revealing what she truly was, and she couldn't go the rest of his life being just his pet cat either. The whole situation was a mess.

"Are you feeling better?"

Nyla jerked, surprised by his sudden question. She glanced over to find him studying her.

"I told you that I'm all right."

He looked back at the road, drumming his fingers along the steering wheel. It was an action he did when he was nervous, and he probably didn't even realize it. He cleared his throat, started to say something, then stopped. Something else he did when he wasn't quite sure what to do.

"Whatever you want to say, Porter, go on and spit it out."

"What happened between us at the motel room?"

She felt her brow furrow. "What are you talking about?"

"I'm talking about there being a moment there when . . ." His voice trailed off as he seemed to search for the right words.

Nyla hoped he wouldn't find them. She was sure he was talking about when the Heat had overtaken her, and she hoped he didn't want to discuss it. It was hard enough keeping her desire under control while sitting next to him. If they talked about it . . .

Before she could finish the thought, he said, "Okay, if we're going to do this hunt together, we need to be straight with each other. You're a pretty hot chick, and a couple times back in the room I thought you might be into me—then you freaked out and locked yourself in the bathroom. What's going on?"

Damn! So much for hoping. But she couldn't help preening over the fact that he'd called her "a pretty hot chick."

"Thanks for the compliment, but I think you're overanalyzing our . . . situation."

"I'm not analyzing," he said, glancing toward her with a scowl. "I need to know what condition your head is in."

She shook her head, confused. "What are you talking about?"

"I'm talking about how you panicked when I had you pinned on the motel room floor." He cut her another glance, and she quickly glanced away. She didn't want to see the question that might be burning in his eyes.

"Nyla, were you ever . . . attacked by a man?"

"I'm a hunter. I'm attacked by a lot of men, not to mention women and things I wouldn't consider either men or women."

"That's not what I meant, and I think you know it."

Yeah, she knew exactly what he meant. She had panicked, but she wasn't about to tell him it was because when he was on top of her she saw herself ripping off his clothes and making love to him right there on the floor.

No, Nyla had never been attacked by a man, or more specifically, she'd never been raped by any. She had, however, had sex with several of them for all the wrong reasons. She'd had sex with strangers to please the pantherian queen, or to appease the Heat riding her body. She'd never had sex to share love, to actually take the time to involve her emotions into the act. If she were to ever have sex for the right reasons, she wanted it to be with Jake.

Unfortunately, the Heat was an uninvited third party. And following on the heels of the Heat was her vampiric need to feed.

"No, I've never been attacked the way you're suggesting," she finally answered, keeping her tone carefully neutral and focusing her gaze out the window. "I just wanted you away from me because I felt sick and, well, kind of claustrophobic."

"Claustrophobic?"

"Yeah."

"Should you be going down in a grave with me?"

She cocked her head, thinking it over. She could handle being in a deep hole, surrounded by dirt walls, but she couldn't handle the close proximity to Jake. The blood she'd savored from her dinner had taken the edge off of her hunger, but it was still there. She needed fresh blood, something warm and flowing.

She couldn't, however, tell him that, so she said, "To tell the truth, Porter, I'm not that keen on the idea of digging up Janie Paxton. The girl died horribly, viciously. We should let her rest."

"She is resting. We're just digging up her shell," he said, his tone matter of fact.

Nyla shook her head. "I know you're not that insensitive, Jake."

"I'm not being insensitive." He made a slicing motion with his hand. "Janie Paxton is dead. Wherever she is right now, she isn't using that body. It's not the flesh and bones that make us live. It's that spark of something inside us. The body is just a shell. If someone wants to dig up my body once I leave it, so be it. Believe me, Janie Paxton could care less what we do with her body. Hell, if it helps us catch the psycho who murdered her, she'll probably cheer us on."

"Do you really believe that? You think she knows what we're doing?"

He shook his head. "No. It was a figure of speech."

"Then what do you believe?"

He sent her a scowl that told her he was tired of the conversation and definitely not happy about the subject matter. Anyone else might have taken that look as a clue that they needed to shut up, but not her. He'd held her for years, telling her his secrets, but he'd only gone so far. There were things she'd wondered about him, but could never ask. Now that she was with him in her human form, she couldn't pass up the opportunity to ask those questions.

"Where do you think we go after we die?" she prodded when he didn't respond.

He shrugged, turning his head so his gaze fell back on the road before him. "Don't know, don't care. As long as they don't stick around as vengeful spirits, it's none of my business what happens to people after they keel over."

"You don't believe there's a heaven or a hell?"

He kept driving, never taking his eyes off the road. If not for the subtle clenching of his jaw, she'd have thought he didn't hear her.

"Do you believe in God?" she prodded again.

He swerved, cursed viciously, then straightened the car before they hit the curb. "Dammit, if you're going to do all this psychoanalysis shit, you can get out of my car!"

Nyla was stunned by the vehemence of his tone and the trembling in his hands as they wrapped around the steering wheel. The rest of his body was rigid, as if struggling to contain his anger. The only time she'd ever seen him this angry was when he was scared. He tended to use it as a security blanket, as though if he could stay angry, the fear couldn't get to him.

"You're scared of dying; really, truly, terrified," she said, amazed. "I never realized that."

Jake turned the steering wheel hard, swerving toward the curb, and slammed on the brakes, screeching to a stop a block away from the cemetery. The heated glare he directed at her was enough to make a weaker person tremble.

"What do you mean you never realized that? We've just met, so you don't know a damned thing about what I think or feel or anything else about me, for that matter."

Her mouth dropped open, and she fumbled miserably for words, coming up short. She couldn't believe she had said something so stupid. Why didn't she just wear a sign saying, *Hi, my name is Nyla, but you know me as Alley, your pet cat. Why don't we talk about this before you kill me?*

Before she could come up with an appropriate response, he growled, "Just how long have you been stalking me?"

She swallowed hard. "I've been following you, not stalking you."

"Same difference. How long? Obviously long enough to think you know me, but you don't fucking know anything about me!"

Nyla was truly shocked, not by his anger, but by the truth of his words. Did she really know him? How much could you know about a person by engaging in conversations in which only they spoke? And yes, she'd observed him for years, but she'd never believed that asking him such a simple question would have sparked so much rage inside him. If she truly knew him, shouldn't she have known that?

"I'm sorry, Jake," she finally managed to say. "I didn't mean to upset you."

"I'm not—"

"Upset, angry, pissed—whatever is the manliest term," she interrupted, her own anger rising to the surface. But was she angry at him or at herself? "I'm sorry, all right? I apologize."

"You haven't answered my question. How long have you been following me?"

She sighed. "A long time."

"How long?"

"Long enough."

He shook his head, anger still burning behind his eyes. "Why?"

Nyla let out a long breath and tried to think. He obviously wasn't going to let his anger be assuaged easily, and they had a job to do, preferably before daybreak. So what was the best way to diffuse the situation they were in?

She decided to go with the absurd. "What if I followed you because I thought you had a nice ass?"

His eyes widened for a second, then he chuckled roughly in defeat, shaking his head. "Is that the best answer I'm going to get out of you?"

"Without torture, yeah."

"Don't give me any ideas, sweetheart. I'm not that nice a guy."

"You can be when you want to be." She raised her hands up in surrender against his heated glare. "I'm not analyzing. I'm just saying that we can all be nice when we want to be."

He shook his head again, letting out a breath while he continued to drum his fingers along the steering wheel. "I don't know why I'm keeping you here. I don't know if it's because my gut says to keep you, or if it's just my own fucking curiosity." He eyed her up and down and said, "Or maybe I keep you around because of that perfect round ass of yours, but don't make me regret letting you stay. And *don't* analyze me. I don't like it."

"I gathered that." Nyla released a breath of relief, feeling as though the end of their partnership had just narrowly been avoided. Without a word, he put the car back into drive, pulled away from the curb, and completed their trip to the cemetery.

"We're not going in through the front gates, are we?" Nyla asked when they neared the cemetery's front entrance. Cave Hill Cemetery wasn't one of the small, unsecured cemeteries she'd been at with Jake numerous times before. It was surrounded by gates and had security guards, as evidenced by the security station placed at the entrance.

"I'm just getting a feel for it, figuring out our best option for entrance."

Jake skidded to an abrupt stop before the main gates, his head tilted to the side. She immediately tensed. Several times she'd seen him tilt his head like that just before a vampire attack. It was as though he could hear voices telling him danger lay ahead.

She started to warn him that stopping in front of the security guards wasn't a good idea, but the warning died when she stared through the gates and realized that wouldn't be a problem. The small security office was located just inside the gates. She should have seen a guard sitting before the window and looking out at the street, but all she saw was a foot sticking out the open door—and a puddle of blood around it.

"Someone's taken out the guards," she said.

"Some *thing* has taken them out," Jake corrected her, his head still tilted, his eyes dark and serious. He was in combat mode. "Vampire, newly changed over, female, well-fed. She's not killing for food. She's killing for battle."

"Where is she?" Nyla asked, shrugging out of her jacket so her weapons were more easily accessible. She didn't bother asking Jake how he knew such specifics. It was a talent he had, and she didn't question.

"In the cemetery. No . . ." He tilted his head further, as though the voices in his mind were yelling something different at him. ". . . she's coming to us."

Nyla searched the area she could see out the window. Nothing. She drew in a breath, and the smell of the guard's blood reached her, but she fought against its pull. She was here to protect Jake, not to go on a vampire feeding spree.

"I don't see her. Are you sure she's coming?"

Something landed on the roof of the car with a loud thud.

"Ding-dong, the wicked bitch is here," Jake singsonged, as he clicked off his gun's safety.

Chapter Nine

"TRY NOT TO SHOOT any holes in my car," Jake said, watching the ceiling of the Malibu, both hands clasped around his gun.

Nyla risked a quick glance at him, just long enough to determine if he was serious. He was.

"Of course. I see how the safety of your vehicle is the priority here," she responded, not bothering to hold back the sarcasm, while mimicking his action with her own gun. Both of her hands were holding it, trigger finger in place. The vampire was on the car's roof; they knew that much. The question was, from which direction was she going to strike?

If it was up to Nyla, she'd just shoot the bitch through the roof, but it was Jake's car and therefore, his call.

With her finger itching to press against the trigger, she glanced from above her to the side windows, the rear, and back to the ceiling.

"Come on," she said, her patience wearing thin.

"Relax," Jake murmured. "I think she wants us to make the first move and actually exit the car."

"You really think she expects us to make such a dumb-ass move?"

"I didn't say she was smart. She expects us to behave like normal people, and normal people would run screaming, leaving a trail of piss along the way."

"You got a point, but I'm getting antsy."

"Step on out then." He chuckled.

"Bite my ass, Porter."

"Oooh, can I spread chocolate syrup on it first?"

She risked going off high-alert long enough to give him the glare he deserved, growing increasingly irritated by his calm, not to mention cocky, demeanor. It was the same attitude which had nearly gotten him in trouble during several hunts she'd been on with him. He'd get cocky and think he could take out more vamps than any one sane person would attempt to handle alone. Fortunately, she could shift forms in a nanosecond and hold her mist form long enough so he never saw his pet kitty sneaking in to help save his ass.

She switched her gaze upward. "You know what? If she doesn't show herself, I'm just blowing holes through the roof."

His eyes widened, all traces of humor vanishing. "All right, don't get your little black panties in a twist."

"I see someone's been in my drawers."

A rough sound came from Jake's throat as he choked back a laugh. "Gee, when you put it that way, it sounds so much more fun." He raised a finger before she could form a comeback and gestured upward. "Evil bitch on the roof, remember? Let's get her good and dead before we get into another round of witty barbs."

Nyla simmered in silence, readying her trigger finger as Jake leaned his head back and yelled, "Hey bitch, er, I mean, witch. Witch, bitch, vampire, I can't seem to tell the three apart. Anyway, why don't you just show your ugly face so we can blow it off and go about our business?" He waited a few minutes, then yelled again. "If you make me blow holes through my car, I promise to make your death long and excruciatingly painful. Do yourself a favor and rear that ugly face of yours."

"She's not going for it, Jake."

He tilted his head to the side again, doing that strange "psychic" thing he seemed to have going for him, and his body suddenly stiffened. "It's a trap!"

"What?" Nyla tightened her hands on her gun, frantically trying to look in all directions at once.

"It's a trap, and more are coming. Her job was to keep us here. Bloodsucking bitch," he added, firing his gun through the roof of the car.

"Oh sure, you get to blow holes through the roof," Nyla muttered, watching the vampire's body roll down the front of the car, jerking in seizure-like spasms. "What's she doing?"

"Get out and get ready," Jake commanded. "We don't want to be trapped inside!"

Knowing better than to argue with him, Nyla followed his barked order, but watched the vampire while she exited the car. The brunette's body jerked on the ground, then her skin started to rot away, murky liquids oozing out while a golden light glimmered from inside her. She screamed through it all.

"Told ya it'd be painful, bitch," Jake said before turning his back on the vamp, obviously feeling no threat from her. "Here they come," he called out to Nyla.

She turned so the car was at her back, same as Jake had done, and readied herself as vampires appeared in the night sky. "Oh, hell. They're fliers!"

"Yeah, I kind of noticed that," Jake responded, his voice strained with tension. "Wait until they get low enough and then start capping them."

"I don't have those nifty, little sun-in-a-capsule bullets you have, Jake."

"You can still slow them down."

Oh, peachy, Nyla thought, watching in growing dread as the three flying vampires started their descent toward her. She didn't dare turn to see how many were closing in on Jake. He was better protected. He could handle it.

If only she could turn into a panther. Unlike a lycanthrope, she didn't retain human features when she shifted. She turned into an actual animal, and the speed of the transition tended to stun the unholy piss out of attackers, dumbfounding them long enough for her to rip out a nice, life-ending chunk of their throat. She'd just have to rely on her feminine wiles this time. In her case, feminine wiles meant uppercuts, spinning kicks, and excellence in weapon handling.

The three vampires came at her in an arrow formation; one in front, two in back. She shot the first one in his face the second he came into close enough proximity, which sent him reeling backward, eventually crashing to the ground.

If she shot the second one, she'd never get a bullet into the third. Knowing she was faster than any gun, she took it in her left hand, extracting her sword from its spine sheath with her right.

The second vampire swooped down on her as the sword cleared the sheath. She swung her arm in an arc, beheading the second vampire in midair and cutting a good-sized slice out of the third one's shoulder.

She'd turned the rest of her body with her arm, effectively spinning around to face the third vampire as he fell to the ground. Once he finished sliding down the side of Jake's car, she staked his heart with her sword, then quickly sliced off his head.

Unfortunately, the move left her back exposed to the first vampire she'd shot. Unlike Jake's special UV gun, hers was loaded with regular bullets. It would cause some pain to a vampire, slow him down, but never deliver a fatal blow, unless it was a big enough round to blow off the whole head or take out the heart.

She heard, rather than felt, him approaching . . . fast. She'd barely begun to turn when an object whizzed past her shoulder, finding a home in the approaching vampire's chest.

She watched in horror as he convulsed violently. Blood and other substances spilled out his mouth and eyes as his skin rotted from his body. The same thing would be happening to her if that bullet had been even a fraction of an inch off the mark.

She spun to face Jake over the roof of the Malibu. He stood in a shooter's stance, three bodies rotting on the ground on his side of the car. He lowered the gun, holstering it with a smug "looks-like-I-just-saved-your-life-there-little-damsel" grin forming across his mouth.

Nyla placed her sword back in the spine sheath, ignoring the dimples Jake's grin formed and the magnetic pull his grin had on her. It wasn't as easy to ignore the call of blood behind her in the security guard station.

"You almost shot me." Even to her own ears, the softly spoken words sounded like a death threat.

"I knew what I was doing," Jake said, the cocky grin no longer there as he watched her round the car and stalk toward him, his eyes wary. "Besides, I have UV-bullets. They wouldn't kill you from just a graze."

Wanna bet? she wanted to ask, but instead smiled sweetly as she closed the remaining space between them. She rested a hand on his chest, gritting her teeth to fight down the passion that touching his body stirred inside her. "I guess I should thank you for your help."

Jake smiled, but it wasn't cocky this time. He was still unsure of her, and he was right to feel that way.

Nyla's smile changed from sweet to predatory as she performed a quick and well-practiced flex of her wrist, which put the small knife in her wrist sheath directly into her hand.

Still giving him a smile that promised pain, she kept her weapon-free hand on his chest in a mockery of affection and slipped her knife hand between his legs.

Jake sucked in a breath, holding it as if afraid letting go would put his testicles even closer to the blade. His eyes were wide, focused only on her face.

"If you ever shoot a bullet that close to me again," she warned in a low and lethal voice, "I'll be using your balls for ping-pong. Is that understood?"

Jake nodded, apparently still not taking a chance on breathing.

"I'll take that as a yes." She backed away, surveying the carnage around them, ignoring Jake's loud gush of air as he started breathing again.

"What the hell is wrong with you?" he bellowed.

Nyla turned back toward him and raised one of her perfectly arched eyebrows. She noticed that he had yet to gain back the color he'd lost during their little "moment of understanding."

"Seriously, are you insane? I save your life and you thank me by nearly Bobbittizing my balls. What the hell is wrong with you?"

"Ever shoot anyone other than a vampire with those UV bullets?"

"No," he quickly snapped, his tone still angry.

"So you don't know what would happen if you shot a person with one."

"They disintegrate into the bloodstream. That's why they kill vampires so effectively. They're just UV."

"And you think having pure UV coursing through your bloodstream wouldn't hurt you? At the very least, you'd probably walk away with some seriously amped up melanoma."

"Nyla, I knew what I was doing. I wasn't going to—"

"You may have known what you were doing, but you didn't know what *I* was doing. What if I'd moved just as you pulled the trigger?"

He heaved out a breath, flexing his hands in irritation. "I wouldn't put your life in danger, all right? I wouldn't hurt you after what I just saw."

She blinked, confused. "What are you talking about?"

"The way you beheaded that vamp in midair. Whatever doubts I had before . . . well, I now know for certain you're a hunter. You have some serious skill."

"Am I supposed to feel honored for receiving your seal of approval?"

He closed his eyes and inhaled deeply, visibly trying to rein in his temper. "Let's not fight, let's just get what we came for."

"This was an ambush, Jake. We need to get out of here."

Jake shook his head. "An ambush would have been larger, with better quality opponents."

"You don't think flying vampires are worthy opponents?"

"They weren't old."

"Do you know how rare it is to cross a flying vamp?" She knew that not every vampire could fly. It was either a talent a particular vamp had, or it was a skill acquired after a very long existence. Centuries long.

"Yes."

"Well, we just faced off with six, no, make that seven of them, and you don't think any of them were old?"

Jake shook his head.

"Were they related or something?"

"How would I know that?"

"You felt the damn things before they could be seen. It stands to reason you'd know other things about them."

Jake shrugged. "Well, I don't. I just know when they're coming and what they're up to."

"How do you know all that?"

He shrugged again. "Practice. Apparently you haven't been on a lot of hunts or you'd get that gut feeling too. It comes with the job."

Nyla just looked at him. She'd always been in cat form when she'd gone on hunts with him before, and she'd always thought it was a gut feeling combined with his hunter skill which helped him perform his job. Now, after witnessing him in action while she was in human form, she suspected there was something more involved. She wasn't about to voice her suspicions, though. If Jacob Porter was what she was starting to think he was, she didn't have a prayer.

"Let's get out of here, Jake. This isn't exactly the boonies, and most likely someone heard the gunshots." She raised both arms, gesturing with a circular motion. "Cops will be swarming this place soon, and I'm sure if they find us standing in the middle of all this blood and death, I doubt they're going to give us the benefit of the doubt."

"The bloodsuckers will be nothing but mush in a few more minutes. The first one already is."

She peered ahead of the car and saw that he was right. The former vampiress was just a puddle of muck. "They might be mush, but the guards won't be."

"We haven't even checked to see whether they're dead or just injured."

"And we're not going to," she said as sirens blared in the not-far-enough distance. "We're getting out of here now."

She rounded the car, quickly making it to the passenger side door, but Jake hadn't moved an inch. He was staring toward the cemetery, determination in his eyes.

"Hey! Do I have to drag your ass into the car?"

He looked at her, glared long enough to make her just a smidge uncomfortable, then finally moved toward the car.

Neither of them even flinched as Jake drove the car over the puddle that was once a living person, but Nyla did count her blessings. She could have easily become one of those puddles.

"YOU REALLY DON'T think it was an ambush?" Nyla asked nearly an hour later, as she sat at the table in Jake's motel room wiping down her freshly washed sword.

"No, I don't. I think it was a test." Jake lowered himself onto the bed, stretching back to rest on his elbows.

They'd both showered and changed, unfortunately Jake had changed into a pair of jeans—*just* a pair of jeans. Whether it was his attire, or the energy she'd spent during the fight at the cemetery, she didn't know, but the Heat had flared back to life.

She sat at the table, busying her hands with the sword in order to keep from tracing that thin line of hair running from Jake's navel down into his jeans, knowing the jeans wouldn't be much of a deterrent in her search to discover just where that line of hair went. She tried to keep her mind focused on the hunter job while keeping her eyes focused on the sword she was drying, but the Heat kept making her itch for Jake.

And no wonder, she thought, realizing she'd spent the past several minutes stroking a phallic symbol.

She set the sword aside in disgust, wondering how she could possibly manage going through two weeks of Heat without pouncing on Jake. The only way she could think of managing that particular task was to have sex with someone else, but every time she did that she lost another piece of her self-respect.

She supposed she could shift into cat form for a while, but the drawback to that was she came back into human form hungrier than when she shifted, and then she'd have to feed.

"You all right, Nyla? You're looking kind of funky again."

She glanced at him, and her stomach did a little flip-flop. Must he lie on the bed all stretched out and barely clothed?

She gave an internal shake of her head to bring her mind away from his body and said, "I'm fine. You were saying about the vampires . . . ?"

"Yeah, if that had been an ambush at the cemetery, somebody older would have been sent for us."

"They were lying in wait for us. Hel-lo. That's the definition of ambush. It might have been a crappy ambush from their end, but it was still an ambush."

"No," he stated quietly but firmly. "It was a test."

"Did the voices in your head tell you that?"

He frowned at her. "What?"

"Nothing." She scratched her arms and squirmed in the chair. Her skin was crawling with the need to touch him. *Dammit!*

Jake shook his head, rose from the bed and crossed over to the window, making sure—for the umpteenth time—that the window was raised.

"You really miss that cat, don't you?" She fought back the grin tugging at the corners of her mouth.

"Yeah, well, animals are cooler than people sometimes." He shrugged, an embarrassed smile adorning his face.

Sometimes it was easier being an animal, Nyla wanted to say, but didn't. She chose to stick to the original topic. "So what were the vamps testing us for?"

"I don't know. I'm not even sure they knew."

"Thanks for clearing that up," she scoffed.

Jake laughed. "What I'm trying to say is that I think someone more powerful than them sent them to test us. To see if any of them came back alive."

"But who would do that? There aren't many master-led vampire gangs around anymore."

"Yeah, but there are some," he said. His eyes took on the haunted look they always got when he thought of his friend Bobby and the night they'd been attacked by vampires.

The night they'd both had the misfortune of meeting Demarcus.

"You all right, Nyla?"

She glanced up as he started walking toward her. She could only stare in awe as his spectacular body crossed the floor to stand before her. His toned abs were right in front of her face. Unable to stop herself, she reached out and traced the taut, muscled lines with her fingertips.

Jake sucked in his breath, obviously surprised by her touch, and if the sudden tightening of his jeans was any indication, he was aroused. The knowledge she'd put him in that state sent a thrill spiraling through her body.

Suddenly, he reached down, grasped her by her nape, and pulled her out of the chair. She stood before him, only a breath away from a kiss, both their heads tilted at the right angles—just her, in her human form, and Jake . . . and the Heat.

Dammit!

"I need some air," she said, fighting with herself not to pull him toward her and pushing him away instead.

"Nyla—" he began.

"Stay here, I'll be back soon," she called over her shoulder before closing the motel room door behind her.

She ran down the hall, dissolving into mist before she'd even hit the parking lot.

Chapter Ten

"DAMMIT," JAKE MUTTERED, watching the door slam shut.

Groaning, he threw himself back onto the bed and wondered whether he'd misread her signals.

It had been a real crapper of a night. They'd faced off with flying vampires, he hadn't gotten to dig up Janie Paxton's body, and just when he'd been sure he was going to get some action with Nyla, she'd practically run out of the room.

It was just as well, he decided with a resigned sigh. He needed to focus on the job and not on Nyla's deliciously rounded curves. She'd proven herself a true hunter, wielding that sword like some sort of barbarian princess. She was a good partner to have, just as long as he didn't piss her off and send her on a quest to castrate him, which she seemed to have a fondness for when angry. Mixing business and pleasure with her, a woman who ran hot and cold faster than he could blink, was not one of his better ideas.

He felt something land on the bed next to him, and he jerked into a sitting position.

"Alley!" He grabbed the cat off the bed, cradling her against his chest. "Where have you been, girl?"

Alley purred softly, cuddling in closer to his chest, and Jake felt a gentle calm wash over him. Some kids had security blankets, some had teddy bears. He'd always had Alley.

"We got company with us on this job, Alley, so if you're sticking around I'm going to have to ask you to behave," he told his cat while stroking the fur along her back. "To tell you the truth, this particular woman kind of scares me. Behave so I don't have to save you. The crazy woman might try to impale you on her sword."

Jake's cell phone rang from where it sat on the nightstand, demanding his attention. He lay back against a mound of pillows, with Alley sprawled across his bare chest, and reached over to grab the phone with his free hand.

"Porter," he announced, continuing to stroke Alley's soft black fur.

"It's Jonah. I have a body."

"Good for you, Ego-boy. Anything else?"

"What? Ugh, I don't mean *I* have a body, I mean I have info on another body."

"Yeah, I figured that, Sparky, I was just twisting your shorts. What'd ya get?"

"You're a pain in the ass, you know that?"

"It's in the genes. You going to give me the information or not?"

"What's got you so irritable?"

"Let's see," Jake began, thinking over the list of things currently ticking him off. "Bodies are piling up, I haven't found Curtis Dunn, I got jumped by flying vampires, and if I don't have sex soon I'm going to bust."

"Those things *fly?*"

"Some of 'em."

"You all right?"

"I'm talking to you, aren't I?"

"You know, you're pretty snippy when you aren't getting any. You should go take care of that."

"Believe me, I have every intention of going to the closest bar and finding someone warm and will—Ahh, *dammit!*" Jake jumped off the bed, letting Alley fall to the mattress.

"You all right, Jake?" Genuine concern laced Jonah's voice.

"Yeah," he said into the phone while checking his chest for blood. "My frigging cat bit me!"

Jake swatted at Alley, chasing her off the bed, while the sound of his brother's laughter poured through the phone.

"I'm glad you enjoyed that," he said, lying on the bed again after determining there was no need for a bandage. Alley had just nicked him.

"Dude, I swear that crazy cat thinks you're her boyfriend."

"That's just perverted. Now tell me about this new victim before I have to drive up there and beat it out of you."

"All right, all right. The body was found just outside Hicksville, a tiny little town not even on the map. Two apparent fang holes, body drained. It's definitely Dunn's work."

"Yeah, and he's moving. I need to move with him."

"I'll email you directions. It's not the easiest place to find."

"Hmm. Sounds like just the type of place a killer would want to go. I'll sniff him out though."

"Yeah, well, if you're going to Hicksville, there's something you should know."

"What's that?"

"Peewee is the sheriff."

He frowned. "Peewee who?"

"Our cousin."

Jake thought back to his childhood, remembering the nerdy little guy. The boy could trip over air and couldn't fight his way out of a paper sack.

"Our cousin Peewee is walking around some town with the right to carry a loaded weapon? That's comforting."

"Jake . . ."

"What?"

"Don't get so caught up in your memories that you give the guy a wedgie or Super glue his butt to the toilet seat."

"Hey, that was a long time ago, but he deserved it. And as I recall, you laughed too," he reminded his brother.

"Jacob—"

"Fine. I'll leave the little twerp alone. What else you got for me?"

"The body was found in a wooded area outside of the town, but it wasn't hidden. It was seen from the road."

"Any markings?"

"I told you, the fang marks were there."

"Other markings, I mean. We were looking at the pictures you sent of Janie Paxton, and Nyla found some strange markings on the fold of her elbow, but we couldn't make them out. We went to the cemetery to dig her up—"

"Whoa, little brother! You're letting this Nyla woman look at the evidence?"

Jake chuckled, amused that of all the things his brother could have focused on, he chose that. "You know, it used to be stuff like digging up bodies that shocked you."

"Yeah, well, I've accepted that you do that kinda stuff. However, I've never known you to partner up with anyone. Can you really trust this woman? What if she's a cop trying to bust you? You know you do some highly illegal crap."

"Believe me, she's no cop. By the way, what did you find out about her?"

Alley jumped back on the bed but kept her distance. Jake eyed her while she curled up next to his feet, gazing at him intently, and gave an amused shake of his head. All he had to do was mention a woman's name, and she was on high alert. Jonah was right. She was a damned crazy, jealous cat.

"Nothing," Jonah answered, ensnaring Jake's attention again. "It would help if you knew where she was born."

"I'll see what I can find out."

"Be careful, bro. If she's a cop," Jonah began, but Jake interrupted him.

"If she was a cop, she probably wouldn't have beheaded a flying vampire in midair."

"She really did that?" Jonah asked.

"In one slice."

"Sweet."

"Yeah, but unfortunately the vamps kept us from doing what we'd set out to do. We couldn't dig up Janie's body, so I don't know what those markings on her were. I need copies of police reports and photos of all the victims."

"That's a pretty big order, Jake."

"I could get them my usual way . . ."

"Dammit, Jake, I keep telling you that you're going to get yourself in one hell of a mess if you keep screwing around like that."

"Yeah, well, I gotta do something. My gut is telling me there is something off about this entire situation. If there's some kind of clue being left behind on the victims' bodies, I need to know what it is."

"Maybe what you and this Nyla chick saw were just scratches. There wasn't anything in the police report about odd markings, other than the fang holes."

Jacob rolled his eyes. "No offense, Joe, but you guys don't know what to look for in cases like this. This is my territory. Now are you going to get me the info I need, or do I have to pose as a fed and march right in to the LMPD and get it myself?"

He watched Alley move up the mattress until she was at his waist so he could scratch the fur between her ears.

"Don't do it, Jake."

"Well, I can't go back to the cemetery and dig up Janie Paxton's body. The vamps might have killed the guards. Even if they didn't kill them, they definitely bled them. The place will be crawling with cops, and I need to head down to Hicksville as soon as possible. I'm not left with much choice."

"Give me a day before you do something stupid."

"I don't do stupid," Jake said, glancing at his watch. It was two in the morning. "I do whatever it takes to get the job done. I'm leaving here at first light, or whenever Nyla gets back. I have to have the pictures by then or I'm going to the LMPD to see what they have."

"Jake—"

"Relax, bro. I do this stuff all the time."

"I didn't hear that."

Jake grinned, amused by how much it bothered his detective brother to hear about the illegal things he did. He seemed to get more upset over that than the fact that Jake was out fighting monsters.

"I'll try to get you the pictures by then, but I doubt I can do it. Are you sure you can't wait?"

"Would you wait if it meant another innocent life might be taken?"

"No, I wouldn't." Jonah expelled a long breath. "Don't get caught, baby bro. Watch yourself."

"Always."

"And play nice with Peewee."

Jake chuckled, and he could imagine Jonah rolling his eyes.

"I'm out. Take care, idiot," Jonah said.

"Back at ya, dickweed."

"Bitch."

"Pussy."

With the dial tone sounding in his ear, Jake snapped his cell phone shut and tossed it on the nightstand, rising to a sitting position. He had a badge in his stash of fake IDs which would get him through the doors of the Louisville Metro Police Department, but it was always risky posing as a fed. He hoped Jonah would come through for him.

"Come here, sweetheart." He gestured for Alley to crawl onto his lap, and he scooped her up in his arms once her little paws landed on his thighs. "You and I are going to have to work on this attitude of yours. I can't believe you bit me."

He raised her in front of his face, meeting her eyes with a stern look. Gazing into her eyes, he realized why Nyla had seemed familiar to him when they'd first locked eyes at the club. "I'll be damned. You both have violet eyes," he murmured softly.

He lowered Alley onto the bed, shrugging off the prickling sensation crawling up his spine. The black cat sat there, cocking her head at him as though trying to figure out what was going through his mind. Good luck, he thought, knowing his mind was a jumble of confusion.

He needed to focus on the job and quit trying to imagine what it would feel like to bed Nyla. It was screwing with his head and messing with his train of thought. Determinedly, he pushed the case to the forefront of his mind.

He knew Curtis Dunn was the killer, but everything inside him said there was more to this situation than he'd first believed. The man had killed a shifter—a creature ten times stronger than himself. And he and Nyla had been attacked by flying vampires, young ones at that. Was Curtis trying to create a better serum? A serum not only promising immortality, but greater strength? Had the man created something that gave those vamps the ability to fly? If so, why would he do that?

He glanced at Alley, sitting there watching him curiously, and he couldn't shrug off the feeling he was missing something, some piece of the puzzle which was probably right there in front of his face, but he was too blind to see it. It had to be his attraction to Nyla throwing him off. He should have caught Dunn by now, but he was wasting precious time playing cat and mouse with Nyla . . . or maybe it was cat and horny dog, he thought wryly, reaching back to pet Alley.

But, to his surprise, Alley wasn't there. Where had the damned cat gone now?

"CURTIS . . ."

Curtis huddled beneath the blue-tinged trees in the open forest, trying to chase away some of the bitter cold enveloping him, but with no success. It was always cold here, in this cerulean world of shadow where *she* roamed.

The Dream Teller.

He'd heard stories about her in his other life, when he was known as Alfred Dunn. She was like the vampires' sandman, only appearing in their sleep, warning them of danger. So why had she started appearing in his dreams?

"You are a part of it," he heard her rough, crackling voice whisper through the trees. "You must call them."

"Why?" he asked, letting his voice float to the sky. He couldn't see her, the fabled old hag with her unseeing platinum eyes, but she saw everything despite her blindness. "Why must I be the one?"

"You must pay for your sins, must make amends."

"I don't want to kill anyone. I don't want anyone hurt."

"Then stop Demarcus."

"I can't."

"You are weak!" Her voice was a roar, rumbling through the sky like the roll of thunder. "You owe us this. You must call them."

"He'll kill me if he knows I'm warning her."

"It is your destiny, Curtis. It has been written since before you were Alfred or any of your other names. Now, you will help them."

"Yes," he whimpered, curling into a ball on the cold, frosty ground. "I will help them."

He lay on the blue forest floor, soaking up the cold from the moon's rays, waiting for the Dream Teller to release him. He knew that when she did, there would be one more body and one more part of the message waiting for him in the waking world.

JAKE WOKE TO THE sound of running water coming from the bathroom. He turned his head, looking for the clock on the nightstand. It was just after ten in the morning.

He pulled himself off the bed, stretching out his tight muscles. He hadn't meant to sleep so long, but he'd had that damned dream he'd had since childhood, the first time shortly before Bobby's death. He was in a blue forest, shivering with cold, and someone was calling to him, telling him it was time.

He raked his hand through his hair, trying to dispel the dream, but it still clung to his mind. He didn't know what it meant or who the old woman was who beckoned him there, but it always creeped him out when he woke up feeling as if he'd really been there. His body was covered in goose bumps, the cold from that blue-tinged dream world still lingering, its only light coming from the silver-blue moon hovering above. He always woke from the dream this way.

He grabbed a black T-shirt out of the duffel bag lying on the floor and pulled it over his head, just as the shower stopped in the bathroom. Apparently, Nyla had come back while he'd been asleep. Looking around the room, he discovered Alley was still gone. Great.

He walked over to the small table and leaned down to boot up his laptop, signing on to the Internet to retrieve the directions his brother had sent him, hoping he'd also sent him some pictures.

A manila envelope lying next to the laptop caught his attention. There wasn't anything written on it, and it wasn't sealed, so he opened it, shocked to find copies of the police reports and photos from not just the first two murders, but the third one as well.

As he laid them on the table, Nyla stepped out of the bathroom, her curvy but slender body encased in snug black jeans and a tight black T-shirt. He felt himself grow hard at the mere sight of her. She raised her hand to towel dry her hair, the action causing her shirt to rise, exposing an inch-wide strip of bare flesh, and he nearly burst out of his zipper. He ignored his libido, reminding himself he had to focus on finding Curtis. It didn't matter how badly he needed to get laid, the job came first.

"How'd you get these?" he asked, tapping a finger against a police report from the envelope.

"I got them from the LMPD. Since we weren't able to dig up Janie's body, I thought we could look at all the victim's pictures to see if there are any odd markings on their bodies. Apparently, another body has been found," she said, obviously referring to the one Jonah had told him about on the phone after she'd left. "Pictures and a copy of the report on that vic had just been faxed in when I got there."

Jake stared at her in disbelief, watching as she casually dried her long, black hair and then folded the towel, draping it over the back of a chair.

"You have no ID on you and no fake badges, and you're telling me you just walked into the LMPD and got copies of this stuff?"

"Yes." She held onto the back of the chair, returning his stare. They stood before one another, only the table separating them, and Jake had the strongest urge to knock the table out of the way and grab her, but that would have to wait. He had to put the job first. He owed it to the victims.

"How did you manage to do this without getting arrested?"

"I showed 'em my boobs."

Jake grinned, then paused. She wasn't grinning, not even a smirk. "You're serious? That actually worked?"

"I have great boobs," she said with a shrug.

Jake couldn't help lowering his eyes to where those full, perky mounds rested. He'd have to agree with her, but she hadn't really flashed the cops, had she?

He cursed inwardly. Staring at Nyla's chest wasn't going to help him find Curtis Dunn, and how she'd managed to get the information didn't matter. It was there, which was all he needed to know. With a shake of his head, he dragged his gaze away from her breasts and lowered himself into a chair to review the materials.

"Curtis is killing women faster than Carter," he mentioned, while flipping through the reports. There was no mention of strange marks on Janie Paxton's body, and none of her pictures showed the inner fold of her elbow well enough to determine what the marking was.

"Not necessarily. Remember, some of Carter's victims weren't found for quite a while," Nyla responded, sitting across from him. Her legs shook under the table, and when he glanced up at her she was fidgeting with her hands.

"Are you all right?"

"Fine. Why?"

"No reason." Jake shrugged, not wanting to set her off on one of her tirades again. She'd made it clear she didn't like being fussed over when she looked sick. He had a feeling she wouldn't like it if he asked her why she was suddenly acting like a junkie in need of a fix. The thought gave him pause, and he glanced across the table at her, again noting the way she couldn't seem to sit still. She kept flexing her hands, then she'd run them up and down her arms. She was either freezing or trying not to scratch. Was she a junkie? Other than the fidgeting, she didn't show any of the classic signs of drug abuse. But there were so many designer drugs these days that he wasn't sure he knew all the signs. However, if she was a junkie, he'd have to find out soon. You couldn't trust a junkie to watch your back.

"What are you looking at?" she suddenly demanded.

"Nothing," he said quickly, returning his gaze to the papers spread before him. "We're going to have to leave for Hicksville soon, where the third body was found. I was just wondering if you were ready."

"No."

"No?" He looked at her again. He hadn't expected her to say that. Her only possessions were her clothes and weapons, and she didn't appear to be high maintenance. From what he could tell, she didn't even wear makeup. "Why can't you leave now?"

She blinked, as if she hadn't expected the question, and shrugged. "We need to stay here and find something. The first two victims were found here. We haven't even scoured the parks for any overlooked evidence."

He smiled wryly. Normally, scouring the parks would have been his first move, but he'd gone to The Crimson Rose on a tip and got hit by Hurricane Nyla. "Yeah, I was going to do that, but I got sidetracked by a woman with a gun."

She rolled her eyes. "It's not my fault that women with guns make you lose focus. We can do it tonight."

"Tonight?"

"Yes, tonight," she snapped. "I haven't slept."

"That's not my problem. You're the one who stayed out all night," he pointed out, more than a little irritated by the memory of how she'd got him all hot and bothered and then ran away, leaving him with a hard-on and nowhere to put it. "What were you doing anyway?"

"Getting you those reports and pictures you're looking at."

He looked at her askance. "And it took you all night? You left here a little after one."

"So?"

"So I didn't fall asleep until around five. That must have been one long tit-flashing session you gave those cops."

She narrowed her eyes at him and fisted her hands. "Whatever gets the job done, right? I got you what you need."

"And then what did you do?"

"What do you think I did?"

"Did you go get a fix?"

Her eyes widened, and she looked at him as if baffled. "A fix? What kind of fix?"

"You tell me. Crack, heroine, meth . . . you're shaking like a video whore. What's wrong? Couldn't find a dealer?"

She was silent for a long moment, and then she burst out into laughter so uproarious that tears ran from her eyes. "You think I'm a drug addict?" she asked between guffaws, as if the thought was the funniest thing in the world.

"You're shaking and acting weird," Jake mumbled, feeling stupid, and he wasn't sure why. She had all the signs of a junkie gone too long without a hit, but she seemed too amused by his accusation for it to be true.

"I don't feel well, you idiot, but I'm not a crackhead." She laughed again, rose from her seat to walk to the bed where she fell onto the mattress. "Wake me at sundown, and we'll check out the parks where the victims were found."

"I want to be in Hicksville before nightfall."

"Then go without me. I'll catch up later."

"Nyla."

"I'm not going anywhere until nightfall, Jake," she stated firmly. "I'm tired, and I'm going to sleep. Good night."

Jake opened his mouth to argue, but closed it, concluding that nothing he said would change the infuriating woman's mind. With a muffled curse, he grabbed the contents of the manila envelope and his car keys. Maybe he'd focus better on the case if he got away from the woman, and it wouldn't hurt for him to patch up the bullet hole in the roof of his car while she slept.

TWENTY MINUTES LATER, Jake leaned back in his car and surveyed his work. The generic patch he'd made from duct tape would have to work until he had time to put his car in the shop. It wouldn't keep a vampire out, but at least it would save his car from a flood if it rained.

He settled into the driver's seat as comfortably as he could, and reopened the manila envelope. Nyla had sidetracked him earlier so he still had material to review, and doing it in his car was safer for them both. There was no way he could control himself in the same room with her stretched out on a bed. He could kid himself into thinking that he was just horny and any woman's body would do, but deep down, he knew he'd still hunger for Nyla.

Forcing thoughts of her perfect body out of his mind, he focused his attention on the second victim's police report. It was the same as the first, only the women had been found in different parks. The second victim was a fair-skinned, blue-eyed blonde named Minnie Davis. She didn't have any strange physical attributes, like claws for nails, so she may have been a regular human being. She didn't have any markings around her inner elbow either. She did, however, have scratch marks around her ankle.

Jake peered closer at the photograph of Minnie Davis's ankle, studying the marks. They swooped out into arcs; one on top, one on bottom. If the scratches were connected, they would form the shape of an eye.

He sat that file aside and lifted the one for the third victim, an unidentified brunette. Only a headshot had been faxed to the LMPD. Like the others, the police report didn't mention any markings other than the fang holes and "typical scratches as found in an attack." He'd have to get better pictures of her from the Hicksville police department, where his cousin, Peewee, ran things. Knowing how Peewee felt about him, he'd probably have to dig up the third victim's body to get any information.

His cell phone rang, startling him. He unclipped it from his waistband. "Porter."

"Hey, bro. What's going on? I called my buddy down at the LMPD to try to get you the stuff you wanted, and I ended up getting questioned. He said someone stole copies of the reports. Tell me it wasn't you."

"It wasn't me."

"Jake . . ."

"Dude, I'm telling the truth. It wasn't me. Nyla got them."

"Nyla?"

"Yes, Nyla. Said she showed 'em her boobs and walked out with copies of the police reports. Lucked out, too, because Hicksville had just faxed a copy of their report over."

"Jake, listen to me carefully. No one handed that woman copies of those reports. One of the cops was attacked."

Jake felt a ball of unease form in his stomach, and he dropped the police report onto the passenger side seat. His brother's tone spooked him. "Attacked how?"

"I don't know. They found him lying in the file room, dazed and confused. He swore he caught some gorgeous woman making copies of the reports, and when he confronted her, she jumped him, bit his neck and drank his blood until he blacked out. The guys thought he was making up a story because someone had gotten the jump on him and stole copies of those reports. Hell, I thought you'd knocked him out and stole them yourself."

"He said a beautiful woman drank his blood?" The ball of unease churned in his gut, increasing in size.

"Yes. Given the fact they're investigating a serial killer who leaves fang marks, it would be easy to believe he'd made up the vampire story to cover his ass, thinking the guys would believe him, but there were no fang marks on him."

And there wouldn't be, because real vampires didn't leave marks. However, the police didn't know that, so if the man had lied about a vampire attack, he would have done something to make it look as though he'd been bitten.

"Gotta go," Jake told his brother and flipped his phone closed, tossing it on the seat. It immediately started to ring, but he ignored it.

His mind raced with the information Jonah had just given him. Nyla had gone to the police station to get the police reports with no fake identification or badge to bluff her way in. Yet she'd somehow gotten them. He thought back to the night he'd met her and the little things that had happened since, which he'd somehow overlooked. He'd met her at night, and she'd been insistent on getting to the motel before daybreak. She had never left the motel before nightfall, and now she was in the room sleeping and had specifically told him to wake her at sundown.

She wanted to avoid sunlight!

Jake ignored the still-ringing cell phone and got out of the car, rounding to the trunk. He opened it and grabbed a UV-blanket and a machete, cursing himself for leaving his gun and specially crafted UV bullets in the room—with Nyla.

His heart and brain battled inside him as he marched toward the motel room, wondering how he would kill Nyla if she turned out to be a vamp. And how he would deal with the fact that he'd fallen for one of those hideous monsters.

Chapter Eleven

IT WAS SO COLD. Nyla's entire body shivered as she stood in a ray of pure blue moonlight, searching the blue-tinged trees around her. Somebody was out there. She could feel them watching her.

This was the Dream Teller's world. She'd been in it many times before, starting the week before she was attacked by Demarcus. Back then the old woman had come to her nightly, and each night she'd given her a direct order: Save Jacob Porter.

The Dream Teller's voice had led her to the alley that fateful night, where she'd crouched atop a Dumpster until the mysterious Jacob Porter arrived. Once Demarcus started for Jake, she knew she had to save him, so she'd leapt from the Dumpster, distracting the vampire by scratching him across the face.

Once Jake was out of immediate danger, she'd shifted to panther form and tore into Demarcus with all her might, using her rage to fight off the fear which had prevented her from doing anything to save Bobby, a regret she would carry until the day she died.

"Nyla, it is time." The Dream Teller's voice seemed to carry on the wind.

"Time for what?" Nyla searched for the old woman, but all she saw were hundreds of trees encircling the clearing in which she stood in the middle. She'd never seen the woman, not even a shadow, and part of her was afraid to see her. Yet, she was tired of being caught in this dream world, given orders by someone who wouldn't show her face. "These cryptic messages are getting old. Just tell me what you want me to know so I can get out of here."

The sound of laughter echoed through the air, followed by the sound of footsteps. Fear snaked its way up Nyla's spine as she listened to the approaching footsteps, unable to determine from which direction they were coming.

"Relax, little cat."

Nyla gave a startled yelp as the old woman's icy cold breath blew against the back of her neck. The Dream Teller was right behind her, had crept up on her too easily.

"Turn around, little cat. I will not hurt you. You have too important a job."

"What do you want?" Nyla asked as she closed her eyes, too scared to look at the mysterious Dream Teller. She didn't know why, but the thought of coming face to face with the woman who'd haunted her dreams for sixteen years was terrifying.

"I am not your enemy, Nyla. You feel afraid because of the coldness, but it is the coldness of harsh truth. Truth you do not want to face. Yet you must face it to conquer it."

Nyla shook her head, fighting to remain calm, trying to slow her heartbeat to its normal rate. She knew better than to attempt escape. She'd tried before. The only way to leave this dream realm was to be released by the Dream Teller. With no other options available, she took a deep breath, released it, and repeated the action twice. Then she turned around to face her fears.

The Dream Teller stood before her in a dark, hooded cloak, looking every bit as old and haggard as her voice. Her face was lined with thick grooves. It wasn't a beautiful face, the nose being entirely too big and sharp, but Nyla couldn't help being struck in awe by the woman whose eyes were two sightless, platinum orbs. There was no pupil, no iris. Just breathtaking platinum. Her skin was thick and tough like leather, and a long rope of thick, wavy white hair escaped from her hood, framing her tired face.

"You're blind," Nyla whispered.

"Only my eyes, yet I see more than most," the old woman replied.

"Are you a witch?"

"Yes."

"Why have you been haunting my dreams, giving me these cryptic messages and refusing to show yourself?"

She smiled, a slight upward tilt of her thin lips. "I did not refuse. You were not ready to see the truth, but now you must face it in order to protect yourself and Jake."

"Protect us from what?"

"The dark ones."

Nyla waited for the old woman to say more. When she didn't, Nyla asked, "Do the dark ones have names?"

The witch's smile widened. She seemed to enjoy teasing Nyla with her cryptic messages. "You must focus on gaining Jake's trust. That is the only thing to concern yourself with now."

Suddenly, Nyla felt warmth spread over her body, cloaking her from the shoulders down. She'd never been warm in this realm. She'd always been bitterly cold. She looked around, confused. The moon was still perched in the night sky, its cold rays lighting the clearing. "Why am I warm?"

"Your physical body is warm, and its warmth has reached you here."

Nyla was even more confused when she thought back to the motel room where she slept on top of the sheets. "I'm not under the covers. I shouldn't be so warm."

"Jake has covered you with a UV blanket."

"He's what?" Nyla frantically looked at her arms, inspecting them for damage. "Let me out of here! He's killing me. I'm going to die! I'm going to melt into a puddle! I'm—"

"Nyla, you are fine."

"I may be fine here, but out there my body is being destroyed!" She grabbed the old woman by the shoulders. "Let me out of here, you old hag before I—"

"Nyla, the sun is not your enemy," the old woman said.

"Of course it's my enemy. I'm a vampire!"

"You're a daywalker."

Nyla released her grip on the woman's frail shoulders and stared at her in disbelief. "A daywalker? What in hell is a daywalker?"

"Exactly what it sounds like. When Demarcus bit you, he infected you with his agelessness and his blood thirst, but not with his weakness to sunlight. UV rays will not harm you."

Nyla took a few steps back, shocked to her core. "You're telling me that I've avoided sunlight for sixteen years, and it wouldn't have hurt me?"

"Yes."

"Dammit, why didn't you tell me?" Nyla didn't bother trying to hide her anger. For sixteen years she'd hidden in darkness, only enjoying the sun's warmth in her feline form and yearning to feel it on her human face.

"You are supposed to find your own way, little cat. I only step in when it is absolutely necessary."

"That's a stupid answer. What was I supposed to do? Risk becoming a crispy critter just to prove that, like all vampires, I couldn't tolerate sunlight?"

When the old woman just smiled, Nyla ignored the desire to smack away her smile and asked, "Why are you telling me this now? What's changed?" Before the Dream Teller could respond, Nyla knew the answer. "You're telling me because Jake is covering me with a UV blanket. Why's he doing that?"

"He thinks you're a vampire."

A new wave of fear crashed through Nyla as she realized this could only mean Jake had discovered something about her. But what? She knew he'd asked Jonah to find out who she was, but there wasn't anything to find. She had no property in her name and had never been arrested. So what had Jake learned that made him think she was a vampire? On the heels of that thought came another one that filled her with such sadness she could barely breathe.

Nyla stared at the old woman, tears suddenly stinging her eyes. "I can't believe he could kill me that easily. And to think I . . ."

"Love this man?" The Dream Teller finished for her when her voice trailed off. "He sees only black and white, Nyla. Good and evil. But he is starting to realize that there is a gray area."

"Is that why he's trying to kill me? Because he's starting to see that there's a gray area?" Nyla snapped, anger suddenly surging through her. "Release me from this damned dream. I have to get back before Jake does something like stake me through the heart."

The old woman shook her head. "He won't. As far as he knows, all vampires are destroyed by ultraviolet rays. He will still wonder, however, if you are something other than human, so you need to be very careful."

"Ya think?" Nyla rolled her eyes, placing her hands on her hips.

"You need to gain his trust, Nyla, and capture his heart," the Dream Teller said, ignoring Nyla's sarcasm.

"And how am I supposed to do that? He just tried to *kill* me, remember?"

"As I said, he is discovering the gray area. He is beginning to understand that not all nonhumans are good or bad. It started with Christian."

"You're talking about the vampire who tied him up?"

The old woman nodded. "And drank from him."

"*Drank* from him?" Nyla's mouth dropped open in shock. She'd had no idea he'd been attacked by the seemingly nonthreatening vamp.

"Yes, dear. Yet, Christian still lives."

"No way would Jake knowingly allow a vampire to drink from him and live." Nyla ran her fingers through her hair as she tried to figure out how Christian had managed the feat. "Was he unconscious? No, Jake would sense Christian. He has that psychic thing he does where he knows when vampires are coming."

"You've discovered that?" The Dream Teller asked, smiling. "It is a wondrous gift he carries. He was born with the ability to sense nonhumans. It was how he sensed evil in that alley all those years ago."

Nyla's breath hitched as she realized the implication of what the witch was saying. "Are you saying Jake's a true slayer?"

"Yes."

Wow, Nyla thought. Slayers were not just average hunters. They had more than skill. They had powers an average hunter could only dream of. They sensed vampires of all ages, could find them easily, effortlessly. They were the only mortals who could truly hold their own against a vampire in a hand to hand fight. And it was their life's mission to destroy all evidence of the vampire race.

"You say I'm supposed to capture Jake's heart, but how can I make Jake love me when it's in his genetic makeup to destroy me?"

"Jake is a special slayer, and you are a special vampire. The two of you are destined to help protect a very important child. Because of this, Jake must fall in love with you, or all will be doomed."

Nyla blinked and shook her head. "We're supposed to protect a child?"

"Yes. A very special child."

"Okay. Since I'm a vampire and can't have kids, I assume that you're talking about some other kid. Are you going to give me a hint as to who it is and why it's our job to protect him—or her?"

The Dream Teller smiled. "Follow me."

The old witch turned and walked toward the thick wall of trees encircling them. A little scared of what might lie inside the heavily wooded area, Nyla hesitated a moment before she did as she was told. What other option did she have? She couldn't leave the dream realm until she was released.

They traveled deep into the forest, the crunching of leaves and the snapping of twigs beneath their feet serving as the only sound in the otherwise deadly silence. Although the warmth from the real world still cloaked her, Nyla could feel the whispers of arctic cold still lingering in the air. She did her best to ignore the cold as they continued their trek through the seemingly endless forest, eventually stopping before a large rock formation.

Nyla looked up in an effort to see the whole mountain of stone. It was tinged blue, as was everything else in this azure world. The rocks were piled atop each other in haphazard layers, reaching high into the heavens. No matter how far back she craned her neck, Nyla couldn't see the top.

"When the time is right, I will bring both you and Jake here," the old witch said, gesturing toward the mountain before them with a frail hand. "You will find the answers you need inside these walls, and the words you find will guide you and the others who have been chosen to guard the child."

"Why can't I see inside the walls now?"

"Because you need your partner with you."

"And Jake is my partner?"

"Yes. He has always been your partner, even before either of you were born."

At the witch's last statement, Nyla recalled the instant feelings of protection that had sprung to life inside her when she first saw Jake enter the clearing that fateful night sixteen years ago.

"It is time for you to go back and face Jake now, little cat. You will awaken burning with the Heat, so be prepared."

"I don't think it's going to be a problem," Nyla said. Her anger had previously kept the Heat at bay, and she would have no trouble being angry with Jake now. The man had tried to kill her in her sleep without even giving her a chance to defend herself verbally or physically. She might love him, and they might be destined to be "partners" to protect some child, but there were just some things that you didn't forgive and forget easily. Almost being murdered was one of them.

"Take care, little cat, and remember to be patient with your partner. He must battle everything he has ever believed to become the hero he needs to be and the man you need at your side. I will call you both when it is time."

Without warning, Nyla felt the warmth around her intensify and realized she was no longer in the dream realm. Pretending she was still deeply asleep, she used her excellent sense of smell to locate Jake's position. Bad idea, she realized as the masculine scent of him steamrolled over her, igniting a fire deep inside her core. She dampened immediately, ready and willing to do anything he desired as long as she could stop the almost painful craving of the Heat engulfing her body.

She fought against the urge to squirm as wave after wave of desire flowed through her body, begging her to do something to end the torture. She grew hotter as the hunger inside intensified, but she realized not all of the heat was coming from inside her. She was still under the UV blanket Jake had draped over her in an effort to kill her.

A mixture of sorrow and rage crept back inside her mind, shoving against the desire currently trying to control her. The emotions waged a war inside her body, but it was two against one, and desire was sent packing as sorrow and rage only strengthened the more she thought about what he'd done. He'd tried to kill her. Not hurt or maim, but *kill* her. Without asking her any questions or giving her even the slightest of chances to defend herself. He'd just wanted her dead and destroyed. The bastard.

Nyla opened her mouth, letting out a soft sigh, knowing it would attract Jake's attention. She heard the creak of a floorboard, followed by careful footsteps. He was being cautious. It almost made her laugh. All the caution in the world wouldn't save his butt now.

She felt him lean over her, his breath softly blowing against her cheek, and after he'd seemed to have observed her for a moment the cover was gently lifted from her shoulders. Was he trying to hide the evidence of his attack? Not a chance, Nyla thought, reaching out to catch his neck in a death grip.

Chapter Twelve

"SURELY YOU ARE joking, Christian," Seta said in astonishment as she paced his living room.

Christian sat back on the couch and watched the skirts of her long crimson dress swirl around her, as did the long, dark hair which set off the Spanish beauty's exotic features. Even the furrowed brow and tightly set mouth couldn't mar her perfection.

He let out a sigh, hating any type of confrontation with the vampire-witch. If there was anything Seta was known for, it wasn't diplomacy, and it sure wasn't her even temper. It wasn't that long ago she'd ripped off a woman's head, throwing it into a roaring fireplace in order to work a spell. Of course, she'd worked the spell to locate Eron, a captured vampire—her sire and love of her life. People did unthinkable things to protect their loved ones. Knowing this, it was hard for Christian to hold any ill will against the dark vampiress, especially since her actions had stopped a greater evil.

"I can't leave my church, Seta. I am needed here."

"And I am needed here as well," she said firmly as she stopped pacing and fixed him with a fiery glare.

"Eron will be fine. Rialto and Aria can protect him."

Eron had been so badly hurt during his captivity, he needed to be put deep into the earth to heal, and it would still be several months, maybe even a year or two, before he could rise again. Seta was worried that an enemy would discover his resting place and try to hurt him while he was unable to protect himself.

"Rialto has to focus on protecting Aria and himself. They are the first set of vampires selected for the Blood Revelation. They have enough enemies of their own to keep them busy. I feel bad enough for asking them to guard Eron's burial site while we have this meeting."

"They will be fine, and so will Eron. It won't take you that long to meet with Jake and canvas the area for a missing vampire, Seta. You have the ability to teleport. You could literally be there in the blink of an eye."

"Why should I help Jake Porter? The man is a slayer. He's killed hundreds of us. He once tried to kill you."

"He burned down my church. It's not like he came after me with a stake," Christian said, casually dismissing Jacob Porter's attack on him several years ago when he was running a church in Pennsylvania.

"You were in the church, you fool."

"Jacob Porter doesn't screw up, no matter who he's up against, yet I survived that night and managed to drink the man's blood the second time we met. He didn't even try to attack me during his most recent visit. You can't tell me fate hasn't brought Porter to us."

Seta made a derisive snort, shaking her head angrily, but no matter how hard she was fighting to dispute everything Christian had told her, he knew she believed in fate.

"Why did the Dream Teller say I had to be the one to help him? Why couldn't we send another vampire?"

"I don't know. I haven't had a visit from the Dream Teller in a long time, but she's just as cryptic and evasive as she's always been."

"Shriveled old hag," Seta muttered, crossing her arms beneath her ample chest.

Christian watched her in silence, observing her obvious irritation. He'd come to realize she was always irritable when the Dream Teller was mentioned. The Dream Teller had saved Seta's life centuries ago, sending Eron to catch her the night she was thrown over a cliff by her married lover, the father of her child. Why Seta didn't seem to like the witch was something he couldn't begin to figure out and didn't dare ask. He didn't want to risk having his own head ripped off and thrown into a fire.

Instead he said, "You know, the Dunn twin is leaving bodies lying around with fang marks, just like his brother did. You remember why his brother was doing it, don't you?"

"To make people suspect our kind were real, to bring out more hunters to destroy us."

"And what was he doing in his lab?"

"Experimenting on Eron," she muttered.

"*Torturing* Eron," Christian clarified, holding back a grin when she glared at him. The vampire-witch clearly knew where he was going with the questions and that she was being backed into a corner. And she wasn't happy about it. "Curtis Dunn is probably doing the same thing right now to another vampire. You can help him."

"By helping Jacob Porter."

"I don't think he's as bad a person as we thought he was."

"He's a slayer, Christian. How can you say he's not a bad person?"

"Your argument is that he's killed several vampires, therefore he is a bad person, correct?"

"Correct."

"How many mortals have you killed?"

"That's different," Seta spat, her face reddening in anger.

"Because you had good reasons to kill?"

"Yes!"

"I'm sure Jacob Porter has always thought he had good reason too. You're both killers. He's killed our kind, and our kind has killed his people. And that's not our only similarity with the man. He believes he is helping mankind, protecting the weak. Why have you killed so many rapists and child molesters?"

"To help mankind," Seta conceded. "To protect the weak."

"He believes he's doing the same thing."

"By slaughtering us all just because we drink blood? By instantly labeling us all bloodthirsty murderers?"

Christian grabbed a small scrapbook off the coffee table and handed it to the vampire-witch, not saying a word. He watched as she opened it, discovering the newspaper clippings inside. He'd been curious about a statement Jacob Porter made the last time they saw one another, so he'd gone to the library to dig up newspapers from the time period Jacob would have been a resident of Baltimore instead of a traveling vampire hunter.

He'd found articles about the murder of a twelve-year-old boy named Bobby Romano. The boy's best friend, the one and only Jacob Porter, witnessed the entire attack and swore vampires did it. Of course, Jacob's parents put him in counseling, and, of course, the doctors all said his young mind couldn't handle what he'd seen so he was making up stories about monsters to help him get through it.

Christian watched Seta's face soften, then turn into a fiery mask of anger as she flipped through the pages of the scrapbook, quickly reading the articles. She slammed the book shut and tossed it back onto the coffee table, looking at him with fury in her eyes.

"Those monsters feasted on a *child*."

"And not only was that child Jacob Porter's best friend, but Porter saw it all. Now, ask yourself this, Seta. What would you do if you'd been him that night?"

"Well, I guess I'd grow up and hunt the monsters down," she snapped. *"Dammit!* No wonder he hates us so much."

"We saved his brother from Carter Dunn, and he knows it. He visited me before leaving town to find Curtis, and as you can clearly see, he didn't kill me. The Dream Teller said Jacob is beginning to see the truth, and we must help him."

"So the Dream Teller is saying that by helping him see we aren't all evil, we'll be saving our kind from one of the world's most dangerous slayers."

"I don't know if that's her reason, Seta, but the Dream Teller specifically requested that you be the one to help Jacob Porter, and she came to me before I ever got the call from him. I think something much bigger is happening here."

She frowned. "Like what?"

"I don't know, but somehow, you, me, Jacob . . . we're all mixed up in it. After thinking about it, I don't think the Dream Teller wants a mere vampire assisting Porter. She wants a witch. I think something major is happening, Seta. Something that involves all of us—maybe something connected to the Blood Revelation."

"You really think that?" Seta asked, her skin paling.

"Think about it. The Dream Teller hadn't appeared to either of us in decades, not until it was time for Rialto to meet his soul mate. Now she's telling us we need to help Jacob Porter. My instincts say there's a connection. The question is, are you going to do this and find out what the connection could be?"

Seta stood there, staring at him angrily. "Do I have a choice?"

"Yes, and I hope you make the right one."

Chapter Thirteen

JAKE'S EYES BULGED as Nyla's fingers tightened around his throat, gripping it like a vice. She forced him onto his back in one swift move, straddling him where he lay on the bed. Once again, she found herself in a position she'd dreamed of for years, but for all the wrong reasons.

She had one hand wrapped around Jake's throat and the other held the gun she'd pulled from his waistband. Jake's hands were free, but he didn't use them. Nyla hadn't thought he would, considering she was holding a gun to his heart, and if she applied even the slightest pressure to his neck, she could easily crush his windpipe. Surely, he felt the degree of her strength.

"I'm going to ease my grip on your throat, but I still have a gun on you so don't try anything stupid," she warned him as she loosened her death grip. "Why would you cover me with a UV blanket?"

He blinked, then wet his lips with his tongue, an action which would normally send her into a hormonal frenzy while in Heat, but it had no effect on her now. She was in survival mode.

"I, uh, thought you might be cold."

"The real reason, Porter. There's a normal blanket on the bed. A UV blanket is a weapon, unless you thought I just needed a tan, which I doubt. What does your paranoid ass think I am?"

He let out a small noise which might have been a groan or a frustration-filled sigh. "A vampire," he muttered, color seeping into his cheeks, and Nyla realized he was embarrassed. Good. Let him feel like a fool.

"A vampire?" She faked a convincing laugh, as if the thought of her being such a creature was completely absurd. "Wow, Jakie. You really are losing your touch . . . your touch with reality, that is. And where did this brainstorm blow in from?"

"A cop at the LMPD said he was attacked by a vampire who made copies of the reports you just happened to get last night. What else was I supposed to think?"

"Uh, that he was lying? Or maybe he was attacked by another vamp? Why would you think it was me?"

"He said a hot female vampire attacked him. You're a hot woman, and you came back here with the reports. It's not that far of a stretch."

"Yeah, except for the whole me being undead scenario," she said, trying not to let her fear show. *Dammit!* She *had* attacked the cop. She'd been so thirsty, and Jake had wanted those photos and reports. It had just made sense to kill two birds with one stone. She hadn't thought the cop's story would get back to Jake.

"Look, I'm sorry. It was a stupid mistake. Can you get off me now?"

"Why? Why shouldn't I kill you? You just tried to kill me."

"No, I didn't."

"You just covered me with a UV blanket, thinking I was a vampire! What does UV do to vampires?"

"It can kill *or* hurt them. I wasn't trying to kill you. I was just seeing if anything happened."

"And what would you have done if my flesh started to burn?"

"Then I would have had to kill you," he admitted with a hard gulp, "but you obviously aren't one of the monsters, so it doesn't matter what I would have done."

Nyla nodded, pretending to consider his words, and slid off of him to stand at the edge of the bed. She allowed him to sit up before balling up her right fist and driving it into the side of his face.

Jake let out a grunt of pain as his head flung to the side, and he raised his hands to his jaw. "What the hell was that for?"

"Don't try to kill me again. It pisses me off."

Jake abruptly stood, towering over her, close enough that she could feel the heat radiating from his body. He glared at her, rage smoldering in his eyes for a moment before he stomped away, grumbling something about her being lucky to be a woman.

The bathroom door slammed behind him, then instantly opened as he barreled through, his gaze zeroing in on her. "Why don't you go out in the sun?"

"What?"

"The sun, Nyla. You seem to go out of your way to avoid it."

Nyla drew in a deep breath and released it out slowly. The Dream Teller said she was a daywalker, and the UV blanket hadn't harmed her. She'd been under the blanket long enough to have at least burned. Her skin was perfect.

"Here," she muttered, walking toward the window as she slipped Jake's gun into the back of her waistband. Her hands started to tremble as she raised the already partially open window higher, but she reminded herself the sun's rays couldn't harm her. She stretched her arm out the window, letting the sun's heat touch it, marveling at the warmth she'd thought she'd never feel again on her human skin.

"So you weren't avoiding the sun," Jake conceded ruefully, rubbing the furrow between his brows.

"You know, I think you've encountered so many monsters, you've started seeing evil in everyone."

"I couldn't agree more," an unfamiliar voice said.

Nyla spun around to see the female vampire who'd been with Jake and the others the night they destroyed Carter Dunn. She stood before them in a long, flowing, black dress with skirts of deep crimson, and black stiletto lace-up boots. She was short but voluptuous, and exuded an energy, a raw power, that made her appear more ferocious than her size would imply. The air around her seemed to crackle with electricity, and Nyla realized she was using her magic at that very moment.

Jake put his hand to the back of his waist, realized Nyla still had his gun, and glared at her as if to say, "Good going, now look what you've done."

Nyla reached around to the where the gun rested at the small of her back and tightened her hand around its butt, but she didn't know if using it on this vampire would be worth the risk. There weren't many people who could scare Nyla, but this woman before her was drenched in power.

"Relax, children," the vampire said, her voice calm and gentle. "And there is no need to search for weapons, Jacob." Her eyes narrowed as she addressed Jake. "Your girlfriend is right. You see evil where there is none."

"What do you want, Seta?" Jake asked tersely. "I haven't hunted you or Christian."

"Yes, and I'm still pleasantly surprised by that. I'm here to help, per your request."

"Christian sent *you?*" Jake's eyes widened in disbelief.

"Why do you sound so surprised? Who better to help you locate a missing vampire than a vampire-witch?"

Jake studied her. "You never struck me as the helpful kind, Seta."

Seta smiled sweetly, her dark brown eyes glistening. "I help when it interests me. And the two of you . . . I find very interesting."

The vampire-witch zeroed in on Nyla, her smile widening as she seemed to study her curiously, those dark eyes shining with the light of fascination, and her brow furrowed in thought. "Are you aware the two of you have the exact same aura?"

"What the hell are you talking about?" Jake asked, then muttered, "Christian *would* send me a new age, hippie vamp, damn him."

"I can see auras, Jacob, because I'm a witch with psychic gifts. I am not a hippie."

"The name is Jake."

"Whatever you wish, Mr. Porter. You may be interested to know that the sharing of auras is rather rare."

"All I'm interested in finding out is if there's a missing vamp, and locating Curtis Dunn before he kills again."

Seta rolled her eyes, obviously irritated that Jake wasn't interested in the information she was trying to give him. Nyla was interested. She'd heard something a long time ago about people sharing auras, but she couldn't remember what it was and didn't want to ask when Jake was obviously very unhappy to be working with the vampire-witch.

"I performed a few spells before I came here," Seta said, "but I couldn't locate Curtis Dunn. I might be able to do so if I could lay my hands on one of his victims, but his brother, Carter, successfully blocked me from tracing him that way, so Curtis has probably done the same. But if he is holding a vampire captive, and I can trace that vampire, I can find him."

"How would you do that?" Jake asked, his interest obviously piqued.

"Find a vampire of the missing vamp's bloodline and track him down by his own blood."

"What if Curtis is draining the vamp of blood, like Carter did to Eron?"

"There would still be an essence I could track," Seta said, her expression hardening in anger. Nyla suspected the vampire-witch didn't like to be reminded of Eron's torture. "Unless, of course, that like Eron he is drained to the point I can't feel his essence until I am just outside the place where they're holding him. I *will* find a way to locate Curtis Dunn, though. I have a wealth of spells at my disposal, and since I've already been through this situation with Carter, I know which spells are more likely to get results. Something will work."

"Do you think Curtis would do the same thing his twin did?" Jake asked the exotic beauty. "Didn't he seem to you that he was appalled by his brother's actions?"

"I never really saw him," Seta replied. "I was upstairs fighting off Carter. But I spoke with Aria, who, as you know, knew Curtis, and she is very confused by the new deaths. She swears Curtis would never willingly do this, but she also said he was battling a demon inside him."

"Still . . . it doesn't seem right to me."

"You may be right, but there is evil here," Seta said, nodding her head in agreement. "I can feel it lurking just outside the city. It doesn't feel demonic. It feels like, well, something dark, but I can't place it."

"Is that supposed to be helpful? I already know there's evil here," Jake snapped. "There's a damned killer on the loose."

Seta laughed. "I sense forces of darkness in a manner similar to how you sense vampires, but I can use my abilities at will to home in on specific areas. While you can sense danger coming at you, I can often locate it before it has a chance to attack. Your abilities work more like gut instinct, kicking in when necessary."

Jake's forehead crinkled, indicating he was in deep thought. Nyla wondered what was going through his mind, if he knew he had a psychic ability and that he was a true slayer, not just an average vampire hunter. He shrugged, as if to say "whatever," and Nyla realized either he didn't know or he wouldn't accept it. He hated anyone who wasn't a "regular" mortal, and having a psychic ability wasn't a normal mortal's trait.

"Whatever, just do whatever you have to do to find the missing vampire—if there is a missing vampire—but don't kill or endanger any humans in the process."

"I prefer the term *mortals*," Seta said, slightly growling the word. "And, unlike some, I don't kill for sport."

"And you're saying I do?"

"Don't you? The last time we met, I believe you said killing me would be a twofer. Tell me, Jacob, how many points would you score for killing me?"

"That was just a smart-assed remark, and you know it," Jake snapped. "If you recall, I was pissed off at that time, and rightfully so, after being tied up and . . ." Jake stopped abruptly, glancing at Nyla for the briefest of seconds before returning his attention to Seta. "I said whatever I knew would irk you."

"Why didn't you finish your statement, Jacob?" Seta asked with the sly smile of a Cheshire cat. "You don't want your girlfriend to know Christian—"

Jake made an abrupt move toward Seta. "Shut your—"

"Stop it, both of you!" Nyla stepped in between the hot-tempered enemies, halting Jake from what looked like a physical attack. She shot a warning glare at him and then looked at the vampire-witch. "Seta, we would greatly appreciate your help. And on behalf of us both, I thank you."

Seta nodded politely, still wearing her sly, amused grin.

"And as for you, Jake," Nyla continued, focusing on him, "try to act a bit more thankful for the help."

Behind her, Seta snorted, but it didn't do anything to alleviate the tension in the room. Jake's gaze bore through her like a laser, his eyes all but screaming incredulity. Nyla couldn't help feeling a little traitorous, but she wasn't going to just stand by and watch the two fight because Jake didn't want her to know he'd been bitten.

"Oh, I like her," Seta said on the tail end of laughter. "I like her very much."

"So you'll help us?" she asked.

Seta nodded, her laughter dying out as she looked at them seriously. "I think I have to."

Nyla looked at Jake, his expression conveying the same confusion she felt, but before either could ask what the vampire-witch had meant, she was gone.

"Whoa," Nyla said, letting out a startled little yelp as the woman literally vanished in the blink of an eye. Nyla could evaporate into mist, but she'd never seen anyone do what Seta had just done. "How did she do that?"

"She's a witch, a powerful one," Jake said gruffly.

Anger still simmered in his voice, and Nyla took a deep breath and turned to face him, ready for yet another confrontation. She wasn't ready, however, for the way his eyes wouldn't meet hers.

"You all right, Jake?"

"Fine," he snapped. "Now that you're awake, and I have the roof of the car patched, can we leave?"

He still wasn't looking at her. He kept himself busy pulling up the directions to Hicksville on his laptop.

"Fine," Nyla said, no longer having a reason to delay the trip since she could go out in the daylight. She was, however, a little anxious about walking out into the sunlight in her human form. "Just as long as you don't try to kill me again."

"Don't give me reason to, and it won't be a problem."

"I didn't give you reason to the last time," she shot back.

She grabbed the bag of clothes and toiletries he'd brought in for her earlier, put his gun on the table and headed for the door. "Come on, Porter. Since you're so anxious to get to Hicksville, let's put a move on it."

She walked out the door, chuckling at the barrage of curse words she heard him muttering beneath his breath. She wanted to correct him by stating she was not a female dog but a cat; however, they were already on shaky ground, so she left it alone.

She walked out into the sun for the first time in sixteen years, not counting the times she was covered in fur, and smiled. From behind her eyes, tears built up and threatened to fall. Free. She was free of the darkness which had plagued her for so long, free to walk in the light.

"Are you all right?" Jake asked, coming to a stop beside her. She'd been so enraptured by the glowing orb in the sky, she hadn't heard him approach.

"Perfect," she said, averting her eyes to hide the wetness glistening there. "Let's go to Hicksville."

CURTIS SNEAKED A glance at Demarcus, making sure the vamp was deeply asleep before he attempted to feed the girl the vampire had captured. Unlike the other vampires in the house, Demarcus was the only one who actually slept in a coffin. He left it open, probably to shock the victims he'd captured.

"Are you hungry?" Curtis asked the teenager. She was shackled to the metal table in the basement of the house Demarcus had acquired. Her eyes were wide and red-rimmed from crying. She couldn't speak because of the gag in her mouth, but she could have nodded or shook her head. She did neither, obviously paralyzed by fear. "I have some food for you," Curtis tried again, showing her the breakfast bar he'd unwrapped.

The girl jerked her head away as he offered her the food, seemingly terrified of it. "There's nothing wrong with it," he said, realizing she must have thought he'd poisoned it. "Eat while you have the chance. He won't let me feed you when he's awake."

Her eyes grew wider, coated with wetness. Tears slid down the sides of her face as strangled garbles erupted from behind the gag. Although he couldn't make out the actual words, he knew she was pleading with him to release her. But he couldn't.

"I'm sorry," he said, knowing his apology would not make up for what he was going to do to the poor girl. "I would let you go if I could, but I'm too weak to fight Demarcus. Please eat before your hunger pains become unbearable."

The girl shook her head vehemently as he reached for the gag, and Curtis realized he couldn't ungag her, not even to feed her. She would scream if given the chance. Fortunately, she was too panicked to have thought to play along until he'd removed the rag.

"I am sorry," he apologized again, helpless to do anything else. He took a bite of the breakfast bar, felt it slide down to his stomach. It landed with a nauseating thud, and he discarded the rest in a nearby receptacle.

The basement was small, dark and cold, the air soured with the scent of mildew and dampness. The girl lay before him on a large metal table. To his left a vampire was shackled to the wall. His head hung down, his body weak and thin.

Cabinets and tables sat in various places, and a couple of old couches and chairs sat off to his right. They'd taken the house from an old couple. Demarcus had satisfied his blood lust by killing the pair, and they'd moved in, using the basement as a makeshift lab.

They'd left the first body in Louisville, knowing a body found there would garner more attention than if it were left in this small backwoods community. They'd strategically placed the second and third bodies so that they were a trail leading straight to them. The next body, the body of the blonde on the table, would be left here in Hicksville.

Demarcus's plan was working. Nyla and her man had killed the vampires in Louisville, which meant the pair would come to Hicksville to investigate this girl's body too. Maybe they'd already figured it out. Maybe they knew Hicksville was the next dumping site and would arrive sooner than expected.

Curtis studied the vampire shackled to the wall. He wasn't an old vampire. An older vampire could take the abuse he was suffering through, but this vamp was fading fast. He would die soon, and Demarcus would have to capture another vampire to replace him. A small voice inside Curtis's head squealed with glee. The death of a vampire was something to be celebrated in Alfred Dunn's mind.

Curtis swallowed down the bile threatening to rise in his throat. Every time he cut into the vampire's flesh and collected his blood, draining the creature of his energy, Alfred grew stronger. Curtis struggled to fight off the hateful old man, but Alfred was too strong.

And the two of them were duking it out inside Curtis's head.

"Come soon," he whispered, sending out a desperate plea to the cat-woman and her man. "Come before Alfred destroys me."

JAKE GLANCED AT Nyla, briefly observing her in her sleep before returning his gaze to the road stretching out before them. She'd been quiet since they left the motel, but she'd made it clear she hadn't forgotten his earlier actions. Before she'd fallen asleep, she'd repeatedly flexed her hand outside the window, seeming to rotate it toward the direct rays of the sun, as if needing to absorb its warmth. She'd acted as if she were the first person to discover the feel of the sun—or someone who'd been away from it for a long time.

She'd reminded him of a movie he'd seen in school about a girl who'd lived on another planet or in another dimension, a place where the sun never shone. Then one day it did, but only for a few minutes, and she'd missed it because her classmates had locked her in a room while they enjoyed it themselves.

Jake shook his head, wondering why he was thinking of movies he'd seen in grade school when there were so many more important thoughts to fill his head right now. Questions in need of answers.

He pulled his cell phone from the charger he kept in the car and punched the autodial button for his brother's number, sneaking another glance at Nyla in the process. If she'd wanted to annoy him with her "I'm so enraptured by the feel of the sun against my skin" routine, she'd succeeded. He couldn't possibly feel any more like an ass.

"Where the hell have you been?" Jonah's voice growled through the phone after the first ring. "I called for an hour after you hung up on me!"

"I had something to take care of," Jake muttered. "You find out anything else about the attack at the LMPD?"

"I thought it was this Nyla woman."

"She's not a vamp."

"Are you sure?"

"She's been in direct contact with the sun, and nothing has happened. She's not a vamp. She's a hell of a fighter though, despite her small packaging. She probably beat the crap out of the cop, and he decided to make up a story so the boys wouldn't laugh him out of the station."

"Did you actually ask her what happened?"

"I already told you what she said. Maybe the guy was attacked by a real vampire, and he got Nyla and the vamp mixed up. Blood loss can make you woozy."

"It sounds like you're grasping at straws, bro."

"I know," Jake conceded, letting out a breath of frustration. Man, he was tired. It'd be nice to switch places with Nyla and take a snooze while they traveled. "I just know she's one of the good guys."

"Man, you are sprung."

"I am not sprung," he growled, despising the thought, especially since his brother might be right. "Just call me if you find out anything about . . . anything."

He disconnected the call without going through their normal name-calling goodbye routine. He was not only irritated by his brother's words but by the memory of standing over Nyla with the UV blanket in his hands. He'd stood there for forty minutes before lowering the blanket over her body—forty minutes of debating with himself about how he would deal with what he'd done if her flesh started to burn when the blanket touched her skin.

If he'd suspected anyone else of being a vampire he'd have killed them without hesitation, but the thought of watching Nyla writhe in pain, watching her life seep away, killed him inside. And the thought of him being her killer . . .

Jake shook his head, struggling to control his emotions. He'd just met the damned woman. Yes, she was beautiful and had a great body. And yes, she could hold her own in a fight and was clearly in great shape. It was a given that she'd be an amazing lover, and that was all he should care about.

But to his dismay, he cared about her more than just getting her into the sack. His stomach did some weird flipping thing when she smiled at him, and he worried about her when she seemed ill. He'd found himself imagining her at his side during future hunts. His brother was right. He was sprung.

He tightened his hands around the steering wheel, longing for something to crush, something to help release his anger. How could he be so stupid?

When you cared for someone, they could die. He already had Jonah to worry about. He did not need another person in his life to care about, another person who could break him if he lost them. He was already barely holding the pieces together.

"I *don't* love you," he said, his voice soft but stern. To his horror, it was also laced with an edge of panic. "I *will not* love you. You're just an ordinary woman."

Except there was nothing ordinary about Nyla.

Thankfully, the sign announcing entry to Hicksville came into view, and Jake breathed a little easier. Now that they were here, he had something else to focus on. The last body had been found just outside of town. Logic said the next one would be in this same area. He had a woman out there to save.

As for the woman next to him . . . well, he didn't quite know what to do with her, and thank heavens he didn't have to make any decisions about her right now.

"NYLA, WAKE UP. You've gotta see this."

Nyla opened her eyes and lifted her head from her arm, which rested against the car door. She must have fallen asleep shortly after she and Jake left the motel. She really hadn't lied to him earlier in the day when she'd told him she was tired.

She raised herself to a full sitting position so she could see what Jake was telling her she needed to look at, but she was assaulted by the Heat before she could focus her eyes.

"This town is aptly named, that's for sure," she heard him say, laughter in his voice, but she couldn't see him. She couldn't see anything. Her body felt as though it barely contained a raging fire, a fire formed from need and want—of unadulterated lust. The feeling was so strong she was sure she'd burst into flame at any moment.

"Nyla, you all right?"

"Yeah," she managed to say evenly, although she wanted to scream in agony. True to the beast inside her, she felt like an animal in heat, desperate for the release of pressure building up inside her. All it would take was one sexual encounter to make it go away.

Dammit! She never should have allowed herself to fall asleep, she thought angrily. It was always worse after sleep.

"Do you see them?"

She strained her eyes until the blur she saw sharpened into a clear picture. They were in Hicksville, she realized, seeing the sign for the Hicksville general store. The town was filled with small buildings and long wide streets, and it looked as if everyone in town drove a pickup truck since those were the only vehicles she saw parked along the streets.

And the town *was* aptly named, she agreed with Jake, noticing the people on the street. A barefoot man sat outside the general store in an old rocking chair, playing a tune on his banjo. He had a long salt-and-pepper beard, a piece of buckwheat hanging out his mouth, and wore old faded overalls. A woman walked up the sidewalk in low slung blue jeans, a thin rope tied around her waist instead of a belt, and she wore a cutoff top that barely covered anything. Her mousy brown hair was bisected into two low braids, and when she smiled at a man passing by, she revealed a large space where two teeth should have been.

"Wow," Nyla murmured, noticing more people dressed in similar fashion, either wearing boots or no shoes at all. And they were all looking at Jake's car as if the two people inside were the oddballs. "It's not Halloween. Do you think they're actors? Maybe we're close to the town theater."

Jake shook his head, laughing. "I've been driving around this town for a good five minutes, and they all look like this. This should definitely be interesting," he added before opening his door and exiting the car. "I'll be right back." He shut the door and walked around the front of the car toward the general store, nodding at a few people as they eyed him curiously.

Thankful Jake was gone and she'd have an opportunity to get herself under control, Nyla closed her eyes and tried to focus on breathing. But deep breathing seemed to make her hornier. *Dammit!* She balled her hands into fists, letting her nails sink into her palms, but the small pain didn't distract her. She wanted sex as badly as a starving man wanted food. She opened her eyes again, and her gaze immediately fell on a short, portly man dressed in frayed overalls that barely covered his enormous belly and a used-to-be-white T-shirt, stained yellow at the armpits. He wore an old, ragged John Deere trucker cap and work boots with a hole in one of the toes. The lower half of his face was covered in stubble, and a thick cigar hung from his stubby fingers. He waved a greeting to the man playing the banjo and smiled, displaying several gaps where teeth should have been. Nyla's need for sex was so great that she tightened her hand around the door handle, ready to pop the door open and grab him the minute he was close.

Oh good lord! she thought in horror, coming back into her right mind. She wasn't so desperate that she would jump a hillbilly!

Unfortunately, she was.

"All right, I found us a place to stay," Jake said, sliding back into the driver's seat. Nyla had been too busy lusting after the pudgy, dirty, and probably smelly hillbilly to notice him leaving the store. She needed to feed the Heat . . . and quick.

"Are you all right, Nyla? You're squeezing the hell out of that door handle."

"Fine," she said too quickly, almost conveying the panic she felt.

Jake studied her a moment, shook his head, and pulled away from the curb. She closed her eyes and slumped back against the seat. She'd waited too long. She'd done it before, tried to ignore the Heat until it became unbearable, until she couldn't control it enough to select a decent partner. At this stage, she'd screw anything that had a functional penis. *Dammit!* It didn't usually hit this fast, but she'd been around Jake so long—Jake, who fed her desire like no one else ever could.

Jake, who was with her now. She cracked her eyes open and let her hungry gaze roll over him. She'd rather mate with him than with the men in this town—or any man in the world, for that matter.

"Pull over," she commanded, the sudden images of his naked body rolling through her mind too much to bear. She needed release, and she needed it now.

"Why? What's wrong?" Jake looked at her, confusion in his eyes.

Nyla glanced around, quickly studying their whereabouts. She couldn't just start doing him on the street while people strolled about leisurely, even if they were in the pseudo-privacy of Jake's car. She looked at the small buildings around them, all of them looking as if they'd come off the *Little House on the Prairie* set. There were no alleys, no dark corners. She looked beyond the town, noting where the road split, a section of it twisting up into a wooded area.

"Up there," she pointed. "Follow that road."

"Why?"

"Just do it," she snapped, her voice a near-growl. Heat was pooling between her thighs along with the pain of not feeding her lust. If she was forced to wait much longer, she'd crawl into his lap while he drove and get them both killed.

Jake looked at her with wide eyes, but followed her order, turning the steering wheel left to follow the road as it wound into the woods. It didn't take long for them to reach a secluded area. They were on top of a hill, no nearby buildings or sidewalks people could come strolling down.

"Pull over and cut the engine," she demanded while analyzing the situation. They had adequate coverage, and, thanks to Jake's height, his seat was already pushed far enough back to allow her the room she needed.

Again, Jake did as she instructed. "What's up? What's go—"

Before he could finish the question, she straddled his lap and fused her mouth with his. She didn't have time for questions, conversation, or gentleness. She needed him inside her, but first she had to kiss him. She had to taste what she'd been longing for, fantasizing about for years.

And it was everything she'd imagined and more. Even through the haze of Heat her heart still sang. Normally, she shut down everything when the Heat took over, numbing herself so that only her body went through the motions, but with Jake, she allowed herself to feel their union on an emotional level, and it was wondrous. Lips caressed, tongues explored, and each stroke sent her spiraling deeper into euphoria.

Although he matched her passion with fervor, it was Jake who pulled away, breaking the kiss. "What the hell got into you?" he asked, his breathing labored. Nyla could feel the adrenaline flowing through his body, most of it was headed toward his erection, struggling to be released from its zippered prison.

"Don't you want me?" she asked, lowering her hands to the snap on his jeans, desperate to let him spring free.

"Wait." Jake covered her hands with his. He licked his lips, and the action stoked a hundred little fires inside Nyla's core. But, dammit, he was stopping her!

"I thought you liked me, Jake," she purred, rubbing seductively against the rock hard lump in his jeans.

"Oh, believe me, I do, and this is a wet dream come true, but you keep coming on to me and then stopping."

"I'm not stopping now. You are."

"Do you really want this? Believe me, I want you, but I don't want you regretting it. We're in a car for one thing, and we still have to work together. Something bad is going down here and I need your help—"

"Quit talking," she murmured against his lips, sliding her hand down to cup him through the fabric of his jeans. "The vampires can wait," she added giving him a little squeeze and smiling as he gasped.

"But—"

"Jake?"

"Yeah?"

"Shut up and fuck me."

His eyes grew wide, his jaw suddenly slack—the complete opposite of the part of him she stroked with her hand. With a big gulp and a nod, he complied.

"Yes, ma'am."

Jake had wanted to make love with Nyla from the very first moment he'd laid eyes on her, but he hadn't thought that when the time came he'd be worried whether the shocks on his car could take it. She'd yanked his pants open so fast that he was surprised they didn't burst at the seams, and had somehow managed to get rid of her own jeans and panties in a matter of seconds before impaling herself upon his erection.

In a state of surprised shock, he hadn't done anything when she started grinding on top of him, allowing him to fill her completely before pulling back, only to ram against him with a force which would have hurt most women. She didn't seem to mind at all. In fact, he thought he'd actually heard her purr once or twice.

Not one to let his partner do all the work, he grabbed two handfuls of hips and angled his pelvis, thrusting into her each time she slid her eager body down the length of his shaft. The car rocked as they ground against each other forcibly, almost violently, and a part of him worried that he might not be giving as much pleasure as he was receiving.

He'd had women of different shapes, sizes, races, and skill levels, but he'd never had one who moved like this. As hard as he tried to match each of her thrusts with one of his own, he found himself falling behind.

She rode him until he found himself wondering if he'd need a penis-splint when it was over, but he never wanted this sweet torture to end. Her teeth nipped at him as her claw-like nails dug into his flesh, but the pain was like a drug. He didn't care if she tore him to pieces, as long as he was still thrust deep inside her when she did it. And when she'd had her fill, he knew he'd want another hit.

He slid his seat back to its limit, allowing her more room to maneuver as he closed his eyes and held on, allowing her to do as she pleased on top of him. He struggled not to come first, to hold out until she got everything she needed.

What she needed was rough and kinky, he realized as she continued grinding against him with the unbelievable speed she'd started with, and then sank her teeth into him. He'd been licked and nipped, but never full-out bitten during sex. He didn't mind it, although she held the skin of his neck between her teeth and bit down just hard enough to hurt. It was like she wanted to eat him alive, couldn't get enough of him. And he couldn't get enough of the fact that it was his body joined with hers that made her growl deep in her throat when she finally came, allowing him to let go and fall over the edge of ecstasy from which he'd been dangling.

Starbursts of color shot before his eyes, and his mind went blank, making him feel as if the only part of his body capable of functioning properly was pumping away inside Nyla. She fell over him, panting heavily against his chest, completely spent.

With the last bit of energy he could muster, he wrapped his arms around her, reaching beneath her shirt to stroke her sweat-dampened back. He wanted to keep her here in his arms, half-naked, satisfied, and full of him. "Damn, girl," he said breathlessly. "You're an animal."

Abruptly, she jerked to a sitting position, her eyes wide and laced with a horror no man wanted to see after having intercourse with the woman of his dreams.

"Nyla? What is it?"

She shook her head from side to side, the unmistakable look of panic in her eyes. She raised her hand to her mouth, whimpering softly, before scrambling away from his body and back into the passenger seat, hastily pulling on her jeans and boots.

"What's wrong?" Jake asked, quickly pulling his jeans back up. He'd obviously done something wrong, but he had no idea what.

She didn't respond. Instead, she finished dressing, opened the passenger side door and ran into the woods.

"Well, so much for cuddling afterwards," Jake griped, finding the shirt he didn't recall being taken off, and exiting the car to chase after her.

Chapter Fourteen

NYLA RAN THROUGH the trees at a blurring speed, desperate to hide herself from Jake. She'd done it. She'd done exactly what she'd wanted to avoid. She'd had sex with Jake—wild, uninhibited, carnal sex, just like a damn animal. He couldn't have pegged her more correctly.

She fell to her knees at the side of a narrow stream, the thought of jumping into the water to cleanse herself running through her mind, but it would be no use. She would still feel dirty.

She shuddered as she recalled using her nails to bring blood to Jake's skin, lapping up the crimson dessert like the animal she was. She'd held his skin between her teeth, barely stopping herself from tearing into his flesh, feasting on him while he allowed her to use him. He'd been her prey, and he didn't even know it. She could have killed him.

How could she face him again? She cringed as she recalled the way she'd mounted him, the way she'd ridden him like a damn mechanical bull. She could only imagine just how cheap he thought she was.

"Nyla?"

She cringed at the gentle, careful tone of Jake's voice. She kept her back to him as she listened to his slow approach, not wanting to see what lay in his eyes. "Go away, Jake."

"No." He stopped walking toward her but made no move to leave.

"Just leave me alone, Porter."

"No."

Damn him! She'd always loved his stubbornness, but at the moment it was chafing her nerves. This was one moment his persistence was not good.

"Why did you run away, Nyla?"

"I don't really want to talk to you right now. Just, please, leave me alone."

"We came here together to do a job, and I'm not going to leave you up here on this hill while I wait in the car for you to get over whatever it is you're getting over."

"Then don't wait. Go."

"What the hell is wrong with you?" he asked incredulously. "We've got things to do."

"Then do them by yourself," she said. In fact, she decided that Nyla should go and Alley should watch over him in case the danger she feared was real.

"Dammit, Nyla. I asked you if you were sure about having sex, and even though you said yes, I knew this was going to happen!"

"Then maybe you should have done something to stop it!"

She could almost hear his jaw dropping open moments before his hand clamped around her arm, yanking her to her feet and wheeling her around to face him. She tried to avert her eyes, but he grabbed her chin, holding her so that she was forced to meet his gaze.

"How was I supposed to stop you?"

She didn't answer. Shame gave her the strength she needed to break her chin free of his hold and turn her head. She didn't want to look at him, to know he was seeing her as she truly was. A whore. She became a whore two or three times a year when she was hit with the Heat. And she hated herself for it.

Unable to pound her fists against her own body, she hit Jake square in the chest. His eyes showed surprise, but he didn't move. She hit him again. And again. Then she started to beat at his chest with both hands while he stood there motionless, taking her assault without a word. She hit him faster, harder, but he stayed as still as a statue.

Finally, she realized she wasn't going to get a response out of him, and she cried, "Why won't you hit me back?"

He looked at her, anger and sorrow meshed together in his gaze. "I'm not stupid, Nyla. You want me to hit you so you'll have a good reason to hate me. I'm not going to give it to you."

"Damn you," she growled. He was going to stay perfect, which only made what she'd done with him hurt that much worse. Shamed and angry, she threw another punch, this one directed at his face.

Jake grabbed her fist before it reached its target and spun her around, using his other arm to catch her around the waist and pulling her back against his chest.

"Let me go!"

"Not a chance," he said, holding on tight. "But I'll consider it when you quit acting like a child."

"Get. Off. Me," she warned, fighting harder against his hold, but to no avail. He held her in a death grip, a grip no other man could have used on her. But what had she expected? He was a slayer. If he truly wanted to keep her here, her strength didn't matter. Still, she'd never given up easily, and she wasn't about to start doing so now.

Kicking one leg behind her, she hooked one of his ankles with her foot and sent them both tumbling to the ground, but he still held on. "Get off me, Porter!"

"So you can run from me? I don't think so."

"Get off of her, Jake."

They both twisted their heads around, focusing on the little man who had joined them on the hill. He stood about five-foot-eight, slender and wiry. His hair was short and a mousy brown color, his nose sharp and pointed. Hazel eyes, full of contempt, stared down at them. If she hadn't recognized him from his boyhood, Nyla would have never known he was related to Jake.

"Well, hi there, Cousin Peewee," Jake said, his tone a mixture of fake joyfulness and genuine irritation. "Would you mind leaving us alone for a moment?"

"No, I will not leave you alone," Peewee responded. "I hope you know the whole town could see your little performance, and I'm not the least bit happy finding out one of the two people up here mating like bunnies in spring-time is my cousin."

"What?" Jake asked. Nyla was too embarrassed to speak as she replayed Peewee's words in her mind.

"You might not have been able to see the town from where you parked your car, but with a good pair of binoculars, they could see you. Miss Harper about died when she looked out her kitchen window and saw the two of you putting on your little show. The woman is an eighty-three-year-old virgin for crying out loud. She liked to have had a stroke."

"Well, maybe Miss Harper should learn not to use binoculars when she takes a glance out her kitchen window," Jake said while Nyla groaned from embarrassment beneath him. She felt as though she were living her childhood dream of walking into school completely naked. Oh, how she wanted to run. She struggled to get up, but Jake wouldn't budge.

"Leave us alone, Peewee," she heard Jake say, followed by the unmistakable sound of his gun's safety being clicked off. From her position, belly down on the ground, Nyla could only see his arm, and the gun in his hand that was aimed at his own cousin. "I'm going to run out of patience soon, and asking won't even be a thought in my head."

Peewee's eyes grew as round as saucers, and he rested his shaking hand on the butt of his own gun, still in its holder at his waist. "Dammit, Jake, I'm the law around here—"

"Goodie for you, you're king of the hillbillies. Now leave. My partner and I were in the middle of a discussion."

"Oh, so that's what you call it now?" Peewee asked, derisively.

Jake cocked the gun, obviously not amused.

"Don't push me, Jake. I could lock you in a jail cell for the night," Peewee warned with a quiver in his voice, but there was determination in his eyes. Nyla prayed Jake wouldn't push him too far. The man was wise enough to know Jake could beat him to a pulp, but he had a badge now and that gave a man like him strength when backed into a corner.

"Peewee, you could lock me in a jail cell for the rest of my life, but it's not gonna make that left nut grow back, is it?" Jake asked, angling his gun so it pointed directly at Peewee's genitalia.

The man let out a curse, his face reddening. "I never did like you."

"Likewise, punk. That's why I glued your ass to the toilet seat. Now, get out of here before I decide to embarrass you in front of your entire inbred town. Besides, the longer you get on my nerves, the longer I just might stay," he added.

"Well, we definitely wouldn't want that," Peewee muttered. "I'll give you five minutes, then I'm coming back prepared to shoot." He gave them both a good glare before turning on his heel and walking away, leaving a trail of muttered curses behind him.

"Well, that was my cousin, the mighty sheriff of Hicksville," Jake said by way of introduction as he stood and helped Nyla up from the ground. "The family is so proud."

Nyla remained silent, embarrassment eating her alive. She'd done a lot of shameful things in her past, but she'd never had an audience. She didn't even want to think about how many people had seen them—or what they must think about her.

It was as if Jake had read her mind. "I'm sorry, Nyla. I had no idea we could be seen."

"I'm sorry too," she mumbled, sitting down on a large rock. She dropped her head into her hands and let the tears she'd been fighting back start to flow. There was no point in running away to keep Jake from seeing her fall apart. He'd just catch her.

"Nyla?" She sensed him crouch before her, felt his hands on her knees. "Nyla, don't cry."

"Why?" she asked between sobs.

"Because I can kill vampires and demons, but I have no clue what to do with a woman when she's crying."

He sounded so serious that she had to laugh at his comment. "It's your fault. I asked you to go away, but you chose to be stubborn."

"I chose to find out what was wrong with you. You make me feel like I've done something wrong, but I didn't do anything I'm ashamed of."

She looked up, gathering all her bravery to meet his gaze. "What do you see when you look at me now?" she asked, bracing herself for his answer.

"Now?"

"Yes."

"Right now?"

She nodded. "Yes."

"A crazy woman."

Nyla stared at him for a moment, then burst into laughter, despite her distress. "Dammit, Jake. I'm serious. I know you must think I'm an awful woman."

"What?" Jake's expression was incredulous. "Why would I think you're awful? Is this about the damned UV blanket?"

"No. It's about me attacking you like a possessed slut."

Jake stared at Nyla's tear stained face, unable to comprehend what he was hearing. "Nyla, I have no idea what you're talking about," he finally said, giving up on the idea of figuring out what was going through her mind. He'd decided a long time ago that a woman's mind wasn't really meant for understanding anyway. "We're both adults and we had great sex, sex that I'm pretty confident was consensual. I don't know what happened to make you suddenly feel so ashamed, but I enjoyed it. Hell, I've wanted you since day one, and I think you felt that way too. But you kept sidestepping what was apparently destined to happen." He wiped a tear away from her puffy, red face, deciding she was still beautiful despite her crying jag. "We all have needs. Only a hypocrite acts like they don't."

"Yes, but now you don't respect me."

"I don't *respect* you?" Jake nearly choked on disbelief. "Are you insane? You are the only woman I know who can kick my ass, you beheaded a vampire in midair, and when you want something, you get it. How in the world could I not respect you?"

She sniffed and ran her hands across her tear streaked cheeks. "Did you just admit that I can kick your ass?"

Jake laughed. "How did I know you'd focus on that part of what I said?" Leaning toward her, he placed a soft kiss on her forehead. "I respect you more than I respect most people, even if you are acting like a girly-girl right now."

She let a small chuckle escape, playfully pushing him away. "Don't you dare call me dirty names like girly-girl, Porter. Remember, I can kick your ass."

"Oh, I knew I shouldn't have let that slip," he said, grabbing her hands and pulling her to her feet. Once he had her up, he held on to her, inhaling her scent, knowing he was feeling way too much for this woman. If any other woman had acted like this after having sex with him, he'd have told them to grow up, but he couldn't do that to Nyla. He didn't want to watch her cry, and he sure as hell didn't want to ever be the cause of her tears. "Are we cool now, partner?"

"Yeah, I'm okay."

"You sure?" he asked, tipping her chin up with his index finger.

"Yes."

"Feel like hunting down some bad guys and kicking ass?"

"Sure."

"Alrighty then," he said, stepping away from her before he gave in to the urge to kiss her senseless. He could still feel her body clamped tightly around his, and he ached to be inside her again, but he knew that wasn't going to happen any time soon. "Well, we have about a minute until my dork-cousin comes back with a shotgun, and I have to break him in two. Let's save him some pain and start moving."

She groaned and looked at him with a heartbreaking, pleading expression. "Oh, Jake, I can't do it. All those people saw me!"

He saw the shame in her eyes, and it undid him. He'd give anything to take it away. "They saw *us*, Nyla, and 'all those people' are probably more like two or three people. Two or three toothless, shoeless hillbillies. It's no big deal."

She shook her head, obviously not relieved by his statement.

"Look, if anyone says anything to you they'll have to deal with me, and trust me, they will regret it." He held out his hand, willing her to take it, to allow him to lead her back to the car. To trust him to take care of her.

Slowly, she reached out and placed her hand in his. He knew he was in trouble when he realized he could feel her gentle touch all the way down to his soul.

NYLA SHIFTED UNEASILY in her seat as she sat outside the motel where she and Jake would stay the night, waiting for him to come out of the office. He'd let her remain in the car while he got them a room.

Although the motel had peeling, peach paint and more than a few broken shutters, it wasn't its decrepitude that caused her to fidget. It was the three portly men who'd gathered on the sidewalk before her, leering at her with that horny-toad-gleam in their eyes that men generally directed at women while they danced around a pole. She didn't have to ask why they were looking at her that way, not when one of them had a pair of binoculars hanging around his fat neck.

Jake exited the office, a room key dangling from his hand. His brow furrowed in concern as he caught her gaze, and then he noticed the men. The biggest one, decked out in bib overalls and a white undershirt, approached him, laughing.

"Shoo-wee, y'all put on a good show," she heard the man bellow as he stopped before Jake. "She as good as she looked?"

Nyla tried to shrink down into the seat, mortified as the men all laughed at her expense. Jake smiled, and the men continued to laugh and congratulate him. Then, without a word, Jake punched the loudmouth in the face, grabbed him by the straps of his overalls, and rammed him headfirst into the hood of a nearby pickup truck.

"You guys have any more questions?" he asked as the man slid down the front of the truck, his face covered in blood.

The two men held their hands up in surrender, backing away from Jake. "No, man" and "No, sir" were repeated in unison as they allowed Jake to pass. Once he cleared them, they hurried to pick up their unconscious friend.

Jake walked over to the car, opening Nyla's door. "Come on, I got us a room."

She didn't want to stay in the hick-town where she'd apparently become the local porno star, but she could tell by Jake's tone that he was going to make her stay whether she wanted to or not. And apparently, he was going to beat the hell out of anyone who gave her any grief.

Reluctantly, she got out of the car and followed him to the room, allowing him to carry her bag. Actually, she hadn't been able to wrestle it out of his hands.

"When was the last time you've actually seen a real motel key?" he asked her as he fitted the key into the lock. "You know, I feel like we're in a *Hee-Haw* episode of *The Twilight Zone.*" He glanced around. "Or maybe this is *Deliverance.*"

"Well, given the dental situation of most of the residents here, maybe we'll get lucky and only meet up with fangless vampires."

Jake chuckled as he opened the door and stepped back, allowing her to precede him. Nyla entered the room, her smile vanishing as her gaze zeroed in on the one queen-sized bed resting in the middle of the room. She looked around, spotting a dresser with a TV set on top, a couple of nightstands, and a small table with chairs.

"Is the other bed in there?" she asked, pointing to the bathroom door.

"All they have are one-bed rooms," Jake said, and she could hear the disappointment in his voice. He closed the door and pocketed the key. "I'll take the floor."

"The floor?"

"You obviously don't want to share the bed with me," he said, a small glint of anger shining in his eyes. "There's just the bed and the floor. You can have the bed."

"You shouldn't have to sleep on the floor."

"I've slept in worse places," he said, walking over to the dresser. He placed their bags on top and started rummaging through his, pulling out a fresh, black T-shirt. "I hope Alley's all right," he added, unfolding the shirt. "I wish she'd been with us when we left Louisville."

"She was," Nyla said, wanting to erase the worry she heard in his voice.

"What?"

"She was curled up on the floorboard behind your seat," she said, lowering herself onto the bed. "I thought you knew she was there."

Jake looked at her suspiciously. "You're telling me that my jealous, insane cat rode with us all the way from Louisville to here and that she was in the car with us when we . . . Oh, hell. Tell me I didn't roll my seat back on her!"

Nyla laughed, although she knew he was seriously worried. "I'm sure she would have definitely let you know she was there if you had. Besides, she got out while we were talking on the hill. She's fine."

"That doesn't make sense," he said, shaking his head. "She'd never ride quietly all that distance with you in the car. She hates women."

"Not this woman," Nyla said smugly. "Back in Louisville, I fed her some tuna and played with her outside the motel before I came in and fell asleep. I would have told you, but I was so tired. Then you were trying to kill me with a UV blanket so it slipped my mind again."

Jake cut her a glare, touched with a bit of weariness, clearly relaying he'd heard enough about that particular incident, and peeled off his T-shirt, wincing as the fabric pulled away from his skin as if stuck to a wound.

Nyla gasped as she saw what she'd done to him. His back was covered in deep scratches. She hadn't noticed before because the black T-shirt didn't show the blood.

"Yeah, you tore me up," Jake said with a cocky grin, when she drew in a sharp intake of air. He turned to admire her work in the mirror over the dresser.

"I'm so sorry, Jake. I . . ."

"I'm not," he said, cutting her off before she could apologize further. He leaned closer to the mirror, seeming to peer at the skin around his neck. "That's weird."

"What's weird?" Nyla asked, unease stirring in her stomach.

"I could have sworn you bit me," he said, searching his skin. "It sure felt hard enough to leave teeth marks."

"You wimp," Nyla said, forcing out a light chuckle she didn't feel. "I might have given you a few little nips, but I didn't try to eat you alive."

She closed her eyes, fear gnawing away at her gut. If he figured out that her saliva had healing properties, he would know she was a vampire.

"Damn, I shouldn't have said anything."

She opened her eyes to find him regarding her, his eyes holding a concern no one had ever shown her before. "You're not going to weird out on me again, are you? We didn't do anything wrong."

"No, I'm not going to weird out," she answered. "I'm fine."

"Good." He let his gaze rove over the bed, and she could clearly see the longing in his eyes. "I'm going to go clean up before we head over to Peewee's office. Don't go anywhere."

"I won't," she promised, watching him walk into the bathroom. "I guess I should thank you for what you did outside," she called to him as she heard the water start running in the sink. "You probably broke that guy's nose."

"Oh, I definitely broke his nose," Jake said matter-of-factly. "Hopefully, I gave him a concussion."

"You didn't have to defend me."

"That's true," he said, turning off the water. He appeared in the doorway, wearing the clean shirt. "Nobody had to defend you, because you didn't do anything wrong, but nobody is going to make you feel ashamed around me." He reached behind him and removed his gun from his waistband. He opened the chamber and checked the ammunition inside. "We need to get a move on. It'll be dark soon, and somewhere out there, a woman is about to die."

Remembering why they were here, Nyla rose from the bed, ready to go to work. She wouldn't waste any more time bellyaching over her problems when a woman's life was on the line. "Let's go."

Jake led her out, allowing her to exit the room first before he locked the door behind them.

"You know," he said, rubbing his neck with his hand. "If not for the daylight thing, I'd swear you were a vamp. Even if you didn't leave a mark, you bit me hard enough for my neck to still be tender."

Nyla gulped as she watched Jake rub his neck, his brow creased. He was a smart man, and a slayer on top of that. It was only by some miracle that he hadn't yet discovered what she was, but she knew she didn't have much longer until he did. Then one of them would die, because a true fight between a pantherian and a slayer would be to the death.

Chapter Fifteen

THE SHERIFF'S OFFICE sat dead center in the town, right across from the small medical center. Nyla didn't even want to think about what credentials were acceptable to practice medicine in this town.

Jake parked the car next to a row of pickup trucks, all of them featuring police decals on their doors. "Time for a little family reunion," he announced as they exited the car.

Nyla didn't look forward to the meeting. Jake and Peewee had never gotten along, and from what she could remember of the few times she'd seen Peewee, he'd been a real ass. Too small to do any physical damage to Jake, and jealous of the bigger cousin's strength and good looks, he tormented Jake by pointing out how the whole family thought he was crazy. Unable to deny the fact he was the black sheep of the family, Peewee's words had hurt Jake, but he'd got his revenge often. Nyla had gotten hers too, scratching Peewee to pieces a couple of times. The memory put a smile on her face.

They entered the building, greeted by curious stares from the staff. A woman in her mid-twenties with blond hair tied up into a chignon and a white button-down blouse sat at the front desk, smiling appreciatively at Jake as they approached. Nyla balled her hands into fists, fighting back her jealousy and wishing the normal-looking woman was as toothless as the rest of the townspeople she'd seen.

The other three staff members—men in khaki shirts and blue jeans—seemed normal as well.

"They must have a good dental plan," Jake whispered, as if picking up on her thoughts. Then he centered his attention on the young woman at the front desk. "Hey there, miss," he drawled, oozing out his signature charm as he approached her. "Would my cousin, Peewee, happen to be in?"

"*You're* Peewee's cousin?" Blondie asked in surprise, her voice full of that lilt women got when they were flirting. "Wow. I never would have imagined Peewee had such a tall, strapping man for a cousin."

"Yeah, well, I snatched up all the good genes."

Between Jake's overabundance of charm and Blondie's exaggerated southern belle accent, Nyla didn't know which one to start hitting . . . or maybe she'd just vomit from all the saccharine sweetness.

"Sheriff Peewee," Blondie practically cooed into the intercom, "your delicious cousin is here to see you."

"Send him in, Luanne," Peewee's voice barked out of the speaker. Clearly, he wasn't as pleased at the prospect of seeing the tall strapping man as Luanne was.

"He'll see you now," the blonde purred, rising from her seat. "I'd be glad to show you to his office."

"We can find it just fine, I'm sure," Nyla said, cutting the woman off before she did something stupid like place one of her pink-nailed hands on Jake.

"Who are you?" Luanne asked, narrowing her eyes on Nyla, acting as if she'd just noticed her.

"I'm the woman the whole town saw *doing* this tall, strapping man on the hilltop," she replied, unable to keep the promise of violence out of her tone.

The three men stopped what they were doing and stared at the two women with the hope of a catfight in their eyes. Their hopes were dashed when an unhappy looking Luanne returned to her seat.

"Come on, Jake." Nyla gave Jake a nudge, starting them off in the direction of his cousin's office and past the men who were now giving him "way to go, man" looks.

"Well, thanks for making me the big, bad stud," Jake said softly, after he'd had a good chuckle, "but I thought you didn't want to be reminded that people could see us."

"Shut up, Porter."

"Not a chance," he replied. "If I didn't know better, I'd say you were jeal—" He stopped speaking, his attention caught by pictures hanging on the bulletin board mounted on the wall they had to pass to get to Peewee's office.

Nyla followed his gaze, gasping as she saw what he'd noticed. Pictures of various men and women were tacked to the board, beneath the word Missing. She focused on a man with dark blond hair, about thirty-five years old.

"Isn't that the guy I beheaded last night?" she whispered, leaning in close to Jake so the audience behind them couldn't hear.

"Yeah," Jake whispered back. "I think it's safe to say he's not coming home—nor are these guys." One by one, he pointed out every vampire they'd killed the night before, including the woman who'd landed on the roof of the car. "Son of a bitch."

"Y'all comin' on in here or not?" Peewee called out as he emerged from the doorway to his office.

Jake stepped away from the bulletin board and started toward the office again. Nyla watched how his forehead creased and was pretty sure she knew what he was thinking. How could all of those freshly-turned vamps have been fliers?

"What are you doing in my town?" Peewee asked without preamble as he closed the office door behind them when they entered.

"Ah, Peewee, you always were such a warm, inviting guy," Jake said, his voice dripping with sarcasm as he lowered himself into Peewee's chair. Nyla leaned against the file cabinets, watching with amusement as Peewee's face turned red.

"Get out of my chair! Y'all sit over here on the other side of the desk."

"Make me move, pipsqueak," Jake taunted, opening the file folder on Peewee's desk.

"Hey!"

"Look, women are being murdered. You can play sheriff all day long when the killer is caught, but until then you need my help."

"Your help? Since when did you become an officer of the law?"

Jake sent an unimpressed glance his cousin's way. "Since when did you?"

"I have a badge." Peewee pointed at his meager chest, showing off the badge pinned to his khaki button-down shirt.

"Big deal. I have experience, and I actually know what I'm going up against. If you truly want to protect your town, the best thing you can do is stay out of my way and let me do my job."

"Why? Are vampires about to invade?" Peewee let out a shrill, high-pitched laugh, turning toward Nyla. "Do you know loverboy here thinks vampires are real?" He laughed a bit more, but sobered as he realized Nyla wasn't laughing with him. "Oh, hell, you're a frigging crackpot too."

"I prefer the title of hunter," she said firmly, narrowing her eyes, daring him to say something else smart to her about Jake.

"I wouldn't piss her off, Peewee," Jake warned. "The woman could kick your ass with both hands tied behind her back."

"Get out of here, both of you," Peewee ordered. "If you want to send me some help, send Jonah. He's a real cop. He caught the last guy doing this."

"No, the last guy 'doing this' caught him," Jake rejoined, "and I was there to help save him."

"What are you talking about?" Peewee looked back and forth between the two of them as if they'd both sprouted second heads.

"Carter Dunn was some sort of demon or devil worshiper, and he was killed by vampires, not Jonah."

"Oh, for crying out loud," Peewee said, rolling his eyes. "Get out of that file and leave!"

"Um, no." Jake continued looking through the contents of the folder despite his cousin's continued ranting, knowing the smaller man wasn't going to do anything to him. "We have a better picture here, Nyla."

Nyla walked over to the desk and leaned over Jake's shoulder to see the picture he held. It was a clear shot of the last victim's naked torso. There was a marking right above the third victim's hip, but before she got a good look at it Peewee snatched the picture and the rest of the file away from Jake.

"Aw, Peewee, I was gonna give it back," Jake said as his cousin stood over him, glaring down at him like he was a cockroach he wanted to stomp on.

"You and your little girlfriend get out before I toss you both into a cell."

"For what?" Jake asked innocently.

Peewee's eyes flared with anger. "For being an asshole your whole life."

Jake laughed, an action which seemed to further anger his cousin. The wiry man made a move toward him, and Jake reached toward the waistband of his jeans.

Nyla instinctively backed up, giving Jake room to maneuver and readying herself should she need to come to his aid, but he wasn't reaching for a weapon. He brought his cell phone up before Peewee could grab him, sticking it in his cousin's face. "Call Jonah. I have him on speed dial."

"Call Jonah for what?"

"Ask him what really happened. Ask him if what I said is true."

"I'm not as stupid as you think I am, Jake. I push that button on your phone, and I'm going to get connected to one of your little accomplices. Whoever he is, he'll sound just like Jonah and yeah, he'll tell me all this crap you're spouting is true."

Jake laughed out loud. "Dude, you have issues. Call him on your own phone if you don't trust me."

Peewee looked between Jake and Nyla, disdain clearly evident in his cold glare and flaring nostrils, before picking up his phone and punching in a number.

"Will Jonah tell him the truth?" Nyla asked, bending down to whisper in Jake's ear.

"If he knows I told Peewee the truth, he'll verify it."

"And then what's our plan?"

"We get all the information Peewee and his merry little band of hillbilly bandits have collected and catch Curtis Dunn before I lose my patience and beat the crap out of my cousin."

"Jake, he really could lock you up, you know."

"Yeah, well, you'll just have to break me out."

Nyla rolled her eyes and shook her head. "What makes you think I wouldn't consider a cage a good place to keep you?"

Jake chuckled good-naturedly before returning his attention to Peewee, who'd just gotten Jonah on the line. They both watched as Peewee's smugness evaporated before their eyes "You're serious?" they heard him ask, his color draining. "Did Jake put you up to this? This is all just a joke, right?"

Jake and Nyla chuckled as they watched Peewee continue to argue with Jonah over the phone, refusing to believe the truth. "You're all nuts," he said, disconnecting the line. "You've turned your brother into a nut case too," he accused Jake, turning on him.

"Call me names if it helps you deal with the truth, Peewee, but vampires are real, and Satan really can control people. The killer who murdered the poor woman whose photo is in that file is not your normal kind of guy. Jonah realized he was in over his head with the guy's brother. If you're smart, you'll recognize that you're out of your league on this one. You need my help, Peewee."

"No, I don't. We know who the killer is. We have the information from Louisville's police department, and we know that Curtis Dunn got away from Jonah and is carrying on his brother's work. All we have to do is catch him."

Jake laughed. "It's that easy, is it?"

"I have a task force on this."

"Ooh, Nyla, did you hear that? He has a task force and everything. And I bet they're real pros."

Peewee walked over to the door, flinging it open. Nyla thought he was going to order them out again, but instead he barked out an order for his task force to come into the office.

Two of the men they'd seen earlier walked through the door, along with a heavyset man wearing jeans, a flannel shirt, and a cargo vest. He carried a rifle in one hand and an open can of beer in the other. Nyla had to blink, swearing for a moment she was looking at the actor who played "Larry The Cable Guy" in the movie. The other two men were tall and slender, a dark-headed man with a mustache, and a baby-faced blond. All three had shoes and teeth, which was a step up from most of the townspeople, although the Larry-lookalike's teeth were a shade of yellow Nyla wasn't very familiar with.

"So this is the mighty task force that's going to bring Curtis Dunn to justice?" Jake asked, not bothering to hide his amusement.

"We sure is," the Larry-lookalike said, stepping forward. "And who is you, pretty boy?"

Jake smiled, obviously enjoying himself. "Me and my partner *is* the people who have come here to replace you boys," he said, emphasizing his bad grammar with an exaggerated twang.

"I don't think so. Petie Joe and Billy Bob here is all the help I need. I've tracked every kind of animal you can think of. This guy won't be no different."

"So you must be Bubba Lee, huh?"

The Larry-lookalike's eyes widened. "How do you know my name?"

"Well, I just met Petie Joe and Billy Bob. What other inbred hillbilly name was left?"

Bubba Lee's forehead crinkled, and Nyla struggled not to laugh while he took his time figuring out he'd just been insulted.

"Hey!" His eyes narrowed as it finally dawned on him what he'd been called. "I don't care who you is, we don't take a likin' to you city folks comin' down here tryin' to make us all look stupid."

"Now, Bubba Lee, why would I waste my time making you look stupid when you do such a fine job of it yourself?"

Bubba Lee's eyes widened, as though surprised someone would say such a thing to him, and judging by his size, Nyla was sure the surprise was genuine. "Oh, you asked for it, boy . . ."

"Stop, Bubba Lee," Peewee warned with a hand held up, signaling the burly man to not take another step. "He's just baiting you. Y'all go on now and find something to do while my cousin and I have a little chat."

Jake sat back in the chair, grinning. "Good idea, boys. Why don't you go clean out your guns or something? Here's a tip—unload 'em, first."

Bubba Lee glared down at where Jake sat calmly, looking smugger than the cat that caught the mouse, and Nyla could imagine the murderous thoughts running through the big man's mind. Finally, realizing the sheriff wasn't going to intervene in his defense, he gestured for his teammates to follow him out, aiming a good, cold look at Jake before he shut the door behind them.

"What was that?" Peewee asked as the door closed. "You can't just come in here issuing orders to my people like you own the place."

"Oh, what? Like you know the right directions to give them," Jake said. "Seriously, who the hell would elect you sheriff? Bubba Lee could probably do a better job."

"Obviously, the town doesn't agree."

"Most of the town doesn't even have enough sense to brush their teeth and put shoes on their feet," Jake retorted. "Did you seriously assign a hunter to go after Curtis Dunn?"

"You two call yourself hunters."

"We don't go after squirrels and deer. There's a distinction."

"Oh, that's right. You're *vampire* hunters. I guess it would be safer if I sent two wackos out into the night fully loaded and ready to shoot. No, wait. You'd stake innocent people to death."

"No, but we *would* kill the vampires."

"Oh, for the love of . . . There is no such thing as vampires!"

"You have a lot of missing people out there on that bulletin board," Nyla interjected.

"Yeah, so?"

"So do you normally have that many people missing?"

"No, but what's that have to do with anything?"

"He really isn't catching on," Nyla said to Jake, who nodded in return. "Women have been murdered. The bodies have left a trail from Louisville to here."

"The last body was found *outside* my town."

"Trust me, the next one—and if we don't find Curtis, there will be a next one—will be *in* your town. So, you have a trail of bodies leading to here, and several people are missing from here. Don't you think the two situations might be connected?"

Peewee shuffled his feet, darting a look at Jake like he expected some sort of help, but Jake merely leaned back in the desk chair, grinning from ear to ear as he watched the man squirm.

"Yeah, it could be connected, but I still don't see how vampires can be involved, seeing as how they don't exist. Y'all know darn well those fang holes are just holes left by some sort of tubes. Carter Dunn was draining his victims to make them look like they'd been attacked by vampires, and his brother is doing the same thing. My boys can handle it."

"Jake?"

"Yes, Nyla?"

"Can I tell Peewee what we did last night?"

Jake's lips twitched. "Sure."

"He won't throw us in jail?"

"No, because if vampires don't exist, we couldn't have killed them, could we?"

"What are you two babbling about?" Peewee cut in, looking between them, not seeming to know which one to glare at longest.

"I beheaded a couple of flying vampires last night," Nyla said. "Jake shot the other five with UV bullets, killing them. Those vampires looked a whole lot like those missing people on your board out there, except they had fangs."

Peewee stared at her, slack-jawed and speechless. Nyla looked at Jake, receiving a shrug for the effort. She returned her gaze to Peewee, finding him in the same speechless state.

"What kind of sick joke is this?" he finally asked, again not seeming to know which of the two he should focus on. "I know those people. They have families."

"And we feel bad for their families," Nyla said, "but this is no joke. We were attacked at a cemetery. We had no choice."

"You sick, psychotic—You're lucky this is too insane to believe, or you'd both be arrested right now! Your poor mother, Jake." Peewee shook his head in disgust. "I won't even bother telling her—"

"He's not going to believe us," Jake said, interrupting what sounded like the beginning of a long insult. "He's not going to help us, and, in fact, he'll probably get in our way as much as he possibly can. We tried."

Jake rose from the chair, gesturing for Peewee to take it. "There's a vampire loose in your town, Peewee, and the bastard is changing your people into vamps. When you want to embrace the truth, you know how to reach me. Hopefully you'll come to your senses before you run out of room on that bulletin board out there."

Nyla followed Jake out the door, choosing to take the high road and ignore the scathing glare she received from Luanne. Instead, she asked, "What do we do now?"

"Stake out the area and review all the information we have," Jake answered, stopping before the bulletin board. "Who the hell is changing over these people?"

Nyla felt a cold chill creep along her spine, and for the slightest of moments she felt a dark presence in her mind. She closed her eyes and focused on strengthening her mental blocks. Now was not the time for Demarcus to enter her head. There was too much going on.

She felt eyes on her back and whirled around impulsively, but her only danger seemed to be the heated glares of the three men Jake had insulted earlier—and Luanne, of course. The woman looked at her with murder in her eyes.

"We should go, Jake. The sun was already setting when we walked in here, and we shouldn't waste time."

"You're right." Jake peeled his gaze away from the bulletin board, giving Peewee's task force a healthy smile before heading for the door.

"I think you made a good impression in there," Nyla commented as they stepped out of the building and into the dark night.

Jake laughed. "Yeah, I should work in customer service."

He unlocked the trunk of the Malibu, removing Nyla's sword and knife sheaths, after glancing around to make sure no one was watching from any of the nearby buildings. She'd left them off since she was only wearing a T-shirt. Country hick-town or not, it was never wise to walk into a sheriff's office sporting major cutlery.

"Better suit up. There is definitely something dark and evil going on, right here in this very town from the looks of it."

"You really think Curtis is here?" she asked, slipping on the sheaths. "You thought he was in Louisville."

"Since that's where the first body was found, that was my original thought, but those vampires who attacked us came from here."

"I wish we'd asked how long those people have been missing. Obviously it couldn't be long enough for them to be fliers, but still . . ."

"I know. It doesn't make any sense." Jake shook his head. "The ability to fly is rare."

"Especially for the newly turned."

"Especially for so *many* newly turned."

"You said Curtis's brother had trapped a very powerful vampire."

"Yeah?"

"So what if Curtis has trapped a very powerful vampire who has the ability to fly? And what if that vampire is being forced to change over the townspeople, and he's passing along the ability?"

Jake seemed to think about it before shaking his head. "I don't think it's an ability that can be passed along like that. The ability to fly is something only truly old and powerful vampires can do, and a vampire can't transfer decades of experience and power to a fledgling."

"What other explanation is there?"

"Carter Dunn was a scientific whiz. Curtis probably is too."

"So you think Curtis is *making* vampires?"

"Maybe," Jake said with a shrug. "It's too coincidental for that many newly turned vamps to fly. We'll ask Seta about it when she pops up again, but I'm pretty sure there has to be some type of tampering going on."

"So you're actually going to play nice with Seta?"

"I know. I can barely believe it myself, but it all comes down to the lesser of two evils. I kind of owe her anyway." Jake closed the trunk, but made no effort to move. He stood where he was, staring up at the night sky, entertaining some hidden thought.

"Seta saved your brother."

"That's right."

"And now she's willing to help you again."

Jake snorted in disgust. "She went into Carter Dunn's house to save Aria and Eron. Saving my brother was an add-on, not something she did purely out of the goodness of her heart."

"Then why is she helping us now?"

"Carter Dunn's plan was to inspire belief in vampires by leaving his victims with fang marks. Once people began to believe in vamps, they'd want them killed, and that would create more vampire hunters. That, in turn, would wipe out vampires, which is what Dunn wanted. Now his brother Curtis is doing the same thing. Vampires kind of frown on exposure since belief in their existence will pretty much guarantee their extinction."

"So you think Seta's helping solely for her own personal gain."

"For her and her kind, yes."

"That's crap, Jake. She could go after Curtis all by herself."

Jake focused his gaze on her. "Don't ever trust a vampire, Nyla. Even if they do a few good deeds, it doesn't change what they are. I don't disagree with Dunn—all vamps should be dead—but I don't agree with his method of trying to make it happen."

He raked a hand through his hair, looking toward the building they'd come from, allowing Nyla the time she needed to tightly squeeze her eyes shut. She had to stop the tears threatening to spill over. Jake was clueless to just how deeply his words had cut her, and if she started crying, he'd want to know why. She couldn't say it was because by wanting all vampires dead, he was also wishing her dead, not to mention the fact that even if he didn't want her dead, he'd never trust her. They'd never be able to build a life together without trust.

"Something else just isn't adding up here," he said after a long pause. "This victim was found naked. That doesn't match the others. They've always been dressed."

"Do you think there's something significant about her nudity?"

"I don't know," he replied. "I saw the last victim's picture long enough to memorize the mark on her, but I really didn't have time to read the file. There was a lot more in there than what was faxed to Louisville."

"Well, Peewee's not going to just let you look at it," Nyla commented, trying to keep her tone emotionless.

"No, but I bet I could butter up Luanne and get it from her."

"Well, don't let me interfere with your dating life," Nyla snapped, a cold bitterness creeping into her blood. "Just don't get so carried away you forget we're on a job."

"What are you talking about?" Jake's eyes were filled with incredulity. "You're the one who flashed your breasts at the LMPD. All I'll flash are my dimples."

Too hurt and angry to come up with a good rejoinder, Nyla growled and spun on her heel, rounding the car. She refused to look at Jake as she opened the passenger door and got in, slamming the door shut.

She'd barely had time to take a deep breath before Jake was in the car with her, nostrils flared. "What is your problem now?"

"I don't have a problem."

"Bull. You're mad at me."

"Most everyone you know is mad at you."

His eyebrows rose slightly, and he nodded his agreement. "Although that may be true, you don't have any reason to be."

"If you say so."

He looked at her for a moment, tightening his hand around the steering wheel. Nyla got the impression he was imagining that hand wrapped around her neck.

"What happened on that hilltop, Nyla?"

"What? You didn't take sex-ed in junior high?"

"You know what I mean. You have sex with me, then run off acting like it's the most shameful thing you've ever done. I try to be nice and give you your space, but you get all jealous when I mention buttering up some woman for information, information which could save lives, by the way. Are there some rules here I'm missing? Are we in some sort of relationship? Forgive me if I'm a bit confused, but I seem to jump from partner to enemy to fuck buddy to . . . I don't know, boyfriend or something, pretty damn quick. My head is spinning, dammit."

"What do you want from me?" she snapped, exasperated.

"I want to know what you want from me," Jake snapped back.

"I want you to shut the hell up and go catch Curtis Dunn."

"That's not what I was talking about, Nyla."

"Look, I don't want anything from you, all right? You can save the where-is-this-relationship-going speech because it's not like that. I already know I'm not your type."

"Really? That's interesting considering I don't recall having a type."

"Trust me, you do."

"What the—"

The sound of men stampeding out of the sheriff's department saved Nyla from having to listen to whatever it was Jake was going to say. Billy Bob, Petie Joe, Bubba Lee and Peewee ran from the building, shouting to each other excitedly as they climbed into their trucks, switching on their sirens before peeling out.

"You think we ought to check that out?" Nyla asked, welcoming the opportunity to end their argument.

Jake glared at her for a moment before turning the key in the ignition. "We'll finish this later," he promised, turning on the headlights.

"Of course we will." Nyla sighed as they pulled out. "If not for arguing and killing people, whatever would we do to pass the time?"

Chapter Sixteen

"YOU'RE GOING TO hit a tree!" Nyla yelped.

"No, I'm not."

"Jake!"

"Would you stop backseat driving? Damn, you're going to *make* me hit something if you keep on fussing!"

Nyla folded her arms, fuming silently as they swerved and careened through the heavily wooded, narrow dirt roads, following the trail of Peewee and his men. She wanted to point out that there were no street lights, and Jake didn't know his way around the town like Peewee and his boys, but she knew he wouldn't listen.

With no other options available, she made sure her seatbelt was securely fastened and prayed Jake wouldn't kill them both. Her faith in his driving abilities became increasingly hard to hold on to as they whipped around sharp corners, trees looming all around them, following the trucks ahead of them.

Finally, they skidded to a stop a short distance away from a small aluminum-paneled house. The trucks parked before the house, their drivers quickly jumping out of them. A woman rushed out onto the porch, wailing, her hands waving frantically.

"You think it's vampire related?" Nyla asked.

"Peewee brought his super-duper task force, so I'd say most likely." Jake tilted his head, listening, or sensing, for something. "I don't think there are any hanging around."

He opened his door, stepping out into the night. Nyla followed behind him, searching the sky for any signs of an air attack. It had barely been twenty-four hours since the last attack, and she wasn't looking forward to another one so soon.

They marched toward the house, knowing they weren't welcome, but she knew that neither of them cared about that little fact. If there was a rogue vampire trying to take over the town, the bumbling idiots in charge of protecting it needed their help. Even if Peewee and his task force shared the IQ of a peanut, they didn't deserve to be slaughtered or changed into another form of life against their will.

As they neared the house, the woman's cries grew louder, more panicked. Something truly horrific had happened. Nyla prayed it wasn't anything to do with children, her mind briefly flashing back to the night Bobby Romano was slaughtered. She never wanted to see a dead child again. Some things were just too cruel to deal with, no matter how tough you were.

"What do y'all think you're doing?" Billy Bob, the mustached, dark-headed member of Peewee's task force asked, stepping out of the front door entry as Jake put his foot on the first porch step, Nyla following close behind.

"You need our help," Jake said. "What happened?"

"None of your damn business, boy."

"You know, I'm eventually going to grow tired of being called a boy and just beat the crap out of all of you, so I'd suggest canning the attitude. Did Peewee send you out here to stop us?"

"Yup," The man answered with an arrogant smirk as he drew back his fist.

"Well, then, you can blame him for this." Jake grabbed a handful of Billy Bob's shirt, bringing the man forward as he lifted his knee, sending Billy Bob toppling over it and down the steps. "Come on, Nyla."

They quickly entered the house before Billy Bob could lift his stunned butt from the ground and attempt to stop them again. Peewee and Petie Joe turned startled glances toward them as they entered the small wood-paneled living room. Their startlement changed to glares as they realized Billy Bob had not thwarted them.

"You two get out of here, now!" Peewee shouted. "This is police business."

"If it's vampires, it's our business," Jake said firmly.

Nyla glanced around the room as the two men continued to argue, taking in the scene. The woman had the ugliest furniture she'd ever seen, but there was no evidence of an attack in the room. Since Bubba Lee wasn't in here, she realized something must have happened in another area of the house. Bubba Lee was probably trying to track the attacker down like he would an animal.

She peered down the hallway, her gaze landing on a young boy peeking around a door frame. Although she could only see his head and arms, Nyla could tell the boy was shaking from head to toe. He'd definitely seen something.

"I'm telling you he *was* a vampire—or at least some kind of monster!" The woman said, jumping up from the ugly couch she'd been sitting on. "Judd wasn't the same! He was crazy!"

"Sit down, Maybelline," Pewee ordered the small brunette. "My cousin here has got you imagining things."

"I know what I saw, Peter Willis Porter! Don't you dare treat me like a child. My husband was a monster. No person acts like he was actin'."

Jake and Nyla exchanged glances, knowing they'd definitely taken a step closer to finding Curtis Dunn.

"What do you mean by 'monster'?" Jake asked.

"You stay out of this!" Peewee warned.

Maybelline looked as if she was ready to smack Peewee before she looked at Jake and explained, "He was crazy, all wild eyes and just plain crazy, like somethin' was in him. He came barreling through the back door, tearing the place apart." A sob shook her before she finished with, "He took our oldest boy. Oh, God, what is he going to do to him?"

"Maybelline, they are *not* police," Peewee said, exasperated. "Let us handle this."

She turned on him wild-eyed and shaking with fury. "How can you handle it when you don't believe me? You didn't find him when he went missing last week, and now he done come back and took our boy! He's not the same man, I tell ya. He's not my Judd!"

Jake and Nyla glanced at each other again, knowing what had happened. The vampire had changed Judd over, and Judd had come back for his own son, who was most likely being changed over as they stood here.

Billy Bob walked back into the house, glaring at Jake. "You want me to shoot him, Peewee? I know the guy is your family, but I doubt anyone would miss him."

"I'd miss him," Nyla answered before Peewee could respond, "and I can guarantee that if you hurt him, you will sorely miss your testicles."

Billy Bob's glare turned on her while Peewee muttered a curse. "Jake, don't make me have to put you in a cell tonight. You are disturbing this poor woman."

"And you're not helping her," Jake said, seemingly unbothered by the threat of incarceration. "Even if you found her husband tonight, you'd be dead before you could blink. You don't know what kind of monster you're dealing with or how to take it out."

"You mean you're going to have to kill Judd?" Maybelline asked, paling.

Jake swallowed hard, his jaw set tightly, and Nyla knew he didn't want to answer the woman's question while looking into her distraught eyes.

"We might have to," Nyla answered for him, "if it means saving your son."

"Oh, for the love of . . . Get out now!" Peewee roared.

Bubba Lee stepped into the room, his shotgun pointed at Jake's chest. "I think you'd better leave, pretty boy, and take your woman with you."

"I think you should take that shotgun and ram it up your ass," Jake responded. "Something is happening in this town, and it's bigger than anything you've ever encountered. Guns with regular bullets will not protect you or anyone else. These aren't animals you're tracking, and Curtis Dunn is not just some wacked-out guy who needs a straight jacket. What you're going up against is pure evil, and you will all die if you don't let me help."

Maybelline let out a startled cry, falling back against her couch cushions. "He's right, Peewee. There was evil in Judd's eyes when he took our boy. Our own son! What if he comes back again for Bobby?"

The little boy Nyla had noticed earlier came running down the hall, quickly launching himself into his mother's arms.

Nyla froze, her heart bursting with pain as she watched Jake's jaw tighten, anger and remorse fusing together in his eyes as he stared at the boy who, though younger, bore the same name as his childhood friend. She knew he was thinking of those hideous monsters getting their hands on this boy and killing him like they had his friend.

"I won't let them get to your son," Jake said firmly, his tone more determined than she had ever heard it. Nyla knew that in those few words he had promised to kill every one of the evil monsters and risk his own life before he'd let them get even close to the boy.

"Jake, I'm warning you—"

"And I'm warning you," Jake said, cutting off his cousin. "These missing people are no longer people. They are being changed into vampires. Hideous, bloodsucking vampires. Seven of them attacked us last night. Now this woman's husband came back to steal his own child. Wake up and see the truth, Peewee. It's staring you right in the damn face!"

"Quit scaring this woman and her child!" Peewee bellowed.

"I don't need to scare them, Peewee. They've already seen one of the monsters in action."

"That's it. You're sleeping in a cell tonight, Jake."

"On what charge?"

"Interfering with police business and pissing me off in general, not to mention assaulting an officer."

"Who, Billy Bob? He tripped on the porch step."

"Yeah, over your knee," Billy Bob said, removing a pair of handcuffs from his belt. "Hands behind your back, boy."

Knowing better than to fight, Jake did as he was told, allowing the grinning cop to cuff him. Nyla watched helplessly, wanting to mutilate the men, but knowing it would only make the situation worse. She and Jake needed to protect the townspeople and that wouldn't be possible if they were both locked in a jail cell.

"And as for you, missy," Peewee said, directing his glare at her. "What's with the knives?"

"Protection," Nyla answered, careful not to let any attitude slip into her voice.

"I don't think letting you wander around my town armed is a good idea."

"I haven't broken any laws."

"Except for public indecency."

Nyla's face heated as Peewee and his boys shared a good sneer, but it wasn't from embarrassment this time. She wanted to stomp on them like the cockroaches they were. She looked at Jake, noting the fury in his eyes. He'd promised that anyone who gave her grief over what had happened on the hill would pay, but she couldn't allow him to attack these men right now. She nodded her head toward him, letting him know she was all right.

"I haven't hurt anyone, and I'm not going to hurt anyone. You have no reason to take my knives, which are all of legal length and size," she said, returning her gaze to Peewee.

"Oh, but I think I do. And I didn't miss the sword at your back," Peewee added. "Call it southern charm, but we don't like arresting ladies in these parts. Hand over the weapons and you can go. Otherwise, you're sleeping in a cell tonight too."

"Nyla," Jake said, drawing her attention before she could protest. "Let him have them."

He subtly directed his eyes toward the door, and she realized what he was trying to say. He had knives and swords in the trunk of his car, along with quite a few other goodies.

"Fine." She removed the knives, handing them and her sword over bitterly. They could have the weapons, but her sheaths were staying. She had every intention of refilling them once Peewee and his toadies were out of view.

"Why can't these people help me?" Maybelline asked. "They seem to know more about what's happenin' here than y'all do."

"They're messing with you," Peewee answered. "The sick bastards enjoy scaring people with these crazy tales of vampires and demons and stuff. Jake's been doing it his whole life. The truth is somebody killed his friend in front of him when he was a kid. He made up stories of monsters because he thought it would sound better than the truth, which is that he'd just stood there and wet himself while thugs attacked his friend, and then he ran away before they turned on him."

Jake let out a growl of rage, lunging toward his cousin with hatred in his eyes, but Peewee's boys grabbed him, holding him back. He struggled against them, slowly gaining ground as they fought to restrain him.

"Jake!" Nyla placed herself between them and grabbed Jake's face in her hands. "He's just trying to hurt you. Don't let him," she pleaded. Then leaning toward him, she whispered in his ear, "Don't let your anger ruin what we came here to do. Don't give him reason to keep you locked up for more than a night. I need you. This little boy needs you. *Bobby* needs you."

He stopped struggling as her words sank in, as she knew he would, but his tense body told her he was still filled to the brim with rage. It hurt her to know what was going through his mind, how badly Peewee had wounded him with the memory of Bobby's death, a memory that would never release him.

"You and I know the truth of what happened that night with Bobby," she whispered softly. "Who cares what these idiots think when they don't even have the sense to see what's happening right in front of them?" She covered his mouth with her own, kissing him softly until the tension in his body drained away.

"That's enough, love birds," Peewee snapped, pulling her away from Jake. "Billy Bob, take Jake to his cell."

Jake looked into her eyes, and she saw the thank you he relayed in the depth of his gaze. He was much calmer, only slightly resisting when Billy Bob tugged on him, leading him toward the door. "Wait. Grab my keys, Nyla."

"I can drive her back," Petie Joe said, his sly grin stating that he was offering much more than a ride. He rolled his gaze down the length of Nyla's body with slow deliberation, making it clear what he wanted to do with her. Nyla simply grinned, knowing she'd break him in two before he had a chance to unbutton his fly.

"Yeah, right, I've seen that Lifetime TV movie," Jake said bitterly. "Nyla drives herself back to town, and if any of you so much as lays a finger on her, I swear before—"

"Jake. It's all right, honey. I can take care of myself," she said, stopping him before he could threaten anyone's life and earn another night in jail. "Will I be able to bail him out?" she asked Peewee, already knowing the answer.

"He stays the night, maybe more, I haven't decided whether I'm filing formal charges, but if I do let him go in the morning, I'll want y'all to leave town immediately."

"Of course." Too bad that won't happen, she added silently while sending Jake an apologetic look.

She took the keys from his pocket, and his cell phone, knowing they wouldn't let him have it with him in the jail cell, and gently caressed his chiseled jaw. "You be a good boy, Jakie. Don't get into any more trouble."

"You take care of things."

"I promise."

"Get him out of here," Peewee barked, and Jake was led out the door. "You need to go now, little lady," the sheriff added, directing his loathsome glare on Nyla.

Although she despised being referred to as "little lady," Nyla knew better than to press her luck. It was nighttime, the time vampires liked to prowl, and there were only two people in the whole town who stood a chance against them. And one of those people was going to be behind bars, stripped of his weapons. She couldn't mouth off to Peewee and wind up in the same predicament.

"I'm leaving," she said, but risked a glance at the woman and child who sat huddling together on the couch. Their frightened eyes beseeched her for help, and she couldn't deny them their request. With a subtle wink and nod in their direction, she turned and left, silently promising to return the minute Peewee left.

"THEY'RE HERE."

Curtis glanced up from the body lying before him to where Demarcus stood in the spill of moonlight shining through the small basement window.

The furry vampire was grinning devilishly and laughing to himself.

"How can you be sure?" he asked, placing his scalpel on the metal table. He'd finished carving his last clue into the victim's deceased body only seconds before Demarcus had awakened, rising from his coffin in a joyous mood.

"My children have relayed to me that there is a small, beautiful, dark-haired woman questioning them about any missing vampires. Who else could it be except Nyla?"

Curtis shivered, unnerved by the fact Demarcus's vampire *children* could telepathically speak to him, even while he slept. What unnerved him more was the fact he was surrounded by the creatures. Demarcus had formed an army of vampires, and all of them lived in the house with him. And at any time, they could communicate with each other without Curtis even knowing it.

He would escape Demarcus eventually, but the whole vampires-sleep-during-daylight thing was only true in movies. Sure, they slept during the day, but not all day long and not all of them at the same time. There was always someone awake in the house, and whether or not Demarcus was sleeping, they could mentally warn him if Curtis tried to make a run for it.

Instead, he stayed with the beasts he'd hated for two lifetimes. The part of him which was Alfred, his great-grandfather, enjoyed dissecting and torturing the vampires Demarcus provided him for experimentation, but the part of him which was Curtis hated it. As much as he disliked what the vampires were, he also felt sorry for them. They'd been people with families and lives before Demarcus turned them, unwillingly, into monsters.

Alfred would enjoy killing them all, but Curtis couldn't do it. He let Alfred control him when he was forced to experiment on the vampire and the victims Demarcus brought to him, but Curtis always took control before the soul of his ruthless grandfather began to destroy the vampires living with Demarcus. Part of him did it because he felt the newly-turned vampires were innocent victims themselves. Another part of him wrested back control from Alfred because he was afraid Alfred would get him killed.

So instead of doing anything to stop the evil around him, he hid clues on the victims' bodies, trying to warn the two who could save him and the rest of the innocent people of Hicksville. That was the one thing Alfred and Curtis agreed on. They had no problem with the cat-woman and her man killing Demarcus.

NYLA DISCREETLY pulled the curtain aside, peering through the motel window. Petie Joe had followed her all the way back to the motel, and apparently he was under orders to make sure she stayed there. With his hawk eyes on her, she hadn't been able to leave the room or get weapons from the trunk of the car.

"You seem anxious to go somewhere," a voice said from behind her, startling a small yelp from her throat.

She whirled around to find Seta, looking beautiful but deadly in a black ribbed turtleneck and black jeans. Her hair was pulled back into a long French braid, the dark mass as sleek and shiny as the black leather boots adorning her small feet.

"You startled me."

"I noticed." The elegant beauty stepped over to the window, sneaking a peek outside. "Why are you under surveillance?"

"Jake's cousin is the sheriff. He arrested Jake and made sure I'm stuck in here. There was an attack earlier, and we think it was a vampire. Of course, the sheriff and his men think we're loons."

Seta's eyebrows arched. "Did Jake sense a vampire?"

Nyla drew back, surprised. "You know Jake is a true slayer."

"Of course I do. I'm a witch. Back to my question, did he sense a vampire?"

"No, but there's something strange going on in this town. There's a bulletin board outside the sheriff's office covered in pictures of missing people. Jake and I killed seven of those missing people last night after they attacked us outside a cemetery. They were flying vampires."

Seta's brow furrowed. "Did you say *flying* vampires?"

"Yes."

"Vampires generally don't develop that skill until they've lived at least five hundred years, unless, of course, they're extremely powerful or carry some special ability."

"Do you think that many recently changed vampires could be fliers?"

"Not without some sort of tampering. They'd all have to be witches or have psychic gifts, and I doubt there would be that many gifted people residing in the same town. We're pretty rare."

"Well, someone is changing over the residents of this town, and they're being made into fliers."

"That doesn't make sense." Seta's brow crinkled in thought. "The Dunns are scientifically gifted, and maybe they could develop something which would turn vampires into fliers, but why? Carter Dunn despised us, and when he kidnapped Eron a few months ago, he wanted to develop an immortality serum, but he wouldn't have done anything that could turn us into a more ruthless race in order to develop it. Like his great-grandfather, Alfred, he wanted our kind wiped out. On the other hand, Curtis didn't seem to want any part of his brother's research, which is one of the reasons we let him go instead of tracking him down. We didn't think he was a danger to us or anyone else. Obviously we were wrong, but that still begs the question, why would he create fliers?"

"Do you think someone else is involved?"

"There has to be. You need a vampire to make a vampire."

"Are you sure?"

Seta nodded. "Yes. A vampire has to drain a mortal to the brink of death, then let the mortal feed on his own living blood. The act can't be mechanically reproduced."

"I'm sure there are other ways."

"Like you?" She shook her head. "You're a rarity."

Nyla gasped, fear creeping along her spine. Seta knew she was a vampire?

Seta simply smiled at her, looking very pleased with herself, as she said,

"Please, Nyla. Did you really think I couldn't sniff the vampire on you?"

"But . . . but Jake didn't."

"True, a fact I find very amusing. The great slayer is fallible after all. Or maybe he wasn't meant to harm you so fate has protected you from his inborn vengeance."

"Why would you think he wasn't meant to harm me?"

"You share the same aura, young one. The two of you were meant to find each other."

"Why?"

"That is for fate to decree," the witch said with a negligent shrug. "Have you seen the Dream Teller?"

Nyla nodded.

"Then you should have your answer soon." Seta sat at the end of the bed, crossing her legs at the ankle, very proper and refined. "Now, what are we to do about this situation? I've questioned local vampires, but none of them knew of a missing vampire. It struck me as odd how new they all were—and how closed off their minds were. Now I know why. They've been tampered with and, in fact, are probably covering for the vampire who made them."

"How is that possible? If you're a witch and they're newly turned, you should be able to read them easily."

"They're protected. Carter Dunn did something similar. It's why I couldn't track him easily. He'd worked with Satan, and when you work with Satan, he has ways of protecting you, but good always wins in the end. We'll win this fight. Now, what did the oh-so-genial Jacob Porter do to get himself incarcerated?"

"One of the newly changed vampires returned to his home and stole his son. We followed the sheriff and his men to the house, offering our help. When we refused to leave, Jake was arrested."

"A vampire returned to steal his own son?" Seta repeated, her eyes dark and cold.

"One of them. The younger one is still there."

"If the vampire took one son, he'll likely return for the other. We have to protect him."

"That was the plan, but I can't leave here with old hawk eye out there watching me."

"Why can't you just shift into a cat and leave through the window?"

"Because I need to get weapons out of the—" Nyla's jaw dropped open as she realized what Seta had said. "How did you know I'm a shifter too?"

Seta flashed her a cat-ate-the-canary smile. "I read you the moment I saw you. I sense you are blocking someone dark and sinister, your sire I suppose. It makes sense. Many do. Anyway, you are blocking him so hard you allowed me to sneak right in."

"So you know everything?"

"Not everything," Seta answered, shaking her head. "The mind protects even when not instructed to, but I know enough. I know you are a pantherian, a race I'll admit I thought a myth, and that you were given vampire traits from a single bite. I also know you saved Jacob Porter's life and have protected him ever since, loving him with all your heart."

"You do understand that I can never tell him what I am, right?" Nyla asked, terrified of what would happen if Seta told Jake about her true identity.

"*Who* you are, dear, not *what* you are. You're not a beast." Seta rose from the bed, laying her hand against Nyla's cheek. "And I know you will have to tell him eventually and trust him to see the truth."

Nyla shook her head sadly. "No. He'll kill me."

Seta looked away, but not before Nyla saw the sympathy in her eyes. "It may be hard, but if fate has declared a union, it will be so. Don't worry so much. Now," she said, returning her dark gaze to Nyla, "let's make sure that little boy is safe, and then we'll go rescue your man."

"I can turn into a cat and get out of here, but how will you . . .? Oh, I guess you'll do that poof thing."

"Poof thing?" Seta looked genuinely confused.

"You know, that thing where you vanish."

"That's teleportation, dear, and it takes a lot of energy. I like to keep my reserves as high as possible so I only use that ability when absolutely necessary."

"So how will you get out of here? That cop out there isn't going to let anyone leave this room."

Seta chewed on the corner of her bottom lip, seeming to mull over ideas. "Okay, I'll do a little magic, and you won't have to shift at all. We'll get your weapons too."

"How?"

"Watch," the vampire-witch said impishly, walking over to the door and flinging it open. "Come along, young one. Trust me."

Shaking her head, Nyla did as she was told and followed Seta out the door. Petie Joe sat straight up in his truck, watching her every move, but she had faith in Seta.

She felt a shift in the wind and heard a faint buzzing. Her skin began to warm as energy crawled across her flesh, and she realized Seta was working some kind of magic. She glanced at the vampire-witch, startled to see she radiated energy while standing perfectly still, her eyes closed and her lips curved into a serene smile.

Seta opened her eyes, looked straight at Petie Joe and blew him a kiss. Petie Joe fell forward against his steering wheel.

"What did you do to him?"

"He's only sleeping," Seta answered. "Now get your weapons and let's go. Unlike you, I have a curfew, you know," she added, looking meaningfully toward the night sky.

Chapter Seventeen

THE DIRT ROAD stretched out before them, seeming to grow along with Nyla's unease. The feeling of impending doom she'd felt before the journey to Kentucky was making a comeback, shooting pangs of warning through her skull.

"Something's wrong here," she said to Seta, bringing Jake's Malibu to a stop. Bright flashes of light darted before her eyes, bringing a blaze of pain on the tail end of each one.

"Do you feel something?" Seta asked, her voice curious.

"Yes. Don't you?" Nyla snapped. Worry was making her short-tempered. "You're supposed to be the witch."

"Yes, but we both have magic running through our veins."

"What are you talking about?" She frowned at the witch beside her.

Seta's lips slowly spread into a smile. "You really have no clue what you are, do you?"

"I'm a pantherian vampire."

"Pantherians are born of magic, Nyla. You were not born a shifter. You were made into one."

"Yeah, I know. Through the ritual." Nyla shook her head. "But what does that have to do with magic? I'm not a witch. I don't get visions."

"No, but you can locate Jacob Porter no matter where he is or how far apart the two of you are."

"So?"

"That's not exactly a normal thing, young one. Both of you have powers you don't realize."

"Yeah? Like what?" Nyla rubbed her temples as little sparks of pain shot through her head.

"Jacob can sense vampires, as you know, and you can sense when you or he are in mortal danger. You're sort of his guardian angel."

Nyla nodded, unable to dispute Seta's claim. She'd become attached to Jake the very first moment she'd seen the twelve-year-old enter that alley so many years ago. "Why? Why should I be the one to watch over him when I'm exactly what he hates?"

"We'll figure that out soon enough. What we need to know now is what danger you are sensing."

"I sense his death."

"You sense that he's dead right now?" Seta's eyes widened until they looked like round saucers.

"No, no. His impending death. Something is going to happen in this town, something fatally wrong."

"You can prevent it. That is why you are getting these feelings. They're omens."

"But I don't know what is happening, so how can I prevent it?"

"You know enough. Curtis Dunn is somehow linked, and there is a rogue vampire involved. We find the rogue, who's the source of these newly turned vampires, and we'll find the answer you need."

"Why do you seem so willing to help a man you know is a true slayer?"

Seta glanced out the window, studying the area. "We should go by foot the rest of the way. If any of the sheriff's men are patrolling the area, we don't want them to hear the engine," she explained, opening the door and exiting the car.

"Seta!" Nyla called after her, exiting the car herself. "Answer me. Why do you want to help a slayer? Are your motives pure?"

Seta turned and gazed back at her, a look in her eyes so grave Nyla's legs wobbled before she pulled herself back together.

"There's rumor of a war coming, a supernatural war between good and evil like no other war ever waged before. Let's just say if the rumor is true, I'd much rather have Jacob Porter on my side than have to go against him."

"I thought you were supposed to be on the good side."

"I am."

"Then why would you fear going against him? He's good."

"He's a true slayer," Seta said, her tone grim. "So far, your presence is the only thing that has kept him from drowning in his own inner darkness. He's as capable of being a monster as any other supernatural being. Maybe even more so."

JAKE SAT ON THE dirty floor of the small cell, trying to sort through everything he'd learned in the past few days. He found it hard to concentrate with images of Nyla constantly appearing at the forefront of his mind, but there were three slaughtered women in need of justice and a woman and child who'd been frightened nearly to death that very night. They deserved his undivided attention, so he would have to shove his feelings for Nyla aside until this case was figured out.

Easier thought of than done, he realized as her beautiful face seemed to hover before him, the passion in her eyes fully ablaze. He kept thinking of how she'd stepped in front of him when he'd lunged for Peewee. He'd wanted to kill the man, to rip him apart and glory in watching Peewee's blood spill from his body, but she'd calmed him, brought him back to his right mind. She seemed to have the same effect on him as his cat. And where the hell was his cat anyway?

Jake shook his head. Alley would be all right. So would Nyla. They were both tough girls. He needed to get out of jail and help protect that little boy . . . Bobby. Of all the names the kid could have, why did it have to be Bobby?

Images from the night of that long-ago attack flooded his mind, and he gritted his teeth against the pain wrenching his heart. He saw Bobby's tear-filled eyes as Lionel grabbed him, the terror on his face as Detra opened her mouth wide, showing her fangs before she bore down on him. Niles sank his fangs in next as the bastard, whose name he still hadn't learned but who seemed to control all the vampires there that night, looked on, his eyes gleaming with some perverse sense of pride.

The memory replayed, and Jake watched the entire scene like a movie, a horror flick he couldn't turn off. He relived that night as though it had only been yesterday that his best friend was taken from him. He heard the old woman's voice telling him to flee, the voice which had followed him into his adult dreams, the voice of the mysterious blind woman in the blue forest. Why hadn't she screamed inside Bobby's mind? Why hadn't she saved Bobby? Why hadn't Alley? More importantly, why hadn't he? His young age was no excuse. He'd known something was out there that night. He'd smelled death on the air. He'd *known* what would happen, and he'd done nothing.

He'd felt the impending doom that night as clearly as he felt it now in this damn jail cell. There was something dark and evil hovering over Hicksville, and that something would be coming for another little boy named Bobby. But this time he wouldn't just stand there and let it happen, and he damn sure wouldn't run away. No more little boys were dying on his watch.

Suddenly, the fine hairs along the back of his neck rose as he sensed a subtle change in the air, and he jumped to his feet. Cocking his head to the side, he listened for the whispers of warning he'd soon hear.

Almost as though his memories had conjured them, vampires were drawing close.

PEEWEE LEANED back in his chair, propping his feet on top of his desk. He decided that all he needed was a big fat stogy to complete his smug victory pose. He'd arrested Jake, and the feeling it gave him was better than sex. Better than money. Better than being elected sheriff. It was his crowning achievement, and he had every intention of basking in its glory.

To his irritation, he only had ten brief minutes to roll around in the afterglow before his office door swung open, smacking against the opposite wall with enough force to send a hanging picture crashing to the floor.

"I hope you have a good reason storming into my office like this, girl," he snapped at the willowy blonde standing in the doorway, not a trace of humor in his voice.

Marilee Mills fumed before him, her meager chest rising and falling beneath her red crop top. Her normally cool blue eyes speared him to his seat like two flaming daggers.

Before he could stop himself, Peewee squirmed in his chair and ran his fingers along his badge for reassurance. He was the law as long as he wore it, and nobody messed with the law. He was the one holding all the power.

"Damn you, Peewee Porter. I've called and called!" Marilee screeched like a banshee, and Peewee felt his courage start to wane. The young girl looked as though she might jump over his desk any minute. "Is it too much to ask you to do your job?"

With a loud sigh and a good eye roll, Peewee lowered his feet to the floor and straightened in his chair. Marilee's grandparents, Joe and Lettie Mills, hadn't answered their door in a couple of weeks, and Marilee had been raising hell ever since, although she knew as well as he did that the elderly couple liked to disappear from time to time on spur-of-the-moment vacations.

"Marilee, you know how your grandparents—"

"Don't! Don't tell me they're away on a trip! Folks are popping up missing all over town, and you won't even look for my grandparents! Something happened to them!"

"How many times have they up and left out of the blue before, Marilee?"

"That doesn't matter. They've never had their windows boarded up before."

Peewee frowned at this news. "Their windows are boarded up?"

"Yes, which you would have known if you'd done your job and went out there to their house like I asked you to do."

"Peewee! Let me out of here! They're coming!" Jake's bellow carried down the hall to Peewee's office, snatching his attention from the angry blonde in front of him.

"Who was that?" Marilee asked, turning toward the direction of the cells.

"My lunatic cousin," Peewee grumbled, wondering what the jerk was up to now. No damn way was he letting Jake out of that cell so Jake could beat the crap out of him. Locking the man in a cell was one thing. If he was forced to shoot him to protect himself . . . well, that wouldn't go over well with the family, even if Jonah was the only one who seemed to actually like the guy.

"What's wrong with him?" Marilee asked, her brow knit in concern as Jake continued to yell from his cell, asking to be released before *they* came. "What is he talking about?"

The intercom buzzed, Luanne's voice soon following. "Uh, Peewee, that cop from Louisville is on line one, and, um, and I think your cousin is going nuts. Should we do something?"

"Yeah, ignore him," Peewee said, pressing the button on his phone to connect with the police officer he'd been speaking with over the past few weeks while gesturing for Marilee to hold tight a moment.

"Sheriff Porter," he announced, holding the receiver close to his ear, his good mood returning. He never tired of hearing or using his title.

"Porter, this is Rooney. I think we found some of your missing people."

"You *think* you found them?" A sinking feeling filtered its way into his gut. If the people found were alive and responsive, the young cop would know for certain who they were.

"Yeah, but . . . well, we kind of lost them."

"What do you mean? Are they alive?"

"They exploded."

"*What?*" Peewee ignored the way Marilee jumped as his voice boomed through the small office, most likely reaching the cells and beyond. "Are you playing with me, boy?"

"No. I . . . I don't know what happened. There was a report of gunshots around the cemetery, so we went to check it out. The security guards were dead, ripped to pieces. There were two bodies lying on the ground outside, decapitated. They looked just like two of the men in the pictures you sent."

Peewee tried to swallow, but found his mouth had gone bone dry. He remembered Jake's girlfriend telling him how she'd beheaded two of his missing townspeople and that they'd shot five others.

"Those were the only bodies found?"

"Yes, except the guards, but their bodies are gone now."

"What do you mean by gone?"

"We had to leave the scene intact until we got all of our evidence together, you know. We had to wait for the coroner. He didn't get there until the sun came up . . ."

"And . . ." Peewee prompted, already having a sneaking suspicion what was coming next, his mind struggling to accept it.

"As soon as the sun hit them, they went up in flames. There was this loud pop, and they just combusted. I've never seen anything like it. None of us have."

"Peewee, damn you, open this cell before you get us all killed!" Jake screamed from down the hall, and the sound of clanging metal could be clearly heard. He was trying to break through the bars.

"I gotta go, Rooney," Peewee said, wrapping up the call before quickly replacing the phone back into its base. "Marilee, I think you need to get out of here."

"What's going on?" Her eyes widened as he grabbed his semiautomatic from his upper right desk drawer and scooped up the ring of keys to the cells.

"I don't know," he answered truthfully. Vampires weren't real, he told himself as he made a shooing motion at the girl. They couldn't be. But people didn't just burst into flame either. "Go home and lock your doors and windows."

He didn't wait to see if she left. Instead, he walked out of his office, striding quickly toward the cell his raging cousin was trying to free himself from. He stopped in front of the last cell.

"Peewee! Let me out!" Jake stopped kicking at the bars and wrapped his fists around them so tightly his knuckles turned a blinding white. "They're coming. I can't protect anyone if I can't reach them. Unlock the cell."

"What happened last night?" Peewee hesitated with the key halfway to the lock. He saw the fear in Jake's eyes, knew the man truly did believe he sensed something, but still he couldn't fully accept that all the monsters he'd heard about as a child were real. They couldn't be real. There was no such thing as a vampire. Was there?

"*Dammit,* we told you what happened last night. Now let me out while there's still time!"

"Two of my townspeople were found beheaded this morning, and they burned up when the sun hit them. What did you do to them?" Jake had to have done something. It was all a ruse. Vampires were *not* real. Jacob Porter was insane.

"The newly turned are highly combustible," Jake growled, shaking the iron bars holding him captive. "Now get me the hell out of here before you meet some vampires face-to-face!" Then Jake went still, all the air seeming to leave his body in a rush as he tipped his head to the side, his eyes glazing over with a cold hardness. The eyes of a killer. "They're here."

A chill ran through Peewee's body, and the keys shook in his suddenly trembling hand. A scream ripped through the air and he jerked, dropping the keys to the floor. Luanne! They'd got Luanne, and they'd be coming for him next!

"Open the fucking door!" Jake screamed, yanking on the bars as though trying to rip them from the floor.

Peewee bent down to retrieve the key ring, his hands and legs trembling. A shadow fell over the floor before him and he knew before looking up that he'd royally screwed up.

"Stay the hell away from my cousin!" Jake yelled. "I'm the only one allowed to hurt him, you bloodsucking bastard!"

With a hard gulp which hurt all the way down, Peewee straightened up, his tear-filled gaze falling on the man before him. It was Billy Ray Dobbs, a man he'd known for years, but not the same man at all. Insanity blazed in his darker than normal eyes, and evil seemed to radiate from his body.

"We've been sent for you, Peewee," Billy Ray said, his grin menacing.

"Me?" he squeaked. "Why?"

"Because there's a new sheriff in town."

As another female scream sounded from down the hall, Billy Ray picked Peewee up by his shirt front. He could hear Jake yelling, but couldn't make out the words. They didn't matter. He was going to die. Jake had been telling the truth all along, and he was going to die at the hands of the very monsters he'd thought were Jake's imaginary enemies.

"I'll be damned," he managed to say before he felt his body connect with the bars of Jake's cell, then he didn't feel anything except the urine pooling beneath him on the floor as he faded into darkness.

"JAKE'S IN DANGER!" Nyla came to a dead stop along the path toward the house she and Seta were heading toward, icy cold fear holding her in its grip.

"What's happened?" Seta asked, standing before her. "What do you sense?"

"He's under attack, and he's trapped." Her head snapped up to meet the Spanish beauty's eyes. "I have to save him!"

"No! You protect the woman and child. I'll go to Jacob."

"No! He needs my help."

"So do the innocent mortals in that house! They won't trust me, but they'll trust you. Help them."

Nyla shook her head, turning away. Jake's life meant more to her than anyone else's on earth. Even hers. She was going to him.

As she turned to head for Jake, Seta asked, "What will happen to Jacob if another little boy dies?"

Nyla halted, guilt washing over her in a tidal wave. "But Jake *needs* me."

"He's a slayer. He can handle himself against a pack of vampires, but even so, I'll go to him just to make sure. You protect the boy. Jake would never forgive himself if something happened to that child because you were protecting him."

"I know."

"So it is settled."

Nyla turned to face the vampire-witch, but she was gone.

"I hate when she does that," she muttered, letting out a deep breath. She had to believe Jake would be all right. Seta was right. He was a slayer. Still, to the best of her knowledge he was locked in a cell, and she was sure Peewee hadn't let him keep his weapons with him. She ached to run back to the car and race off to fight at his side, but Seta was right. The abduction or death of another little boy named Bobby would be Jake's undoing. And since he couldn't be in two places at one time, she'd have to guard this particular fort while he battled at another.

The house was close enough to see. Reluctantly, she pressed on, stepping carefully. She had no idea if anyone from Peewee's task force was guarding the perimeter. If there was, she didn't want to alert them to her presence. This whole night would go a lot smoother if she could get into the house without being seen.

She heard a scuffle to her right as she neared the house, and she jerked her head to the side, holding her breath as she listened. Footsteps. *Dammit!* She willed her body to dissolve into mist, shifting into cat form seconds before Bubba Lee stepped out of the trees to stand before her.

"Where'd you come from?" he asked without dislodging the cigarette in his mouth. He seemed to study her for a moment before lifting his shotgun to his shoulder, training it on her. The crazy hick was going to shoot her!

Nyla dissolved into mist as the bullet was fired, sliding her way behind him where she shifted into panther form. With a growl deep enough to send vibrations through the earth beneath them, she jumped on his back and knocked him to the ground. He looked behind him and screamed like a girl, his eyes widening until they looked as if they would pop right out of his face.

Nyla growled at him as he struggled to scoot away, then grabbed his shotgun in her mouth, flinging it into the woods. Go fetch, you mutt, she thought to herself before turning and racing toward the house, shifting into cat form before she reached the porch.

She pattered around to the back of the house and looked around. Petie Joe was sleeping in his truck in front of the motel, Bubba Lee was looking for his gun, and she was sure Peewee was back at the jail with Jake. That left Billy Bob unaccounted for. Assuring herself that Billy Bob wasn't close enough to see her, she shifted back to human form and rapped hard on the back door, announcing who she was at the same time. If Billy Bob was in the house, she'd just have to deal with him.

A moment later, the door swung open, and Maybelline looked at her with tear-filled eyes. "Oh, thank goodness you came back. We've been just terrified."

"Apparently not terrified enough," Nyla commented. "Is it just my imagination, or did I *not* hear you unlock the door?"

"Billy Bob and Bubba Lee said to keep it unlocked so they could come in and out if they needed to."

"Idiots," Nyla muttered, stepping into the kitchen and locking the door behind her. "Are the other doors locked?"

"Yes."

"Windows?"

"Yes. Actually, they're painted shut."

"Unfortunately, that won't stop them from breaking, but it's a start. Where's Bobby?"

"Watching his programs," Maybelline said, pointing toward the living room. Nyla made a quick study of the kitchen, noting the huge mess, but rooms usually were a mess after an abduction took place in a home, and headed for the living room.

Bobby half-sat, half-lay on the couch, covered in a raggedy blue afghan, watching television and simultaneously chewing his nails down to the quick. Nyla reached behind her, touching her sword. *Jake's* sword. It wasn't the same weapon she was used to, but its presence was just as comforting.

"Do you think he'll come back tonight?" Maybelline whispered behind her.

"If he wants Bobby," Nyla answered, then turned to face the woman. "What exactly happened during his last visit?"

"He came in here, acting strange, like he was hopped up on drugs, but . . . worse, you know? Judd Jr. put up a fight, but he couldn't hold him off." The small woman cried soundlessly, and Nyla was sure she'd used up all the heavy sobs her body could make. "Then Bobby got the rifle and shot him. That's when he took off with Judd Jr."

"Bobby shot his father?"

Maybelline nodded, wiping tears from her cheeks on the collar of her taffy-pink robe. "It didn't kill him, but it chased him away. I swear he moved so fast, it was like he flew away or something. I went to the door, and there was nothin' out there. He was gone, with my boy. Can you get my boy back?"

Nyla avoided the woman's gaze, not wanting to see the desperate hope she knew was there. Hearing it in the mother's voice was heart-wrenching enough.

"I don't think so," she answered honestly, "but I'll make damn sure no one takes Bobby."

Not this time, she added silently, looking at the small tawny-headed boy on the couch, but remembering a twelve-year-old kid with darker, curlier hair and a best friend who had loved him like a brother.

A man screamed somewhere in the distance, and the sound of a shotgun firing repeatedly came from another direction. Nyla took an educated guess and figured one of the task force members was a goner, and the other would be soon enough.

Bobby screamed and ran to his mother. Both of them huddled together, shaking from head to toe.

"Do you have a basement?"

"No," Maybelline answered.

"You two need to hide some place where they can't break in through a window or door."

"There's a crawlspace. We can get to it through that closet there." Maybelline nodded toward a closet door standing between the living and kitchen area. A shotgun hung on the wall next to it.

"Is the closet the only way in or out?"

"Yes."

Nyla grabbed the shotgun and handed it to Bobby. "You two need to get in there. It appears that Daddy just came home," she said as several thuds hit the ground surrounding the house, "and from the sound of it, he's brought some buddies with him."

Chapter Eighteen

PEEWEE'S BODY HIT the door of the cell hard enough to break the lock and send the set of bars careening open. The vampire had unknowingly allowed Jake the access he needed to reach the monster and send him back to hell where he belonged.

"Thanks," he growled, stepping through the door and over the crumpled body of his cousin. He couldn't check Peewee's vitals until he cleared the area, so he didn't waste any time on the fallen man. His weapons had been taken from him, and he wasn't about to try looking for them. There were more vampires. He knew this without the women screaming nearby. He could feel them. Three newly-turned, bloodthirsty freaks.

The vampire who'd attacked Peewee watched Jake's movements as he circled him, readying his hands for a fight. Jake recognized the vampire from the missing persons' bulletin board, although he couldn't recall his name. It didn't matter. He was going to kill him in a moment.

"Silly little man," the blond, mustached vamp with a mullet haircut said, "I'm a vampire. You can't do nothin' to me."

Jake smiled, not bothering to correct the two-inch-shorter vamp on his reference to size. "Oh, I know what you are. I probably know more about your kind than you do, newbie. After all, I've killed plenty of you."

The vampire's eyes widened for a second before narrowing into small, dark slits. "If you caught us in the day, that could happen, but you're helpless now, boy."

Jake shook his head, once again getting the feeling he was on the hillbilly version of *The Twilight Zone*. He'd seen vampires in all shapes, shades, and sizes, but he'd never seen one with a mullet and southern twang. He wished he could say this was the first vamp he'd ever seen with missing teeth, but they were all there, strong and pearly-white, and he remembered for a fact that this particular missing person hadn't had many teeth left in his picture.

"So, suck-face, did you decide to sell your soul for immortality or the dental plan?"

The vampire didn't answer, choosing to run his tongue over his new teeth instead, seeming to enjoy the feel of them. "I must kill you now."

"Funny, I was thinking the same thing about you."

Jake had barely gotten the words out before the vampire rushed him, most likely thinking Jake wouldn't know what hit him. Most non-vampires wouldn't expect the quick burst of speed vamps could use against them, but Jake was a seasoned pro. He stepped aside before the vamp could plow into him, and instead the monster slipped in the puddle of sour-smelling urine pooled beneath and around Peewee's body. A combination of the speed and the slippery floor sent the vampire skidding the entire length of the hall, out into the main area of the sheriff's department.

The women's screams had stopped so Jake assumed their deaths could not be prevented. Any second he would be swamped by three vampires, and the one whom he'd already met was going to be very pissed off. He quickly checked Peewee, feeling a pulse in his neck. In addition to the pulse, he found a Ruger GP-100 seven shot .327 Federal holstered at his side. It wouldn't contain UV bullets, but unlike most revolvers, which only had six shots instead of seven, it was better than nothing.

Straightening up, he cocked his head to the side, trying to determine the vampires' positions. He still sensed them, and not one of them was more than a few weeks turned. What was going on in Hicksville that would suddenly turn it into Vamp Central?

Shoving the questions aside for when he would actually have time to think them over, he took a step forward, nearly slipping in urine himself. "Remind me to rib you about this later, pissy-pants," he said to his unconscious cousin as he straightened himself again and pressed forward. As he walked the length of the cell-filled hallway slowly and cautiously, he swept his eyes from side-to-side in search of anything he could use as a weapon.

He heard a horrible screeching sound as he neared the end of the hallway and felt the presence of one of the vampires fading. As he stepped out of the hallway, he came to an abrupt halt, momentarily shocked to see a leggy blonde in a red crop top and cutoff jeans impaling one of the vamps with a chair leg. The girl couldn't be any older than nineteen at best, and she showed no fear, just an overabundance of pissed-off determination.

"I'm not alone after all," Jake said to himself, scanning the room. Desks and chairs had been upturned all over the room. Apparently his helper had given them one hell of a fight.

While he was looking to the right, he sensed an approaching vampire to his left. Young, new, thirsty and female. He kicked out without looking, catching the brunette by surprise and sending her flying across the room.

He watched her land and quickly turned toward the first vampire he'd fought, who was now rushing toward him in another burst of speed. He chuckled to himself despite the danger and, once again, simply moved aside as the vampire lunged for him, allowing the vamp to run headfirst into the wall, momentarily stupefying himself. If the idiot wasn't careful, which was exactly what Jake was hoping for, he was going to wear himself out quickly. The newly-turned didn't have the same stamina as the older vamps. Fortunately for him and the girl, these jackasses didn't seem to know it, or were too stupid to consider it.

No sooner had he completed that thought than the brunette rushed toward him in the same manner the mustached vamp had. This time, instead of moving aside, he rammed his fist into her face as she closed in on him. The force of the blow, combined with the speed at which she was going when he struck her, sent her flying in an arc and crashing into the opposite wall.

"Damn. Nice punch," the young blonde said, stepping back from the vamp she'd staked with the chair leg.

"Pull the chair leg out."

"What? Won't that defeat the purpose?" she asked with the same country twang everyone else in Hicksville used before looking back at the vamp's body. "Ain't he supposed to be smoking or something?"

"Those are movie vampires. These are real ones, and he's not dead, but he's getting there. Pull the stake out to allow him to bleed out faster. That's what's killing him, not the stake in the heart itself."

The girl's mouth rounded into an O, then she nodded and gripped the broken off chair leg with both hands, grunting as she pulled it out.

Jake sensed the brunette and the other remaining vampire rising to their feet and refocused his attention on them. He now had one twelve feet in front of him and one six feet to his left. Common sense said to take out the closest one before worrying about the second, but there was another person in the room to think about, and either of the vampires could head for her in the blink of an eye.

"You did a good job, kid, but I think you need to get out of here now," Jake called to the girl across the room, steadily flicking his eyes back and forth between the two vampires, waiting for one or both of them to make a move.

"I ain't goin' nowhere until these freaks are dead, and the name is Marilee," the girl said. "Call me kid again and you might wind up plucking this chair leg out your butt before the night is through."

Jake had to laugh at the girl's spunk. Hell, she was a better partner than any of Peewee's task force would have been, he conceded. "All right, Marilee, but watch out. They're fast, they're hungry, they have unbelievable strength, and they're unpredictable."

"I know. That bitch killed Luanne."

The vamp she referred to turned her head, a pretty face despite her evil disposition, and smiled maliciously before saying, "You'll be next, Marilee. I'll drain you just like your grandparents were drained."

Marilee's face paled, and Jake felt his heart thud, wondering how he was going to fight off two vampires without adequate weapons and defend the girl if she was unconscious and an easy target. Fortunately, she didn't faint. She visibly banked down her anguish and glared at the brunette vamp. "Go to hell, Peggy Sue. I didn't like you when you were alive, and I'll have no problem seeing you die twice."

Peggy Sue grinned malevolently for only a split second before rushing

Marilee. Although she'd managed to stake one of the bloodsuckers, Jake knew she wouldn't be able to do anything against a speeding vamp. They moved in a blur, too quick for most people to see. He shot the gun, blowing a hole through the vamp's chest seconds before she reached Marilee. It wasn't a killing blow, of course, but it knocked her backward, giving Marilee a chance she wouldn't have had otherwise.

The other vampire took advantage of the fact Jake's attention was on the female and jumped him from the side, knocking him to the floor. As the mullet-topped vamp opened his mouth wide, angling toward his throat, Jake raised a knee to his groin. Vampire or not, he still had balls, and getting kneed in the groin hurt like hell for any kind of man. Add to the fact vampires tended to feel pain greater than regular humans, Jake felt pretty smug about the move, especially when the vampire howled in pain and paused in his attack long enough for Jake to shove him off him. Jake jumped to his feet before the vampire could do the same and shot him in the heart.

The sound of laughter pulled his attention to the female vamp, who was holding Marilee by the throat. The girl had fought hard, but in the end she was just a spunky girl. Now she was in deep trouble.

"Put her down, and when I say down, I don't mean throw her across the room."

"What are you going to do? Shoot me again?" The vampire's eyes gleamed. "Bullets won't kill us."

"Yeah, but they still hurt like a bitch, don't they?" He backed up as the male vampire stood, giving himself enough room so the man couldn't easily jump him.

Marilee tried to speak, her voice coming out in small garbles. Her face was turning blue, the result of not enough oxygen. The longer he stood there, deciding what to do, the closer she came to death.

He trained the gun on Peggy Sue's face and pulled the trigger twice, taking out her left eye and then the right. The vampiress screamed, dropping Marilee as her hands flew to her bloody eye sockets.

He knew the male would rush him as soon as the bullets started flying, so he quickly turned in his direction, steadily pulling the trigger, but the bullets missed as the vampire streaked past him in a blur, disappearing down the hall.

He started to run after him, but Marilee screamed, catching his attention. Although he'd blinded her, Peggy Sue could still smell and hear. All of a vampire's senses were far greater than any human's. She'd caught Marilee again and was ready to sink her fangs into the young girl's throat.

Jake pulled the trigger again, lodging a bullet in Peggy Sue's throat. She screamed, but retained her tight hold around Marilee's neck. Jake could see blood spilling from the girl's throat, where Peggy Sue's long nails had punctured her skin. Marilee looked at him, her eyes begging him to save her.

Rage crept into Jake's body, strengthening a thirst inside him similar to the vampires', but he didn't want to drink gallons of blood. He wanted to watch it spill. He shot the vampiress again, this time in the chest, and boldly walked across the room to her.

She dropped Marilee in a crumpled heap, sensing his nearness. She turned toward him, waiting for him to come near her, and then when he reached her, she jumped, hovering over him in the air.

Jake grabbed her foot and, with a rough tug, brought her body slamming back to the floor, where he unleashed his rage, kicking her wherever his foot could find a place to land. He broke her nose, busted her lips, and cracked bones. And still, it wasn't enough. He loved the screaming, the sounds of pain coming from her. He longed to see more blood spilling out of her. What was pouring from her face wasn't nearly enough.

"Big, bad, tough guy," the vampiress taunted him, pausing long enough between words to spit out blood. "You get off on hurting women."

"I didn't hurt a woman, bitch, I hurt you," he responded, giving her another good kick to the ribcage. Anger boiled inside him, hot and suffocating, as he replayed the woman's words over in his mind. He could hear Marilee whimpering . . . and knew she was whimpering because of what he was doing.

But he couldn't stop. He had to kill the monster. He searched the desks around him, knowing Peggy Sue wasn't going anywhere. Her body was broken. He didn't know where his guns were so he had to find something else. The bitch would bleed out, but he didn't want to wait on her to do that.

He found a lighter in one of the overturned desk drawers and flicked it, a perverse joy coursing through him when the flame formed.

He grabbed a handful of Peggy Sue's hair and pulled her across the room toward the hall of cells. As he'd feared, Peewee's body was no longer in the hall, and the mullet-topped vampire was gone, a man-sized hole in the wall the only evidence of his escape.

He took his rage out on the vampiress, dragging her into one of the cells. "Why did you come for my cousin?" he asked, hatred burning a hole through his chest. It grew as Peggy Sue lay crumpled on the floor of the cell, refusing to answer. Or maybe she couldn't. He'd smashed her face in.

"Suit yourself," he said. "I was going to keep you in here until I found my gun so I could kill you quick and fast with some UV, but now, you can fry, bitch."

He flicked the lighter, watched the flame grow strong and tossed it into the cell. The fire found her body and she went up in flames, sounds of unbearable pain coming from her bloody mouth.

He sensed the presence of another vampire and drew the gun, pointing it before he turned. He barely managed to ease his finger off the trigger, realizing who the vampire was.

Seta looked toward the cell, her eyes widening and her upper lip curling in disgust, before turning her disapproving gaze on him, giving him a good once-over before saying, "So besides this, the dead woman lying under one of the desks, another dead vampire, and the girl with the crushed larynx, what else did I miss?"

"A vampire took off with my cousin."

"Is that why you felt the need to destroy this one so viciously?"

"It got what it deserved," he answered, allowing his hatred for the monsters to slip into his voice, not giving a damn about the disapproval in the vampire-witch's eyes. She should be thankful he hadn't blown a hole through her face, which was exactly what he felt like doing. She was a bloodsucker too, and despite their little truce, he couldn't forget that.

Seta again looked him over, seeming to analyze him. She was probably doing that mind-reading thing witches were so good at. If he wasn't so enraged, Jake would have cracked a smile at how she must feel seeing all the different things he was thinking of doing to her kind.

"I healed the teenager," she finally said, her voice low and laced with a hard bitterness. "I couldn't do anything for the other woman. Nyla is with the boy. Put the fire out, and let's go." She gestured for Jake to precede her down the hall toward the fire extinguisher, and he knew she was making sure she didn't turn her back on him.

Smart witch.

NYLA CLOSED THE closet door, instructing Bobby to shoot anyone who poked their head through, just in case any of the vamps managed to slip past her. She inhaled deeply and blew the breath out slowly on the wings of a prayer. Her heart threatened to burst through her chest despite the breathing exercise.

She'd fought vampires before, but fliers were harder to deal with, and judging by the thuds she'd heard outside, these bloodsuckers had flown in. And she was all alone with the lives of a mother and child to protect. Lovely.

She touched the knives sheathed on her arms for reassurance, then pulled free the sword she wore on her back, familiarizing herself with its weight. It was slightly heavier than the one she normally carried, but she could handle it. She would have to handle it. The only other option was letting the flying monsters get their claws on an innocent young boy, and that option simply didn't work for her.

She heard the doorknobs jiggling, both the front and back, and instinctively grabbed for one of the guns strapped at her side. She'd brought two of Jake's guns, both loaded with the specially crafted UV bullets he liked so much, and fortunately for her, she was ambidextrous when it came to firearms.

She stood in the living room with a sword in her right hand, a gun in her left, and waited for the first fanged face to come into view. "Come on, you evil sons of bitches," she said under her breath, growing antsy. She really didn't want to fight a horde of vampires all by herself, but the longer she waited, the quicker her heart raced. And if she was busy covering her own butt, she could worry less about Jake's.

She heard glass breaking in the kitchen, and she quickly positioned herself between both rooms. She could see that the window over the kitchen sink had been broken, and a set of arms reached in, gripping the counter. She waited with bated breath until she got a clear view of the vampire's head and shot a UV bullet into it, killing the first intruder.

Howls of rage quickly followed the fallen vampire's screams of pain, and Nyla knew she'd just royally pissed off the vampire army surrounding the house. They'd come in more forcibly now, knowing there was someone armed inside. She couldn't shoot in two different directions with only one gun in one hand, so she sheathed the sword, replacing it with the second gun.

Time seemed suspended as she waited, a gun pointed toward each room, her index fingers poised over the triggers, waiting for her enemies to appear. She could hear her heartbeat roaring in her ears and briefly closed her eyes, willing it to slow down. When she reopened them, she breathed easier. For the sake of the child in the closet, she'd fought back the last tremor of fear trying to shake her.

And then all hell broke loose.

JAKE BROUGHT Peewee's hot-wired truck to a screeching halt outside the house where Nyla was protecting the kid. His protective instincts went into overdrive. He'd sensed the small army of vampires before he even reached the house, and since he couldn't see any outside, that meant they were all in the house . . . with Nyla. And if she wasn't alive when he marched in there, he'd send the monsters to hell and then follow them there where he'd rip them to pieces every day for the rest of damnation.

"Stay in the car," he ordered the teenager in the backseat as he opened his door.

"What if those *things* come out here?" Marilee asked, shooting a cautious glance toward Seta, who narrowed her eyes at her.

"We gave you a gun," Seta reminded her. "Now stay out of our way."

"Can you sense them in there?" Jake asked Seta as they simultaneously slammed their doors shut.

"Yes. I sense Nyla too. She's alive, and fighting her heart out."

Relief flooded through Jake, and it was in that moment he realized he was trembling. He glanced over at the vampiress next to him as they marched toward the house, wondering what was going through her mind.

"Are you going to be able to do this, or should I go in alone?"

"Do what? Slaughter everyone in sight?"

Jake picked up on the disgust in her tone and found it amusing coming from a bloodsucking witch. "They're your people."

"So every non-vampire in this country is *your* people? Even the serial killers and rapists?"

He ignored her last remark, wrapping his right hand around his gun, which he'd finally found locked away in a small room next to Peewee's office. It wasn't the right time to be getting into an in-depth debate with the vampire-witch. Nyla's life, and the lives of two innocents, were at stake. "I just want to make sure this isn't going to be a conflict of interest for you."

"My only interest is in protecting the child and his mother."

"It better be," he warned, bounding up the porch steps.

The front door had already been kicked in, and most of the windows were busted out. He kicked what was left of the door aside and with his gun pointed straight ahead, stepped into hell.

NYLA SWUNG HER sword in an arc, having dispensed all of her bullets within the first five minutes of the attack. Vampires had rushed in from all directions, kicking in doors and breaking through windows. She'd shot at them first, taking out as many as she could, before having to rely on her sword. If not for the fact she could evaporate into mist whenever too many of them closed in on her, she'd have been dead long ago.

She heard the front door being kicked off of its one good hinge, and thought, *Oh no, not more of them.* But dread turned to sweet relief when she saw Jake and Seta barrel into the room. Jake was alive, and, except for some gashes, bruising—and blood that she was sure wasn't his staining his clothes—he looked good.

"Thank you," she whispered to the heavens before decapitating another vamp. The beasts were beyond determined, never backing down, as though they were on a mission with strict orders to not turn back, no matter what. And the damned things seemed to be multiplying.

"Is the boy all right?" Jake called to her while he fired UV bullets into the crowd of bloodthirsty vamps, successfully turning several of them into rotting piles of gunk.

"He's secure," Nyla answered, noticing the horror in Seta's eyes as the vampiress watched Jake's victims dissolve. She understood the vampire-witch's reaction, remembering the fear that had run through her the first time she'd seen what the UV bullets could do.

Nyla turned just in time to avoid having fangs sink into her shoulder, and impaled a portly, middle-aged vamp with her sword. Just as the crowd of vampires started to thin out, thanks to her sword-swinging, Jake's bullets, and Seta's fireballs, more poured into the house.

"Where the hell are these things coming from?" Jake yelled over the commotion of the fight, dropping his empty gun in favor of a lamp stand and impaling one of the vampires on it.

"Jake!" Nyla threw her sword to him, filling her hands with the knives she'd kept sheathed to her forearms. He caught it and swung just in time to protect Seta from one of the charging vamps. The vampire-witch seemed to be weakening, her energy drained by the power needed to produce the fireballs with which she'd been killing vamps.

"Seta! Get behind me," she instructed. "Only use your fireballs when too many are on me. I have to bring them in closer since I only have my knives." Of course, she could change into mist if they got too close, but it was too risky to chance doing that around Jake.

"Keep one of them alive," Seta requested as she fought her way to Nyla, standing back to back with her. "It'll take the last of my energy, but I might be able to read one of them and figure out who sired them."

The battle continued, blood splattering over walls, furniture, and them as she continued hacking vampires to pieces. Seta used her fireballs only when necessary, and Jake swung his sword like a man possessed. Nyla couldn't help shuddering at the violent sound of his guttural cries as he ended each vampire's life.

"Touch him," Seta said softly from behind Nyla.

"What?"

"Touch him. He's losing himself to the rage inside. When I walked into the sheriff's department, he'd just set a vampiress on fire, after she was already near

death. If he gets any farther gone than he already is, I might not make it out of here without one of us dying. I'm too weak to teleport, and I seriously doubt you could kill him to save me. I don't want to kill him, but I won't allow myself to die either."

Nyla gulped, knowing she couldn't kill Jake, even if he was in the wrong and about to take an innocent life. She also couldn't stand by and watch Seta kill him in self-defense.

"Touch him, Nyla. Your touch has the power to diminish his darkness."

Nyla rammed one of her knives into the gut of an attacking vampire, pulling it up until she reached the heart and successfully cut it out. She closed her eyes as the organ fell to the floor. She had enough awful memories from the night to last her a lifetime. Too many.

The vampire's body fell to the blood-soaked floor with a sloppy-sounding thud, and Nyla stepped over it to make her way to Jake, sensing Seta following behind her. She swung her knives, effectively carving out a pathway to the man she loved, the man whose eyes were filled with a rage that chilled her to her marrow. Reaching him, she put her back to his, and Seta stood angled between them.

The three of them stood together in an imperfect circle, fighting at each other's sides, and she took the only moment she had to place her hand on Jake's thigh, relieved to feel some of his anger drain out of him and into her.

"They're going to swarm us this way," Jake warned, his voice closer to normal but still not quite there.

"Yeah, but at least none of them can creep up behind us."

Nyla took her hand away as a vampire charged her, needing both knives to stop his advance. She had to have faith that she'd done enough to make Jake less of a threat to Seta.

The vampires thinned out as the trio fought with everything they had inside them. Finally, with the walls and carpet soaked in blood, they won. Only one vampire stood before them, determined to fight until the very end.

"No!" Seta yelled as Jake raised his sword in the air, ready to decapitate the last surviving enemy. "Restrain the vampire, but don't kill him. I need to put my hands on him and see if I can determine who sired these fledglings."

Jake seemed oblivious to Seta's words, and Nyla grabbed his arm, successfully stopping him from killing what could be their only chance of discovering who had turned the residents of Hicksville into a vampire army.

The vampire charged them, but Seta quickly raised her hands, using her power to pin him against a wall.

"Sweet move," Nyla commented as she watched Seta approach the thin, dark-headed man.

"Yes. Too bad I'm going to drop like a sack of rocks after I'm through with him," the vampire-witch said, her voice haggard. "I didn't feed before all of this. Big mistake."

"What are you doing?" Jake asked.

"I'm going to pull his memories," Seta said simply as she stopped before the man and placed her hands on his body.

Nyla looked around the room as they waited, nearly gagging at the sight.

Blood was everywhere, including on them. Bodies littered the floor, some whole and some an assortment of chunks. The place would never be clean, would be better off burned.

"Bobby? Maybelline? Are you all right?" she called to the people waiting in the closet.

"Yes, can we come out?" Maybelline answered.

"No!" Nyla said quickly, then added to Jake. "We'll have to cover the boy's head with something when we take him out or he'll be in therapy for the rest of his life."

"Is my daddy dead?" Bobby's small voice came from the closet.

Nyla looked down, not wanting to answer. Bobby's dad had been one of the first she'd killed.

Her thoughts were interrupted as Seta screamed, falling back from the vampire's burning body, her hands aflame.

Nyla stood speechless as Jake ran from the room, quickly returning with a sheet. He batted the vampire-witch with it until the flames were doused and pulled her away from the vampire's burning body before the fire could spread to her.

"What the hell was that?" Jake asked, looking at Seta's charred arms.

"Hellfire," the vampiress answered, her voice laced in pain. "Lucifer uses it to protect his minions."

A scream and a series of gunshots sounded from outside the house, diverting their attention.

"Vampires are outside," Jake said, jumping to his feet.

"Who's the woman screaming?" Nyla asked, and more importantly, she thought, who was out there with a gun? She was sure Billy Bob and Bubba Lee had been killed.

"Marilee," Jake answered, already halfway out the door.

"Marilee?"

"Another hunter we picked up," Seta explained with a pain-filled laugh.

Nyla bent down to the woman and checked her burns, which looked as nasty as they apparently felt. The burning vampire had turned into ash and somehow put himself out.

"I saw a vampire with fur," Seta said, her voice a thin rasp.

"With fur?"

"Yes. And I saw you. These vampires were made to destroy you."

"What?" Nyla's heart skipped a few beats. "Why?"

"I don't know. The hellfire prevented me from seeing more."

A roar cut through the air, turning Nyla's blood to ice. It was Jake, and he was screaming in pain and rage.

"Go help him," Seta prodded. "I'll be fine here. I don't sense any vampires near."

Nyla nodded and ran out the door as fast as her legs would carry her. Jake and a blonde teenager stood over a woman's body twenty-four feet from the house. Jake's hands trembled with rage as he fell to his knees over the woman's body, screaming "No" over and over, his voice growing in ferocity.

Nyla skidded to a stop beside them, realizing the latest victim had been practically dumped at their feet. Whoever was killing these girls was taunting them now.

"Jake . . ." She reached out to comfort him, but stopped as she realized who lay on the ground before him. As she looked into the pretty, young face of the latest victim, she realized where his pain and rage were coming from. It was Chrissy, the fourteen-year-old girl he'd met at The Crimson Rose, the girl she'd found him manhandling in the alley the night she'd shown up as herself.

She knew Jake well enough to realize he was blaming himself for the girl's death, that he was railing at himself for not taking her home that night. If he had, she would be alive and well, not lying on the ground before him with two fang marks in her neck.

Fang marks that were *not* closing.

Chapter Nineteen

"JAKE." NYLA REACHED out to him, but he shoved her away.

"Don't touch me."

"Jake, please." Nyla tried to hide the pain in her voice, feeling rejected, but understanding he was angry with himself and lashing out at her because she was within reach. "Jake, it's not your fault. There was nothing you could—"

"Don't!" He rose to his feet, turning away from the body of the young girl. "I had her, Nyla. I had her right in my hands! I knew she was a runaway, and I knew she was in trouble!"

"And you did all you could do."

"No! I didn't do all I could do, Nyla," he snarled, "because the moment I saw you my dick started doing all the thinking for me. All I could think about was what it would be like to be inside you, and I just let the girl go."

"Um, I'm going to let you two hash this thing out," the blond teenager murmured from beside them, glancing uneasily between them when they both turned their gazes on her.

As Nyla watched the girl walk backwards a few steps and then turn and run toward a truck, she carefully chose her words. "If you want to blame me for this, go ahead and—"

"I don't blame you. I blame me. I let her go."

"What was your other option? Take her with you? That would have been just beautiful if the cops found you, a twenty-eight-year-old man with a fourteen-year-old girl. You warned her of the dangers of the streets. It's not your fault she didn't listen."

"How do you know she didn't listen? She could have been grabbed that same night, and all because I let her walk away."

Nyla looked down, unable to deny the possibility of that scenario. If she recalled correctly, Chrissy hadn't had the same twang as the residents of

Hicksville. She was most likely from Louisville and had been abducted there. Whoever had done this to her had kept her alive for awhile. "We'll get the bastard who did this to her, Jake. That's all we can do."

"It's not all we can do," Jake said, his voice a low growl, as he picked up the sword he'd dropped on the ground and turned back toward the house.

"What are you doing?" Nyla asked, fearing she already knew the answer.

"She died because of vampires. I say we kill them all."

"Jake, no!" Nyla ran to catch up to him as he steadily marched across the yard. She grabbed the back of his blood-soaked shirt and tugged him back, forcing him to turn and look at her. "You can't kill Seta. She helped us."

"I don't give a fuck what she did. They're all animals, all predators. Get her hungry enough, and she'll suck us dry."

"You don't know that, and she's hurt in there because she helped us!"

"She's helping her own kind. They don't want the exposure, Nyla. If more people believed in their existence, there would be more hunters. That's all her help is about! I should have never called Christian in the first place; a vampire minister for crying out loud. If that's not the most twisted—"

"Believing in God is twisted? Did Christian ask to be a vampire, Jake? Did Seta? Did any of these people who we've just killed? Have you ever bothered trying to find out?"

He glared at her. "What is all this bleeding heart crap? You're starting to sound like one of them! They claim they're people, but they're not people, Nyla. They're parasites. Killers!"

"Says the man who just killed a roomful of them," she stated dryly. "And if Seta and Christian are so bad, Jake, why did they let you and your brother go? They could have tried to kill you in Baltimore."

Jake continued to glare at her, the fury in his gaze hot enough to burn flesh. "That doesn't change the fact that they're killers."

"Newsflash, Jakie. Tonight we were all killers. And you seemed to enjoy it more than anyone."

He drew back, as though her words had lashed him across the face, and in a way, she supposed they had. But she needed to make it crystal clear that he was the one who had been the most blood-hungry. "I love you, Jacob Porter," she said, filling her hands with the bloody knives she'd sheathed after the last vampire went down, "but I won't let you kill an innocent woman."

Jake's eyes went wide, and he looked stunned for a moment, then he looked at the knives, his hand tightening around the handle of his sword. "You'd fight me over *her,*" he stated, his eyes full of an identifiable emotion which seemed to reach out and squeeze Nyla's heart.

"She's an innocent in this, Jake. I won't—I *can't*—let you kill an innocent."

He shook his head, muttering something too low to hear, but undoubtedly crude. "If I see her now, I'm going to kill her."

"Then take the girl home. It's too late to protect Chrissy, but the one in the truck can still be saved."

"It's daylight now. She'll be fine."

Even though he stood in a relaxed stance, she felt the anger and stubbornness writhing inside him. "Jake."

"What?"

"I'm not letting you near Seta when she's too weak to defend herself. Go."

"I'm not leaving without the boy." His eyes widened in alarm. "She's in there with them!"

"Jake, you'd have heard screams if Seta had attacked them! Just chill out. I'll get him." She pointed her finger at him. "You stay!"

She walked toward the house, pausing outside long enough to make sure he was doing as she'd ordered, and then stepped into the bloodbath which used to be a living room. She'd thought Maybelline had ugly furniture before. Now it was downright gruesome.

"He wants to kill me, doesn't he?" Seta asked, her voice a pain-filled rasp.

"I won't let him," Nyla promised, squatting before the fallen vamp, careful not to give in to the urge to kneel. Her jeans were already covered in blood, but she still didn't want to kneel on the drenched carpet. "Can you heal yourself? I've heard witches have that power."

"I healed the girl, Marilee, earlier. Crushed larynx. Took a lot out of me."

"And then the fireballs and the reading. When was the last time you drank?"

"Too long. I probably couldn't heal this damage anyway. Hellfire is Lucifer's weapon, and it's a good one. Hopefully, I'm powerful enough that the day sleep will heal it. I'll have scars for a good while though."

Nyla nodded, pity mingling with anger inside her chest. Someone would pay for this. "I'm going to get something to cover Maybelline and Bobby's faces as I lead them out of here. After I hand them over to Jake, I'm going to take you somewhere safe."

"Protect Jacob," the vampire-witch whispered.

"You want me to protect him knowing he hates you?" Nyla asked, surprised.

"There was a time I hated him as much," Seta said, a small laugh escaping her. "But I understand him now. There's so much pain inside him, so much rage. He honestly believes he's doing the right thing. He tries to fight against the darkness inside him, but he needs you to bank it down. You must stay with him, Nyla. He needs you far more than I do."

"Why?"

"Because, as I told you earlier, your touch diminishes the darkness inside him. Go with him. Let him hold you."

Nyla shook her head wearily. "I don't think he wants to hold me, Seta. He's pretty upset with me right now."

"Then you hold him. You can't let him drown in the darkness. If you do, he'll become a monster far crueler than anything he's ever hunted," Seta warned before closing her eyes and slumping against the wall. Nyla knew she'd blacked out from the pain.

"ALFRED!"

Curtis cringed as the sound of Demarcus's voice reverberated around the basement laboratory. The vampire was angrier than he'd ever seen him, stomping around the room and cursing as the few vampires who'd returned cowered in the corner.

The one named Billy Ray had returned first, with the scrawny sheriff draped over his blood-soaked shoulder. The smaller man, now strapped to the same metal table the young girl had recently vacated, had apparently urinated on himself some time during his capture and still reeked of the foul-smelling scent.

Two other vampires, both female, flew away from Judd Smith's house when they realized they didn't stand a chance against their three opponents. Demarcus had been ready to kill them for abandoning their mission, but then he realized that they'd brought him valuable information.

"Alfred!"

Curtis shuddered as he carefully placed the test tube he'd been working with into its holder, smiling slyly. He'd finally perfected the serum on which his brother had worked so painstakingly. He'd known how to do it all along, but he'd pretended he hadn't, afraid whose hands the serum might fall into. But now he had to do it. The witch with the platinum eyes who'd come to him in his dreams had told him so.

He left his work area to answer the volatile vampire, knowing it wouldn't take long before the impatient beast would direct his anger at him. "Yes?"

"I thought you made my children stronger!" Demarcus barked, whirling around to face Curtis as he approached.

"I did," Curtis answered, shrugging. "I gave them the ability to fly and revved up their stamina, but that's all I can do artificially. I can't make them better strategic fighters. That only comes with time and practice."

"How am I supposed to defeat her if she's killed off my army?"

Curtis would have suggested Demarcus ask for help from other powerful vampires, but he knew doing so would only anger him further. Demarcus had no vampire friends or associates, and except for the vampires he'd created or captured to be experimented on, he wouldn't want any other vampire to see the hideous, fur-covered creature he'd become after the pantherian had attacked him.

"Answer me!"

Curtis jumped at the harshness of Demarcus's tone, barely managing to suppress a whimper. "She wasn't alone. She had help from her man, correct?"

"Yes."

"It's been your plan all along to capture him and make her come to his rescue so we can ambush her. Let's just stick to that. She won't be as powerful by herself."

"The man killed two of my children and would have taken out Billy Ray had he not run."

"Actually, the girl killed Lou," Billy Ray interjected from the corner he remained huddled in, earning a glare from Demarcus.

"I did not expect a mortal man to be so much trouble," the dark vampire said, swinging his narrowed gaze from Billy Ray to Curtis. "I have three children left, and now those three hunters are protecting the town, so it won't be easy for me to make more. How did they get a vampire-witch to help? That was definitely unexpected."

Curtis quickly schooled his features before a smile could escape him, remembering how it was the vampires who'd destroyed his twin. Leaving the bodies had brought the catwoman's man to them, as Demarcus had planned, but it had also brought one of the vampires. Another who stood a chance at destroying Demarcus.

"I suppose the vampiress followed the bodies, just as Nyla and her man did. You forgot it was vampires who killed Carter. Obviously, it is vampires who will seek me out as well if they think I'm killing these women."

"You *are* killing these women," Demarcus reminded him, causing a sharp pang of guilt to slash through Curtis's chest.

Behind Demarcus, the sheriff started to moan on the metal table, flexing his fingers. Then his eyes flew open as he jerked his wrists against his shackles, and he screamed.

Demarcus bent over the man and smiled, flashing elongated fangs for effect, and the man's scream became shriller. Liquid spilled from the table, and Curtis groaned, realizing the man was wetting himself again, making more of a stinking mess for him to clean up.

Demarcus straightened, laughing at the terrified man. "And to think I was told you might present a problem for us. Sheriff Pee-Pee, is it?"

"Peewee," the sheriff corrected him, anger apparently giving him some semblance of courage. "And you do have a problem."

"Oh, really?" Demarcus cocked his head, peering down at the strapped man. "What would that be? Your special task force has been dismantled, and you, the man in charge of protecting this town, are now at my mercy."

"My cousin is going to kill you."

"Ah, yes, your cousin. The man who killed many of my children. I fully intend to meet this cousin of yours. Who is he?"

Don't say anything, Curtis silently pleaded with the scrawny captive, trying to catch his gaze. But the sheriff wouldn't look at him. He was too busy watching Demarcus, most likely fearing an attack. Curtis couldn't blame him for being scared. It was bad enough finding yourself at the mercy of a vampire, let alone one with fur, claw-like fingernails and patches of decaying skin. But Nyla and the man's cousin could be their way out of Demarcus's prison. They were doomed if the sheriff gave away too much information.

"His name is Jake," Peewee answered, "and he's been killing you monsters for years."

"Is that so?" Demarcus's mouth twisted into a sinister grimace, which was probably meant to be a grin but came off far too ugly.

"Yes."

Curtis watched as Demarcus rolled the information over in his mind, repeating the man's name. He couldn't tell what he was thinking, but there was definitely something going on inside his head.

Suddenly, the vampire's eyes flew wide, a look of dawning recognition etched into his face. "Your name is Porter," he said to the sheriff.

"Yes."

"Your cousin. His name is Porter?"

"Yeah."

"Jacob Porter?"

"Yes," the sheriff said smugly, apparently thinking Demarcus had heard the name because of the many kills he'd just boasted of, but Curtis could tell there was something else sparking Demarcus's memory.

Demarcus threw his head back and let out a deep roar of laughter, the sound rumbling through the house like a roll of thunder. "The fool! He doesn't even know!"

Peewee visibly squirmed on the table, despite his restraints. The sheriff had come to the realization something was wrong, just as Curtis had. They both watched the laughing vampire, who now had streams of water running from the corners of his black eyes. "He doesn't know!"

"There's good news, master?" Billy Ray timidly asked from the corner he remained cowered in, breaking into Demarcus's laughing fit.

Demarcus glared at the mullet-topped blond, obviously not pleased with the intrusion, but his glare quickly softened, followed by a slight upturn to his mouth. "Yes, my child, there is good news." He leaned over Peewee once more, offering a predatory smile. "Your cousin, brave sheriff, is the same boy who escaped me sixteen years ago. I've always wanted to meet him again, and now it appears that I will."

"You're one of the vampires who killed Bobby Romano," Peewee said, his pupils dilated with fear.

"Yes."

The sheriff started screaming again, loud and shrill, like a woman in panic. He fought against the restraints, but couldn't do more than jerk.

"Silence him," Demarcus instructed Curtis as he turned away to pace beside the metal table, clicking his long nails together as he thought.

Curtis retrieved a sedative from the small area which had been set up as his laboratory and injected it into the screaming man's blood stream.

"You look as though you've thought of a way to get to the woman," he said, watching as the strong sedative quickly took effect in the young sheriff's body, silencing him almost instantly.

"Jacob Porter is a slayer," Demarcus said almost happily, which was odd considering slayers were the vampires' greatest fear, next to UV and fire.

"Wouldn't that be bad news then?"

"Normally, yes, but considering who he's with . . . and the fact that he obviously has no clue what she is or she'd be dead, it's wonderful news. It's our ticket to both of them."

"What are you planning?"

"I can't send vampires to retrieve him. He'd sense us before we could get close enough to touch him."

"If that's true, how can he not know what the woman is? You said she became a vampire after your bite."

"She did. She drinks blood, and I don't sense that she's aged at all since that night."

"So maybe he does know what she is and doesn't care. He was working with the vampire-witch too."

"No," Demarcus said, shaking his head. "She dropped her guard for a split second earlier today, and I was allowed a quick peek. He was inside her, pleasuring her. He wouldn't do that with someone he suspected of being a vampire. Somehow, he doesn't pick up on her scent."

"And you know how to use that against him?"

"Against them both," the vampire answered, a devilish smile spreading across his hideous face. "Slayers are born with a deep, consuming hatred for my kind. If he were to find out who he has become close to . . ."

"He'll kill her himself, saving you the trouble."

"And he'll probably kill himself for screwing her," Demarcus added with another deep, booming laugh. "I didn't know how to capture her, not after reports that she can shift faster now than she did sixteen years ago. There'd be no way to hold her. Now I won't have to."

"How can he kill her if she shifts that fast?"

"He's a slayer. If anyone can kill her, it's him."

"So that's the plan? Wait around for him to discover what she is and kill her?"

"Maybe, maybe not," Demarcus said as he walked over to the table where Curtis had left out his research materials. Curtis had scoured the Internet for information regarding the therian race, finally coming across bits of information after several weeks of searching. He'd also come across information regarding large cat diseases, information which could possibly help in curing Demarcus, but he hadn't printed out that information. "I felt the strength of her emotions coursing through her as they fucked. It'll happen again. I just need her to let go enough to drop her shields, just long enough for me to take control."

"To possess her."

"Yes."

Curtis's stomach rebelled. "You'll use her body to kill Jacob Porter and then make her commit suicide."

"If she allows me the opening. If not, we'll just have to figure out a way for Porter to see what she truly is. As a slayer, he has immunity to mind tricks, so I can't get inside his head with any spells, not even with a blood sacrifice. Anything I do, it has to be done through her."

Curtis struggled to think of a way to protect the hunters. They were his only hope of being freed from Demarcus, and the witch had promised him Alfred could be exorcised from his body if he helped them. He glanced toward the vial containing the serum he'd created. "Can Jacob Porter sense me?"

Demarcus glanced up from the folder of papers he was sifting through. "You turned away from Lucifer, so I don't think he'd sense a demonic presence, especially with your wiring so screwed up," he added, referring to the fact there were two souls inside his body. Alfred and Curtis overlapped one another, canceling out any chance of anyone getting a clear reading from him. It was that little fact which had kept his plans hidden from Demarcus.

"I've created something which could slow him down," Curtis lied, focusing on keeping his voice steady. Demarcus might not be able to see the lie in his mind, but he still stood a chance of hearing it in his voice. "Why don't I go to them?"

"Are you trying to escape me?"

"No!" Curtis said too quickly, realizing the mistake as Demarcus's eyes narrowed.

"Liar! You may have created something to slow him down, but you wouldn't go to them, you sniveling coward. You'd take off in the opposite direction as fast as you could. Nice try, but you won't be using your little creation unless they come hunting for us."

"You know it's only a matter of time before they do. Wouldn't it be more to our advantage if we hunted them down first?"

Demarcus didn't answer. Instead he continued to focus intensely on a paper from the research folder. "You know, if we get lucky, Nyla will find herself in a position where she can't shift, and we'll be able to capture her after all. Maybe then you can dissect her living body and speed along the hunt for the cure for my . . . condition. And Mr. Porter would, of course, come for her. Oh, the fun we'd have then."

Curtis gulped, realizing what information Demarcus was reading, and hoping it didn't come true. Of course, if it did happen, Jake would come for her and give him the chance he needed. Somehow, before Demarcus could carry out his plans, he'd have to inject Jake Porter with the serum.

NYLA PLACED A pair of pillowcases over Maybelline's and Bobby's heads, then led them out of their home, which had so recently become a slaughter-house. The sun fell on her face as she stepped out into the morning light, but she could barely feel it through the stickiness of blood clinging to her skin.

Jake stood with his feet braced apart, his hands fisted at his sides, struggling with some inner turmoil she didn't want a closer look at. The lower half of his face was covered with a fine shadow of hair, bits of dried blood clinging to the scratchy-looking stubble. His clothes, arms and everything else, for that matter, were soaked in the substance. Two large bags hung from below his tired eyes, which were red around the rims. He was probably bruised and battered from their recently fought battle, but she couldn't find any evidence of such injuries beneath the caked blood drying on his skin.

"Take Maybelline and Bobby to the motel and secure them," she suggested as she uncovered their faces, listening to their sharp intakes of breath as they saw Jake, blood-splattered and almost as scary-looking as what had invaded their house. "Get cleaned up, shave, take a nap. It's been a long day."

"Where are you taking Seta?"

"I can't tell you that."

She saw the flinch he tried to hide and felt horrible. He wasn't a murderer, not in the sense she knew she'd just made him feel like, but she knew his mind wasn't in the right place at the moment. After what they'd just been through, she couldn't hold that against him though, and hoped he'd understand. She was protecting him as much as she was protecting Seta.

"Did you kill my daddy?" Little Bobby asked her for the second time, and as she gazed down at his small, innocent face, she found she couldn't lie to him.

"I had to."

"Thank you," he said, lowering his eyes to the ground as he reached for his mother's hand and led her to the truck.

Nyla glanced up quickly enough to see the pain in Jake's eyes before he could hide it, knowing what it cost him to hear the small boy's words, and know they hadn't been able to protect the child's innocence.

"We saved his life, Jake. A few nightmares are worth that."

He nodded, taking a deep breath. "Take care of Seta then. I'll take care of the women and . . . Bobby."

"And yourself," she reminded him, unclipping his cell phone from her waistband. "Your brother has been calling, but I didn't answer. I was kind of busy."

Jake nodded, taking the phone from her. It, too, was caked with blood splatters. "I'll piece together the messages on the bodies of the girls they've killed. I think I know what the symbols are."

"All right. But get cleaned up first," she instructed, knowing she felt worse every second she felt the blood on her skin, and he was more caked with it than she. She also didn't like the weird look in Jake's eyes. It was as though he were shell-shocked, and that couldn't be good. Removing the blood should help him to come out of it.

"Nyla?"

"Yes?"

He looked at her, hundreds of words seeming to flow from behind his eyes, but nothing came out of his mouth. Finally, he pulled her toward him and held her in an embrace, completely devoid of any sexual promise, shocking in its almost childlike manner. "Thank you," he whispered before stepping back and quickly turning away, marching determinedly toward the truck he'd commandeered.

"For what?" Nyla wondered aloud as she watched him leave, feeling deep in her heart that something was terribly wrong.

Chapter Twenty

OVER AN HOUR later, tired, sore, and desperate enough to sell her soul for a hot shower, Nyla pulled Jake's Malibu to a stop in front of the small motel. She'd hoped to find him fresh, clean and asleep in bed. Instead he was sitting in a plastic chair outside their room, still covered in enemy blood.

She stepped out of the car and rubbed her neck. Blood couldn't have healed Seta instantly, but it went a long way in speeding up the process, and the vampire-witch had been in need of it. She'd gone far too long without feeding and had more than overexerted herself in order to help them. As far as Nyla was concerned, giving Seta her blood was the least she could have done for her since Seta had helped save their lives. She only hoped donating her blood to Seta wouldn't spark her own hunger. She'd controlled her urges amazingly well, especially when she'd been in a bloodbath a few hours earlier and not once had the urge to taste the freely flowing blood.

As she approached Jake, he didn't move or react to her presence in any way. He was leaning forward with his elbows resting on his knees and his large, powerful hands clasped together. He didn't look up as she stood over him. He kept his gaze on the ground a few feet before him, but she could tell he wasn't seeing the dirt or the few stones scattered among the blades of grass.

"Jake?"

He remained still long enough that she was about to repeat his name when finally, he crooked his neck, turning his head just enough to offer her an empty glance. "Yeah?"

"What are you doing?"

"Sitting."

"I can see that. How long have you been sitting out here?"

He shrugged, focusing his gaze on the far off distance, disturbingly nonchalant. Jake was never this mellow, and no one in his right mind would just calmly sit outside while other people's blood dried on his skin and clothes.

"Bobby and his mom all right?" she asked.

"They're in the next room with Marilee. Trust me, that girl will shoot any-one stupid enough to try and get in there with them."

"That's good," Nyla commented. Seta had filled her in on who the girl was, and she didn't doubt Jake's statement. "Then you don't need to be out here standing guard."

"I'm not."

"Get cleaned up, Jake."

"I'm fine."

"You're covered in blood," she pointed out.

"So are you."

"Yeah, and it's about to come off. Come on."

He glanced at her briefly, his eyes moist and weary, before shaking his head. "You go ahead and clean up. I'm going to sit out here a while longer."

Nyla stared at him, trying to figure out what was going through his mind. She'd seen him after dozens of slayings. He'd always cleaned up immediately afterwards. For him it was just a job. Then he would talk to her in her cat form, or sometimes he'd pull her onto his lap and pet her until he fell asleep. He never dwelled on what had happened, so what was different this time? True, this particular incident had been a full-on battle in horror-flick proportions, but . . .

The answer slammed into her. This time he didn't have Alley to help him deal with the aftermath. *Damn.*

"Come on." Nyla grabbed his arm, pulling him out of the chair.

"What are you doing?"

"You're in shock, Jake, and I'm not leaving you out here."

"I'm not in—"

"Shut up."

"Get off me." He pulled away as she opened the door to their room, starting back for the chair, but she grabbed his wrist and forced him inside.

"You don't know what's best for you right now."

"Woman, I said I'm fine. I have killed more bloodsuckers than this."

"This many in the same night?"

"Leave me alone, Nyla!"

"Why, so you can sit outside in broad daylight, covered in dried blood, waiting for someone to see you and report you to the police? We have enough problems right now, thank you very much!"

"What police? They're all dead. Peewee's probably dead or a vampire right now too!" His voice almost cracked on the last word.

"Well, that's all the more reason why you need to be in the right state of mind. The people in this town who've managed to avoid being changed over need somebody to protect them."

"Yeah, and I'm *so* good at that," Jake muttered. "They took my cousin, my own flesh and blood!"

Nyla started to point out that he'd never really liked Peewee and had recently threatened to shoot him himself, but thought better of it. She didn't know anything about familial love firsthand, but she knew enough from observing Jake's family to realize he loved his cousin, even if he didn't *like* him.

"You protected him the best you could, Jake. You were outnumbered, and instead of listening to you, Peewee stripped you of your weapons and locked you in a cell. It is not your fault he was taken."

"Is that supposed to make me feel better?"

"No. I know you well enough to know the only thing that'll make you feel better is getting the bad guy, and you're not in any condition to do that right now. You need to get out of those disgusting clothes, shower, shave, eat something and sleep."

She held up a hand when he started to argue and led him to the bathroom. She turned the shower on full blast and gestured for him to start taking off his clothes, but he stood still before the tub, gazing at the water raining down from the shower head.

"Oh, for crying out loud," she muttered as she peeled the stiff T-shirt from his body and unsnapped his jeans. "I don't know if this is some sort of subconscious punishment you're putting yourself through, but I'm growing tired of it."

"You said you loved me," he said abruptly, grabbing her wrists before she could slide his jeans down. "Did you mean that?"

She forced herself to look him in the eyes, her face growing warm as she recalled blurting out those words to him a few hours earlier. She started to speak, but the fear, rage, guilt, and doubt she saw mingling together in his eyes silenced her. Tears welled in her eyes. She wanted to cry for him, knowing he'd never allow himself that release.

"Nyla? Did you mean it? Is it the truth?"

His eyes were so full of anguish that she nearly choked on her own returned emotion. "Yes, Jake, it's the truth. I love you."

"How can you? How can anybody? If you could see what's inside of me—"

She silenced him with a kiss, the pain in his voice becoming too much for her to bear. As their mouths met, she sensed the pain and confusion inside him diminishing and remembered what Seta had told her. She'd said that Nyla needed to take his anger and hurt away before it destroyed him. Why hadn't she noticed her empathic ability before? She didn't know. But now that it had been pointed out to her she found herself focusing on it, and let his emotions pour from his body into hers where she absorbed them, freeing Jake from the burden.

In need of air, she finally pulled away from the embrace, but she knew there were still too many mixed emotions coursing through Jake, hurting him worse than any weapon could.

"Come on," she said softly, peeling off her own clothes. "We'll both feel better when we're clean."

The Jacob Porter she'd known before would have tossed his cares to the wind if offered the chance to share a shower with a naked woman, but this version of the man seemed to crave affection more than sex. Sweet as it was, Nyla wasn't used to this side of Jake, and she wasn't sure how to handle him.

If there was anything she'd learned during her years spent under the pantherian queen's rule, it was how to sexually satisfy a man. But as she washed the blood from Jake's skin, watching the red streams escape down the drain, she found herself at a loss for how to cure his pain. He needed more than just physical pleasure. He needed someone to help him to slay his own demons. He needed a friend, she realized with sudden clarity.

She remembered the many times she'd been away from him over the years and somehow sensed he was in trouble. She'd come running back to him, always finding him engaged in battle with vampires or other creatures of the night. Foolishly, she'd thought all this time that he'd been in danger of his enemies, but he'd really been in danger of himself. After those fights, he would wash away the blood, the remnants of the cruel things he'd done, and he'd pour his heart out to her as she curled up on his chest, listening to his heartbeat. She now knew that she'd been absorbing his anger and sorrow. As Alley, she'd been the best friend to him she could be, but Alley had limits. Jake had never had anyone who could tell him the things he needed to hear.

"Do you feel better?" she asked as the water flowing toward the drain turned clear again.

"Yes," he answered, his beautifully sculpted body free of any evidence that he'd mercilessly killed an army of vampires mere hours before. "Thank you, Nyla, for . . . Well, I guess I should say catching me."

"You had me scared for a while there, Jakie."

"Me too."

He wrapped his arms around her waist, and she could feel the tension inside him giving up the last of its hold, but there was still a heart-wrenching need for companionship inside him. He'd always been a loner, a rogue hunter. She'd never realized it wasn't by choice.

"I'll leave you to shave, and then we can talk," she said, giving his mouth a small, innocent peck before stepping out of the tub. She wrapped a towel around her body and stepped out of the tub and over the pile of ruined clothes.

Closing the bathroom door behind her, she let out a deep sigh, her heart aching for Jake. She'd thought she'd known everything about him, but in cat form there were so many things she hadn't picked up on. She quickly dressed in underclothes and one of Jake's many black T-shirts. It hung around her like a nightshirt, comforting her with his scent.

She had just crawled into the big, inviting bed and leaned back against the pillows lining the headboard when the bathroom door opened and Jake emerged, a towel slung low over his hips and his face freshly shaved.

"Ouch. That's one heck of a shiner," Nyla commented as she noticed the blue and purple marking spread across the left side of his face. She hadn't noticed it before because the heavy beard stubble had camouflaged it.

"Yeah, you have a hell of a right hook," Jake answered as he pulled a pair of boxers out of his duffel bag sitting on the table.

"Oh, sorry," Nyla apologized, wincing slightly. "I forgot about that. Man, it's been a long day, and night."

"Yeah, it's all running together."

She couldn't help watching as he stepped into the boxers, dropping the towel in the process. The Heat had been sated, but Jacob Porter did things to her body that were equally as bad. If not for his fatigued expression, she might have forced him into a chair so she could have her way with him again.

"Come on, Jakie. You need to sleep."

He shook his head, but crawled into the bed anyway, laying close against her so she could wrap him in her arms. "We've got too much to do. There's no time for sleep."

"You have to sleep, you're running on empty," she advised, feeling the fatigue herself, and thanks to her therian blood, she had far more stamina than Jake. With Jake's head resting against her breast, his back against her chest, she ran her fingers through his short hair, combing it away from his face, feeling the loneliness engulfing him. "Tell me about your friend."

He stiffened instantly. "It was a long time ago, and it wasn't like Peewee said."

"I know that. Tell me about it. Tell me about your friend. Quit holding it all inside you."

She felt him resist, but he finally took a deep breath and let it out slowly. She could feel a jumble of emotions inside him, warring with each other, and decided he wasn't going to speak. Then he opened his mouth and started speaking. He started out slowly, but the words sped up as his story progressed. As he shared his most painful memories with her, she offered words of comfort, something she hadn't been able to do as Alley.

"I pissed my pants and ran," he said in disgust, balling his hands into fists.

"You were just a boy, Jake. And running that night saved your life."

"But I left Bobby there to die," he said, shaking his head. "I knew what was out there, I felt it, but I didn't stop him."

"You tried to, but he made the choice not to listen. You didn't know vampires were real before that night. You didn't understand what you felt until it was too late." She leaned forward to kiss his temple. "What happened is not your fault. You need to let go of the guilt."

"I can't. I let my best friend *die*. He was just a kid!"

"And you were just a kid yourself. You weren't physically equipped to do anything to help Bobby. But think of all the children and other people you have saved since then. Think of the boy next door who we protected tonight. I couldn't have done it alone. You saved the day, and you need to acknowledge just how great you are."

"Great?" He let out a derisive snort. "I'm a freak. Ask anyone who knows me. My own parents were ashamed of me, their weirdo-kid who believed in monsters. Bobby's parents never forgave me, always wondering why I'd gotten away and their son didn't. They knew I left him there."

"Jake, don't."

"Don't what? You wanted to know what happened, and I'm telling you. I'm a freak, Nyla. Everyone knows it. Even my brother didn't believe me until he came across Seta and her son while working a case."

"Your brother loves you."

"Yeah, but he's paid the price for it. As a kid, he got into fights all the time defending his baby brother. I was no good to anyone."

"Don't say that, Jake. Who cares that Bobby's parents weren't able to accept the truth or that your parents weren't worth a damn? You were their son, and you'd been through a traumatic experience. They should have nurtured you, no matter what. To hell with them all. You have me, and you have a brother. We love you, and people out there need you to protect them."

"You shouldn't love me, Nyla. I'm no good inside."

The pain in his voice squeezed Nyla's heart, threatening to crush it. "You are a good person, Jake. Don't think that you aren't."

He let out a small strangled sound. "There's nothing good about me. You were right earlier. I enjoyed killing those vamps. They were people once, and as you pointed out, they were most likely turned against their will. Still, I killed them without mercy. Hell, I set a woman on fire tonight because she had fangs. She could have been someone's mother. Do you think I cared?"

"She would have killed you if you hadn't killed her first. And I killed the father of the little boy in the next room tonight. Am I evil for doing that?"

"No, but you didn't enjoy it either. You didn't let your rage get out of control."

Nyla held him tighter, wishing she knew the right words to say. "You're a good person, Jake, but you can only face evil so many times before it starts to sink into you, to make you react the same way. But you've never killed anyone who you didn't believe was evil, and those people tonight were ravenous. They would have killed anyone in their path. You saved many people by killing them. It's a horrible job, but you're good at it. And I know you can—and do—control your darkness."

He turned in her arms, raising himself so they sat eye to eye. "Thank you for . . . everything," he said, his voice a soft rumble as he leaned in to lightly kiss her mouth. "We can rest a bit, but then we need to get out of here."

"What are you talking about? You want to leave?"

"Yes."

"But what about—"

"It's a trap, Nyla."

"What's a trap?"

"The markings on the bodies were warnings," he explained, leaning back against the headboard, his shoulder touching hers. "After I saw the one on Chrissy's body . . ." His voice trailed off at the mention of the girl, and his eyes clouded over in a mixture of emotions.

"Jake?" Nyla reached out to touch his face, searching his eyes. The guilt and anger she saw in their depths fueled her own anger, filled her with a feeling of vengeance. She would kill Chrissy's murderer, just to take that look out of his eyes.

"I'm fine," he said, shrugging her hand away. "I just wish I could have protected her. She was so young." He let out a deep breath and continued. "After the fourth marking, I realized they were Egyptian hieroglyphics. I checked the 'net when I came back tonight and found them. They're part of the Egyptian alphabet. T-R-A-P."

"Trap?"

"Yep."

"You're saying that someone put those markings on the bodies to spell the word trap?"

"Yes."

"Assuming it is a trap, why would someone take the chance that we'd figure out what the markings are?"

"Damned if I know, but the bodies of women with fang markings left a trail to this town which just happens to be under some sort of vampire infestation. It's all deliberate."

"We were lured here."

"*I* was lured here. You came along for the ride. Think about it. I've got more vampire kills under my belt than I can count, and a fact like that tends to get around in the vampire community. I think someone has set all this up so they can kill me."

"Who would do that? And why would any vampire go to such lengths to get one man, regardless of the number of kills you have under your belt?"

"I don't know why, but I do know that this is a trap. I also don't know if what we faced tonight was the whole army or just a part of it. There was that small group of vamps watching over the victim's grave in Louisville. There might be small groups scattered all along the trail."

"And you're saying that because it's a trap we should just leave?" Nyla cocked her head, studying him. His expression and eyes were now as unreadable as white on white.

"How many more ambushes can we walk into and still be able to walk out of alive?" he asked.

She didn't buy into his answer. "What's going on, Porter? I know you.

You won't leave your cousin behind without a fight, regardless of whether or not you like the guy. You'll either rescue him, or if he's been turned into a vamp, you'll . . ." As she spoke, it suddenly hit her what he was up to, and she pulled away and glared at him. "You want me out of here so I'll be safe, and then you're going to go find the brains behind all this and take him down. Well, Jake, you can forget your protect-the-little-woman proclivities. I'm staying by your side until this entire mess is over."

"It's not your fight, Nyla."

"Bull." It was more her fight than he realized, she thought as she recalled the images Seta had pulled from the vampire's mind before the hellfire stopped her. There was a vampire behind the murders, a vampire with fur.

Suddenly, it all fell into place for her. Demarcus had bitten her sixteen years ago, and she'd walked away with immortality. What if she'd given him something in return? What if he'd taken on some of her feline traits? If Demarcus was behind this, then the trap wasn't for Jake. It was for her.

And she'd just let the love of her life walk right into it with her.

"We're going in together, Jake," she stated firmly.

"No, Nyla. I can't take the chance of losing you. When I reached that house tonight and found it ambushed there was a moment when I didn't know if you were . . ."

"I was fine tonight, Jake, and I'll be fine tomorrow, and the next day, and for as long as I need to get this job done," she cut in, noticing how he was struggling to finish his sentence. "As touched as I am by your concern, I can't let you do this alone. We're stronger together, and you know that as well as I do."

"Yeah," he conceded, albeit reluctantly.

"So it's settled."

"I don't like it."

"I don't either, but the alternatives are letting innocents die or get changed into vamps against their will. Those are not options I can accept."

"Me neither." He raked a hand through his hair, his eyes growing wearier by the minute. "I just wish we knew what we were up against. Curtis Dunn is involved somehow, but apparently there's also a vampire in the mix."

"You said Alfred Dunn was reincarnated in Curtis Dunn's body but that Curtis has his own soul."

"Yeah. He's supposed to be two souls inside one body, and they're battling each other."

"Well, if that's true and Alfred Dunn hated vampires so much, he wouldn't willingly do anything to help them, would he?"

"I don't know. When Carter Dunn captured Aria Michaels in Baltimore, he'd killed several women there while trying to invent an immortality serum. According to Aria, Curtis didn't seem to want to have anything to do with his brother's work, wouldn't even help his twin torture a powerful vampire, but she also said he acted weird sometimes, weird enough to scare her."

"Was that when Alfred was trying to take over?"

"I don't know, but probably."

"So if Alfred hates vampires, and Curtis doesn't want to hurt people, but they're still doing something to make vampires in this town and killing people in the process, they must be under a vampire's control."

Jake arched a brow. "They?"

"Whatever," Nyla said, rolling her eyes. "I'm not up on the proper multiple personality terminology. He, they, Curtis, Alfred, or a combination of all that, must be doing someone's bidding against his will. The vampire controlling him obviously wanted to make his newly formed vamps more powerful, and they were certainly that."

"Yeah, the ones I went up against at the jail had more stamina than any newly-turned vamps I've ever had the displeasure of meeting, and the whole flying circus was a nice touch."

"So it would be an old, powerfully strong vampire," Nyla deduced, thinking how Demarcus fit that description perfectly. "Someone scary enough to make even old Alfred, the reincarnated, vampire-hating spirit, do his bidding."

"And the hellfire tells us whoever the vamp is worships the devil," Jake added.

"So we're looking for an older, powerful, devil-worshiping vampire with a grudge against, um, one of us," Nyla muttered, realizing why she'd seen a raging inferno and dancing demons on one of the unfortunate occasions she'd glimpsed inside Demarcus's twisted mind before learning how to shield herself from him. "How in hell do you beat a vamp with the devil on his side?"

Jake shrugged. "Christian defeated Carter, and he was supposedly under Lucifer's protection."

"Are you thinking what I think you're thinking?" she asked.

"Don't rub it in," he grumbled, shooting her an irritated look.

"I wouldn't tease you about asking for Christian's help. Heck, I'd commend you on the proper use of your common sense. Maybe the minister can get some of his other vamp friends to help," she added, fearing the thought of Jake going up against the very vampire who'd birthed Jake's hatred for the entire race. The vampire she'd vowed to protect him from.

"Maybe," Jake said, seeming to contemplate the idea.

Nyla looked away, her mind a mass of indecision. She knew she should warn him about who she thought the vampire was that was orchestrating the trap. But how could she tell him without revealing how she knew—and what she was. He'd seemed so concerned for her safety, as though he truly cared for her, and she cringed inside at the idea of seeing repulsion in his eyes if he discovered she was his pet alley cat let alone a vampire to boot. But on the other hand, she couldn't allow him to go up against Demarcus blindly. She glanced over at him, biting her lip. She couldn't do it. She couldn't stand the thought of losing him. She'd just have to get him to sleep and go after Demarcus herself. Take out the psycho before Jake could get near him.

"You should get some sleep, Jake. We'll be able to formulate a better plan if we're rested, and it's been over twenty-four hours since either of us slept."

"Yeah, there's one problem with that," he said, an undercurrent in his tone heating up her blood.

"What's that?"

"I'm wide awake."

"Doesn't look like it to me," she said, looking pointedly at the darkened areas beneath his eyes.

"I'm talking about little Jakie."

"*Little* Jakie?" she parroted, trying to keep the laughter from her voice, her suddenly raging hormones giving her the urge to giggle.

"Not *that* little," he responded, a warning tone in his voice as he leaned over to press his mouth to hers.

Their lips fused together, igniting a fire inside Nyla's body similar to the Heat, but gentler in its assault. Her heartbeat kicked up a notch as his hand slid over her thigh, stopping at her hip so he could dip his fingers into the waistband of her little black panties.

He wants me, she inwardly screamed with glee as he pulled the small scrap of black lace from her body. She was not a wild animal throwing herself at the closest male in response to a curse which possessed her body seasonally, and he wasn't some guy just going along for the ride. He was seeing her as a woman, and he wanted her. He was coming to her purely by his own choice, and she poured herself into their kiss in order to keep from crying out in overwhelming happiness. It was the moment she'd been dreaming of since realizing her love for him so many years ago.

He freed her of her remaining clothing, taking a moment to gaze appreciatively at her naked body, a nimble finger following the path his eyes formed, causing goose bumps to form in its wake. "Is this all right? You're not going to weird out on me again?"

"No weirding out," she promised, pulling his head down for another taste of his talented mouth. Instinct kicking in, she reached down to stroke him intimately, but found her fingers quickly laced around his.

"Not that I didn't thoroughly enjoy your dominance our first time," he said, freeing his mouth long enough to speak, "but this time you're going to lie back while I take care of you."

She'd been with more men than she cared to remember, but Nyla had never experienced anything like what Jake did to her body. She struggled to control herself as his clever mouth explored her, breathing over, kissing or licking various points along her body which seemed to be directly linked to her core. Each intimate caress sent a shower of sparks rushing through her system, creating a torturous tingle which threatened to consume her.

Sex had always been a matter of fulfilling a need for her. Not in her wildest fantasies did she know it could be this wonderful. Jake continued to caress her body with mouth and hands, drawing out her pleasure until it became almost unbearable, continuing to put her needs before his own. It was an offering she'd never thought she would receive.

What seemed like hours after he'd first begun, and Nyla reached the point she was about to beg, Jake finally drove into her, filling her body with even more pleasure than she could have imagined. He continued to work her body with his hands and mouth as he rocked back and forth, pleasuring her from the inside and out until the sensations spiraling through her became too intense to contain. She dug her nails into his skin, biting down on his shoulder to keep from screaming as he thrust inside her one last time, his entire body shuddering as he let out a deep cry, sharing her orgasm.

Nyla felt some place deep inside, where she'd never felt anything before, come alive, and she choked back tears. She tried to understand what was happening, but couldn't think clearly, her mind a mottled mess of pleasure and joy. Joy like she had never known could exist.

"I love you," Jake whispered, his voice hoarse as he struggled to talk over his labored breathing.

Nyla's heart felt as though it would burst as adrenaline filled her. Tears fell from her eyes as she replayed Jake's words, words she would have given anything to hear and could hardly believe that she'd finally heard them. "I love you, Jake."

Then she gasped as, suddenly and without warning, something dark and cold forced its way inside her body, turning the joy she'd so recently felt into chilling fear. The foreign, yet terrifyingly familiar, entity snaked its way through her body, holding her prisoner inside her own skin. She realized too late that while she'd been consumed with elation over Jake returning her love, she'd dropped her guards against Demarcus. It had only been for a moment, but it was long enough for him to push his way in. She tried desperately to re-erect the walls she'd had in place, but it was too late. He'd invaded more than her mind; he'd taken over her body.

She opened her mouth to scream, but the sound of Demarcus's deep, rumbling laugh tumbled out instead.

Chapter Twenty-One

SOMETHING SHIFTED in the air, drawing Jake out of the sex-induced fog he'd been lost in. The fine hairs along the back of his neck stood on end as he realized something dark had entered the room. He slowly pulled away from Nyla's body, ready to warn her of the danger, but deep, rumbling laughter of someone dark and achingly familiar fell from Nyla's lips, killing his words before they could form.

"Your little friend tasted so sweet," she whispered against his ear in a menacing, male voice. A voice he'd never forgotten.

He jerked away from her, wondering what kind of cruel game she was playing, but froze when he saw her eyes. The woman lying on the bed looked like Nyla, but someone else was staring at him from behind her eyes, eyes which should have been the color of lilacs, not onyx so deep and dark he felt as if he were gazing into a bottomless well. And there was a cruel set to her mouth that was disturbingly out of place.

"I've always loved tasting the blood of young ones," she continued in that menacing voice as she rose from the bed. "They always taste so much better, so delicate, but Bobby . . . well, he was a real treat."

"Nyla?"

"Yes, lover?"

Jake balled his hands into fists as he stood opposite her side of the bed, every muscle in his body tense. He stared at the face of the woman he loved, the woman he'd poured his heart and soul out to, and fought to keep from taking her life with his hands. "Get out of her, you sick son of a bitch."

She tilted her head back and laughed, the sound growing deeper as she returned her dark gaze to him. "I don't think I'll do that, Mr. Porter. If you want to kill me, you're going to have to kill her."

Jake stared at Nyla, or the shell of Nyla, in horrified disbelief. The voice of the monster he'd spent every waking moment of the past sixteen years wanting to kill was coming out of her mouth, looking at him through her eyes. He knew it wasn't her, that she was being manipulated by the sick bastard who'd taken his friend's life, but he still struggled to control his homicidal craving. The beast was inside her body, within reach.

"Bobby's cries were a symphony, so melodic and—"

"Shut up!"

"I never got the chance to thank you for leaving him there for us."

"I said shut up!" Jake yelled, trying to think past his need for vengeance. He wanted to kill the thing, to destroy it mercilessly, but it was in Nyla's body.

He looked in her eyes, and the rage intensified. Nyla's eyes weren't looking back at him. He was being leered at by the black eyes of a murderer, a demon. *She's still in there*, he reminded himself, tearing his gaze away. He grabbed a pair of jeans and quickly pulled them on, figuring whatever was about to go down was best going down in clothes.

"So modest."

"Screw you." He straightened himself as she walked toward him, readying himself for a fight. "How did you get inside her?"

"She let me in."

"Liar." He backed away as she continued to approach him, snagging a knife from the table at his back despite the fact he didn't want to hurt Nyla. "You're the psycho who's taken over this town. We came here to kill you."

"Go ahead."

Jake smiled, shaking his head. "I'm not that stupid, bloodsucker. You've possessed her body, and you're controlling it, but you wouldn't die if she did. You're *not* going to make me kill her."

"Have it your way then," she said, and lunged for him.

Jake sidestepped her, causing her to fall to the floor. He backed up, placing the bed between them again while he looked around the room for something he could use. He needed a way to detain her without inflicting bodily harm while he figured out a way to get the vampire out of her body. He eyed the tangled sheet spread across the bed just as she rose from the floor.

"I've wanted to do this for far too long," she said, quickly walking around the bed.

Jake reached for the sheet, but halted as Nyla's body jerked unnaturally. He watched as she grabbed one of the bedposts, seeming to pull and push it at the same time, making moaning sounds of pain while she struggled.

"Jake!"

"Nyla!" Her eyes were hers again, purple and filled with terror. He forgot about the sheet, rushing towards her.

"No! He's going to make me kill—" Her warning died as her eyes bled to black, her mouth twisting back into a smile. "I'm sorry. Nyla had to leave."

She lunged forward, grabbing at his collarbone, sinking her fingernails in when she met flesh. Jake let out a cry of pain, grabbing her by the waist as he fell onto the foot of the bed. As his back connected with the mattress, he pushed her upward, effectively tossing her over him, toward the head of the bed. As she catapulted past him, he jumped up, turning to prepare for another attack.

She was on her knees, facing him. Her forehead was red, the aftereffect of slamming headfirst into the wall. "Why don't you just kill the bitch quick and clean instead of beating her first?" she asked with that evil laughter bubbling up her throat.

"Go to hell," Jake growled as guilt assaulted him, but he couldn't let it tear him apart. If he allowed the vampire controlling Nyla to kill him, he'd never be able to save her from its clutches, and he knew she'd never forgive herself for killing him while being controlled. If he had to hurt her to save her, he would just have to deal with it and beg forgiveness later. "I'm not killing you until you're out of her body. I lost Bobby to you. I'm not going to lose Nyla too."

"You stupid, love-struck fool!" She threw her head back and the vampire's laughter poured out of her. "You don't even know what she—Jake!"

Jake started for her as the sound of Nyla's true voice called his name, sounding so scared and desperate. He halted when her eyes once more returned to dark, soulless black pits. "Nyla, I know you can hear me in there! Fight this son of a bitch!"

"She can't fight me. I made her."

"You sick motherfucker!" Jake threw himself at the creature inhabiting Nyla's body, the knife in his hand tightly enclosed within his fist. He grabbed her by the shoulders, holding her down on the bed, aching to drive the knife into her chest, if only to take the smug grin off her face. He raised the knife in the air, ready to plunge it into her heart, then realized what he was doing.

"No!" He threw the knife down, desperate to keep himself from hurting Nyla. "I won't kill her just to hurt you, no matter what lies you spew."

"Lies? She's the liar. You don't even know what she—" Her body bucked beneath him, cries of rage coming from her mouth as her eyes seemed to flicker, black and purple swimming in her irises. "Jake, please don't listen . . . help . . . help . . ."

She let out a painful cry, and the voice changed back to the deep, menacing tone of his tormentor, as black eyes glared up at him. "She was there, too, that night. She is how I found you again," the vampire said through Nyla's mouth as he used her body to shove Jake to the floor.

Jake rolled as she rose from the bed, careful to put space between them before he stood. "I don't believe you. You've hunted me down because not only did I escape you that night, but I've killed two of the vamps who were with you. You knew it was only a matter of time before I got to you and the other one."

"The other one is already dead. This bitch killed him."

Jake's mouth dropped open, surprised by the news. He'd been on the trail of Niles eight years earlier, had closed in on him when all of a sudden the trail just stopped. It was as though the vampire had vanished into thin air. Assuming what the monster said was true, Nyla had beaten him to the killing. "I'll have to remember to thank her for that."

"I guess you'll want to thank her for saving your life that night too."

"I don't know what you're trying to do, but it's not going to work. She had nothing to do with anything that happened that night."

"Jacob, Jacob, why do you refuse to see what is so clearly in front of you? How do you think I've gained control of her body? She's mine."

"No."

"Yes."

Jake's body shook with denial as he let the vampire's comment sink in. He knew a person couldn't be possessed unless there was some sort of entrance to their mind. They either let the host in willingly, or there was some sort of link. Nyla wouldn't let this monster inside her, he knew she wouldn't . . . but the alternative couldn't be true either. "You work for Satan. He has a hell of a bag of tricks."

"And that's what you think this is?" the vampire asked, laughing as he forced Nyla's body to walk toward Jake with a look of murderous intent in his eyes. "This is all a trick?"

"Yes," Jake answered, taking a step back for every step she took forward.

"I actually tried to do you a favor by giving you the opportunity to kill this woman. You've wanted to kill me more than you've ever wanted to do anything else. She protected me from you, Jacob. She could have found me for you at any time."

"No," Jake said, his voice barely audible as he struggled to contain his emotions. There were too many thoughts racing through his mind, too many doubts. He loved Nyla. He'd do anything for her, and she loved him. She wouldn't lie to him, or hurt him. She *wouldn't*. But how did this thing get inside her? How did it find entrance? What connection could there be? "What's your name?"

He laughed before answering. "Knowing my name makes it easier to hunt me, doesn't it?"

"I'll kill you either way. I'd just like to know the name of the demon I'm going to send back to hell."

"That's not going to happen," he said, "but I'll tell you my name since it's only fair you know the name of your executioner. It's Demarcus."

Jake rolled the name around in his mind, trying to place it. "You're very old, Demarcus. The few occasions I've come across your name, it was in tales of your death."

"Widely exaggerated tales, as you now know."

"They won't be exaggerated for long."

"You won't live to know the difference." Nyla's arm raised, revealing the knife he'd thrown down earlier held firmly in her grasp.

Jake positioned himself for attack, expecting her to lunge toward him with the knife, ready to bury it in his chest, but she turned her wrist, directing the blade toward herself.

"What are you doing?"

"Killing you would be too easy, Jake. I want you to suffer the loss of the woman you claim to love first."

"No!" Jake barreled into Nyla's body as her arm swung in a downward arc, managing to knock her to the floor before any damage was done. He grabbed her wrist, beating it against the floor until she dropped the knife. Her knee jerked upward, smashing into his groin with enough force to dispel his breath from his lungs.

They rolled around on the floor, each grasping the other's neck, struggling to choke them into submission. Jake didn't want to hurt Nyla, but he couldn't let Demarcus hurt her either. If Demarcus killed him now, he'd kill Nyla soon after, and she wouldn't be able to stop it from happening.

They rammed into the legs of the small table his gym bag was resting on, sending it crashing to the floor beside him, and several items rolled out. He was on top now, able to pull back a little from his opponent's grip, but she still held on tight. He increased the pressure of his hands around her throat until her eyes swam with color.

She struggled to speak, fear emanating from violet eyes and tears running down both sides of her face. Jake let out a cry of anguish, realizing he was killing Nyla, not the black-eyed bastard who'd possessed her. He immediately released his grip, and the black eyes returned as she raised the upper half of her body to attack him.

She fit her mouth to his neck, sinking all of her teeth into his flesh. Crying out in pain, he tried to push her off of him, but she wouldn't budge. She was attached to him by her teeth.

Out of the corner of his eye, he saw a small bottle on the floor, which had rolled from his gym bag, highlighted by a ray of sunlight streaming through a crack in the window blinds. He grabbed for the sports bottle as Nyla continued to gnaw through his neck, and opened it with his thumb.

"Take this, you bloodsucking bastard," he said from between teeth clenched in pain as he pulled himself as far away from Nyla's mouth as he could get and raised the bottle above the spot where they were joined. He let the holy water pour between them, aiming to get as much as possible inside her mouth.

She hissed in pain, breaking away from his neck, a small chunk of his flesh still in her mouth. He fought down the bile threatening to escape him and poured the holy water down her open mouth, holding her body as she struggled against him.

Her cries changed from rage to agony, switching from masculine to feminine, as he effectively exorcised the beast from her body. She let out a howl of pain and began to shiver on all fours, tears streaming down her face. Thankfully, Jake could no longer feel a trace of the evil darkness Demarcus had brought into the room with him.

"You're all right now, baby. He's gone," Jake assured her as he grabbed the sheet from the bed and wrapped her in it, trying to ward off the tremors wracking her body.

Nyla gagged, spitting out the chunk of flesh she'd torn from his body, and looked at it in horror. Her face paled as she realized what she'd done, and she tore out of Jake's embrace, running toward the bathroom with her hand over her mouth. The bathroom door slammed behind her and Jake gave her privacy as he heard her retching.

Warm blood dripped down his chest, but he didn't want to barge in on her while she recuperated in the bathroom, so he grabbed the T-shirt he'd taken off of her earlier and used it to wipe away the blood, balling it up against his wound. He sat on the edge of the bed, a hundred questions running through his mind.

How in hell had Demarcus gotten inside Nyla? Possession was a very rare skill, and although many fictional accounts suggested it, not many vampires could play mind tricks. And when it came to mind tricks, possession was the biggest, baddest bitch of them all. He doubted that even Seta could pull off a possession, and she was a born witch.

Of all the possession cases he'd ever heard of, the possessor was invited inside the host or had some sort of mental or blood tie. A tie similar to the bond between a fledgling vampire and its sire. Extremely powerful vampires could get inside a person's mind if they'd recently drank of their blood, but a full-on possession was stretching that theory a little thin. So what had just happened?

He glanced at the bathroom door, listening to the sound of running water, and nibbled on his bottom lip. He was probably bleeding heavily, but he needed to make sure Nyla was doing well before tending to himself.

"Nyla? Are you all right in there?" he called.

Her answer came in the form of a shaky, somewhat affirmative grunt, followed shortly after by more retching. He glanced at the glob of flesh still lying on the floor and quickly turned his head away before he vomited himself.

He needed to clean the wound, and judging by the size of the disgusting chunk of flesh lying on the floor, it was going to be one big, nasty bitch of a wound too. "Just what I need," he muttered, rising from the bed. Figuring Nyla wouldn't want to be barged in on while she heaved up what sounded like everything she'd eaten for the past week, he walked over to the spilled contents of his gym bag, looking inside to see what he had to work with. He grabbed a bottle of holy water and a package of antiseptic wipes and took them over to the dresser.

Standing before the mirror which hung over the dresser, he held the balled up T-shirt firmly against his wound, delaying the moment of truth. He wasn't the type to faint at the sight of blood, or vomit at the sight of it, for that matter, but when a chunk of meat was bitten out of your neck, the damage couldn't be anything but utterly disgusting. He had a feeling the wound, which didn't hurt that much at the moment, was going to hurt like hell once he saw the actual damage.

Taking a deep breath and letting it out slowly, he removed the wadded-up shirt to inspect the damage . . . and felt his heart come to a screeching halt as he took in what he saw in the mirror.

NYLA CONTINUED TO heave, although she'd ejected the complete contents of her stomach several minutes before. She'd never gotten sick from human blood before, but she'd never ripped away flesh. She'd practically tried to eat Jake! She knew she'd been possessed and unable to control her body, but she still felt the horror of it, the shame of doing something so vile.

She rinsed her mouth with water from the tap, wondering how she was going to face Jake after what she'd done to him. Tearing his neck open wasn't even the worst part. She'd brought Demarcus to him, and the bastard had nearly revealed her secrets to him. Jake wasn't stupid. He knew about possessions, and, more damningly, he knew about the relationship between sire and fledgling. He had to be wondering if what Demarcus had said was true. The only thing saving her now was her ability to walk in daylight, but it wouldn't take long for Jake to put two and two together and know she was really a vampire.

Maybe it would be for the best if he did, she conceded, thinking back over what had just happened. If Demarcus had gotten inside her once, there was a possibility he could do it again, even though she would work twice as hard to keep her mental blocks in place. She couldn't take the chance of letting the psycho control her body again, using her to hurt Jake. Although it would break her heart, she'd rather Jake leave her than die trying to protect her. She was the one Demarcus wanted. Jake was just gravy.

She looked in the mirror, decided there wasn't much she could do about her green pallor, and allowed herself a moment of meditation. Deciding her stomach was as calm as it was going to get, and knowing Jake was either worried sick or ready to fire away a dozen or more questions which she could only hope of having good answers for, she turned for the door. Nyla took a deep breath, knowing the next few minutes would either seal or destroy her relationship with Jake.

After opening the door, her eyes immediately fell to the spot on the floor where she had recently spit out a meaty chunk of Jake's neck. She was relieved to find it had been cleaned up. The last thing she needed was a visual reminder of what she'd done to the man she loved.

Jake sat at the small table, staring at the screen of his laptop, a deep frown line bisecting the smooth skin of his forehead. When he raised his eyes to acknowledge her presence, they were filled with chilling accusation. "You feel better now?"

"Yes," she answered weakly, wishing her voice didn't shake so badly. It made her sound guilty, and that wasn't the impression she needed to make.

"So what the hell just happened, Nyla?"

"Someone possessed me," she answered, a ball of dread forming in her gut. Something was wrong, and she suspected she wouldn't find out what until she stepped right into it. "The vampire who changed all these people."

"The vampire who killed Bobby."

"Yes. That's what he said." She chewed her bottom lip, wishing she knew words that could take away Jake's pain from hearing the awful things Demarcus had told him. "I'm sorry."

"You killed Niles," he pressed on.

She shrugged, not wanting to reveal too much information. "Maybe so. I don't always know the names of the vampires I kill."

Jake sat back in the chair, one hand rotating a switchblade, the other holding a wadded up T-shirt to his neck. He'd gotten dressed while she was in the bathroom, right down to the black boots and leather shoulder holster, although the look in his eyes was far more dangerous than any weapon he could have holstered. It cut into her far deeper than the knife in his hand would have, and she had the feeling he was thinking of putting that comparison to the test. "When did you meet him?"

"Who?" she asked, knowing that playing stupid wouldn't help, but she couldn't think fast enough for a good answer. Fear kept her brain from functioning at full capacity, and standing before him in nothing but a thin bedsheet tied tightly under her arms made her feel extremely vulnerable, especially when he was dressed to kill. Literally.

"You know who, Nyla! When did you meet Demarcus?"

"I don't—"

"Don't do it, Nyla. Don't *lie* to me," he yelled, rising from his seat to stand before her. "You know him. He couldn't have gotten inside you otherwise. You've been acting strange since we met, which means you've been fighting him off this whole time. When did he claim you?"

"Jake, I'm not what you think I am."

"Oh, really? Explain this then!" He removed his makeshift bandage, throwing the T-shirt across the room to reveal smooth, unmarred skin where there should have been a deep wound. "And before you try to conjure up some excuse for this, I know that the only physical changes which take place during a possession are voice, facial expression and eye color. You have healing properties in your saliva, and there's only one way to get that. When we had sex in my car, I was sure you'd bitten me, but there were no teeth marks, so I decided it was my imagination. Now I know that I was right. You did bite me. You had the nerve to *drink* from me!"

"I didn't drink from you! I know how you feel about that, and I would never—"

"Oh, that's considerate of you. You lie to me, screw me in the ugliest sense of the word, and protect that evil son of a bitch."

"I have never protected him! I've been protecting you all along!"

Jake threw his head back and laughed, a sound full of humorless anger. "By toying with me? I poured my heart out to you, trusted you in a way I've never trusted anyone, and you're just a filthy bloodsucker! Tell me, how does it feel to be that big of a heartless bitch?"

"Jake . . ." Nyla fumbled for something to say, something that could make everything right, but couldn't think of words and fight back tears at the same time. "I'm the same person I was an hour ago. Everything I've done, I've done to keep you safe."

"Save the lies, Nyla. You've been hiding this monster from me, knowing that for the past sixteen years of my life I've wanted nothing more than to kill him. And you're a . . . a . . . what the hell are you?"

"I'm not a vampire," she said through a sob, as her tears broke free. "You've seen me walk in daylight for extended lengths of time without any sunscreen."

He frowned, studying her. "That's true, and that's the only thing that's thrown me off thus far, but you have a mind link to that sick freak, and your saliva heals. What are you? What connection do you have to that monster?"

"He bit me, years ago," she admitted, no longer seeing any advantage in denying a connection. "I wasn't changed over in the normal way. I never drank from him. He bit me one time and passed along some of his . . . traits."

"So you're some kind of half-breed?" Jake asked, turning up his nose in distaste while scrutinizing her with hate-filled eyes.

Nyla turned her face away, unable to bear seeing the disgust in his eyes, and retrieved clothes from her duffel bag on the floor. "Yeah, something like that," she answered as she quickly dressed.

"I don't buy it. No one known to man has ever turned vampire by just a bite."

"I didn't turn full vampire. I gained traits."

"Do you drink blood? Do you have the thirst?"

She sat on the edge of the bed and kept her eyes trained on the boots she pulled onto her feet, not wanting to see his revulsion. The sound of it in his tone was demeaning enough. "Yes, but I can't help what I am, Jake. I didn't ask for any of this, just like you didn't ask to be what you are."

"A hunter? Believe me, sweetheart, I chose what I am. As far as I'm concerned, the greatest job in the world is killing bloodsuckers."

"You're not just a hunter, Jake. You're a slayer," she advised him, raising her eyes to meet his gaze, fresh anger squashing her moment of shame. "And a slayer isn't a normal human being. You're an outcast, just like me. Just like the people you hunt!"

His eyes darkened, both nostrils flaring as he tightened his grip on the switchblade. "Don't ever insult me like that again. I'm nothing like the things I hunt!"

"No, you're not, because if you knew what I was you would have killed me the moment we met, and that makes me just a little bit better than you." She walked past him, her heart threatening to crumble as she headed toward the door, knowing she was walking out of his life.

"Where the hell do you think you're going?" Jake clamped a hand around her arm and wrenched her back, nearly causing her to fall. "You can't just put me through hell and leave."

"Put you through hell? How have I done that?"

"You conned me, Nyla, and you did a damn good job of it too, but you're not getting away with it. You're leading me to Demarcus."

"No!"

"Yes! You claim you love me, so prove it."

"I've been proving it for sixteen years!"

Jake's mouth dropped open, his eyes growing wide in shock as he loosened his grip on her arm and stepped away. Nyla realized her mistake too late and felt her heart race with the onset of panic. She tried to think of a way to take back what she'd said, or say something to throw Jake off, but she came up with nothing.

"Just how long had you been following me before we met outside The Crimson Rose?"

"A while."

"Sixteen years?"

Nyla looked away, not wanting to answer, knowing once she did it would all come together.

"That freak was telling the truth. You were there that night. You were one of his minions—"

"No!" Nyla's head jerked up to face him before he could complete the horrid accusation. "I was never his anything. I'd never even seen him before that night!"

Jake's face reddened, the muscles in his arms bunching as he tightened his hands into fists. "You're telling me you were there the night Bobby died, and you expect me to believe you weren't on Demarcus's side?"

"Yes! I'd never be on the side of anyone that evil! I was sent there to protect you!"

"By who?"

"The Dream Teller!"

Jake stumbled backwards, his mouth agape. "The Dream Teller? The old blind woman in my dreams is in yours too?"

"Yes," she answered, surprised to hear Jake had also been visited by the old woman.

"Bullshit! I don't know how you know about that, but it's a lie! All of it!"

"Jake, I'm telling you the truth! I was sent to protect you that night, and that's exactly what I did!"

"How the hell do you expect to convince me of that? I remember everything about that night, Nyla, and everyone I encountered in that alley. There was Demarcus and his three minions, Niles, Lionel and Detra. Bobby died, and nobody jumped in to save him! Nobody jumped in to save me, either, except for an alley cat who jumped in the psycho's face. If anyone protected me that night, it was . . ." His voice trailed off as he looked at Nyla with a mixture of realization and denial. "No. You can't be . . ."

"I've watched over you for sixteen years, Jake, and I've been in love with you for the last eight of them."

"No." He stepped backward, seeming to want to escape. He was so desperate to get away from her, away from the truth that he didn't watch where he was going and backed into the small table, almost stumbling. "You can't be Alley. I'd sense lycanthropy."

"I'm not a lycanthrope. I'm a therian, pantherian, actually."

"What the hell is that?"

"We're a purely female race of people who can shift form, but only if we survive a ritual we're subjected to during infancy. My true animal form is the panther, but I can also take on the appearance of a small, black cat."

"No," Jake said, shaking his head vigorously. "You can't be my pet alley cat."

"I was sent to that alley sixteen years ago to protect you, Jake. After you ran I shifted to panther form and attacked the vampires. Demarcus bit me, somehow passing on some of his vampiric traits in a single bite. He is, in a way, my sire, and he can get inside my mind and, apparently, if he tries hard enough, my body. I've been fighting him off for sixteen years."

She tried to approach Jake, but he continued backing away, moving away from her until his back hit the wall. "All these years when I've been talking to my pet cat, I've really been talking to you?"

"Yes."

"And you rode with me from Baltimore to Louisville? You faked the stolen car, the other motel room, everything?"

"Yes."

"And when we . . . oh, man, I thought it was bad that I'd slept with a vampire, but I . . . *I fucked a cat?* There are laws against that! People go to the frigging loony bin for doing nasty stuff like that!"

"I'm not an animal, Jake. It's just a form my body can take."

"But you're a cat!"

"Jake, you made love to a woman, to me."

"No, I screwed a damn cat! And you let me! Hell, you didn't even give me much choice that first time in the car. You just jumped on me like a damn . . . cat in heat. Oh, that's just so twisted it's almost funny. You were in heat, weren't you? I guess you have nine lives too."

She flinched, his words hurting far worse than she'd been prepared for. "Just one—one which has been devoted to you for sixteen years."

"Save it, lady, or . . . whatever the hell you are," he snapped. "You conned me. Love isn't about lies."

"Is it about turning your back on someone when you discover something about them you don't like?" she countered, anger and desperation making her tone sharp. She was losing him, and at the moment, she didn't know whether to be mad at him or beg him to stay. "You said you loved me an hour ago, and I know you meant it. Now, just because I can shift form, you're taking it all back? I help you through the aftermath of the killer you become when your hunter rage takes you over. Why can't you see me through my abilities?"

"How do you expect me to?" he asked, incredulously. "You've lied to me since day one. Even now, I don't know what's real or make-believe."

"I couldn't tell you what I was. You'd have killed me on the spot, and you know it." Fresh tears slid down her face as she clasped her hands together, praying for the right words to fix the damage her avoidance of the truth had done. "I understand there is a lot of evil in the world, but you let your prejudice label us all bad without any consideration that we might be different. Demarcus is evil, yes, and he deserves to be killed, but Seta and Christian—and most of all, me—we've done nothing but try to help you."

"It figures you'd take up for your friends." He glared at her as his nostrils flared.

"Yes, I consider Seta a friend." She threw her hands in the air, wishing Jake could get past his blind hatred and distrust of the entire vampire species. "If I ever get to meet Christian, I'm sure he'll be a friend too, but Demarcus has never been a friend. I killed Niles because he hurt you. I've fought against evil with you more times than you could imagine over these past sixteen years. My life has been devoted to protecting you."

"If that's true, why have you been protecting Demarcus?" His glare grew hotter.

"I've been protecting *you*. I've seen inside Demarcus's mind, and I know the evil that lies there. I don't want you near it. It's me that he wants. I'm the one he set the trap for. You just got swept up in it. This is my fight."

"No." He shook his head hard, and his jaw clenched tight.

"Jake, just leave here. Let me deal with Demarcus. Please," she added, voice cracking.

"You've been able to find him all along, but you've let him live. Why should I trust you now? You didn't even save Bobby!"

"I know," she admitted, lowering her gaze to the floor, feeling the shame deep in her heart. "I should have moved quicker. I can't apologize enough for my failure."

With a rush of speed, Jake barreled into her, knocking her to the floor before she could react. Her head hit the floorboards, sending a burst of stars shooting before her eyes. Her vision cleared, and she saw him kneeling over her body, using one hand to pin her down while the other held the opened switchblade, poised for attack. "Jake, don't do this," she pleaded, gazing helplessly into his crazed eyes.

"You let Bobby die," he growled, his voice full of rage. "You let that sick bastard inside you, and I could have been killed while trying not to hurt you. You lied to me. You made me care about you, knowing how I feel about what you are." He growled the words out while his eyes smoldered in rage.

"Jake, please." She could buck beneath him, throw him off, but she didn't want to fight him. She knew it would be a fight to the death, and she couldn't kill the man she'd loved for more than a decade of her life. Not even if it was to save her own life. "Please, Jake. *Please.*"

He brought the knife down in an arc, letting out a roar of pain-filled fury, and Nyla forced herself to remain still. She would willingly die if it would bring him peace, but she knew he'd never find peace if he spent the rest of his life knowing he'd killed the woman he loved. So she put her faith in him and prayed that love would stop his hand in time. She gasped in relief as the blade dug into the floorboard beside her, and even though he wiped viciously at his eyes, a tear fell upon her face.

"I can't even kill you!" he cried, his voice thick with anger as he stood and backed away from her.

"Jake . . ."

She didn't get to say anything else because he fled the room, silent tears falling like hot rain down the sides of his face.

Hours later, she sat on the bed with her knees pulled to her chest, arms wrapped tight around them, wondering if Jake would ever return. She knew she'd hurt him, despite her best intentions, and he'd probably never again look at her with love in his eyes, but she didn't want their relationship to end with such an awful experience. He'd tried to kill her. She didn't want that to be the last memory for either of them.

She heard footsteps just outside the room and leaped off the bed and ran to the door, throwing it open. She gasped in surprise as a beaten and bloody Peewee slumped against the doorframe.

"Peewee! How did you escape?"

"Where's Jake?" His voice came out as a rusty rasp.

"He left. How did you get here?"

"I'm sorry, Nyla."

"Sorry for what?" An alarm bell rang in her mind, but the warning came too late as she felt the prick of a needle in her side.

"He said I had to do this, or he'd kill me," Peewee said, catching her falling body as she toppled forward, darkness closing in around her.

Chapter Twenty-Two

"SETA."

The vampiress opened her eyes to find herself in a forest filled with warm, earthy hues of green, brown and orange. Leaves danced in the breeze, their soundtrack provided by brightly colored birds. Above her, the golden sun was large and magnificent. She stood in one of its rays, wrapping herself in its warmth, a pleasure she hadn't experienced in far too long.

"It must feel wonderful to embrace the warmth of the sun without fear after all these centuries."

"Yes, it does," she responded to the blind, platinum-eyed witch standing before her. While it was true that not all vampires immediately burst into flame once the sun touched their skin, they could still burn to death if they remained in its presence for too long. She knew that in this realm, however, the sun would not harm her, no matter how long she basked in its warmth and beauty. "It's been a long time since you've brought me into your realm, Dream Teller. I don't recall it being so warm and beautiful the last time."

"You were afraid of the truth the last time you were here. You've changed over the last century. You don't scare easily."

"So that's why this realm is all sunshine and rainbows now?"

"The realm reflects what it finds inside you. You're strong, Seta, which is why I've summoned you here. Something has happened."

"What?" Seta asked, noticing a cloud move past the sun as trepidation crept inside her. She immediately thought of Eron, where he lay healing beneath the earth in Baltimore, and feared for his life.

"Eron is fine," the Dream Teller said, reading her mind. "Your son is perfectly capable of protecting both him and Aria. Right now, they are not the ones being threatened. Jacob and Nyla are."

"Are you saying what I think you're saying?" she asked, curiosity replacing her fear.

"Yes. They are part of the Blood Revelation."

Seta crossed her arms and cocked her head, studying the ancient witch. She didn't appear to be joking. "Correct me if I'm wrong, but doesn't the Blood Revelation state vampires will save the world from the ultimate evil?"

"That is correct."

"If Jacob Porter is turned into a vampire, he'll go mad."

"Most likely."

"So how can he be a part of the Blood Revelation? If Nyla changes him over—"

"Nyla won't change him over. She couldn't, even if she wanted to. She's not pure."

"I hope you're not suggesting that I change him over."

"No one is changing Jacob Porter over."

"Then how—"

"You will see in time. Right now, there is a more pressing matter. Nyla has been captured by her sire, Demarcus."

"I thought that beastly rogue was dead."

"Interesting term you've chosen. He is far more beastly than you recall."

"He is the fur-covered vampire whom I saw in my vision," Seta said, suddenly understanding what she'd seen. "He passed along vampire traits to Nyla, and in return, she passed along feline traits to him."

"Yes."

"Serves him right," she said with a chuckle, enjoying the man's misfortune.

"It is not so funny, Seta. He has grown madder. Nyla is a genetic carrier of a feline disease. It's a recessive gene in her bloodline, and if she has children, it will be recessive in them and their children, et cetera. But when Demarcus bit her, he somehow contracted it as a full-blown disease, and he is steadily growing more dangerous because of it. The fever is affecting his brain."

"So you need me to kill him before he can harm Nyla?"

"No. Jacob Porter must save Nyla. It is his destiny."

"It's a slayer's destiny to save a shifter-vampire hybrid and have a child with her?" Seta asked in disbelief.

"Yes. Like your grandchild, their child will be one of the three who will be charged with saving this world from Satan's wrath."

"So why did Aria have to be changed over if Jacob doesn't have to be?"

The blind witch smiled. "Everything will be revealed in time."

"Why can't you just be straight with people when they're brought here?" Seta snapped, her voice elevating with irritation. "You always make everything so mysterious. Just tell me straight out what is going to happen."

"It is not the way, little witch. You know that."

"Yes, I know it. My baby was ripped away from me because of it!"

"You got him back. As for what is going to happen, I cannot tell you everything because no one knows the future. The chosen must follow their hearts to fulfill fate's design, and only time will tell if their hearts will lead them to fulfill their destinies. It is the way fate works."

Seta expelled a hot, angry breath, balling her burnt, but fortunately not aching, hands into fists and placed them on her hips. "Fine. So why am I here if I'm not supposed to kill Demarcus? What am I supposed to do?"

"Give Jacob guidance. He has discovered what Nyla is, and he has run from her. He's confused."

"A slayer in love with a pantherian vampire? I'd say confused is an understatement. How am I supposed to guide him? He hates my kind, remember?"

"During your battle, while your energy was waning, you were nearly attacked by a charging vampire. Jacob swung his sword just in time to save you. He followed his instincts, and his instincts have always been to protect the innocent. On a deeper level, he knows you aren't evil. And he knows Nyla isn't evil. He tried to kill her, but he couldn't do it."

The witch stepped forward, reaching out for Seta's hand. She ran her own leathery, wrinkled hands along the skin of Seta's burned arms. Electrically charged magic crackled between them as she healed the burns, returning Seta's skin to the flawless beauty it had always been. "This should help you."

"Thank you, Dream Teller."

"It is my duty as your guide to protect you and lead you in the right direction."

"With only the bare minimum of information."

"It is the way," the old witch said, smiling unapologetically.

"So, what am I to do with Jacob Porter?"

"Find him, set him straight, and then send him to me. I have important information for him, but I cannot get him to fall asleep."

"Well, I don't know if I can set him straight, but I can definitely put him to sleep."

"Seta . . ." the witch said, her tone full of warning.

"Oh, don't worry. I'm not going to euthanize the poor bastard," she assured the older woman, adding with impishness, "Killing someone painlessly just isn't my style."

"JACOB."

Jake raised his head and swiped at dried tears that had left sticky tracks on his skin. "Go away, Seta. I'm not in the mood for you right now."

"Too bad. You can finish licking your wounds like a beaten mongrel later. Right now, we need to talk."

"Look, lady . . ." Jake abruptly stopped speaking, noticing how the vampire-witch stood before him in broad daylight with smooth, unburnt skin covering her recently fried hands and arms. The electric buzz of power crackled around her. "How in hell . . ."

"The Dream Teller healed my burns, and I'm not really here. I'm astrally projecting myself."

"Just what the world needs, a vampire who can be in two places at one time," he responded with disgust. He sat on the hood of his car and leaned back against the windshield. He'd driven away from the motel as fast as he could, no real destination in mind, until he'd reached the point he couldn't see through his own film of tears and had to pull over in the woods. Then he'd climbed out of the car and perched on the hood, crying more tears than he'd shed in his entire life. He hadn't felt so much loss since the night he saw his best friend die before him.

"Quit sulking, Jacob."

"Stay out of my mind," he warned the vampiress, wondering why she could read his thoughts so easily when he'd always seemed to be immune to vampire mind intrusion.

"You are immune to vampire mind intrusion, and tricks, for that matter," Seta said, as though he'd asked the question aloud. "Slayers are born with that measure of defense, but since I mean you no harm—and since we're all a part of something bigger than us—I've been allowed access to your psyche."

"What the hell are you talking about?"

"You're a slayer, Jacob. That means that you are not a normal mortal man, and you shouldn't hold it against Nyla that she isn't a normal mortal woman. The two of you are more alike than you realize."

"I'm *not* an animal," he snarled.

"Nor is Nyla. It's just a form she takes on. I saw you battle the vampires the other night. I could say you're a bloodthirsty killer, but would that be true?"

"I'm a hunter," Jake said defensively.

"No, you're a slayer. You possess the psychic ability to sense and read supernatural beings. Along with that ability, you carry a darkness inside you far worse than the darkness inside vampires. Our darkness comes from fear, survival instinct, and the loneliness of existing for decades in the shadows. Your darkness is born of pure, cold hatred. You're like a ticking bomb, but Nyla counters the darkness inside you. She's an empath, and she was sent to you the night that your friend was killed because the elders knew you would make a mighty warrior for the side of good, but only if you could control your darkness."

Jake started to deny everything the vampiress said, but knew in his heart there was a grain of truth to it. Whether in cat or human form, just the slightest touch from Nyla seemed to drain his violent urges. And he knew he'd reached the brink of madness many times before, only to have been brought back after talking with Nyla in one of her forms, of touching her in some way. "You make me sound like the things I hunt."

"Because you are. Slayers are supernatural beings, just as vampires, shifters, and witches are. And you have the potential to be far more dangerous than any of us. So far, the only thing that has stopped you from becoming the true beast you were designed to be is Nyla's love and her empathic ability. You need her. And right now, she needs you."

"She can defend herself, believe me."

"Perhaps, but you're supposed to be bonded."

"What does that mean?"

"The Dream Teller will tell you more, but basically, Nyla was sent to you to keep you on the side of good so you can fight with us in an oncoming war between the supernatural forces of good and evil."

Jake blinked in surprise. "Fight *with* you? The vampires?"

"Most of us are good, Jacob. You've just had the misfortune of meeting some truly horrific ones."

"Yeah, and I had the pleasure of killing them. It's what I do, Seta. It's what's inside me. I can't change that, and I proved that tonight. I almost killed Nyla."

"Almost is the key word." She smiled. "You failed because your heart knew it would be wrong. There's still goodness inside you, and Nyla will help you hold on to it."

Jake shook his head, not seeing how the things the vampiress was telling him could be true. His whole life he had felt different, and he knew there was something inside him that wasn't normal, something dark that shouldn't be there. Now Seta had confirmed it, and he felt completely out of control.

"You can still be a good man, Jacob. You can love, which is unusual for a slayer. It's why you were chosen."

"I don't believe in all this destiny crap you're spouting," Jake bit out in irritation. He needed answers, not a bunch of warm and fuzzy Hallmark card crud about fate, love, and destiny.

"Then I suggest you start, because it believes in you," the vampiress stated sternly. "Rialto, Aria, me—we were all fated to be what we are, and you are fated to be a warrior, not just a bloodthirsty slayer. You only have to follow your heart, and destiny will guide you the rest of the way."

Jake raised an eyebrow as he studied the vampire-witch. "Do you know how weird that inspirational stuff sounds coming from you?"

Seta's eyes narrowed briefly before she gave in to the quirk flexing at the side of her full lips, allowing herself a small grin. "I'm not completely ruthless, Jacob, and I know how all of this must sound, but it's true. Over a century ago I went over a cliff and landed in the arms of a vampire. I allowed him to sire me so I could watch over my son, who'd been taken from me by his father."

"You're talking about Rialto?"

"Yes. Then, twenty-eight years to the day after I went over that cliff, I sired my own son in order to save his life. Over a century later he found his mate, setting in motion a prediction that was made over a millennium ago. I was sired so I could sire Rialto, when his time came. And he was changed over so he could be here to sire Aria when it was her time."

"I hope you're not saying I'm supposed to become one of you," Jake said, his heart threatening to burst from his chest. He didn't exactly fear vampires, but becoming one of them was something totally different. He recalled the feel of Christian's fangs sinking into his neck and reflexively tightened his hands into fists, ready to fight Seta. All his hunter instincts for self-preservation were on full alert. He knew he couldn't be changed over by a vampire's astral projection, and Seta was the only vampire he sensed in the immediate area, but he still couldn't override his instincts.

"None of us are going to try to turn you, Jacob. Frankly, we don't think you would survive it without going mad."

"So if I'm not going to be changed over, what's all this mumbo jumbo about me being destined to fight with you?"

"You'll find out in time, as we all have. You must go to the dream realm now. The Dream Teller has been trying to bring you to her, and she sent me here to make sure you go to her."

"I don't have time to sleep. Those freaks have my cousin, and I have to get him back." He slid off the car's hood, ready to go look for his cousin.

"I'm sorry, but I have orders," the vampiress said, letting power build around her before blowing him a kiss.

Before Jake had time to ask the vampire-witch what she was up to, he found himself standing in the bitter cold of the dream realm, slivers of pale blue light slicing through the silvery trees surrounding him.

"Son of a bitch. Seta!" He screamed the vampire's name to no avail. She'd put him to sleep, but she hadn't come with him, he realized as cold wind whipped around his body. "Dream Teller!" he then yelled. He waited for a response, but none came. *"Dammit!* Let me out of here! I have lives to save!"

After several minutes passed, he realized the whistling wind was the closest thing he was going to get to an answer. He strained to hear any indication that the Dream Teller was near, but the only sounds he picked up belonged to nature. Muttering a choice selection of curses, he began walking, having no idea where he was going, but it beat standing in one spot with his thumbs in his pockets waiting for something to happen.

"If I don't get to my cousin in time because of this little game you're play-ing, Dream Teller, you're gonna regret the day you met me," he vowed as he marched on.

He cleared the forest, coming upon a large rock wall. "What's this?" he asked aloud, gazing toward the sky. The formation seemed to go on forever, farther than the naked eye could see.

A sense of familiarity, warm and inviting, came over him, and he closed his eyes, trying to decipher what he was picking up on. Warmth, security, love—home. "Nyla," he whispered, realizing she was here, somewhere close to him.

He felt himself being pulled toward her, as if tied to the end of an invisible rope, and his pace quickened when he gave in to the tugging sensation. Then anxiousness suddenly mounted inside him, and he broke into a full-out run. He didn't know if he'd ever be able to fully digest the truths he'd discovered about Nyla, but he still cared for her safety, and his gut was telling him she was in danger. He needed to get to her, needed to do whatever the Dream Teller wanted so she would release them from the dream realm.

The stone wall began to curve, and Jake careened around the bend, desperate to find Nyla and a way out of the realm. As he rounded the corner, he realized the ground was suddenly ending, and he skidded to a stop, nearly toppling over the edge of a cliff.

He bit out a curse as he held on to a jagged rock for balance and leaned forward, taking in the hundred foot drop. "I am so kicking somebody's ass before I get out of here," he muttered before straightening back up and trying to dislodge his heart from his throat.

He felt the pull again, the unmistakable presence of the woman who'd completely turned him inside out in only a few days time, and followed it. Finally, he came upon a dark tunnel, the entrance cleverly hidden among the stones forming the large mountain.

It started out narrow, but widened as he traveled down its length, eventually opening into a large, circular space lit with torches. And there, sitting on the ground with her knees drawn to her chin, was the woman he'd confessed his love to and nearly killed in the same day.

"So, are you really here in the realm with me, or are you a part of my dream?"

"Which answer would make it easier for you to kill me?" she questioned, the sadness in her voice far more cutting than her words.

"I'm sorry about that. I kind of lost it for a moment there."

"Well, at least you have the decency to apologize. Where's the Dream Teller? I'm ready to go."

"Haven't seen her." He inched closer to Nyla, slowly and awkwardly, afraid any sudden movements would scare her off.

"You don't have to creep up on me, Porter. I'm not in panther form. I'm not going to attack you."

Jake let out a frustrated breath, torn between soothing her hurt feelings and defending himself. He'd said hurtful things to her. He knew that, but she'd deceived him. Surely she had to realize a man needed time to come to grips with what she'd thrown at him. "Nyla, I'm not trying to treat you like an . . . an . . ."

"Animal. You can say it, Porter. The cat's out of the bag, no pun intended."

"Nyla."

"*What?*"

Jake jumped from the ferociousness she'd put into that single word and tried to think of something to say to calm her. He gazed down at her, taking in the oddly fragile way she held her knees to her chest, the mixture of sadness and anger swirling in her deep violet eyes. She'd always looked so strong, and it hurt him that he'd made her feel this way. He looked into those eyes, which had watched over him for the past sixteen years, and saw the evidence of recent tears. He couldn't help feeling like an ass, even though his anger had been based on Nyla's deception.

He lowered himself to the ground, sitting before the woman who'd thrown his world into a tailspin and really looked at her. He took in the angelic face, the eyes which seemed to see right into his soul, and the body which set his aflame, and he realized he had no clue what he was going to do about her. As wrong as it should be, he still cared for her.

"Nyla, I don't know what to say to you. I've never felt this way about another woman, but you dropped a bombshell on me. I look at you, how beautiful and great you are, and I want to hold you. Then I remember all the times I've held my pet cat, and now that I know I was really holding you, I just can't wrap my mind around that."

"Then don't. I'm not worth it."

"What the hell are you talking about?"

"I love you, Jacob, but I don't want you anymore."

His mouth fell open, a small sound of disbelief slipping out at the same time a sharp jab of pain speared his heart. For the second time that day, he felt his heart breaking.

"You don't know who I really am, Jake, and believe me, you wouldn't want the real me. So let's just get the hell out of here and move on with our lives." She raised herself from the ground and turned her back to him, walking a few steps away before Jake was able to scramble up and grab her elbow, turning her around to face him.

"Wait a minute. What are you talking about? I know the shifter and vampire stuff now. And yes, I know you were sired by the bastard who killed my friend, but I'm not holding that against you. I don't know if you and I can be a couple, but you sound as if you want away from me for good."

"You tried to kill me, Jake. Why do you care whether or not you ever see me again?"

"Because, whether or not I knew what you were before now, you're my best friend. In fact, you're the only friend I have. And maybe eventually we can be . . ." Jake let his voice trail off, confused by his emotions. Part of him wanted to declare his love for her, but the logical part of him kept seeing her as a cat, and he just couldn't get past that.

"You don't know everything about me, Jake. If you did, you could have never looked at me the way you looked at me this morning, and if I can't see love in your eyes, then I don't want to see you at all."

"What don't I know about you? You're a vampire and a shifter."

"I'm also a whore."

"Come again?" he said, not expecting that kind of declaration.

"I've been with a lot of men, Jake. Pantherians serve a queen, and she commands her servants to have sex often and indiscriminately, since it's so hard for us to get pregnant, and she wants the race to continue."

"And you did this until sixteen years ago?"

"Yes." Her voice cracked, tugging at his heart.

"But you haven't since the night you . . . met me?"

She looked away, her bottom lip quivering as she spoke. "I've been away from my family for the past sixteen years, but I haven't been a much better person. I dealt with the Heat the best I could, and the best I could meant I grabbed random men off the street when the need arose."

Images of Nyla wrapped around the bodies of assorted men entered Jake's mind, and he reflexively balled his hands into fists. "Why are you telling me this?"

"You should know who you've developed feelings for."

"So out of the blue, you just blurt out that you sleep around when in heat?" he said, starting to realize what she was doing. "What's really going on?"

"Nothing," she answered, but the desperation in her eyes gave her away.

"You're going after Demarcus alone! Forget about it. I'll take care of Demarcus"

"It's not your fight!" Her eyes darkened with determination.

"He killed my friend!"

"Bobby's dead, Jake. No matter what you do, he's not coming back, so just go. Let me take care of Demarcus. *I'm* the one he wants."

"And *I'm* the one he's going to get."

"No! Bobby is gone, and you can't do anything for him now. Today you decided that you don't love me, so defending me isn't an excuse for you to get mixed up in this. Besides, I can take care of myself."

"You're protecting me," Jake murmured in sudden understanding. "Even after I attacked you in rage, you're protecting me, just as you've done all these years. Why are you so scared for me?"

"Jake, just go away, and let me take care of this."

"Why? I fight vampires all the time."

"This isn't just any vampire." She licked her lips. "This is Demarcus, the vampire who killed your friend, and he is pure evil."

"So he's evil, and he killed my friend. I'm not going to piss myself like I did when I was twelve, Nyla."

"I know that. You're going to go after him, too mad to think, and get yourself killed!"

"No, I'm not!"

"Yes, you are," she yelled. "I've already seen it happen!"

"What?" Jake asked, taken aback.

"It was just a feeling at first," Nyla explained, lowering her voice to a normal tone, "but I've had a vision. You're going to die if you go up against Demarcus."

"Since when do you have visions?"

"Since the two of you started to form your bond," the Dream Teller said from behind him.

Jake spun around to face the old witch. "It's about time you showed. Why did you bring us here at a time like this? There are innocents in trouble, and they need us."

"I brought you here because I promised Nyla I would explain some things to her when the time was right. That time is now."

"What are you talking about?"

"During one of her visits, I told Nyla that the two of you would discover the truth here. Your destiny is written on these walls." The witch snapped her fingers, and the torches blazed brighter, casting off enough light to show words etched into the walls of the cave.

Jake glanced at Nyla, noting the uneasiness in her stance and the fear in her eyes. "You've already read the walls, haven't you?"

"Yes."

"What do they say that has you so frightened?"

"See for yourself," the Dream Teller answered for her, drawing Jake's attention to one of the walls.

The wall was covered in words from some ancient language, but as he stared at them, they transformed into English. The words may have been easier to read in English, but they were no easier to grasp.

"Three sets of immortals will produce children who will set forth a motion to save the world from the ultimate evil," Jake read aloud, summarizing the lengthy passage the best he could. "One of these children will save the world from Lucifer's wrath." He glanced at the witch. "Vampires are going to have children?"

"Yes," the Dream Teller said. "But as many before you have done, you have misunderstood the wording. There are other types of immortals besides pure vampires."

"Like Nyla?"

"Yes."

Unease coated Jake's stomach, and he gave an anxious wave toward the wall. "Seta said I fit into this somehow."

"You do. You and Nyla are one of the sets."

"I'm not a vampire, and I'm not going to allow myself to be changed into one," Jake said adamantly. "All other immortals are immortal from birth."

"There are other ways to achieve immortality than birth."

"He's going to die," Nyla said, anger making her voice rough. "He's not immortal. He's just a slayer, and he's going to die! I've had the vision, and I've read the words. Read on, Jake."

Jake glanced between the two women, feeling trapped inside the tension formed between them, and continued to read the writing on the wall. The words went on, covering each wall of the cave. He'd journeyed farther into the cave and had gone full circle by the time he found the part which had frightened Nyla.

To save the life of his mate, one of the chosen will have to die a mortal death at the hands of their enemy. The death will save his mate and their child.

"I'm the one who's going to die?"

"Yes," both women answered in unison.

Jake swallowed, feeling Nyla's uneasiness creep inside him. He looked at the old woman. "If my death saves the life of our child, then that means . . ."

"Your child has already been created," the Dream Teller finished.

Jake tried to breathe, but all the air seemed to have escaped the cave. Nyla was pregnant. The woman he'd attempted to kill was carrying his child inside her. "That's impossible. We were only together two times."

"Once is all it takes," the Dream Teller said, a hint of laughter in her tone.

"You know what I mean," he muttered irritably. "Both times were within the last twenty-four hours."

"Pantherians have a difficult time getting pregnant, but once they do, their body has a way of letting the mother know about her condition immediately."

Jake returned his gaze to Nyla. She stood and wrapped her arms around her midsection, looking back at him with a dozen different emotions shining from her eyes. Fear was the most prominent.

"I can't shift," she said, her voice barely above a whisper. "As soon as a pantherian becomes pregnant, we can't shift, not until the child is born."

"My child is growing inside you right now?"

"Yes."

Awe and fear slammed into him at the same time. "Will it be a shifter?"

Nyla's eyes narrowed, and her body faded in and out, like an electronic image dying.

"Nyla? What's happening?"

"They're waking me," she explained, her body fading in and out again. "Don't come for me, Jake. I'll find a way out, despite what these walls say, and I'll raise our child with love, something I don't think you can do."

"Nyla!" Jake ran to her, trying to hold on to her, but his hands went through her body.

"For what it's worth, I'll always love you," she added, fresh tears streaming down her face before disappearing for good.

"What happened?" Jake asked, whirling around to face the Dream Teller. "Did you release her?"

"No. They awakened her."

"Who awakened her? I left her alone at the motel."

"She's been captured. In her pregnant state, she can't shift and escape, and she's been drugged to diminish her physical strength."

"Drugged?" Jake repeated, panic coursing through his veins. "By who? Where is she? What drugs? Will they harm the baby?"

"The baby will be safe—if you save him."

"Him?"

"Nyla is carrying your son, Jacob. She will be the first pantherian to give birth to a male child, but then, she's not your average pantherian, and your son won't be an average child."

"He'll be a shifter too?"

"Does it really matter?" Her tone sounded disapproving.

Jake thought about it. He was going to have a child, a son. Pride swelled in his chest, but then he imagined the boy shifting into a panther, and his emotions became a jumble of confusion.

But confused or not, he wasn't going to let anything happen to Nyla or the child. "Time's wasting. Tell me where she is and let me go, Dream Teller, or pretty soon the answer to that question won't even matter."

"I haven't been given her location, and she doesn't know, either. She was unconscious when Peewee took her from the motel."

"Peewee? That son of a—"

"He had to do it, Jacob. His own life was on the line, and this was fate's design."

"Whatever. I've had about all I can stomach of this fate and destiny crap." He threw his hands into the air. "Let me out of here so I can find Demarcus."

"There is one thing you must know first. You must not kill Curtis Dunn."

"Are you serious? If he hadn't survived the first time, none of this would be happening."

"He is just a puppet for Demarcus. And Alfred, the demon that possesses him, killed the girls, not Curtis."

"They're the same person," he reminded her.

"No, they are two entirely different people sharing the same body. Alfred is the killer. Curtis tried to tell you what was going on by carving the letters on the bodies. It wasn't much, but he did try to help. I've shown him a better way to help. You must let him live so he can do it."

"And what about Alfred? If Curtis lives, Alfred lives."

"Alfred will be dealt with. You must remember that you cannot harm Curtis."

"Fine, whatever." He'd agree to anything if it got him to Nyla quicker. "Just let me go."

"All you have to do is leave the cave."

"*Now* you tell me." Jake turned for the exit, quickly making his way out. He paused at the entrance of the narrow tunnel and turned to face the old witch. "Am I really going to die?"

"Only if you truly love Nyla," the witch answered.

FIFTEEN MINUTES later, the Malibu skidded to a stop outside the motel, and Jake jumped out, gun loaded and ready. The door to his and Nyla's room was ajar, and although he knew the Dream Teller hadn't lied to him, he checked inside the room anyway. He'd hoped his time in the dream realm had been just a dream, not reality, but his hopes were dashed when he called Nyla's name and received no response.

He ran to the next room and banged on the door. "Marilee, it's Jake. Let me in."

He heard a muffled cry from beyond the door.

"Marilee?"

The muffled cry came again, louder, and was joined by another. Maybelline.

Jake kicked in the door to find the willowy, blond teenager and Maybelline gagged and bound together in chairs whose backs had been placed together.

"Where's Bobby?" he asked, removing Marilee's gag.

"Peewee took him," she blurted, eyes wide and wet-rimmed. "He said to tell you Demarcus said it would be just like old times. I'm sorry, Jake. I didn't think Peewee would do this!"

Jake tried to restrain his anger enough to keep his head clear. He had to think of a plan, and quick. Demarcus would be stronger when night fell, and now there was another innocent victim to protect—another victim whose chances of survival diminished with every second.

Maybelline threw herself into his arms and screamed in anguish when he released her from her bindings, intensifying the guilt inside him. He could not let another mother lose her son.

"Take care of her," he instructed Marilee, turning Maybelline so she fell into the girl's arms. He couldn't deal with the emotional woman right now. He needed to think. "Did Peewee say where they were holding Nyla and Bobby, or did you see in what direction they went?"

"No," she said, shaking her head while rubbing Maybelline's back in a consoling manner, allowing the other woman to cling to her while she keened for her son.

Jake bit out a curse, then paused as something clicked inside his mind. "At the sheriff's office you told Peewee your grandparents were missing, and that the windows of their house are boarded up?"

"That's right."

"That's where they are. That's Demarcus's lair."

"I'm coming with you," she said determinedly as she eased Maybelline onto the bed.

"No, you stay here and take care of Maybelline."

"No, dammit! They killed my grandparents!"

"And they'll kill you. This isn't child's play, Marilee. These freaks are monsters."

"And my grandparents were decent, innocent people. With or without you, I'm going."

Jake stared at the young girl, noted the determination in the set of her jaw, and sighed. "Fine, but you follow my command," he said. "Get Maybelline calmed down, and I'll be right back."

"Where are you going?"

"I'm calling in backup."

Jake reentered the room he'd shared with Nyla and pulled out his cell phone. He pushed the button to connect him to Christian.

"Hello, Jacob," the vampire said, answering the phone on the first ring.

"You were expecting my call?"

"Yes. Seta's here, and she had a vision of you calling."

"She's there already?"

"She teleported back after speaking with you. Unfortunately, coming back used the last of her strength."

"When will she be able to come back?" he asked, heart sinking.

"She said she can't help you," Christian advised apologetically. "You and Nyla must fulfill your own destiny."

"Damn. I guess that means you won't help either."

"The great Jacob Porter is actually asking for my help?" At this, the vampire seemed a little amused.

"Don't be a wise-ass," Jake snapped, lowering himself onto the bed. Nyla's scent wafted up from the sheets, and as he inhaled it, his heart ached with regret. "Seta was hurt by hellfire which means Demarcus is obviously one of Lucifer's toadies. He's going to be a hard vampire to slay, even for me. I saw you take out a devil-worshiping psycho with prayer alone. I . . . I need you."

"I didn't destroy Carter with prayer alone," Christian said. "I had faith as well, which strengthened my prayer. You can do the same thing."

"No, I can't." Jake didn't know the first thing about faith.

"Yes, you can. You believe evil exists. You only have to believe that goodness does also."

"I've seen evil, Christian. I've never seen goodness."

"Yes, you have. You fell in love with her, too."

Jake closed his eyes as the reminder of what he'd lost burned through him like a hot lance. "Christian, please."

"I'm truly sorry, Jake, but I can't help you, either. This is your fate, your destiny."

"Dammit, my fate is to die!"

"Just believe, Jacob."

"In what? What am I supposed to do?" He couldn't believe it. He was whining, and he never whined.

"I'm not the one you should be asking for guidance. I've pointed you in the right direction. The rest is up to you," the vampire said before disconnecting the line.

Jake threw the phone across the room, letting out a growl of rage before rising to pace the floor. The lives of Nyla, Bobby, and his unborn child were resting on his shoulders, and no one would help him.

God listens, Christian's voice said inside Jake's mind. Jake stopped pacing, recalling the conversation he'd had with the vampire in his Baltimore church. *Some darkness is so evil we can't possibly understand it. We aren't supposed to. We merely believe, keep our hearts true, and know deep within our soul that everything is for a reason, and if we only ask, He will not give us more than we can handle.*

Jake reflected on those words while recalling the night Carter Dunn had been destroyed. Christian believed in those words, and it was his faith which had saved their lives that night. If a vampire, a creature not even human, could do it . . .

Jake fell to his knees, bowing his head as he placed his hands together. It made sense. If there was going to be a supernatural war, and Lucifer led one of the armies, there was only one being he could imagine leading the other. "It's been a long time," he started, "and I know I've done wrong over the years. I also know I'm unworthy, but I really need your help."

Chapter Twenty-Three

NYLA OPENED HER eyes, feeling as if she were drowning in grogginess and trying to swim through it. Her heart ached with sorrow, remembering the frightened look in Jake's eyes when he'd asked if their child would be a shifter. She'd once thought she could reach Jake, help him to understand that not all immortals and shifters were evil, but his prejudice ran deeper than she'd realized. Still, she loved him. He couldn't help his ignorance. He was a slayer and it was inborn.

But she'd worry about all that later. Right now she had to save her own life, and the life of her unborn child, and by doing so save Jake's life. She couldn't allow Jake to die out of revenge for Bobby, the friend he'd lost over a decade ago, and thereby fulfilling the prophecy written on the dream realm's cave walls. He might not love her the same way she loved him, but she'd never be able to live with the knowledge that his death had saved her life.

"Nyla."

She struggled to focus, blinking away the blurriness clouding her vision. A thin, redheaded man with piercing green eyes stood before her, an empty syringe in his hand.

"Curtis Dunn, or should I call you Alfred?"

"Curtis would be preferred," he whispered, wincing. "I don't care much for Alfred."

"Why are we whispering, Curtis? You're one of my enemies. Remember?"

"I tried to warn you."

"Right before whipping up the drugs Peewee injected into my system, I suppose."

His cheeks reddened. "I had to. The drugs I've used won't hurt the baby."

"How did you know I'm pregnant?" she gasped.

"Demarcus felt new life inside you when he possessed your body. He knew you wouldn't be able to shift, and that your metabolism would be slower, allowing the drugs to work in your system."

Nyla studied her surroundings. She was bound to a wooden pole, her wrists tied together above her head, both ankles secured. To her right, Bobby was strapped to another pole in the same manner. Peewee lay on the ground before him, bound at the wrists and ankles. They seemed to be inside some type of underground earthen cave—earth which appeared to have been freshly dug.

"Where is this place?"

Dunn looked around the area. "Demarcus killed an old couple and took their home. The first few days here, he had the vampires he'd created dig out this area under it."

"So the couple's house is a cover for this underground prison."

"Yes. He knows your man will come for you, and he hopes his minions will catch him inside the house before he ever finds the entrance to the tunnels."

"Why does he think Jake would come for me after what happened this morning? Jake knows what I am now."

"That's why he took the boy."

"Smart move," Nyla commented, looking at the boy. His eyes were full of fear, but to his credit he wasn't crying. She had to respect the boy's toughness, even while her heart skipped a beat with fear for his life. "So why did you kill the girls?"

"He made me, but it wasn't me. It was Alfred. I couldn't kill a fly."

"Your hands did the killing, Curtis. You're just as responsible."

He looked down at his feet, shame coloring his cheeks to match his flaming red hair. "If I could have done things differently, I would have. I'm just not strong enough."

Nyla's body stiffened as she felt a dark presence draw near. "He's coming," she warned Curtis, unsure if the man could feel Demarcus's presence as well as she, the beast's fledgling, could.

Curtis tapped his hand against the pocket of his cargo pants, seeming to make sure something was there, before backing away from her and turning to face his master as Demarcus entered the room.

Nyla gasped when she saw her dark tormentor. He had the same eyes and face shape as she'd remembered, along with the same tall, muscular build, but his body was covered in patches of fur. Some of the fur around his face was spotted with blood and seemed to be falling out. The air around him was rank with the smell of decay.

"Well, no wonder you're pissed at me," Nyla said, noting the scratches she'd embedded across his cheek sixteen years before. They should have healed the next day.

"You gave me a disease, catwoman, and now you are going to pay," he said as he approached.

Nyla frowned, trying to figure out how she'd given the vamp a disease when she was disease free. "How could I have made you ill? Pantherians can't catch diseases. For that matter, I thought vampires couldn't either."

"I thought the same thing, but you cursed me with your lycanthropy, somehow weakening my system and allowing this disease that you obviously carry, to enter my system."

"First, I'm not a lycanthrope. I'm a pantherian, and that isn't contagious."

"Well, apparently you're wrong, since I've been like this since I bit you," he said, stopping in front of her, his body's foul smell stirring waves of nausea inside her.

"Well, that's what you get for putting your filthy mouth on me," she said, unable to resist sparking his ire.

His hand shot out, and she felt pain explode through her head as it connected with her jaw, whipping her head to the side. "Watch your mouth, bitch. I can still make your inevitable death slower than it needs to be. I could allow you to live long enough for the child inside you to form, then cut it out and make you watch as I kill it before putting you out of your misery."

"You are one sick bastard," she said, tasting her own blood well inside her mouth.

"Thank you, I try," he said with an evil smile. "Your lover should be here soon, and then the fun times will really begin."

"Why are you doing this?"

His smile never wavered. "Because I'm evil. I thought we'd established that already, and I'm very vengeful."

"So you're going to kill all these people because I somehow passed a disease to you?"

"Yes."

"Why not just kill me?"

He grinned. "Because killing multiple people and watching their deaths weigh on your conscience is so much more satisfying. I loved my appearance as much as you love your little slayer. You took my face, and now I'm going to take your man."

"Why the girls? Why did you imitate the Dunn murders?"

"Because you let your guard down for a moment in Baltimore. I've always known you followed a vampire hunter, but I couldn't find out who it was. Then, when you let your guard down, I saw he'd followed the trail of bodies of those women. Lucifer helped me find Alfred and recreate the killings. I knew he'd follow that trail, too, and that you'd follow him."

"And you killed Chrissy just to torture him?"

"Chrissy?" He turned toward Curtis. "Who was Chrissy?"

"The last girl," Curtis answered.

"Your man knew the girl?" Demarcus asked, returning his black gaze to Nyla before erupting into a fit of laughter. "Oh, that's priceless! And to think, I just picked her at random." He threw his head back, letting the laughter roar from his throat. "And the little boy named Bobby, your lover turning out to be the boy who'd gotten away from me sixteen years ago, and the sheriff his own relation . . . absolutely priceless! I couldn't have planned it any better."

No, you couldn't have, Nyla realized. Everything was unfolding the way it was because of the words etched into the dream realm's cave walls, the way it had been planned before either she or Jake were born. She'd led Jake right to his killer, and he was going to come here to save the little boy and his cousin, getting killed to fulfill their destiny. Jake had given her a child, and in return she was going to be forced to watch the man she loved more than life itself die.

"STAY LOW, AND do everything as I say," Jake instructed the headstrong girl at his back as they crept toward the boarded-up house. "And shoot everything that moves."

"Honey, that's one command you didn't have to give," Marilee said, her finger poised over the trigger.

Jake paused outside the door and opened his senses. Nyla was here, scared and weak, deep inside the house, or . . . below. "Did your grandparents have a basement?"

"Yes."

"How deep?"

"It's just a regular-sized basement," Marilee said with a shrug.

Jake focused on Nyla, trying to pin down her location. "Is it the same length as the house?"

"Yes."

"Dammit. They've built tunnels beneath the house. I hope you can see good in the dark."

The young girl looked at him, fear in her eyes, but she quickly banked the emotion. "Come on. Let's go kill some undead guys."

Jake allowed himself a moment to determine the whereabouts of Demarcus's minions, and then he busted down the door.

HE'S HERE. NYLA'S eyes welled with tears as she sensed the man she loved nearby. He'd come to save the lives of innocents, just as the vampire in front of her had known he would, and he was walking right into his own death trap. She ground her teeth, trying to keep her tears at bay. She didn't want to give away the fact that Jake was in the house above them. She had to give him a fighting chance, despite already seeing his death in a vision.

"How is killing Jake and me going to help you find a cure?" she asked her tormentor, trying to gain his undivided attention.

"It won't, but it'll make me feel better for a little while."

"And then you'll be left with fur all over your body."

"Who said I'm going to kill you right away? Your punishment will be watching the man you love die, but we're going to dissect your living body.

Find a cure for my ailment."

"I won't let you."

"It amuses me how you think you have a choice. I can do anything to you I want," he said, placing his hands over her breasts as he leaned in close to her face. "Anything."

"Get off of me, you disgusting freak," she cried, squirming in effort to escape his touch as he continued molesting her.

He abruptly darted away from her, and pain exploded inside her chest. Nyla let out a scream, glancing across the room to see Marilee standing opposite her, one of Jake's guns poised in her grasp, her face twisted into a classic look of horror. "Oh, shit! I'm sorry! Oh, shit! Oh, shit, oh shit!"

Jake appeared behind her. "I told you to stay behind . . ." His admonishment was cut short as he looked across the room, meeting Nyla's gaze. "No!"

Nyla looked down and saw her own blood gushing from her chest. She let out another scream before pulling her head up to look at Jake. Her gaze found him just in time to see Curtis barrel into him as he tried to run toward her. They rolled on the ground until Curtis came out on top, a syringe gripped tightly in his hand.

"No!" Nyla screamed, watching helplessly as the man drove the syringe into Jake's body.

Nyla.

Seta? Nyla jerked, surprised to hear the voice inside her mind. *Seta, is that you? Where are you?*

Nowhere near. The blood you offered me is still in my system, giving us this mental link. You've been shot.

Yeah, I kind of noticed that.

You must focus on the bullet.

It's kind of hard not to.

Not the pain, Nyla, the bullet itself. Imagine the flesh around it squeezing tighter, pushing it out. DO IT !!!! Seta screamed inside her head when she started to black out.

Nyla forced herself to ignore the action around her, closed her eyes and focused on the area of her body where the bullet had penetrated. It seemed to be lodged inside her chest wall, right over her heart. She imagined the flesh around it, just behind the tip of the bullet, swelling. She imagined the bullet being pushed out from her body, and in a rush of pain, the foreign object fell from her chest as the area behind it closed.

Good girl. I knew you could do it.

Nyla opened her eyes, surprised to find herself lying on the ground. Marilee was at her feet, untying the ropes around her ankles, crying madly. "I didn't mean to shoot you. I swear, I didn't. I was aiming for the guy in front of you."

"Nyla!"

Jake leaned over her, checking her chest for signs of a wound.

"I pushed the bullet out," she explained. "Seta helped me. What did Curtis inject you with?"

"I don't know," he said. "I knocked the little bastard out before he could tell me. Your wound is closing." He helped her to her feet and gave her a push toward the exit. "Get out while you can, and take the others with you."

"No! You're going with us."

"I can't do that. Demarcus has to be stopped."

"Jake, please!"

"I have to, Nyla." He cocked his head to the side. "I can't sense him. Why can't I sense him?"

"Because your girlfriend's feline traits have blocked my vampire scent," Demarcus's cruel voice said from four feet behind them.

Jake whirled around, placing himself in front of Nyla. "You're furry? Dude, you are *fucked*." His statement intensified the rage shining out of Demarcus's black eyes, and Jake ordered, "Marilee, get Bobby out of here now!"

The girl had just finished untying the boy, after freeing Peewee first, and jumped at Jake's command. She quickly pulled the child toward the exit. Demarcus rushed toward them, but both Jake and Nyla lunged for him, tackling him before he could reach the escapees.

They all hit the ground with a thud, and Nyla rolled off the vampire, her body filled with pain from the force of the impact. She managed to raise herself to all fours before recognizing the sense of déjà vu washing over her.

"Oh, no," she gasped, realizing she'd lived this moment before, even if only through a vision. *"No, no, no, no, no!"* She forced herself to turn her head in Jake's direction, screaming as she saw her vision come to life.

Jake and Demarcus stood face to face. Blood poured around Jake's hands, which were gripped around the hilt of the small sword Demarcus had hidden from them until the moment he'd sunk it into Jake's chest. She watched helplessly as Demarcus twisted the sword, effectively destroying Jake's heart.

Jake fell backward when Demarcus gave him a small push. His head lolled toward Nyla as his body connected with the ground, blood pooling beneath him. "I'm . . . sorry," he said, struggling to speak through his own blood coming up through his throat. "R . . . run."

"Jake!" All of the pain in Nyla's heart came out through her voice, erupting into an excruciatingly sorrowful scream.

Demarcus pulled the sword from Jake's lifeless body, smiling in victory. Nyla rushed to Jake's side, feeling his throat for a pulse, but there was none. Just as she'd feared, he'd been killed, and she'd failed him exactly as she'd failed his best friend sixteen years before.

"Kiss him goodbye, bitch. I have plans for you before I go catch your little friends," Demarcus said from above her, laughter accompanying his words. "None of them are going to survive to see a new dawn."

"That includes you," Nyla growled, quickly twisting around to face the beast who'd taken from her the only man she'd ever loved. "Without Jake, I don't give a damn if I live or die," she said, "and you don't know how dangerous that makes me."

She saw a glint of fear in Demarcus's eyes seconds before she struck. She couldn't shift due to her pregnancy, but she was still quick, and she was filled with a rage she could barely contain, a rage which surpassed anything she'd ever felt emanating from Jake's body.

She barreled headfirst into Demarcus, knocking him to the ground, disarming him before burying her elongated fangs into his throat, ripping the flesh out with her teeth. He let out a scream of pain before backhanding her, effectively removing her from his body.

She flew backward, smacking into the wall with enough force to shake the underground room, causing dirt to fall from above them. "You won't beat me, bitch," Demarcus said, rushing toward her with a speed which surpassed her own. "I made you."

"You only gave me immortality and a thirst for blood," she spit back at him. "Two things which will make it easier for me to kill you!"

She moved aside in time for Demarcus to run headfirst into the wall, causing more dirt to rain down upon them. "You'll pay for killing Jake!" she cried, kicking the vampire in the midsection, causing him to howl in pain. She attempted to kick him in the face, but he reached out too quickly, grabbed her by the ankle and pulled her to the ground.

"I told you, you can't kill me." He gripped her throat in both hands, squeezing the air out of her lungs. "I'm your sire. You'll never be stronger than me. You can't kill me."

"I guess it's moments like these you hate having a slayer in the room with you," a deep voice said from behind the vampire.

Nyla blinked, unable to believe her eyes as she gazed past Demarcus's shoulders to see Jake standing behind him, Demarcus's sword raised in his hands.

"You're dead," Demarcus said, his voice full of disbelief.

"And you're still ugly as hell," Jake retorted. He swung the sword in an arc and sent Demarcus's head careening across the room.

Nyla quickly scooted back, avoiding as much splatter of Demarcus's blood as she could when his decapitated body fell forward. "Jake!"

He pulled her to her feet, quickly checking her body with his hands. "Are you all right? The baby's not hurt, is he?"

"I'm . . . You . . ." She glanced toward the area where she'd watched him die and saw his blood still puddled on the ground. His T-shirt was ripped, but as she pulled it up to inspect his chest, she found the skin unmarred. "I don't understand. I saw you die."

"Yeah, well, now we know what Curtis injected me with. It looks as if the crazy bastard created the immortality serum his brother was trying to make. Come on," he added, pulling her toward the exit as the dirt roof above them started to fall. "This place is going to cave in."

A FEW MOMENTS later, they emerged into the blazing sunlight of the summer day, walking side by side with Curtis Dunn draped over Jake's shoulder. Jake lowered the still unconscious man to the ground and walked over to his cousin, who stood next to the Malibu, shaking like a leaf.

"Are you all right, cousin?" he asked the smaller man, holding him by the shoulders.

"Yeah, I'm fine. Thank goodness you found us."

"You should have believed me in the first place," Jake said, letting his anger coat his words. "And you should have never put my woman in danger. Jonah called before I got here. The feds are on their way. Have fun explaining this mess."

Peewee stared up at him horror. "What? How am I supposed to explain all of this?"

Jake only smiled as he hoisted Curtis back over his shoulder. "Don't know and don't care. I have some people to get home."

MARILEE, MAYBELLINE, and Bobby waved goodbye as Jake maneuvered the Malibu out of the motel parking lot, heading toward the city limits.

"I can't believe he's dead," Nyla said, watching the trees whiz by as they sped out of town, trying to get well away from the aftermath of everything that had happened in Hicksville before the feds showed up. They didn't want to be anywhere near the town when the slaughtered bodies they'd left behind were discovered.

"I can't believe that one helped," Jake responded, inclining his head toward the backseat where Curtis Dunn lay unconscious.

"You knocked him out pretty good."

"Yeah, well, I don't like it when people stab me with things."

"And why are we bringing him with us?" Nyla looked back at the unconscious man, uneasy with his nearness after all that had happened.

"I need to find out what, exactly, he put in me, and I just have this gut feeling that leaving him back there was the wrong move. I have the feeling that I'll be getting a visit from the Dream Teller instructing me what to do. She was adamant that he not be killed."

Nyla nodded. Jake's gut was never wrong, and she trusted him, so she accepted the fact that Curtis was coming along for the ride. But there were other issues weighing heavily on her mind. "Can we be serious for a moment, Jake?"

"Sure. What's up?"

She glanced at him, noticed the tight set of his jaw as he kept his eyes focused on the road in front of him, and sighed. "What are we going to do about this situation?"

"What situation?"

"The baby."

"Well, I guess the first thing we'll do is get married." Jake continued to look forward, but finally turned his head in Nyla's direction after a few moments of stunned silence had passed. His brow furrowed as he looked at her, and she knew she'd gone slack-jawed. "What? I didn't exactly have time to get a ring, and since the baby's already been conceived, I didn't think you'd hold me to some sort of romantic formality."

"Did you just say we should get *married?*" she asked, sure she'd heard him wrong.

"Uh, yeah."

"But you don't love me."

Jake slammed on the brakes, bringing the car to a skidding stop along the side of the highway. "Where did you get a stupid idea like that? I just *died* for you back there."

Nyla sat speechless, unable to do anything but blink as she stared at his angry face.

"Well?" he prodded.

"I . . . You . . ." She shook her head, trying to clear her thoughts. "The baby could be a shifter."

"And? He could also be a psychotic lunatic, a male ballet dancer, or hell, he could really go bad and become a Republican. That doesn't mean I won't love him anyway."

Nyla blinked, unable to wrap her mind around his sudden change of attitude. "I thought you hated me for what I am."

"I've never hated you. I admit I didn't deal well with it when I learned you were the cat I'd been pouring out my secrets to for the past sixteen years, or that you were there the night Bobby died, but that's old news." His eyes grew soft and warm. "I realize you couldn't stop his death because, whether or not I like it, it was simply his time to die. You weren't even able to save me today."

"Jake . . ."

"No, Nyla. It's fine. I was meant to die so I could save you."

Nyla held back the tears burning her eyes. "You really had no idea you'd been injected with immortality serum, did you?"

"No. Now that I do, I kinda feel bad about knocking Curtis out," he said with a laugh.

"Jake?"

"Yeah?"

"Why did you die for me? Earlier today you tried to kill me."

He turned his body so he faced her fully. "I love you, Nyla. This morning I was too stunned, or scared, or . . . I don't know. Whatever I was, I didn't see things clearly because my true nature was trying to win out over what my heart was telling me. I actually prayed today, and I followed what my heart told me to do."

"Which was?"

"If I want to fight with the good side, I need to fight at your side."

"So you don't think I'm a freak?"

He shook his head. "Not any more than I am. When you were captured, and before we came to save you, I was alone, and it felt awful. You've been my best friend for most of my life, and you've given yourself to me in so many ways, done everything you could to protect me. I suddenly realized what a mistake I'd made, and that I'd never love anyone as much as I love you."

"Even though you know the truth about my past?"

"You served a queen, Nyla. You did what you had to do to survive, and that was before we met. Well, before we officially met. I understand now why you reacted the way you did after we made love in the car. You despise that part of you."

"I never wanted to share that ugly part of me with you. Especially not the first time." Nyla lowered her gaze to her lap.

He tipped her chin up with his fingertips. "I understand, but you don't have to feel ashamed. I don't care who came before me, just as long as no one comes after me."

"There'll never be another man, Jake."

"I believe you." He smiled, the gesture reaching his eyes. "So let's get married and give our baby a little bit less of a dysfunctional family."

"Well, when you ask so sweetly."

"Hey, romance isn't one of my special skills," he said as he pulled back out onto the highway.

"I think you're better at it than you think," Nyla commented, resting her head on his shoulder, love blossoming inside her chest.

"Hey, Nyla?"

"Yeah?"

"How old were you that night you saved me from Demarcus?"

"About the age you are now," she muttered.

"So you're like, forty-something now?"

She groaned. "Shut up, Porter."

"Wow."

"Shut up."

"Why? You obviously haven't physically aged since that night. I probably won't age anymore now, either. Damn, when that happens, Jonah's going to freak!"

Nyla chuckled, his amusement spreading to her. His merriment, rare that it was, had always been contagious.

"So, uh, just out of curiosity, how often does this heat thing happen?"

"More than you can handle," she quipped, chuckling at his typical maleness.

"Dude, *I'm the man!*" He laughed with glee at his good fortune. "And you're pretty hot for an old la—Ow! Why'd you hit me?"

"For the same reason I always hit you. Sometimes, you're just the jerk I love," she said, grinning at him.

The End

Printed in Great Britain
by Amazon

44123455R00111